DAEMON OF TITAN

A FANTASY ADVENTURE

PAUL MOUCHET

PAUL MOUCHET PUBLISHING

To my wife, who believes in me, even when I struggle to believe in myself. Without her support and infinite patience, I would have never realized my dream of becoming an author.
And, to my big sister Louise, thank you for helping me bring my stories to life.

CONTENTS

Chapter One

DRAGON BRANDY

Kit and Mukale were in the war room poring over maps, when General Rusty Karter barged in. She had worn the same deep frown for the past three days. Her drab, waterlogged tunic and trousers did nothing to improve her appearance or demeanor. A thick layer of muck covered her knee-high boots, which tracked a trail of water and sludge behind her.

"You need to talk to them, Sister Kit." The woman's voice and demeanor were even sadder than her apparel. Rusty was a hearty woman of limited stature. She drummed her fingers on her thigh, waiting impatiently for a reply. With a tired sigh, Kit looked up from the map covered dining table.

"Let me guess. We lost some more recruits?" It wasn't like Rusty to let her appearance suffer. Kit glanced down at herself and the tight-fitting black leather breaches and the dark burgundy surcoat. She had been wearing the same clothes since she had given her speech to the people of Cormorant.

It's time to take better care of myself. She tucked her tangled mass of bright red locks behind her ear and ran her hands over her coat, trying to smooth out the wrinkles.

"If you would speak to them." Rusty's words snapped Kit out of her ruminations. The general's normally braided hair was loose, soaking wet, and plastered to her face. "They're not soldiers and they're refusing the training."

Kit sighed and pushed one of the stone carvings across the map. "It won't do any good. I might be able to get them fired up again, but you can't expect Berrat to fight like humans. It's not their way."

"If they won't wear armor and practice with shield and spear, how am I going to put them to use?" Rusty's voice trailed off as she turned her attention to the map Kit was working with. It was of Arnnor, Berrathia, and Lycos, with each city of the major slave houses identified, including Silverhawk and Templeton. At Cormorant, there were seven small black ship carvings, along with pieces that resembled human infantry and wolves.

"What you're asking goes against our nature." Mukale never looked up from another map covered dining table. The Berrat male, at under four feet tall, was short even for his kind. His bone white hair, with shots of red, was tied up into several severe looking braids which hung to the top of his shoulders. He was dressed in light, sleeveless leathers that showed off his sinewy arms. "We don't wear iron armor and we don't fight with shields. The spears you use are too big for most of us to wield. We prefer bows and hand weapons that are fast and light."

"Who exactly is this man?" Rusty's face was turning red. The woman's tone and choice of words made Mukale stand taller.

"He's my friend." Kit practically barked out the words. "He helped me rescue Treedale from the slavers in Silverhawk." A flood of memories came roaring back. The day the boy was kidnapped was when she'd met Lin's grandmother, Grams, and the sprite, Feigh. She had seen none of the sprites nor Ashkey, the other boy they'd rescued, since they left Grams' house.

Rusty stared down at the muddy mess at her feet, and her frown deepened even further. "I need the Berrat to fit into my army; to be part of something bigger. If they won't fight the way I need them to, they're of no use to me."

"And that's the problem." Mukale's nostrils flared. "You expect them all to change to fit your idea of a soldier, but you're unwilling to even consider any alternatives."

"And what alternatives am I not considering?" Rusty retorted, planting her hands firmly on her wide hips.

"That they aren't front-line soldiers." Kit glared at Mukale, trying to calm the waters before he exploded. She really didn't need more conflict, especially with her own people. With a heavy sigh, the young priest turned her attention back to Rusty. "The Berrat don't fight by meeting an enemy head on. They survive by being invisible, melting into the background, striking from the shadows."

"How do you know how Berrat fight?" Rusty crossed her arms over her ample bosom and cocked an eyebrow. "You grew up in a temple devoted to Titan. You were taught how to fight with a hammer, ax, and shield."

"Actually." Kit moved closer to her general, tilting her head back slightly to stare into her eyes. "I grew up in northern Berrathia, in a Berrat village. When the slavers came, I watched my people defend themselves. When they came into our homes to steal us away, I watched the Berrat spring from the shadows; they struck out and disappeared just as quickly."

Rusty's face was turning bright red, her ears even brighter. She was fighting on two fronts, and she was losing on both of them. "Then tell me, how am I supposed to use them? We don't fight like that."

"Surely there must be some warriors among the hundreds of people you're trying to train," Mukale said. "They would likely be the ones telling you that you're doing it wrong."

Rusty's face went blank, her shoulders slumped. "Yes, there were a few outspoken individuals."

"Maybe you should listen to them." Kit rubbed her face. Her eyes were stinging from staring at the maps. "Maybe they can teach you something about fighting Berrat-style."

"Fine!" Rusty threw her arms in the air. "I'll fix this." She stormed towards the door, slamming into Lin as she entered the room. The robust general sent the woman sprawling, knocking her into a set of stacked chairs. They had been moved to the side to make more room around the tables. Rusty didn't even slow down. She continued out the door, leaving a trail of muck and water behind her. "Argh!" The woman's voice echoed down the manor's hallway, her frustration coming out in shrill screams.

Mukale bugged his eyes out at Kit, trying to suppress a laugh. "I'll go speak with her. Maybe I can offer her some suggestions."

"Go," Kit said, running her fingers through her tangled mass of dark red hair. "Try not to make things worse, okay?" Mukale nodded and took off.

"Your girlfriend is awfully tense." Kit offered Lin a hand up, a small smirk cutting across her face.

"She's not my girlfriend." A thick pout tempered the sharpness in Lin's voice. "It won't work." She had recently cut her once mid-back-length hair. It was now a short, chin-length bob. It made her face appear rounder and her brown eyes larger. She had some dark circles under her eyes. Either she had been crying again, or she hadn't been getting much sleep.

Kit suddenly regretted having teased her friend. "Oh, I didn't know. What happened?"

"It doesn't matter," Lin shook her head, holding up Fury, Kit's sentient war hammer. "This is more important."

"What's more important than your happiness?" Kit asked.

Fury, the dragon soul trapped within Kit's hammer, spoke out in his typical arrogant fashion. "I am, of course. Those Hobgoblins are crafty. They say they can pull the piece of me held in that soul cannister and add it into the hammer." Fury paused for a few moments before continuing. "But they hate doing necromancy spells."

"But they'll teach me how to do them," Lin interjected. The excitement in her voice was palpable. "I'm going to learn my first necromancy spell."

Kit's eyes went wide with revulsion. "I forbid it. Necromancy spells are unnatural. They're evil."

"It's the only way I'll be whole again," Fury said. "Why are necromancy spells any different from any other spell?" He was trying to sound innocent, but Kit wasn't buying it. The sour expression on her face made it perfectly clear.

"Well then, thankfully, it's not your decision," Fury finally stated. "We need somebody we can trust to cast the spell, and unless you're going to do some celestial magic, there's nobody else who can do it."

Kit glared at Lin and walked back to the map covered table.

"I need to borrow some of Indie's dragon brandy to boost my magic," Lin said. "Do you know where he is?"

"You're going to what?" Kit could feel her inner fire swelling in her chest. Ever since she ignited her dark celestial self, the little priest had been struggling to maintain control over it.

Fury chuckled. "You're flaming again. It's a good look on you."

Kit closed her eyes and calmed her breathing. The flames on her hands died out. After a few more moments of concentration, she took one final cleansing breath. "Are you suggesting that Indie is drinking the dragon brandy?"

Lin clamped her mouth shut and shrugged. Without a word, Kit stormed past her, heading down the hall towards Indie's bedroom.

"Don't set him on fire again," Lin shouted out. "Control your emotions."

⌘

Kit burst through the door, ripping it off its hinges as she did. "Where is it?" Brimstone's acrid fragrance followed as she stepped inside Indie's room. When her eyes fell on him, her breath hitched. His half-naked body was drenched in sweat. His long black hair was loose, sticking to his face and chest. *Sweet Titan.* She gasped as she took in his physique, his sweaty, well-muscled physique. Lump, who was in human form, switched back to his natural golden retriever self.

"What are you two doing?" Indie paused at Kit's question. He stole a quick glance at Lump before turning back. "We're... training. I'm... um... Lump's teaching me how to fight bare handed."

"He's a dog. He fights with his teeth," Kit said, tilting her head to the side. "How can he be teaching you unarmed combat?" The question hung in the air for a few moments. She tried to ignore the man's chiseled physique. He looked incredible. He seemed more muscled. His dark, tanned skin had an almost golden quality to it.

"Um, Kit, you're flaming." Indie threw up his hands and took a quick step from the young woman. "I'd really prefer that you not set me on fire again." Ever since the *incident* a few nights ago, Indie had been distant, sullen.

"And that's why you've been drinking the dragon brandy?" Kit asked, her flames subsiding. "Because Fury said it might give you resistance to fire?" Indie could not maintain eye contact. "You don't need that." She reached out to hold the man's hands.

"You set me on fire." Indie retreated; his fists clenched at his side. "Because you couldn't control it."

"How many times do I have to say that I'm sorry?" Kit said, pushing Indie's hands away. "It's the first time I've done *that*, and I lost control."

"You lost control and set me on fire. You nearly burned down the entire manor."

Kit threw her hands up in exasperation. "That's a total exaggeration. I healed you as soon as my flames died down. The bedsheets were hardly even scorched."

"Do you not remember how much it hurt you to heal me?" Indie's knuckles cracked as he tightened his fists further. "I was on fire and while I burned, you worked at putting out your own flames. While you did, I kept on burning. My skin was melting off my body."

"I said I was sorry. It won't happen again."

"And while you're learning to control yourself, I'm taking steps," Indie said, his own fury suddenly becoming playful.

"Steps?"

"Yes, steps. I want to finish what we... started." He managed a coy grin, his left eyebrow twitching.

"Where's the brandy?" Kit asked, trying to not let her fire ignite again at Indie's words. When his eyes drifted over to the tall wardrobe in his room, she shook her head. Opening the door, she had no trouble spotting the tall skinny bottle on the top shelf. Unable to reach it, she jumped and flailed at the bottle, hoping to snag it from its lofty perch. After several attempts, and a few chuckles from Indie, Kit finally made contact, knocking the bottle from the shelf, sending it flying across the room. It struck the wall close to where Lump was standing, dislodging the cork, spilling its contents all over the stone floor.

"Lump, leave it!" Kit screeched out as the wolfdog licked the spilled liquid. As fast as she was, she couldn't pull the dog off before he had lapped up the honey-sweet liquor. "Oh, Lump. What have you done?"

"Well, that's going to be interesting." Fury floated at the entranceway to Indie's room. "First, he drank the magicked water from Titan's statue, and now he's had the better part of a bottle of dragon brandy."

"Shut up!" Kit growled at the levitating war hammer, clutching the golden retriever to her chest. "If he dies, I swear to Titan I will destroy every bottle of that brandy, and then I'm going to wipe every single dragon from the face of Orth. You included."

"Kit, you're on fire again," Indie said. An inferno wreathed Kit's entire body, engulfing both her and Lump. She could feel the flames seeking any poison that might be in the dog. They were searching, probing, seeking anything that might harm him. The golden retriever's eyes were unfocused, but otherwise he seemed unharmed.

"I told you it would be interesting," Fury said. "If he survives..." Kit's death stare cut off the hammer's words before he could finish his thought.

"And that's why I've been drinking the brandy," Indie said, kneeling down beside Kit and Lump, taking care to stay away from Kit's flames. He regretted his words when he saw the tears staining his love's face.

Hours passed in silence as Kit continued to hold Lump's head on her lap. Even though her flames had long since died away, the tears had never stopped. "You can't die, Lump. You just can't. Why did you do that?"

Lump's eyes opened, and he gave Kit a weak doggie-smile. The smile on his face faded away as his eyes closed.

"Lump, no. You can't die," Kit pleaded as her body became engulfed in a golden aura. She pumped every bit of her healing energy into the dog, desperately searching for his injuries. She could feel her power coursing through him, seeking something, anything, for her to repair, but there was nothing there. There were no injuries. "Lump!" she sobbed, clutching at his fur while tears continued to stream down her cheeks.

"Kit." Indie knelt on the floor next to her, keeping his voice soft. "Look. He's still breathing."

"What?" Kit pulled her face from Lump's neck-ruff. "Lump, you're alive!" The golden retriever responded by licking Kit's hand, a weak doggie-smile returning to his face. His eyes were dull, but he was alive.

"Let me move him to my bed." Indie slipped his hands between Kit and Lump. With little effort, he lifted the large dog and placed him gently on his bed. "You rest now, buddy. You've been through a lot, I think." He turned back to find Kit still on the floor, her knees tucked up to her chest, clutching onto her ankles. "He's going to be okay, Kit."

"I nearly killed him." Kit's forehead continued to rest on her knees. "I let my anger get away from me and I nearly killed him."

CHAPTER TWO

THE RESPLENDENT DRAKEN

The evening sun was streaming through the stained-glass windows of the war room, creating a kaleidoscope of colors on the walls. There were still several clouds in the sky, but none of them looked threatening. It was nice to see the sun again after three days of wind, rain, and ice pellets. The double doors to the balcony were wide open, filling the room with crisp air.

Kit was sitting on one of the meeting room's couches with Lump laying beside her. The pup still wasn't himself since lapping up the spilled dragon brandy. He was lethargic, even for him. If he moved, it was to find a cool place to lie down. Much worse, he barely ate. Kit had tried, repeatedly, to use her powers to cure him, to help him feel better, but at no point could she find anything to heal. It made her stomach feel like it was filled with snakes, writhing and twisting her gut until she couldn't bear it any longer. Indie, despite his desperate need to comfort the young woman, kept his distance. He and Coldforge, their dwarven prince comrade, were sitting far enough away to leave her alone, but close enough to tend to her if she needed anything. Several times, Indie had moved to get up, and each time, Coldforge grunted and pointed at his chair.

"Hello Kitten," a honeyed baritone voice said from the balcony. Those two simple words pushed away the subdued, almost morose mood.

"Sweet Titan," Kit squealed, and raced over to her friend, nearly landing on her face as she tripped over Lump, who was also on his way to greet Danny. She bowled the young Berrat over when she leapt at him, wrapping her arms around his neck, kissing him about the head and face. Kit never heard Indie's teeth gnashing together.

"I'm happy to see you, too," Danny said, a broad smile splitting his face from ear to ear. "Hello, Lump, ol' boy," he said, giving the dog a good scratching.

"What are you doing here? Were you looking for me? Are you well? How did you get up here?" Kit's brain was a mess. Questions were coming out of her face quicker than her mind could process them. "What are you doing here?" she asked for the second time without taking a breath.

"What we're doing here is a bit of a long story," Danny said, still rubbing Lump's ears, fending off the exuberant pup's slobbery affection.

"We?" Kit's eyes popped from her head when they fell upon the beautiful red headed Berrat standing off to the side.

"I'd like you to meet Breayn," Danny said, struggling to get the words out. Between Kit and Lump, he wasn't being given much of a chance to breathe.

"I'm pleased to meet you," Breayn said with a slight bow. "I've heard a lot about you in the past few days." Kit continued to gape at the woman. Breayn tugged at the thick silk rope that hung over the edge of the manor's massive balcony. "Sorry to show up like this. There were too many guards posted. Sneaking in was our only option."

"Oh, I'm so pleased to meet you, too," Kit said, her face reddening. She grasped the woman's hand, shaking it wildly. "Are you Danny's...?" Kit asked, waggling her eyebrows at her. "I'm so happy to meet you. It's so nice that Danny has found someone."

"Our mothers are sisters. I'm his cousin," Breayn said with a flat smile.

"Oh," Kit said, her eyes darting back and forth between the two of them. "I guess that's why you have the same flaming red hair?"

"I guess," Danny said, taking a hold of several strands of Kit's own bright red hair. Your liquid-gold eyes are new.

"It's a long story, too." She brushed his hand away, wanting to keep the story fixed on her friend. "Why are you here? When did you arrive? How long can you stay?"

"We've been in the city a few days now. It's a shame we didn't know you were here. It would have saved us a lot of time and effort."

"We spent the first two days skulking about," Breayn added. "We had not expected to see free Berrat in a slaver city. They told us of a woman they called *Frelser Dronning*."

"They're calling me the *warrior queen*?" Kit's hand rested on her breast while a deep scarlet crept up her neck. She had never heard the phrase before, but the library's book of languages had taught her every known dialect used in the north. Every one, except Berrabbithi, the language of the Berrats' ancestors.

"Others were calling you, *The Slayer*," Danny said with a small laugh. "Strangely enough, nobody referred to you by your name. From what we could see, the slavers had been overthrown, but we couldn't verify it." Danny's face brightened as he gazed past Kit. "Hello, Indie. Still by Kit's side, I see."

Indie and Coldforge were standing at the doorway to the balcony. Indie kept his arms tight to his body and glared at the well-muscled Berrat. An ugly chuckle escaped his lips as he puffed his chest out. Coldforge was jubilant as he thrust his thick, meaty hand into Danny's face.

"The name's Coldforge. If'n yer a friend of Kit's, then yer a friend of mine," he said, before his eyes fell on Breayn. "Praise be to Gimlie." The dwarf turned from Danny, reaching out to greet the attractive woman. "Yer a fine-looking woman, if ya don't mind me sayin'."

"Thank you," Breayn said, gingerly accepting the dwarf's hand. "I am pleased to meet you." Before she could say another word, Coldforge led her inside, past the growling Indie.

"What are you doing here?" Indie demanded, giving way to the dwarf and the Berrat woman as they walked past. Danny popped up to his feet and patted Indie on his chest as he followed his cousin inside. Kit glowered at her Nomad boyfriend as she pushed past him. Lump was also through the doors before another word was spoken.

"Well," Danny said with a stretch as he surveyed the opulent room. His eyes fell on the tables covered with maps. "We came here to fight some slavers and get

Breayn's mother, but visiting with old friends is a welcome respite. We've been to Helja and back over the last ten days."

"What's been going on?" Kit asked, giving Indie one last death stare before centering her attention on her newly arrived friend.

"Well," Danny added, running his fingers through his mass of red hair. "We've been putting it to the Split Crows. We haven't removed them yet, but I'm guessing they're in the middle of a blood bath right now with House Byssus."

"Who are the Split Crows and House Byssus?" Kit was exhausted trying to remember all the players in this game. There was always another name to learn and remember.

"House Byssus had taken control of Lilloet and Taseko," Danny replied. Kit gasped at the declaration. A scowl pulled the corners of her mouth down as she wrapped her arms around her belly.

"What's wrong?" Indie asked. Kit's reaction to the question forced whatever his issues were with Danny to take a back seat. "Why does it matter if this Byssus person has taken Lilloet or Taseko?"

"Taseko is where Danny was born." Kit continued to maintain a grip on her waist. Her breathing was shallow, and she was on the verge of vomiting. She took a deep breath, attempting to regain her composure. "I was so sorry to hear that your village had fallen. It's why you left the Temple. I understood why you left me behind."

"Thank you," Danny replied, his chest heaving. He turned his gaze onto Indie, his posture stiffening. "Lilloet is where Kit's village is," he said, annoyed with Indie that he didn't know that about her. "Lord Damil Byssus was the ruler of Wantage, a city just east of Lilloet. His cruelty there was so bad that a group of Berrat slaves rose against him and drove him out. That group has named themselves the Split Crows. You'd have thought they'd have been happy after liberating the city, but they simply took over where Byssus left off."

"There are Berrat slavers?" Indie asked. He had no trouble following the story, but it was so incredible, he had to make sure he was hearing it correctly. Danny's face sagged, and he nodded.

"And they are as cruel as Byssus, except they're much smarter and better organized." Breayn pulled herself away from the dwarf, who seemed way too interested in her. She had a bit of a grin, despite how grim the story was. "But, like the six other major Auctioneers' slaver houses, they are greedy and self serving, and they don't trust any of the other slaver organizations in Berrathia. They are vying for the top spot, desperate to gain the support of King Faol."

"Taseko may still be in the hands of the Split Crows." Danny's expression brightened somewhat. "But at least we freed Lilloet, and Lord Byssus has been captured." A hint of arrogance spread across his face, along with a crooked grin. "Breayn and I, and her mate Ryn, helped to liberate the city. We also killed The Wing, one of the Split Crows' leaders."

"You freed Lilloet?" Kit asked, her eyes wide and glassy. Indie moved to her side, wrapping his arm around her shoulder.

"They were already on the verge of a revolt," Breayn said. "We just gave them a nudge in the right direction. Even though the Split Crows drove House Byssus out of Wantage, I think they were controlling him. Lord Byssus behaved like a lap dog, bending to whatever The Wing wanted."

"Who's The Wing?" Indie asked, pulling Kit closer to himself.

"The Split Crows have three leaders. The Wing was their top assassin. If anybody of any importance got in their way, he made them disappear, permanently."

"The Beak," Danny continued, "is their mouthpiece. She is the face of the organization. When she speaks, people listen and obey. The last leader is the Claw. He is a brutal warrior, and he leads the Crows' armies."

"We captured Lord Byssus and killed The Wing. As soon as we did that, the soldiers swore fealty to Lord Byssus' daughter, Lady Kandyce. She's a good woman who wanted nothing more than to return home and free her people. When we left, she was sailing to Wantage with ten warships and four thousand soldiers. I expect they've already retaken Wantage by now. That's why we think the Split Crows are in a blood bath. They will not take losing two cities within a week's time lightly."

Danny's hazel-green eyes brightened. "I think we met an old Berrat friend of yours." Kit's face screwed up at the comment, wondering what Berrat friend she might have in Lilloet. "I believe his name is Old Sky Eyes." Kit's mouth dropped open at the mention of the elder's name.

"Sky Eyes lives? You met him?"

"We did," Breayn said. "He spoke highly of you. Because you've unseated King Karter from his rule over Cormorant means he wasn't exaggerating."

"And we also put the boots to operations in Ravenlord," Indie added, quick to show off all they had accomplished as well.

"You attacked House Nobilis?" Danny asked. There was a heavy dose of awe in his voice.

"Not directly." Indie deflated. "We took seven black ships, the slaves, and all the equipment that was being transported. But a big part of the shipment was silvered weapons destined for Ravenlord."

"Those little blue freaks are amazing." Lin strode into the room, holding Fury, the sentient dragon hammer, aloft in triumph. Her joyous expression fell away at the sight of Danny and Breayn. She gave the red headed Berrat a half-hearted smile and an even less enthusiastic nod.

"Hello, Aithlin." Danny's voice dripped with sarcasm. "I'd like you to meet my cousin, Breayn."

"The Hobgoblins wouldn't appreciate you calling them *little blue freaks*," Kit replied, cutting off the banter before it started.

"I don't think they'd care," Lin said, returning her attention to Kit, twirling the large double-headed mithril hammer in her hands. "There isn't a sane one in the bunch."

"Did they get Fury out of the soul cannister and into the hammer?" Indie asked, his eyes never leaving Kit.

"Am I not resplendent?" asked a sonorous voice with a slight lisp. Kit covered her mouth with a badly shaking hand. Fury's appearance was exactly as it had been when the Fate, Tyr, had transformed him into a draken inside the secret library. He was nearly seven feet tall. His skin-scales were an iridescent blue, the blue of a mid-day sky. He bowed deeply to Kit, his colors shifting as he did, reflecting the different hues coming through the stained-glass windows.

"You're a dragon again?" Indie asked, his mouth agape. "How?"

"Oh, no, my fine young man. I am neither a dragon, nor am I even truly in draken form, but I *can* project myself from the hammer to create this wondrous manifestation of myself." The draken lowered his head. "So long as I am within ten paces of the hammer."

Lump jumped down from the sofa he had been curled up on and leapt towards Fury, landing a few feet from him. The golden retriever put himself into a play-bow, his front feet stretched out with his butt high in the air, his tail spinning in slow, lazy circles.

"At least someone knows how to address me properly," Fury said with his weird lizard-like grin. "Who's a good dragon-puppy?"

"He's not a dragon-puppy." Kit growled and craned her neck at the draken visage. "But you are as beautiful as I remember."

"Well, of course I am." Fury put his body on full display. He chuckled as he ran his clawed fingers across his iridescent scales. "But I appreciate hearing you say it."

"Fury? Is that really you?" Danny blinked in disbelief. "You look just like you did in that secret library."

"Well, of course it's me," Fury said with a small bow. "Nobody can match my splendor."

"You're *the* Fury?" Breayn stepped back so as to see the draken in his entirety. She chuckled lightly, narrowing her eyes. "The Dragon Lord, second only to Ouroboros himself?" she added, her voice dripping with doubt.

"In part, yes," Fury responded, this time bowing much more deeply. "It's nice to meet somebody who recognizes greatness when they see it."

"You're full of surprises," Breayn said to Danny.

"He's full of something," Indie mumbled, earning him a stiff jab in the ribs from Kit's elbow.

"Does this mean you can return the other trapped souls?" Indie asked, wrapping his arm around Kit. Lin grimaced at the question.

"It won't be easy. We must find their bodies first.

"Who are in the other two cannisters?" Kit asked, finally tearing her eyes away from Fury.

"Well," Fury said, "one of them is Robyrt Karter and..."

"Sweet Titan," Kit said with a whistle. "Does Rusty know?" Fury shook his head and grinned his creepy, lizard-like grin.

"I doubt it. I haven't spoken of this to anyone else."

"How can you know that? How can you know it's her father in there?" Indie crossed his arms in front of his chest. Kit couldn't help noticing that both his chest and arms looked bigger. "How can you possibly know whose souls are in the other canisters?"

Fury smiled and wiggled his long-clawed fingers in front of himself. "Dragon magic," he said with dramatic flair.

"C'mon, be serious." Kit rolled her eyes at the wondrous creature. His draken form may have been mesmerizing, but it was the same arrogant dragon on the inside.

"I am serious." Fury flinched at his assertion. "I can sense who's been trapped in the cannisters. Maybe it's because I was kept in proximity to them these past years."

"Somebody needs to tell Rusty," Kit said, looking straight at Lin, who was staring down at the floor. A moment passed before Lin exhaled deeply and nodded.

Lin sighed. "I'll tell her. I'll go right now." She slowly headed for the door. After several pensive steps, she picked up speed and disappeared in a few moments.

"Who's in the other cannister?" Indie asked, seemingly oblivious to Lin's pain.

"Somebody by the name of Amka Fox-Dancing." Fury gave Kit a quizzical look when her jaw practically bounced off the floor. The draken cocked an eyebrow at Kit's reaction. "I take it you know her?"

"No, not really," the little priest replied before turning her attention to the Berrat cousins.

"But I do," Breayn said, her legs wobbling beneath her. She grasped the corner of a chair for support. "She's my mother." While the others reacted to her revelation, the woman regained her strength. She took a purposeful step toward the draken. "She's why we're here. When we were dealing with Lord Byssus, he told us that her soul had been taken from her body; to be sent to King Faol. I plan on righting the wrong."

"Why was it taken?" Kit asked, her gaze flitting between Breayn and Danny.

"Because we are Berrabbithi," Danny said, his fingers running over his long red mane. "Somehow, King Faol thinks we are the secret to creating better vampires. Too many of those he sires lose their mind to bloodlust. They become unstable creatures, unable to follow orders. He thinks that, with Berrabbithi blood, the vampires he turns will accept the change more easily."

"And yet, she remains here," Fury said, stroking his fingers over his blue scaled chin. "If she was a gift to Faol, why wasn't she taken to him?"

Coldforge had been standing in the background, watching and listening. "Whoever is in King Karter's body wants her for himself, and he's not working to help Faol. I'd say that he has his own interests in mind."

Chapter Three

Family Souls

The moon was rising in the crystal-clear night sky. The group had been pondering the situation for several hours. No one could arrive at a plausible explanation as to why holding onto a Berrabbithi soul was so important to King Karter. When food was delivered to the war room, it gave everyone an excuse to stop talking, at least long enough to fill their faces. Kit was at one of the dining tables, filling up her third helping of food, when Rusty came charging into the war room. The wet, mud-covered uniform she had been wearing earlier in the day had been replaced with a snappy gold on red surcoat with white enameled armor. Her hair was pulled back in a set of severe looking braids, creating an imposing air of authority. Lin stood a step behind the general. Her eyes were red and swollen.

"Lin, are you okay?" Rusty glared at Kit, her words rushing out of her mouth before Lin could answer.

"Is it true? Do you have my father in one of those gold cans, the ones Lin took from his private office?" Rusty scowled at the group when all they did was gawk at her. "Well?"

Rusty nodded her head curtly at the two new guests before turning her attention back to Kit. "I asked if you have my father. Is it true?"

When the seven-foot visage of Fury materialized behind Kit, Rusty staggered backwards a few steps before drawing her saber.

"No need for that, friend." The draken gave the woman an ingratiating smile. "I am Fury, and yes, the essence of your father is contained within a soul cannister."

"It's why your father hasn't been himself," Kit finished. "His body has been inhabited by somebody or *something* else." At Kit's words, the general shook badly. She dropped to her knees, burying her face in her hands. In a heartbeat, Lin knelt down beside her, grasping her in a deep hug. Rusty fought to push her away, but she maintained her grip. Lin held the woman in silence until she raised Rusty's chin, giving her a bit of a crooked smile, her eyes swollen with tears.

"I told you, we can return him to you." She couldn't hide the emotion in her voice. "If we can get your father's body back, we might be able to reunite him with his soul."

"That's impossible." Rusty shoved Lin away and got up from the ground, her take-charge persona instantly reappearing. "If my father's soul has left his body, then he's dead. His soul would have returned to the Great Cycle."

"That's not entirely true." Danny put his plate down and strode smoothly across the room to greet the general. "Our soul's disposition is a common misconception. Those of us who are native to Orth, we pass into the Beyond. Only those created by the gods will pass into the Great Cycle. The essence of those people returns to the god who created them."

Fury chuckled. "You read that in the library, didn't you?" When Danny gave the draken a blank stare, his laugh increased. "And the information only comes to you when you need it to?"

Danny nodded lightly. "It was one of the three books I picked." His attention returned to Rusty. "Humans, Gigas, and the Berrat, are the original races. They all lived here before the gods came to torment us. There are other less known races, but they live secretive lives, in the mountains, in the seas, or beneath the surface."

"And the rest? They're all made by the gods?" Kit asked.

Danny shook his head. "No, not all. But the powerful races, the Elves, the Dwarves, the Trolls, the Orcs, and the Arachne." He was counting them off on his fingers as he listed the peoples of Orth. "They are all children of the gods."

"Arachne?" Kit asked.

"The spider folk, the Anansi, and Arachne, are children of the god Bael. They are part spider and part human, but they are mostly evil. It was from the Anansi that Bael created Arachnielle." Danny stretched and yawned. "It's all quite sad, really. They don't know they're play-things. These people are just living their lives, oblivious to what the gods had intended. They're no different from us."

When Danny stopped talking, the room fell into a somber silence. Mouths opened and closed without a word until, finally, Coldforge broke the quiet.

"Okay then, so yer souls are all going to live on, but me and me kin will return to whichever god created us."

Danny nodded. "You and the Elves will all return to Ollin."

"That's not true." Fury gave the sad-faced dwarf an uncharacteristically warm smile. "That's where you should go, but Ollin isn't *himself* anymore. He is so entwined with the earth that he's a part of Gaia now, along with his mother, Orth." The draken chuckled at the stunned expression on everyone's faces. "I also read some interesting texts in the library."

"I'll return to The Mother?" Coldforge asked. His massive mustache and beard were vibrating.

"Unless something changes," Fury replied with a nod. "The future has not been written, but if things remain, then yes, I believe you will."

"How?" Kit asked. "How can the son of Titan and Orth be a part of Gaia?"

"It would take me days to explain it to you in a manner that you'd understand," Fury said, his condescending tone of superiority leaking out. "But I will try to explain it briefly." Most everyone was waiting patiently for his tale, all except for Rusty, whose scowl had been deepening ever since the conversation moved away from her father.

"And when I am finished explaining this," Fury said to the general, "I will tell you about your father and how we can get him back." Rusty's scowl remained unchanged.

Fury dramatically cleared his throat, ensuring everyone's undivided attention before he began.

"Titan and Orth are of a race known as the Travelers, and they are but bored children. Their parents left them in the care of the Fates, whose sole job was to entertain them and watch over them to ensure they didn't destroy the universe. After an immeasurable length of time, the Fates grew tired of their duty and sought a way to unshackle themselves from their charges."

Fury paused for a moment to survey his audience. His tale had mesmerized all of them, including Rusty. Smiling inwardly, he continued.

"But, even as children, the Travelers are beings of astounding power, capable of creation or destruction with nothing more than a thought. If the Fates abandoned their duties, the Travelers would have eradicated them. It took the Fate, Tyr, to develop a plan, a strategy to separate himself and his cohorts from the children."

"And here I thought Tyr was supposedly a mastermind," Indie scoffed. "It took him how long to come up with an escape plan?"

"Creating a plan to escape from erratic people with nearly limitless power is no small feat, my young apprentice."

"What do you mean, *your apprentice*?" Kit growled, her hands almost instantly igniting into flame.

"That's not important," Indie and Fury responded in unison.

Danny's eyes bulged. "Since when can you do that? Can you ignite more than your hands?" The questions drew a look of ire from Indie. "What?" he asked, genuinely surprised by Indie's reaction. "You don't like that Kit can do that?"

"She can't control it," Lin interjected, a wicked smile crossing her lips. The comment wiped the scowl from Rusty's face, and the two of them shared a grin. "It shows up at *inopportune times*." When Lin giggled, Rusty slapped her shoulder with a backhanded swing, which made Lin laugh all the more. It only took Danny a few seconds to catch on, joining in the chorus of laughter.

"What's the joke?" Coldforge asked, his eyes dancing with merriment. "Ye got ta let me in on it."

"I'm the joke." Indie's face contorted with anger and embarrassment. "Laugh it up, all of you."

As Indie stormed for the exit, Fury tried to cut him off, but as soon as the visage got out of range of the hammer, he winked out of existence.

The entire episode made Coldforge laugh. It started off as a childish giggle, and built into a roaring, thunderous belly-laugh.

"Frook you!" Indie's voice echoed from somewhere down the hallway, likely on the way to his room.

"Will Fury be coming back?" Danny asked Kit, trying to suppress his own mirth. "I'd really like to hear the rest of his story."

"It's not his story to tell," Tyr said as he popped into the group, absent of his typically cool demeanor.

"And yet, tell it I will, Trickster," Fury said, popping up beside Kit.

"Get back into the cane." Tyr charged across the room as he became ensconced in a deep, green aura.

"Make me," Fury laughed. "You have no hold over me any longer, Trickster."

"We'll see about that," Tyr said, just before popping out of existence. In the distance, a coyote howled.

"Why does he do that?" Kit asked, shaking her head.

"You mean treat me like his property?" Fury's head swiveled about, perhaps searching for Tyr. The altercation had clearly set him on edge.

"Well, that, too, but I meant that stupid coyote howl thing he does when he disappears."

"Because he's a narcissistic morsel of refuse who needs to always have the last word." Fury grinned at his comment and preened the shimmering scales on his head and neck.

"The world is full of those types of people," Indie grumbled as he walked back into the room. Apparently, his short time away from the group wasn't enough to soothe his irritability.

Kit growled as the man drew near. "You and I need to have a serious conversation. I don't know what's crawled up your butt, but we're going to work it out." The momentary respite of humor disappeared, and Rusty's face turned a deep shade of purple. The cords in her neck pressed against her skin, threatening to burst out.

"Is anybody going to tell me how we can get my father's soul, his essence, or whatever else you want to call it, back into his body?"

⌘

The moon was high in the night sky by the time the discussion about getting the body of Rusty's father, Robyrt Karter, came to an unsatisfactory conclusion.

"So, even though you think you know how to reunite my father with himself, you have no idea how to locate his body." Rusty turned to each member of the group, but ultimately, she directed her question at Kit.

"We don't know who's in his body," Kit said for what felt like the tenth time. "He can teleport at will. We don't have any way of tracking him and even if we did, we don't know how to make whoever is possessing him vacate."

"At least he has a body to return to." Breayn had become increasingly frustrated with Rusty's inability to think beyond her own personal needs since she had come into the room several hours before. "My mother may be forced to live out her life in someone else's body."

"What would happen if my father was put in my body?" Rusty asked, ignoring the Berrat woman's obvious annoyance with her.

"Your father would compete with you for dominance." Lin grimaced, placing her hand lightly on Rusty's arm. "According to the little blue freaks, it can be a horrific experience."

"Do you think you could live with your mother?" Danny asked Breayn. "If you two could work together, perhaps it could solve your *problem*."

"My father was a good man," Rusty said, talking over Danny. "He would not fight me."

"How do you think it would work, having your father with you, when you are... um... amorous?" Lin said, raising her eyebrows, causing Rusty to blush furiously.

"Humans are way too hung up on sexuality." Breayn pursed her lips, trying to stifle a laugh.

"Can we get back on topic?" Kit asked, with no hint of humor in her voice. "We've got places to be tomorrow and we're burning through the hours like we've got all the time in the world. If we're leaving for Templeton at first light, I need to know what we're walking into." She held out the ledger. "I think it's written in Berrabbithi. It's King Karter's ledger, and it describes everything about his operation. The problem is, I can't read it. Nobody can."

"And you think I can, because of the phoenix bone inside of me?" Danny asked. "Like I could read the documents that Father Hoarfrost gave you?"

"I'm hoping you can," Kit said. "If not, we're going to be going in blind."

"Wait right there." Rusty wagged her finger like a mother scolding her children. "It's my ledger, and I'll decide who is going to see it and when."

The gold in Kit's eyes swirled. She closed the distance between her and the general, her hands clenching tighter with each step she took. "You have sworn fealty to me," the young priest said in an unnaturally deep, resonating voice. "Again, you let your own petty desires, your feelings of jealousy, your disregard for the greater good cloud your judgment."

Rusty stood defiant for a moment, unsure of what she should do. Just before she was about to speak, she lowered her gaze and took a knee. "There is no excuse for my outburst, Mistress Kit. I... I... I'm lost right now. Never have I been in charge of so many. I've always had someone to give me orders. You... you give me latitude, leeway. You tell me what you want and leave it to me to decide how to make it happen. If my father was back, my true father..."

"And if he was here with you now?" Kit asked, her gold eyes pushing away the darkness.

"He was a good man, an outstanding leader, somebody worthy to lead your army."

Rusty's voice had never wavered like this before. She had never shown this side of herself.

"You would give up yourself, your privacy, possibly your life, to get your father back?" Lin asked, her emotions now running amok. "You would give up any chance for *us*?"

"In a heartbeat," Rusty squeaked out, lowering her eyes so nobody could see her despair.

"As would I," replied Breayn. "In a heartbeat."

"It sounds like it's settled then," Kit said. Something inside was telling her this was the correct path, *the way to Titan*.

From the corner of the room, Coldforge yawned loudly, accidentally kicking Lump, who had been sleeping beside him. The sleepy dwarf gave his orange beard a hard tug. "What'd I miss?"

Chapter Four

The Ledger

The remaining group sat in silence after Rusty, Breayn, Lin, and Coldforge left for the Hobgoblin's alchemy lab. Coldforge had accompanied the ladies to make sure the Hobgoblins took their request to transfer the souls seriously and acted promptly. The temperature had dipped after the sun had gone down, so Indie had lit fires in two of the four fireplaces in the war room.

"How long until sunrise?" Kit asked, finally breaking the silence.

"Not long, two hours at most," Indie replied, not bothering to lift his chin from his chest.

"Maybe I should look at that ledger?" Danny tried to stifle a yawn. "If you're planning on heading out at sunrise, we don't have a lot of time." Indie picked up on the sadness in Danny's voice. He raised his head high enough to show everyone his scowl.

"You can't be serious," Danny said, slamming his hands on the arms of his chair. "She's with you, and I couldn't be happier for you both. We're friends, best friends, and that's never going to change. If you have a problem with that, well, that's your problem. It's not mine, and it's certainly not Kit's."

"I set him on fire," Kit said, shaking her head. "When we tried to be *together*."

"Kit!" Indie popped up from his chair, a snarl on his lips.

"Indie's not jealous of us. He's jealous of you and that you cannot be hurt by fire." Kit gave her boyfriend a death stare, challenging him to deny it.

"Whoa." Danny's chuckles made it difficult to get any words out. "That's… Titan's snowballs. That's the funniest thing I think I've ever heard."

"If you hadn't wasted my bottle of dragon brandy, I'd likely be impervious to fire," Indie growled at Kit, ignoring Danny's outburst. "In fact, I might already be... resistant."

"Would you like to prove it to her?" Danny said, standing up from his chair. He called upon the phoenix spirit living in his body. In a moment, his hands were ablaze.

"No!" yelled Kit. "You, put out the fire and sit, and you, let it go, we'll figure it out. Can we please get back to the ledger?"

"Sure thing, Kitten." Danny stared at Indie with a cocky expression.

"I'll get it," said Indie. "Afterwards, I'm going to beat this little freak over the head with it."

"Indie, I swear to Titan..."

Indie picked up the ledger from one of the dining tables and expertly tossed it across the room to Danny. As Kit moved over to sit next to her Berrat friend, Indie moved next to the heat of the fire burning in the hearth. He reached in, letting the flames lick his fingers. After leaving them there for several seconds, he finally reached in and grabbed a good-sized log.

"I'd say that I have a decent amount of resistance to fire." Indie gave a smug smile. He held the flaming log out in front of himself. Seconds later, the young man's eyes widened before he tossed the log back into the fire. He surreptitiously rubbed his palm on his trousers. "It barely hurt at all."

Kit raced across the room, taking his hand in hers. "What were you thinking?" Her voice was a mixture of pity and anger. "Let me see." Kit inspected his hand, inhaling sharply. "Sweet Titan, your hand is covered in scales, golden scales. They're faint, but they're there."

"Fire brings them out." Indie caressed Kit's hand. "In a few minutes, they'll be gone."

"This ledger has everything about the Auctioneers' operations in northern Berrathia. I mean *everything*." Danny got up and headed to one of the dining tables. "It will take me weeks, if not months, to go through it all."

"You can read it?" Kit lead Indie back to where Danny was standing.

"Easily," he said. "There are several symbols used on each line, but there is a chart at the back of the ledger that explains them all."

"What about the shipment that was to go to Templeton?" Kit asked. "It was due to leave port here three nights ago... or was it four? I've lost any sense of time these days."

Danny flipped through the pages of the ledger, looking for the entry that Kit was talking about. When he found it, he let out a low whistle. "There were five hundred Berrat to be delivered, along with three crates of gold, and a letter of Lordship over Aarall to be provided by King Jordain."

"There is no lord of Aarall," Indie chimed in. "That role was filled by Father Hoarfrost and the Temple. Who's it supposed to go to?"

"Somebody by the name of Lord Renay Aster, the current lord of Templeton."

"We got played," Kit growled, her hands igniting into flames. Indie, seeing the fire licking up around Kit's fingers, grabbed her hands, squeezing them tightly. As Kit struggled to pull free, her anger at Indie's foolishness made her flames burn brighter. Sucking in a breath, Indie finally released his grip and shook out his hands. Golden scales were now easily visible, along with the large blisters covering his hands and up his wrists.

"Let me see that," Kit said, rolling her eyes at the foolish man. She winced briefly as her golden aura washed over Indie's wounds, healing them instantly. "You don't need to change," she whispered. "I just need to learn to control myself."

"You never even prayed to Titan," Danny stammered out. "Whatever you've got going on, it's impressive."

Kit ignored Danny's comment and returned to the item at hand. "If the king was planning on giving control of Aarall to Aster, then what will happen to Hoarfrost and my father?"

"Your father?" Danny asked. "You found your father?"

Kit nodded, and Indie answered. "Captain Harding."

Danny blew out his cheeks and laughed. "Hard-case Harding's your father? That explains a lot."

"Ha, ha," Kit said with narrowed eyes and a mock grin. "Can we get back to the ledger, please? What else did it say about the shipment to Templeton?"

"Only that it was due to arrive today," Danny said.

"Well," Indie said, shaking his head. "It's going to be late."

"It doesn't have to be." Breayn walked in with Coldforge, Rusty, and Lin, who was mindlessly twirling Kit's war hammer in her hands. Kit had smiled inwardly when Fury had insisted on attending the procedure. It had been good to be away from him for a while. His ability to manifest and chatter on endlessly was grating on her.

"The Hobgoblins were successful?" Danny asked, his face a picture of concern. Neither Breayn nor Rusty appeared to be particularly well. Their eyes were bloodshot, with dark circles under them. Both women nodded in response.

"If the ships can handle the speed, I can get them there before end of day," Breayn said. "I should be able to fill your sails with enough winds..." The woman wobbled. Danny rushed to Breayn's side and escorted her to a chair. Indie followed suit, offering to guide Rusty to a chair as well.

"Ah, chivalry is not dead," Rusty said weakly. "Thank you."

"If you don't mind me saying," Danny said, stoking Breayn's hair. "You look horrible."

"The process was much harder on them than it was on me," Fury declared as he manifested beside Lin. His pompous, self-important mannerisms were non-existent. "I suppose, when they merged my pieces together, it was easier because I was joining with myself. It's so much more taxing to have another soul stuffed into your body. The Hobgoblins made them rings to suppress the foreign soul, to keep them quiet when necessary."

"My mother had many questions," Breayn said, taking a deep breath. "But after a little while, she slowed down long enough to give me a chance to get used to her being in my head."

"I had to use my ring," Rusty said, her eyes full of tears. "My father tried to take me over. He's got an incredibly powerful personality."

"Like father, like daughter." Lin laughed and patted Rusty's shoulder.

"Will you be okay to help Kit get to Templeton?" Danny asked. "You really don't seem up to it."

"Rusty?" Kit asked. "How many soldiers can be safely carried on one of those black ships?"

"Bango would know for sure." Rusty closed her eyes and leaned comfortably into Lin, who had taken a seat beside her. "But if I was to guess, if there was no other cargo, three hundred or so."

"But they were scheduled to carry five hundred Berrat slaves, plus oarsmen." Kit said.

Rusty shrugged, never bothering to open her eyes. "Berrat are tiny, and they're not all carrying weapons and wearing heavy armor." After letting out an enormous yawn, she reiterated Bango would know more about such things. "The harder problem will be to keep the number of volunteers low enough that they don't sink the ship. I'm going to have to beat them off with a stick to convince them all to not go with you."

"Okay," Kit said with a grin. "I'll go find Bango, and the rest of you get some sleep."

"Do you think I can hold on to this ledger?" Danny asked. "It's going to take me a long time to read through it all."

"Rusty will probably object." Kit smiled at the woman, who was now snoring loudly. "But since you're the only one who can read it, it makes sense that you keep it with you." Kit reached into her pocket and pulled out the dragon tears. She tossed one of them to Danny. "Report your findings back to me if you find something important."

"What's this?" Danny asked, rolling the tiny blue and white crystal ball in his hand. When a light glowed from within the dragon tear, Danny's eyes widened. "I can see you in it."

"And speak to me as well," Kit said with a grin. "Over extremely long distances. Now you won't have to leave me any letters. You can speak to me directly." Danny grinned and stuffed the crystal into his pocket.

"You mustn't let that fall into the wrong hands," Fury piped up. "They have powerful magic within them, and they can be easily used against us."

Danny nodded knowingly and patted his pocket, burying his nose back into the ledger.

⌘

"Bango?" Kit called out, knocking on the door of the new harbormaster. Once Rayan Staul had passed along everything he knew to his successor, he left to take up residence with his family at the plot of land Aurora's Guard had offered him in return for his cooperation.

"Yes, Mistress Kit?" a bleary-eyed Bango responded, opening the door to her quarters. She had taken a room in the manor, rather than stay in the harbormaster's residence. During the transition phase of things, she thought it would be better to be nearby, in case Kit needed her at a moment's notice, like now.

"I'm sorry to wake you," Kit said, pushing past Bango, not waiting for an invitation. "We will leave port in a few hours with a black ship. How many soldiers can it safely carry with minimal cargo?"

"What's the purpose of the soldiers?" Bango asked.

"I am going to overthrow Templeton."

"Okay," Bango said, still rubbing the sleep from her eyes. "Including a crew and oarsmen, you can take three hundred soldiers. You can bring heavy arms and armor for half of them, and light arms and bows for the rest. Make sure none of them are wearing the armor during the voyage. If they were to fall overboard while dressed in iron and steel, it would be bad for them."

"And if I want them all to be in heavy armor?" Kit was considering the city's layout and the likelihood they'd have to breach the temple if the enemy hid behind its walls.

"Two hundred and fifty, at most. I've already assembled a ship's crew for you. They are at the Rusty Anchor, awaiting your orders."

"Yes, if you could. I'm going to see about getting the soldiers. I'd have asked Rusty to do that, but she's sleeping. She had a rough night." When Bango was going to ask about it, Kit waved her hands to dismiss any questions before they started.

Chapter Five

The Mysty and the North Wind

The first rays of the sun were showing over the horizon when Kit made it to Captain Tym Windspeak's modest residence. Of all the military leaders who had sworn fealty to her, she figured he'd be the best man to assemble an army for her to bring to Templeton. She could have sent somebody to bring him to her, but Kit looked forward to having some alone time and soak up the crisp morning temperatures. She had spent no significant time at a port before, and she was growing to love the tang of the salty sea air.

Before Kit could even wrap on the captain's front door, it swung open, revealing a young girl of nine or ten cycles. Her jet-black hair was in long braids that hung down in front of her frilly nightgown.

"Good morning, Mistress Kit Standing Bear." The small girl greeted her warmly. "My father will be down shortly. Would you like to join us for breakfast?"

A Nomad woman bustled up behind the girl, shooing her from the door. Like her daughter, the woman had long jet-black braids hanging down over her frilly nightgown.

"Mistress Kit, you grace us with your presence. Please excuse my daughter, Elisa's, boldness."

"Please, just call me Kit. She's a delightful girl. She clearly takes after her mother." Kit gave the woman a broad grin. "Elisa has offered me some breakfast."

The woman's eyes went wide with joy. "Oh, yes. Please come in and join us. I was about to put it on the table. My name is Finnigan, but everyone calls me Fin."

Kit was already on her second plate of eggs, ham, and biscuits when a bare-chested man, scrubbing his face with a thin hand towel, walked into the kitchen. "Have either of you seen my dress lapels? I want to look my best when Mistress Kit leaves this morning." The captain had not feigned the deep seductive voice he'd used during Kit's interrogation of him. At the sound of his wife excessively clearing her throat, and his child giggling wildly, he pulled the towel down from his face, which turned bright red.

"Holy Helja, my apologies, Mistress Kit. I wasn't expecting you." Kit chuckled when the man tried to hide his bare chest with the tiny hand towel.

"Dear," Fin said, "maybe you should scoot upstairs and finish dressing."

"No need." Kit motioned for the man to take a seat. "I need to get back to the manor, but I have a request of you."

The captain sat at the table as his wife placed a large plate of food before him. He paused momentarily, waiting for Kit's approval to begin. As soon as she did, he shoveled the food into his mouth.

He didn't say a word until he had finished half his plate. He was either starving or he was trying to calm his nerves. "What do you need me to do?"

"Round up an army of two hundred and fifty soldiers with heavy arms and armor. I want to bring them with me to Templeton this morning. We're going to overthrow it."

The captain continued eating, clearly trying to think through the logistics of putting an army together in a few hours. His head bobbed as he swallowed his last mouthful. "If I may, I would suggest that I put together two hundred infantry and fifty archers. If you're planning on attacking a fortified location, you're going to want missile support." When Kit chuckled to herself, the captain gave her a questioning look.

"Bango also said I needed to include archers as well, but she suggested half of the soldiers be heavy infantry and the rest be archers."

"Not a bad call, if you have to breach a fortified wall, like we have here. But if you're going to fight inside a city, you're going to get into melee and heavy troops will suit you better. Using archers to soften up the target is always a good thing."

Fin brought a couple more plates of food, replacing the now empty plates in front of both Kit and her husband. Kit tried to wave it off, but the woman wouldn't take no for an answer.

"I will leave one of my commanders in charge during my absence." The captain struggled to swallow a fresh mouthful of food. "I'll make sure he squares away a training regime with General Karter while I'm away."

"You want to come?" Kit's voice was muffled as she pushed another forkful into her mouth.

"Are you kidding?" The captain tried to not to spray food. He nearly succeeded. "For a chance to fight by your side, I would—"

"Yes, dear? And what exactly would you be willing to do?" His wife's eyebrows shot up. She still had the questioning look when she delivered two mugs of fresh steaming coffee that had just finished brewing. The captain ducked his head and shoveled more food into his mouth. "Men!" With a loud harrumph, she headed back over to her cookstove.

The rest of the conversation was light, with Kit asking Elisa what she liked to do to fill her day. The little girl turned into a chatterbox, rhyming off all the different things she enjoyed doing, but she got most excited when she talked about training with her father, swinging wooden swords and shooting haystacks with her bow. Fin didn't seem to appreciate that aspect of her hobbies, but the child was so animated in her storytelling that her mother could only smile at her.

As soon as Kit had finished her coffee, she thanked her gracious hosts and headed for the door. As she stepped out, she asked the captain to have his men boarded and ready to leave in two hours.

When Kit got back down to the harbor, the sun was up, and the Gaelinora sea was dead-calm. There wasn't nary a wisp of wind, and the sun reflecting off the water lit up the hulls of the ships still at dock. Most of the fishing vessels would have left hours ago, leaving only pleasure ships, merchant vessels, a few barges and the seven black ships. Bango, along with several other Port Authority personnel, were busy loading the *Mysty* with supplies for the journey.

"The crew is still having breakfast at the Rusty Anchor," Bango said when Kit approached. "They'll be set and ready to go at a moment's notice."

"Excellent." Kit surveyed the docks and the endless sea beyond while the Port Authority loaded supplies onto the ship. "Captain Windspeak will assemble an army of two hundred heavy infantry and fifty archers. It seems you know more about military tactics than you let on." Bango gave Kit a small grin and shrugged her shoulders. "The captain will come along. He's going to leave a commander in charge while he's gone, to make sure the rest of his soldiers continue their training. Maybe you can look in on Rusty to make sure she's aware of the temporary change in command?"

Bango's chin dropped low. "I wish I was going with you, too. Watching you in combat was... exhilarating."

"Sorry, I need you here. My friend Danny showed up last night. He can decipher the ledger." Bango's eyes lit up at the news. Knowing what was in the ledger would be the key to gutting the Auctioneers' trade. "If my mother, Aurora, returns, she'll want to know everything in that book as well."

Kit and Bango walked in silence toward the manor. Bango's pace was far faster than usual, spurred on by the idea of getting detailed info on what the slavers had been up to.

Bango spoke. "I'm assuming that Lin and Indie will also be joining you?" Kit nodded without a word, lost in her own thoughts of what the day might bring. "Do you want me to have your horses loaded as well?"

"Yes, of course." Kit snapped out of her trance. "I would suggest that the captain's horse come along as well, assuming there is room onboard."

"Will do, and I'll ensure the animals have ample supplies."

The *Mysty* was docked with the other six black ships that Kit's army had commandeered from the slavers. Even moored, their black-stained hulls and massive size gave them an imposing look. The sun was now low in the east, turning the sea's dark waters into a brilliant shade of blue. The surface was so still the entire sea resembled a giant mirror, reflecting the bright blue sky and the puffy white clouds that hung lazily in the cool morning air.

With no winds to drive them off, the heavy scents of decaying sea life and sewage hung heavily. The only respites were the briny salt-air and the acrid scent of wood fires that were burning at the shore's edge. Kit stared out at the great blue vastness. The sailors and soldiers alike were becoming agitated by the delay, but none would speak their displeasure aloud.

The morning continued to burn on, but Kit held the *Mysty* at dock. She had no plans on leaving without Runt, and when she finally spotted him racing up the docks with a pack of gray wolves at his heels, she breathed a sigh of relief. Her dire wolf pup had left with Fenrir and Amilta to search for Shade, Amaruq's Omega, three days earlier. Apparently, the wolf god thought Runt's presence would be necessary if they found him. Kit could have sworn he'd grown a great deal since he'd left, but it was likely just her imagination, after having only Lump around for the past few days. But based on the pup's exuberance, knocking Kit to the ground and giving her a thorough tongue-bath, Runt was still the same puppy at heart. He finally climbed off Kit when Lump joined into the fray, the boys rejoicing with their own doggie-reunion.

Amilta shed her wolf form. "We could find no sign of Omega or Ymir. We will continue looking while you're away." Even though Fenrir had been with them on their search, Kit was inwardly happy they hadn't found them. She desperately wanted to be there for that encounter, and she guessed Indie would as well. He was still nursing that sore spot, thinking the worst of his father, who had worshipped the traitorous god, Ymir.

Breayn smiled warmly at Amilta. "Will you be joining us?" Even though they were meeting for the first time, Breayn took an immediate interest in the child, connecting with her at a spiritual level. When Amilta shook her head in reply, Breayn appeared genuinely disappointed.

"If you're still here when I return, I'd enjoy a chance to speak with you."

The young Berrat girl smiled sweetly back at Breayn, pleased with the attention she had received.

"With no scent to follow, I expect I will be here for at least a few days. My pack will patrol the new village that's being built outside the city walls. Fenrir asked me to help guide any of the Berrat there, to teach them how to spirit bind."

"If you could," Kit said, "that would be wonderful. I know in my home village in Lilloet, almost nobody could take the form of anything more significant than a small animal."

"They have lost touch with Gaia," Amilta and Breayn said in unison. The two Berrat laughed at themselves.

"With Gaia?" Kit couldn't figure out why the earth god would have anything to do with their shifting ability.

"Gaia is nature," Breayn said. "It was through the Berrabbithi's connection with her that they learned to embrace the animal spirits. We could bond with animals without harming them. Now, the only way for most Berrat to spirit bond is to separate the animal's spirit from their body by killing them. I suppose the outcome is similar, but the animal suffers for it."

Coldforge rubbed the sweat off his hands. "Not that I want to be at sea, but the sooner we leave, the sooner I can get off this accursed boat."

And with that, Amilta said her goodbyes and exited the docks with her pack.

⚬⚬⚬⚬⚬◈⚬⚬⚬⚬⚬

With the *Mysty* loaded with soldiers, their gear, the horses, and enough supplies to keep them fed and watered for several days, the oarsmen finally pulled the well-laden ship out of port. Filled to capacity, the ship ran low, the water surface not too far below the ship's deck. There still wasn't so much as a ripple on the water, so when the crew unfurled the sails, they laid limp and lifeless.

"Okay then," Breayn said from her place on the ship's quarterdeck, a few feet behind the helm and the ship's captain. Her hands shook as she concentrated, calling on the wind to push the boat to their destination. The Berrat woman presented no sign that she was performing any sort of magic, and yet, a light gust of wind came from nowhere, filling the ship's sails, propelling it forward at a slow but steady pace. As soon as it was underway, Makara jumped along the sides of the boat, following along in the ship's wake. Many of them were huge, nearly the length of the ship itself, their blue-black skin glistening each time they broke the surface. Their single, blue-white spiral horns looked to have been carved from ice.

Once the *Mysty* was at a suitable distance from port, Breayn called more heavily upon the winds. The small wake coming off the ship's prow turned into a tremendous wave as the hull cut deeply through the water. The mainsail groaned as the winds continued to build.

Kit cupped her hands around her mouth. "You're going to break the ship." Much of her voice was blown away, but Breayn got the message. She let her eyes shut and raised her face into the spray of water coming off the bow of the vessel. With effort, she redirected some of the wind to the stern of the ship, creating a massive wave, propelling the vessel even faster. With the push from the water's surge, the pressure on the mast reduced somewhat.

Kit couldn't help but chuckle when the boys, Indie, and Lin were all standing at the prow of the ship, enjoying the full-face sea air. Coldforge was standing near the side rail, looking like he was going to hurl. "How long can you keep this up?"

The Berrat had to scream over the rush of the wind. "With my mother's help, until we arrive."

"How long do you think it will take to get us there?" This was the first time Kit had ever been on a boat of any kind, giving her absolutely no sense of how fast they were traveling. And, since she had never seen Arnnor from this perspective, she had no sense of where she was.

"I have no idea." Breayn couldn't hide her annoyance. It appeared to Kit that trying to carry on a conversation was an unwanted distraction, so she gave the woman a pat on the shoulder for support and left her to the task at hand.

When Kit got to the side rail to check on Coldforge, the Makara were still following along with the boat, leaping from the water like a pod of dolphins.

"Why don't we go below?" Kit tried to pull Coldforge from the railing. He was gripping it so tightly that the wood was splitting in multiple places. When he shook his head adamantly in response, Kit tried to offer him encouragement, but it was lost on him.

She walked up to the ship's prow, joining her friends, letting the sea air fill her nostrils with its tangy goodness. After a good long while of standing in silence, Kit suggested they join Captain Windsong below deck and prepare for their arrival at Templeton.

Chapter Six

Lady Kandyce and Lieutenant Regnor Barclay

Icy winds had whipped the North Sea into a froth. Massive waves relentlessly pounded against the hulls of the ships, constantly throwing them off course. The captain of the *Narwhal* never stopped cursing. Despite his protestations, the well-seasoned sailor led the fleet through wind and waves. It had been three days since they'd set sail from Lilloet. They should have arrived at their destination in two.

"I tell ya, the sea is against us. The wet bitch doesn't want us to make port in Wantage." Captain Ruckham's voice was swept away by the heavy easterly wind. The man was too heavy for his height, but he was far from fat. Thick unruly hair covered his face and a thick layer of frozen salt clung to it. Whatever hair he had was either cropped short or tucked up under his thick wool cap.

"How far are we from the city?" Lieutenant Barclay yelled at the captain as he shielded his face from the sea's icy spray. "Lady Kandyce wants to get home as soon as possible."

"If'n it wasn't for the mist, we'd be able to see port." The captain pointed off the ship's starboard side. "It's only two leagues from us, but the sea keeps pushing the *Narwhal* north..."

Kandyce shielded her eyes from the wind and stared off towards the south. She could see no sign of land; only water, rain, and a thick gray mist that obscured everything. How the captain could know where he was, was beyond her.

"Regnor, can we drop the sails and row in?" Kandyce wasn't much of a sailor but if the wind was working against them, it seemed reasonable to let the oarsmen take over. The lieutenant shrugged and turned to the captain. The man stared at the thick fog, facing directly into the wind, his long white beard whipping about his face.

"We'll need your soldiers' help," he said, sucking in a deep breath of tangy sea spray. "To make any headway in this, we're need to achieve ramming speed. The oarsmen's backs will give out long before we reach port."

"To get us ashore, my soldiers will paddle with their hands if they have to." Regnor stole a glance at Kandyce who nodded her approval. "Give the word and my people will take over."

"Get below deck and tell the coxswain." The captain renewed his grip on the helm's spoked wheel. "Ye should take shelter, too, Lady Kandyce. The open deck is no place for a woman of your station. I expect you'll find my quarters much more comfortable." The woman's long black hair was plastered across her face as she nodded in agreement. She took Regnor's hand and allowed the lieutenant to lead her from the quarterdeck to the stateroom.

It took the *Narwhal's* crew several hours to row into the sheltered port of Wantage. The coxswain switched out the ship's crew, replacing them with soldiers when their arms and backs gave out. It appeared the soldiers were ill-suited to the task, requiring relief every twenty minutes. The other seven ships laden with Lady Kandyce's troops followed the *Narwhal's* lead, switching from sails to oarsmen. They may or may not have also been using soldiers to help row, but they arrived into the port well over an hour later.

The port of Wantage was a natural deep-water harbor, sheltered on three sides by tall, rugged peaks. A narrow valley cut through the mountains to the city's south. A road ran south from the city through the valley. It was the only way in or out of Wantage, except by sea.

"Where are all the ships?" Kandyce asked the captain, moving in beside him at the helm. "Outside of our fleet, the harbor's empty."

"They set sail for Taseko," he replied. "I thought you knew."

"Knew what?" Kandyce strained to see past the docks to the city beyond. A heavy fog lingered, making it impossible to see anything beyond the shoreline.

"The Beak," the captain said, "she took the rest of the fleet to Taseko. The entire population of the city has been moved there."

"When?" Regnor shared the same look of confusion as Kandyce. "Why did the Split Crows empty the city?"

The captain shrugged and shook his head. "Not my business to ask. I do as I'm told. I live longer that way."

"What should we do?" The lieutenant nudged Kandyce. "There's no city left to take over." The woman paused, considering her options. She twisted her salt-stained hair into a ponytail and tied it in a knot.

"How long to sail to Taseko from here?" she asked.

"With fair winds, three days," the captain said. "But with the winds we're facing, a fortnight at least."

"How are the ships fixed for supplies?" Regnor asked. "Is there enough food and water to get us to Taseko?"

"There's enough on board to get us to Cormorant," the captain said. "It's where we were supposed to go before you waylaid my vessel."

"Cormorant?" Kandyce said, her brow furrowed. "Why would my father be sending soldiers to Cormorant?" The captain shrugged yet again.

"I go where I'm told ta go. Like I said, I'd don't ask questions and I live longer."

"Signal the other ships," Kandyce said. "We'll make sail for Taseko." The captain puckered his lips like he had just sucked a lemon. "Is there a problem, Captain?" The man's expression went flat, and he shook his head briskly.

"No, m'lady. I am here to serve."

"Speak, Captain. I wouldn't have asked if I didn't want to hear your opinion," Kandyce replied, pushing her nose so close to the captain's that his beard tickled her chin.

"M'lady," he said, holding her gaze. "The winds we're fighting are unnatural. The North Sea is treacherous on the best of days. But I will take this fleet wherever you tell me to."

"Why don't we spend the night in the harbor," Regnor said, as the last of the warships were coming into port. "It will give everyone a chance to rest, and with any luck the sea will be in a friendlier mood come daybreak."

"Does that work for you, Captain?" Kandyce asked. "Tell me true." The captain's shoulders slumped at the question.

"The crew would be grateful for the rest, m'lady. Perhaps the morn will bring favorable winds."

"Signal the other ships," Regnor said. "We'll make anchor here. I don't want to be at dock, in case the Crows left any people behind. I don't want someone sneaking aboard under the cover of darkness."

"As you wish," the captain said, motioning for one of his crew to join him. "I'll set sentries to keep watch through the night, to make sure no boat finds its way to us while we sleep."

"No, Captain," Kandyce said. "Just signal the other ships. My soldiers will take watch."

⬟

The night in Wantage harbor had been quiet and uneventful. The smells of meat cooking in the galley woke Kandyce from what had been a remarkably deep sleep.

"Coffee?" Regnor asked, coaxing Kandyce's eyes open. She had slept in the captain's quarters while Regnor had spent the night in the hold with the captain, the ship's crew, and the rest of the soldiers. A smile crossed her lips as she reached out for the heavy earthenware mug. She was bringing it to her lips when the ship heaved, causing her to spill the glorious hot beverage onto herself.

"I take it the seas are no better today than yesterday?" she asked, ineffectively trying to wipe the brown stain from her shift.

"The seas are as favorable as I've ever seen," the captain said, entering his cabin. "We've been at sea for several hours."

"We have? Why didn't anyone wake me?"

"Your lieutenant suggested you needed your rest." The captain raised his eyebrows. "Perhaps *suggested* is too soft a word."

Regnor forced out a smile, his hands clenching into tight fists by his side. He turned his attention back to the woman. "We've got several long days ahead of us. Take sleep when you can. You never know when the next peaceful night might be." Kandyce nodded and took a sip of her coffee. The bitterness of the drink chased away the last of her slumbering mind.

"So, three days to Taseko, Captain?" she asked, brushing her fingers over the deep brown stain on her clothing.

"Maybe two, if the weather stays like this. The skies are clear, and we've got a favorable wind at our back. It seems Triton wants us to get to our destination."

A frantic sailor burst through the doorway. "Captain. Black ships are headed for us."

"How many?" the captain asked, already heading for the door.

"Maybe twenty," the sailor replied. "Hard to tell for sure. They're bunched close together."

"How do you know they're heading for us?" Regnor asked, following the captain towards the door.

"They changed direction to intercept us," the sailor said. "They were hugging the coastline until they headed our way."

"Captain?" Kandyce asked, downing the rest of her coffee.

"Get dressed and get on deck," he said. "We're going to need every pair of hands at the ready."

⌘

"Can we outrun them?" Kandyce asked as she moved up beside the captain.

"Yes and no," the captain replied, just after yelling at his first mate to arm the aft ballista with scatter shot. "The big merchant vessels are no match for us, but the cutters will run us down. Our only hope of escaping them is to destroy their mainsails."

"Are the cutters the ships at the front of the fleet?" Kandyce asked, pulling her cloak tighter around her neck. "They're not big."

"Each vessel holds about seventy-five sailors," the captain replied. "They're either going to disable our sails or ram us. Their job is to slow us down. Those big tubs likely hold a thousand soldiers each. If they board us, we don't stand a chance."

There was a loud twang, followed by an even louder bang. The ballista stationed not ten paces behind the helm had just fired off a bag of stone shot at the cutter nearest the *Narwhal*. Dozens of fist-sized stones landed nearly a hundred paces short of the target. Two thick-armed sailors were already winching the giant crossbow's steel cable back while three other sailors were dropping sacks of stones into the huge leather cup suspended between the cables. The weapon's configuration made it look like an enormous slingshot. Before the ballista had again been fully locked and loaded, the cutter swerved, changing its angle of attack.

"Make yer next one count," the captain called out again. "She'll soon be too close to hit."

There was another loud twang followed by a colossal bang. The stone shot flew at its mark, the top of the cutter's mast exploding on contact. Most of the small ship's sail went limp, but the vessel continued to close on the *Narwhal*. A second and a third twang announced two more loads of stone shot. The first came from the bow of the *Narwhal*, its projectiles flying over the approaching cutter, landing harmlessly into the black water. Another volley came from the *Wave Runner*, the *Narwhal's* sister ship. A staccato of loud cracks filled the air when the shot found their target. The cutter's main mast and jib both exploded, fully dropping its sails. When the jib sail hit the water, it acted like an anchor, spinning the fast-moving cutter away from the Narwal and into the prow of the

Wave Runner. The much larger ship slammed into the smaller vessel, cutting its hull in two, sending its crew into the icy waters.

"Drop the skiff," the captain yelled out, motioning for his crew to step into action.

"Captain, they're the enemy," Kandyce said, raising her voice to make her point. "They'd not do it for us."

"The sailors are doing as they're told. Those who survived the collision don't need to freeze to death in these waters. I know most of the men in the Crows' navy and I will not let them be fish bait."

"Captain! We are not here to rescue our attackers."

"When the battle's over, ye can keelhaul me if you wish, but I'll not let those people drown. Not if I can help it." He motioned to his sailors to follow his instructions. They moved swiftly, dropping the skiff into the water, calling out to the sailors who were desperately clasping onto floating debris.

"Cap'n," another of the sailors yelled, pointing to another of the cutters that was headed for their ship, a massive wake spraying from its prow. "It's the *Sea Wind*. She's gonna ram us!"

The sailors had almost finished lowering the skiff when the cutter neared. Before impact, they dropped the small vessel the last few feet to the water before running for cover. A huge, pointed timber stuck out from the vessel's bow, narrowly missing the Narwhal's hull. As it swerved to port, it missed striking the quarter deck by only a few feet. The two ships scraped against each other, the wooden timbers screeching in protest as they rubbed together.

The *Narwhal* lurched from the contact. Any unprepared sailors were sent skittering across the deck. When the ship listed heavily, it sent five deckhands overboard into the black, frigid waters.

"Sailors overboard," somebody shouted, racing across the main deck, snatching up a long coil of rope. Two more deckhands moved in beside the first as he tossed the longline into the water. Those who could swim made for the lifeline. With frozen hands and stiff muscles, they took hold. With effort, the crew dragged their cohorts aboard the boat.

The *Sea Wind* dropped its sea anchor, slowing the vessel. Its crew readied their own skiffs, lowering them into the water to help those floundering in the choppy seas. A bright red ball of flame shot up from the ship. It arched across the sky, leaving a yellow-orange trace behind.

"What are they doing?" Kandyce yelled to the captain. "Why are they stopping their attack?"

"Because we are not enemies." The captain moved to the railing along the ship's rear castle. He doffed his hat to the *Sea Wind's* captain who returned the gesture in kind. "We are of the same navy, and we do not kill our own, not if we don't have to."

"You're turning us over to them?" Regnor said, drawing his sword.

"Put that blade away," the captain barked. "I am not turning you over to them. But I am going to have a parlay with the man." The lieutenant put his sword away, shaking his head.

"I will talk with the other captain as well," Kandyce said, her jaw jutting out. "I want to hear what you two have to say to each other."

"If'n you insist, I will relent," the captain said, gripping the railing. "But it'll go easier if I'm talking with the man by myself."

"Why? Why would it go better if I'm not there?"

"Because as far as he's concerned, you're a slaver. If you're with me, he'll hold his tongue for fear of losing it." The captain made a signal with his arms to the captain of *The Sea Wind*. Within a few moments, his crew were busy tossing ropes across to the crew of the *Narwhal*. "M'lady, I'm asking you to trust me as I have trusted you."

"You were forced to trust us when five hundred of my soldiers climbed aboard your vessel," Regnor said, his eyebrow cocked. "What choice did you have?"

"You know nothing of the sea, lieutenant," the captain said with a smirk. "Had I wanted, you'd all be resting deep beneath the waves. When you brought Lord Byssus aboard wrapped in chains, I decided you were on the right side of things." Kandyce caught her lieutenant's attention and nodded her agreement.

"I think he's bluffing," Regnor said as he led Kandyce from the captain. "I don't think he could have overpowered us, but he's right. We know nothing of the sea and what he could or could not have done to us once we were under sail." Kandyce leaned in close and dropped her voice low.

"Either way, make sure our people are armed and ready to fight if we have to. If this turns into a boarding party, we will not be caught unprepared."

Captain Ruckham strode across the aft deck with the captain of the *Sea Wind* at his side. The two men had matching crimson jerkins over white linen shirts and dark gray breeches. The way the second captain stayed a step behind Captain Ruckham suggested he was, at least to a degree, a subordinate.

"Lady Kandyce, Lieutenant Barclay, this is Captain Nelsyn of the Sea Wind." The captain bowed respectfully as he was being introduced. "We will await Captain Robyrts, and at that point, we will decide what will happen next."

"You call Robyrts, captain, and he'll likely throw you overboard," Captain Nelsyn said. A wicked smile crossed his clean-shaven face.

"Just because the Crow bitch put him in charge, doesn't make him an admiral," Captain Ruckham said, spitting on the deck. "The man's a menace."

"An absolute picaroon," Captain Nelsyn laughed, "but he has friends among the other captains. You'll need him onboard if you're going to get them all to side with Lady Kandyce. You'll need to give him something, something bigger than calling him *admiral*."

"I'm not giving him the Narwhal." The captain spat out the words, his nostrils flaring, his eyes bulging. The man's antics made Captain Nelsyn laugh all the more.

"I don't think that's what he'll want." The man's eyes fell onto Kandyce, eying her up and down. Regnor's face reddened, and his hand went to his sword.

"He'll not lay a hand on her body," Regnor ground out, his face continuing to redden.

"The man has no interest in her body," Captain Nelsyn laughed again. He looked down his nose and appraised the lieutenant. "You are more his type. All he wants of Lady Kandyce is her hand." Regnor's face drained of blood, turning from deep red to a pasty white.

"It would seem the admiral is a man of ambition," Kandyce said, her tone guarded. "My father was an ambitious man and look where it got him. What could he hope uniting with me would give him? Wantage is empty and Lilloet wanted me gone."

"The admiral is low born," Captain Ruckham said. "Not that his heritage matters to any of us true sailors, but low born, such as himself, cannot rise to power. The city's elite simply wouldn't allow it, and he'd face blockades at every step. But, with you at his side and an army at his back, the snobs may consider him *worthy*."

"But I have no city," Kandyce said with something of a sneer.

"He wants to rule Cormorant," Captain Nelsyn said, shaking his head. "House Hanse is weak and falling apart. They suffer from too many lords and not enough leaders. The youth are rising against the existing hierarchy. They are ripe for the taking."

"That was Lord Wing's plan for my father's soldiers?" Kandyce said, clutching at her breast. "The Crows had planned on expanding their power to include Cormorant. Sweet Titan." The woman gasped at the thought. "They're planning on taking Ravenlord. They're planning on conquering the entire Berrathian kingdom."

"How many soldiers are the black ships carrying?" Regnor asked, his eyes looking across the choppy seas to the six black ships that were heading their way, their hulls riding dangerously low in the water. "How many slaves are aboard those vessels."

"Including crews, we are near twenty cohorts of soldiers and twice that many in slaves," Captain Nelsyn replied. Any joviality he previously had shown slipped from his face.

"Eight thousand men and sixteen thousand slaves?" Captain Ruckham's jaw flopped open. "And you risked their lives to attack us. Why?"

"How could you have known we were against you?" Kandyce asked. "As far as you knew, we were acting on Lord Wing's command."

"I didn't know," Captain Nelsyn said, "but when The Beak speaks, we listen. Everybody listens or bad things happen. If it weren't for Ruckham's act of kindness, we'd have scuttled every one of you." Captain Ruckham scoffed at the comment. "No, my friend, you'd have not survived. The cutters would have slowed you enough for the command ships to draw near. They each carry at least one elemental wizard. As soon as you were in range of their magic, the battle would have been over."

"What are elemental wizards?" Kandyce asked.

"People who can manipulate water, air, fire, and earth," Captain Ruckham said, his head hanging low. "How could the Split Crows have gotten them to join their cause? How did they convince them to leave their homes and come north?"

"Who are they?" Kandyce asked. The captain's explanation was far from helpful.

"Hobgoblins," Captain Ruckham said. "They are some of the most gifted spell casters on all of Orth, second only to the elves."

"They're better than the elves," Captain Nelsyn interjected, "when it comes to manipulating earth and water. But we can save that argument for another day."

"Hobgoblins?" Kandyce said, her head snapping back. Her gaze shifted between the two captains. "Do you mean the blue dwarves that my mother told me stories about as a child? They're... real? The way she told the stories, they were all mad."

"Their crazy laughter sends chills up my back," Captain Nelsyn said. "And I hear the Crows had many of them shipped to Cormorant, along with hundreds of dwarves."

"How could the Crows get them? They are not *that* powerful, are they?" Regnor's brow was furrowed to the point his eyes had all but disappeared. "They are being helped by someone. They have to be. Somebody who wants the slave trade unified. We know King Faol is gathering his forces at Ravenlord, but I doubt even he has a long enough reach to snatch dwarves from the Mithril

Mountains. That's dragon territory, home of the dragon lord, Ouroboros, himself." The two captains shrugged at the lieutenant's comments.

⌦⌦⌦◆⌦⌦⌦

Even in the now dead-calm sea, the *Narwhal* and the *Black Witch* worked in tandem to bring the two ships side by side. Two short stocky blue creatures stood at either end of the *Black Witch*, their eyes closed, and their hands extended before themselves as they concentrated on their task. As soon as the two vessels were latched together, a man dressed in a long crimson cloak swung from a rope across the main deck, landing lithely onto the quarter deck. He touched down, barely making a sound.

"Bloody Helja," Captain Ruckham swore under his breath. "Perhaps we should throw him a parade in honor of his arrival." Captain Nelsyn laughed behind his hand, desperately hoping the admiral hadn't noticed.

"Admiral on deck," the first mate bellowed out. "All hail, Admiral Robyrts!"

"Hail," the rest of the crew echoed back.

The admiral threw back his hood with a flourish, revealing his powdered wig, hawkish nose, razor thin lips, and his distinct lack of chin. "Captains," the man called out, his voice shrill and grating. "I'm assuming there is a good reason this ship is not at the bottom of the sea." The two captains cleared their throats, preparing for a response.

"Admiral Robyrts," Kandyce said, gliding up to the man, slipping into her air of ladyship. The woman's long black hair glistened, catching the rays of the midday sun. A small gust of wind blew her locks out behind her until they settled gracefully upon her bare shoulders. She had unbuttoned the top of her blouse enough that she could pull it down, exposing as much skin as she dared. The man standing before her was far from attractive, but her eyes lied, telling the man that he was, without a doubt, the most beautiful creature she'd ever witnessed. "I am Lady Kandyce Byssus, the ruling member of House Byssus. It is my pleasure to meet you." The woman held her hand out to him, palm down.

"Is it just me or did she suddenly become... more beautiful?" Captain Nelsyn whispered. "She's stunning."

"It's a gift she has," Regnor whispered back. "She can alter her appearance at will, to a minimum degree. Truthfully, I find her most beautiful when she's herself, without the glamor." The two captains gave each other a knowing glance.

The admiral placed his hand to his belly and bowed deeply. He held the pose for an extraordinarily long time before straightening himself. With polished grace, he took her fingers in his hand and brushed her skin with his lips. He inhaled deeply as he did, enjoying every moment of the intimacy. As he raised his head, his cheeks flushed.

"Lady Kandyce, the moon and stars hide from your beauty, ashamed to be but a reflection of your luminance. The sun itself pales at your radiance." The man pressed his lips together and blinked.

"You speak most eloquently for a low-born," she replied, the sharp edge in her voice wrapped in layers of obsequious pandering. "It is an honor to meet someone who lifted himself from obscurity to take a station of such renown. You are truly a man bound for greatness."

"It's funny how she managed to insult the man and ingratiate herself to him in the same sentence." The two captains sniggered at the lieutenant's whispered remark, covering their mouths so they wouldn't be heard. "I both hate and admire the politician in her."

The admiral's face became stoic while his bushy eyebrows danced around on his forehead like a pair of wooly bear caterpillars. A sneer appeared for a moment before it melted away, to be replaced by a sycophantic smile.

"We could do great things, you and me," the admiral cooed. "With your station and my political prowess, we could rule the northern lands." Kandyce pouted, her lower lip sticking out like a great pink lump.

"You disappoint me, sir." Her eyebrows shot up. "I would have expected you to offer me all of Berrathia, not just this stretch of frozen waste." The admiral's eyes brightened, and his lips pulled back in a grin wide enough to split his face.

"For you, Lady Kandyce, I would deliver any kingdom your heart desires. I would make King Faol himself bow before you." The woman batted her exquisitely long eyelashes at the man, slapping him playfully on his remarkably muscular forearm.

"And I suppose you'd sweep me off my feet with your manly physique as well," she replied, a deep red blush appearing on her chest, neck, and cheeks. "We've only just met, and you would offer me the world?" The man snatched up the woman's hands and drew her in close.

"First, I will deliver Cormorant unto you. Then I will deliver Ravenlord, all tied up in a pretty bow. If you would take me as your mate, I will deliver whatever city you ask next." Kandyce moved close enough to the admiral that she could taste his wonderfully sweet breath.

"Let's start with Cormorant," she said, her lips brushing his. "When we take King Karter's manor from him, I will show you why I am worth your effort. I know it is power that you seek, but with me at your side, I can give you... oh, so very much more." Kandyce pulled away from the admiral and blew him a kiss. The man's legs visibly buckled.

Chapter Seven

TEMPLETON

The *Mysty* continued to cut along the Gaelinora Sea's glassy surface at an unnatural speed. Below deck, the group gathered in the captain's stateroom. It was quite large and well appointed with hand-polished teak and, what appeared to be, dragonwood accents. The enormous wave pushing the boat along was visible out the aft windows, threatening to come crashing into the ship at any moment.

"What do you think we can expect upon our arrival?" Tym asked, pinning down a large sheet of parchment, then handing a quill to Kit. "If you can draw me a map of what we're heading into, I can help organize the soldiers to be their most effective."

Kit started making something of a map, but Indie groaned at her. "What? You don't like my drawing?"

"The scale is off," Indie replied gently. "There is a greater distance between the docks and where the sea-gate is at the back of the village, and there is a huge line of fir trees obstructing the view of the docks from the town."

"And that's why you are the tracker and I'm the blunt instrument," Kit said with a smile, passing the quill over to the young man.

In a few minutes, Indie produced a remarkably accurate map of the town, its streets, and the temple itself. He also gave a remarkably accurate recollection of Xin and the lord's personal guard, including what weaponry they were using, their numbers, and their state of training.

"You should be in the military," Tym said with admiration. "You're a natural."

"My father, the captain of Aarall's City Watch, would agree with you," Kit said, taking Indie's hand in hers. "But I would prefer him to be with me."

"Your father is Captain Harding? Captain Ray Harding?"

"Do you know him?" Kit asked.

"I've never met him, but I know him by reputation. His defense against the Gizmo uprising is legendary."

Kit laughed at the captain's comment. "It caught my mother's attention, too. That's where they met. I was born some nine moons later." When everyone went silent, she chuckled. "No, it wasn't on the battlefield. I asked my father the same question." This may or may not have been what had silenced everyone, but Kit's explanation brought on multiple bouts of laughter, starting up repeatedly each time it seemed like it had finally died down.

"Okay then," Tym said, trying hard to hold back another outburst. "It would be nice if we could get the soldiers off the ship unseen, but if they're expecting slaves to be delivered today, I expect Xin and her soldiers will all be at the docks."

Indie pointed to an area on his hand-drawn map, a small way up the coast. "If we deploy the infantry here, they can march up along the shoreline under cover, for at least most of the way. It won't be a simple walk, but I think it might be possible. We can keep the archers on the ship, and if a fight breaks out, they can keep Xin busy while the infantry moves in."

"A bold plan," the captain said, raising his eyebrows in surprise. "We've only got two small skiffs on this ship, so it will take some time to offload the infantry and their gear, but it's a solid strategy, assuming the shoreline is conducive."

"And if that doesn't work, Kit and Fury can just set them all on fire, like she did during the battle in Cormorant," Lin suggested with a wink. "With the improved Fury, I'm thinking they'll be pretty effective." When neither Kit nor Fury responded, Lin shrugged. "Okay then. Let's call that a backup plan."

⁂

At Indie's suggestion, Breayn slowed the ship down as soon as the town's docks were about to come within view. Coldforge was on his hands and knees at the port side of the ship, having never really left his spot. His face was a horrible shade of green, contrasting with his bright orange beard, fouled with the remnants of vomit that hadn't quite made it over the side of the vessel.

Even though the water was dead-still, the coast was far too rugged to land the skiffs there. Tym looked out at the coastline and rubbed his hand over his stubble covered chin. "Even if we offloaded the soldiers, traveling along the shoreline would be nearly impossible."

"I can scout up ahead," Breayn offered when she saw Kit's disappointment. She took the time to explain to Kit that, with her mother to help keep Boreas, the North Wind, in check, she could transform herself into a hawk and scout both the harbor and the city.

In less than ten minutes, Breayn returned from her foray over Templeton.

"I saw seven women at the docks, all dressed in light armor. There are several other people there as well. If I were to guess based on their activities, I'd say they're all dockhands. I also flew over the city. There was no sign of other soldiers. The townspeople all appeared to be going about their daily lives. There were many Berrat there as well. I saw no obvious signs of slavery going on at all."

Breayn wobbled a bit, using the captain's shoulder to steady herself. "Indie's diagram of the town, the docks and the small pine forest near the shore are very accurate."

"Are you okay?" Kit asked as Breayn's brow furrowed.

"Boreas, the elemental spirit I've bound with, is struggling to break free. When I changed into a hawk, my mother tried to control him, but he's extraordinarily strong. She wasn't prepared to deal with it. I just need some place where I can concentrate and help my mother regain control over him."

Coldforge and Lin guided Breayn to the captain's quarters at the aft of the ship while the captain got the oarsmen to work, to bring the ship the rest of the way into the harbor.

While the *Mysty* moved towards the docks, Kit decided, after dealing with Indie's objections, that she and Tym should be the ones who step off the ship to assess the threat level, and to be the Auctioneers' representatives. Nobody at the docks would know Captain Windspeak, and it would be unlikely that they'd recognize Kit, especially with her dramatic change in physical appearance. The biggest unknown was if Captain Muul, the *Misty's* former captain, who was busy feeding the crows back in Cormorant, was known to the people here. If he were, they would question his absence.

When the ship's crew members pulled the vessel in close enough, the archers tossed the mooring ropes out to a dock-crew, waiting to tie them off. There were no soldiers on the dock, but Xin and a contingent of six female guards were standing near the shoreline. With the weather being warmer, Xin had donned light armor, exposing much of her honey-colored Easterner skin. As soon as the gang plank was set, Kit and Captain Windspeak headed down to make their greetings.

"Hail," Xin called out, striding confidently toward Kit and the captain, her chin-length straight black hair swaying with each swing of her hips. Even though the woman was lithe and well muscled, she still had a womanly shape, unlike the rest of her female soldiers, who all could have passed for young boys. "Will Captain Muul not be joining us today?" Kit's heart sank at the question, but Captain Windspeak took charge.

"I'm afraid that Muul is no longer with us," the captain said with a slight inclination of his head. "King Karter did not take kindly to the state of the slaves he delivered to Cormorant at the new moon. They were... in poor condition." With practiced grace, the captain pulled his hat from his head and bowed more deeply. "Captain Tym Windspeak, at your service. My ship's hull is full of fresh and healthy Berrat, along with several chests of *recompense*, for Lord Aster's help in this transaction."

"I'll have my people unload them immediately," Xin said, waving her guards forward.

The captain held up his hand and clucked his tongue at the warrior. "I'm afraid that my instructions are to deliver my cargo directly to Lord Aster. I don't plan on joining the former captain in the Great Cycle."

Xin's face turned gray, and her green eyes turned solid black. "I speak for my lord, and you will allow my people to board your vessel to unload my lord's property."

Captain Windspeak wavered, his eyes becoming vacant. Kit placed her hand on his forearm, offering her support. A moment later, the captain set his jaw and raised his arm above his shoulder. The *Mysty's* deck bristled with archers, their bows knocked and readied. "I would truly prefer that things not go poorly for you and yours."

When Kit's hand landed on the haft of her battle hammer, Xin nodded her understanding. "If you would follow me, I will bring you to see my lord."

"No," the captain replied. "I will stay here with my ship and your lord will come collect his cargo personally. I will not break from King Karter's orders."

"We could just kill them all and keep the chests for ourselves," Kit offered with an evil grin. "I'm sure King Jordain would gladly accept his cargo directly from us."

Xin's bright green, almond-shaped eyes narrowed when Kit spoke. "Have we met before?"

"Unlikely," Kit said, her voice flat and even. "This is the first time I've been to Arnnor."

"Titan's grace upon you," Xin replied. When neither Kit nor the captain responded, the warrior sneered. "I'll return with my lord shortly."

The captain gave the woman a small bow. "We'll be onboard, awaiting his arrival."

Kit and the captain waited as Xin and her soldiers departed. As soon as they were out of sight, Kit let out a long breath. "She recognized me."

"Perhaps," the captain responded, turning back towards the *Mysty*. "We'll know soon enough, I suppose."

⌘

"Xin's a vampire, and so are her guards," Indie said as soon as Kit and the captain were back onboard. "None of them are strong, though."

"I know," Kit replied. "I felt it as soon as I stepped off the ship. We have to assume it was Pental who sired her, but that makes no sense to me. He would not strengthen the slavers. I'd have expected him to wipe them out, like he had tried the last time we were here."

"Not that you couldn't handle yourself without help, but the vampires you've fought so far... they didn't expect you to fight back. Xin will.

"Captain Windspeak?" Kit asked. When he didn't reply, she gave him a nudge. "Tym? Any thoughts?"

The captain scrubbed his face with his hands, groaning all the while. "I think they were expecting us, and I think that gives them the advantage.

"You think Lord Aster is expecting our attack?" Indie asked.

"Maybe. I don't know. But our encounter with that Xin lady." Tym took another deep breath. "It just felt like something was off. I couldn't put my finger on it."

"She was using compulsion on you," Kit said. "Even if she wasn't particularly good at it, the magic in her voice could have been unsettling. Did concentrating on your wife and child help?"

"It did," the captain replied. "I'm guessing the ring Lin gave me helped as well."

"The ring?" Kit asked, her eyes darting over to Lin.

"The little blue freaks helped me," Lin said. "They said it wouldn't be fool-proof, but that it would help." Lin showed her the sparkling pink-diamond ring on her own finger. "They made one for me, too."

"Let's just attack," Coldforge said, crunching the knuckles of his fists. "We'll know soon enough if they are expecting us or not. If we immediately offload our soldiers, we can seize control of the beach before they return."

"The tactics sound good," Tym said, "but there are better options. I think we're walking into a trap."

"Then we set a trap of our own." Lin broke out in a wicked smile.

While waiting for Lord Aster to make his appearance, Kit stared out the aft windows. The winds had picked up significantly, with dark clouds rolling in from across the sea to the north. The bright, warm afternoon was turning dismal and gray.

"Is this your doing?" Kit asked Breayn, who had just come out from the captain's quarters. Her eyes were dark and bloodshot, and her skin was unnaturally pale. She walked across the deck to the railing, and turned her face into the stiff, northern breeze that was carrying a storm their way. She drew a deep breath and nodded her head slowly.

"When I shifted," the Berrat woman said, her voice strained, "I lost control of Boreas. My mother was trying..." The woman winced and called out, "I... mother, I'm coming!" Breayn's face sagged before she collapsed against the railing. In a flash, Kit was by her side, offering what support she could. The woman became deadweight, falling limply into the young priest's arms. With little effort, Kit swept her up and carried her back to the captain's quarters and laid her on the bed with its soft feather mattress. Even though the woman was unconscious, she continued her internal struggle. Perhaps it was a battle of wills against the North Wind. Based on how badly contorted her face was becoming, she appeared to be losing.

"Kit," Lin yelled, sticking her head in through the doorway. "Xin's coming up the path from the sea gate."

Kit gave Breayn one last check before heading out the door and up onto the ship's deck. The woman's face was still looking strained, but Kit couldn't stay with her any longer. She could only hope that between Breayn and her mother, they could get the situation under control.

"And she's got plenty of reinforcements," Captain Windspeak said, as Kit approached him. "I'd guess she's got at least one hundred archers and another hundred skirmishers."

"Skirmishers?" Kit asked, as the group of soldiers approached.

"Light infantry," the captain continued, scanning for any other soldiers who could follow them. "They're often used as the vanguard, a screen for a larger force."

"Okay then," Kit said. "I'd say that means she recognized me. Indie, you and Coldforge stay out of sight."

Xin and her soldiers marched out onto the beach, spreading into formation with the skirmishers taking the front and the archers taking up the rear. None, save for Xin's personal guard, were particularly well armored. The archers in the back were all wielding longbows, and the skirmishers were carrying javelins and short swords. Once they had finished forming ranks, Xin and her guard approached the docks.

"Where is Lord Aster?" Captain Windspeak called out, loud enough to be heard over his feet banging down the gangplank to the docks.

When Xin didn't reply, Kit drew her battle hammer, letting it dangle down by her hip, as she, too, pounded down the gangplank.

"If I have to turn this ship back to Cormorant, it's exactly what I'll do," the captain called out, his long black hair now whipping about his face.

"I will take our cargo now," Xin yelled. "My lord is otherwise engaged, and he will not tolerate any further delays."

Kit ignited her hammer; blue flames licked up the handle and around her hand.

"Where's your boyfriend?" Xin called out. "Or has he been replaced by this fine-looking man?"

"I'm right here," Indie yelled, running down the gangplank with the boys right behind him. The captain slapped his forehead with the palm of his hand.

"Well," said Xin, "I can't help but wonder why the savior of Aarall would have suddenly turned slaver."

"We all have our reasons," Kit growled, and spun around when yet another pair of feet bounced down the dock-boards behind them. Lin gave her a quick smile as she stepped past, taking the lead on the way to Xin.

"My people want to know where Aster is?" Lin challenged, despite the noises of disapproval coming from both Kit and the captain. When Xin didn't reply, Lin drew her twin long swords and ignited their flames. "If I have to go look for him, my father will not be pleased." The woman continued pounding down the dock until she was face-to-face with Xin on the sugar-sand shore. A powerful gust of wind whipped her now rain-soaked hair about, a good amount sticking to her cheeks.

"And you are?" Xin ground out, taking a step forward to accept Lin's challenge, her six guards fanning out close behind her.

"I am Aithlin, daughter of Lord Arthure and Lady Jaquine, and if your pompous lord ever wants to see another shipment of *special weapons* ever again, you're going to drag his sorry ass out here."

"He no longer needs your family," Xin said with a sneer. "He has the support of King Jordain himself."

"Unless you've got three times as many soldiers hidden behind that treeline, I'm afraid the king is going to be of little use to him right now." Lin called back over her shoulder. "Captain, call out your infantry."

At the captain's command, the infantry poured out from the long line of pine trees and the deck of the *Mysty* bristled with archers. Lin chortled at the sight. "I suggest you tell your soldiers to lay down their arms. This day will not go the way you'd hoped."

"Enough!" A man bellowed behind the line of skirmishers.

As the ranks of Xin's soldiers parted, Lord Aster came stumbling through wet sand towards the group, his face contorted with rage. "What's going on? Why hasn't my cargo been unloaded?"

The man continued moving towards Lin until he was standing nose to nose with her. "I don't know you," he said to Lin, poking her in the shoulder with his finger. "I don't know you, either," he said, turning to the captain. "But I know you, *little priest*. Changing the color of your hair isn't much of a disguise, but the golden eyes are an interesting touch."

Before Kit replied, Lin spoke up. "You don't know me, but you know my father and my mother, Lady Jaquine."

"Ah," said Lord Aster, "you bear a striking resemblance to her. And you appear to be as much of a shrew as she is. Maybe you can tell me why my cargo is still aboard your ship then, and why you have this little priest with you?"

"You've got it all wrong," Kit said with a smirk. "I'm the one holding the reins. Fury, seize him."

The lord's eyes bulged out of his head when all seven feet of Fury materialized in front of the man, grabbing him by the throat, lifting him until he was eye-level with the draken's. Xin's guards brought the point of their spears to bear, directing them at Fury.

"Xin, unless you want to see your love die," Kit said calmly, "have your people lay down their arms."

For the briefest of moments, a worried look crossed Xin's face. It disappeared just as her eyes turned black and a thin smile appeared. She called out with a disembodied voice, cutting through the wind and rain, echoing in Kit's mind. "So young. So naïve. He's merely a puppet, a handsome, playful puppet to be sure, but just something for me to keep on a string and parade around. Have your pet kill him if you like. It makes no difference to me." Lord Aster made an odd gurgling noise at Xin's declaration, his face now turning a brilliant shade of purple.

"Let him go, Fury," Kit said, never taking her eyes off Xin. "He's not the one we need to worry about."

"Naïve, but not stupid," Xin laughed, as Fury dropped the lord and vanished. "I just couldn't tell which side of things you were on, and that troubled me greatly."

The wind whipped up; sprays of rain mixed with sleet pelting everybody. The soldiers from both sides, now less than forty paces apart, were all shivering badly. Xin, dressed in light armor and little else, appeared unaffected by the elements.

Xin stifled a feigned yawn. She flicked her wrist towards Kit and her cohorts. "Kill them. Kill them all."

The six women guards standing behind Xin dropped their spears, their fingers elongating into wicked claws. Kit could hear the captain yelling something, but his words faded to nothingness as three vampires converged on her.

Indie's instructions to Kit on dealing with vampires flooded back. She swung her hammer in a wide arc. When the hammer connected with the head of the nearest vampire, there was a blinding flash of light, obscuring the gore when its head exploded on contact. Kit instinctively threw her free arm up in front of her face, just as another vampire fell on her, biting into her forearm. She screeched out in pain as a dark power surged into her. Numbness spread through her arm, radiating out from the bite.

As the third vampire landed on Kit, its eyes bulged as Lump's jaws closed on her shoulder, ripping her away before she could get a bite in. Still holding off the vampire who had her teeth in Kit's arm, the small priest brought her hammer back around, ramming it into her attacker's ribs.

"Burn!" Kit growled, instantly igniting Fury's blue flames.

When the flames burst forth, a dark shadow passed before Kit's eyes. The vampire lurched backward, bewildered by what had just happened. She drew back her wicked claws, her face contorting with rage.

There was a whiz-thud as an arrow struck the vampire in the chest. In a moment of indecision, the creature paused long enough for Runt to attack, crashing into her with his full weight, his crushing jaws finding purchase on the vampire's wrist. Annoyed by the dire wolf's attack, the vampire raked him across the face with her free hand. With a flick of her wrist, she tossed Runt across the sand like a giant rag doll.

When her wolf fell lifelessly to the ground, a sudden calmness spread through Kit's mind, everything snapping into clear focus. One vampire was closing in on her. The woman's movements were slow and exaggerated. Kit glanced over her shoulder. Her cohorts stood like statues, frozen in time. It was only at that moment the little priest noticed that the wind-whipped rain was falling so slowly that she could see every drop. She could see the incoming arrow flying over her shoulder. Her eyes followed the projectile. It embedded itself into the vampire's chest, a tiny burst of blood exploding outwards as it made contact. In the time it took for the woman's expression to change from disdain to horror, tiny red lines appeared on her neck, spreading up to her face, her eyes going dead.

A shadow emerged from the now-dead vampire, traveling to the body of the woman currently engaged with Indie. Where Indie had been winning, the tide turned. The vampire's attacks were coming so quick and so savage that all Indie could do was try to block or evade. With each attack, the man's defenses were weakening.

Coldforge tried to engage, to split the vampire's attention. She struck the dwarf with a backhanded swing, knocking him across the sand, sending him head over feet. With a look of detached amusement, the vampire reached up and snatched an arrow, mid-flight, aimed at her chest. A sneer crept at the corner of her mouth as she snapped the shaft in her hand.

Kit closed in, throwing her hammer out in front of herself, calling upon its brilliance. A blast of light poured forth, striking the vampire, bathing it in a dazzling white luminescence. As Kit was about to strike with her hammer, Indie's blade broke through the vampire's defenses, burying its point into the creature's throat, his sword tip protruding out the top of her head.

Again, the shadow emerged, vacating the vampire's lifeless body. It swirled about, as though seeking another host, before merging with Xin.

"Impressive," Xin huffed. She turned to where her army was, recoiling at the sight of them all having dropped their weapons and taken a knee. The bulk of Kit's army were standing behind them, weapons at the ready. Xin turned into a cloud of ash, and was blown away by the gale-force winds. Seconds later, the storm died off and the seas turned dead calm.

"What just happened?" Lord Aster asked, visibly shaken by what he had witnessed.

"Captain Windspeak," Kit said, still focused on where Xin had disappeared. "Bind Aster and have him stowed below deck. I'm going to want to have a talk with him. Lin, interrogate Xin's soldiers. Find out who needs to be sent to the Great Cycle and take care of it."

In an instant, Kit was kneeling beside the fallen dire wolf, her hands awash in a golden aura. "We've got a lot more to do, my friend," she said as she laid her hands upon the wolf's broken body, her healing abilities at full power. The girl's head snapped back as she took his pain, his wounds disappearing as though they had never been there.

Chapter Eight

The Rise of the Veil

After having taken the time to heal everyone's wounds, Kit returned to the captain's quarters to check in on Breayn. Within the cabin, the woman was sitting upright at the side of the bed, her eyes looking focused and alert once again. She gave Kit a half-hearted smile.

Kit took a seat beside the woman. "How are you feeling? Do you have everything under control again?" Breayn shrugged and blew out a breath. She put about as much effort into her response as she did her smile.

"I'm tired," she said, her shoulders slumping. "My mother is too, I think. I'm so thankful to have her with me, but sharing this body is harder than I had expected, on both of us." Kit placed her hand on the woman's knee and gave her a comforting smile.

"Is there anything I can do to help?"

Breayn just shook her head in reply. "I just need to rest some more."

"Does anybody have any idea what that shadow was?" Indie asked, staring out the porthole window.

Fury scratched at his chin. "As best as I can tell, it was a shade, and a very strong one at that."

Kit's mind raced back to the shadow demons she'd faced on Mount Toka; the ones Eris had set upon her. This one didn't seem to be the same. "So, not like the one that Eris attacked me with?"

The big draken shook his head. "Shades are manifestations of demons, the creatures created by Bael in the bowels of Helja. With the Veil up, demons cannot leave their plane, but it would appear they can send a silhouette of themselves to Orth. These shades can inhabit people and force them to do their bidding. However, if the host can control their possessor, they can become insanely powerful, harnessing the strength of the demon. It is rumored that King Faol controls the shade of Gorgaraeth, the demon god himself, which is why he's so extremely dangerous."

Kit groaned and sank her face in her hands. "Another god?"

"There are more," Fury said. "Would you like me to tell you about them?" Kit pulled her hands away and rolled her eyes.

"No!" she said, her voice sharp. "I really don't."

Fury cocked a thick, scaly eyebrow. "Do you want to hear more of Gorgaraeth?" The little priest wrapped her hands behind her head and drew her forehead to her knees.

"No," she muffled. "But I'm guessing you're going to tell me, anyway."

"It might be helpful for you to understand what you're facing, what your mother has been trying to deal with since before you were born." Fury smiled when Kit lifted her head with renewed interest.

"My mother?"

With a broad smile, Fury looked out over his audience and told the tale of King Faol and Gorgaraeth, the demon god.

"During the last cycle, after Ollin and Bael had broken their own rules..."

"During the last cycle?" Indie asked, drawing a low growl from Fury for the interruption.

"During the gods' last game," Fury replied. The draken's eyes shot upwards when Indie and Coldforge both stared blankly back at him. "You don't know about the game, the one played by the gods?"

"Titan and Orth," Kit interrupted. "They came here to play games. They created races of peoples, allowed them to live for hundreds of cycles, sometimes thousands. After each race was sufficiently advanced, they'd unleash challenges upon them. The gods then spared whichever race survived and allowed them to play in the next game, the next cycle. The gods then reset their game board.

They destroyed all the other races and started the game again, creating new races, spreading them across the lands."

"Did you learn this from the library as well?" Indie asked. Kit slumped and lowered her eyes.

"No. I learned most of it from the box of papers that Father Hoarfrost had given me. I picked up other bits and pieces along the way."

"Ah, but that is but a part of the tale," Fury said with smug satisfaction on his face for knowing more than everyone else in the room. "Most of what I am going to share with you is true, to the best of my knowledge. Some of it is conjecture and supposition based on what makes the most sense to me and mine."

"I might be able to fill in some holes," Coldforge added, his whiskers twitching, his eyes full of wonder. "Me and mine are good at keepin' our ears to the ground." Fury stared blank-faced at the dwarf.

"From what I know," Fury said, almost daring the dwarf to interrupt him, "the Fates drew Titan and Orth to this world, intent on either destroying them or at least weakening them to where they could escape them without repercussion. To do this, the Fates created a game for the Travelers to play and designed it so that they could never win. Each time they played the game, the Fates would do everything they could to ensure the humans always survived."

"You're saying they cheated?" Kit asked, drawing a glare from the draken.

"Perhaps," Fury said, "but since they were the ones who set the rules, it's hard to say that the Fates were cheating."

"And why would the humans' always winning hurt Titan and Orth?" Indie asked, ignoring Fury's obvious annoyance with him.

"It wouldn't," Fury stated with a glare, "but if you will let me finish my tale, then maybe you'll learn something." Indie rolled his eyes at the draken, motioning for him to continue.

"As I was saying, the Fates made sure the humans always won. This infuriated the Travelers, goading them into making new, more powerful races. To do so, the Travelers needed to use more and more of their essence. By doing so, by using up so much of their essence, they weakened themselves."

"Did the Fates create races, too?" Kit asked. The information was coming in too fast, and it was making her sleepy. She wanted to close her eyes, but the tale was too interesting. "Is that how they helped the humans win?" Fury shook his head.

"No, never. The Fates are powerful, but they do not have the spark, the ability to create life from nothing. The Fates made sure the humans won by creating challenges that put the Traveler's races at a disadvantage. I can't say for sure how they did that, but I'm quite certain that is how they helped the humans to victory, game after game.

"That is pretty clever," Indie said, remembering back to when he considered perhaps Tyr was not as smart as he believed he was.

"It was clever," Fury said, blowing a puff of blue flame past Indie, close enough that it made his dragon scales appear, but not hot enough to set the ship on fire.

"Each game, the Travelers put more and more of themselves into their creations. Each game, regardless of how devious Titan and Orth thought they were being, the humans still always won." Fury held a finger in the air like he was about to make an important point. "And this created the first wrinkle in Tyr's plan. Because they were continually losing the game, Titan and Orth believed that if there were more players, they'd have a better chance of defeating the humans. So, they created children of their own. They split off huge amounts of their essence and created Ollin and Bael."

"Children created more children?" Kit asked. "I thought that Titan and Orth were only kids and that's why the Fates were forced into looking after them."

"It was more like gods created more gods. They may be children, but they are children with nearly limitless power. They created their offspring as easily as they created the different races to play their game."

"That's just wrong," Indie said, like somehow the Travelers were doing something unnatural. With a huff, Fury ignored the young man's protestations and continued telling his tale.

"When Bael and Ollin started playing, Tyr sowed discorded between them and their parents. He planted a seed of doubt. He made them think that Titan and Orth were cheating and the only way they could win was by creating more and more powerful creatures. They tricked them into putting even more of their essence into their creations. Over the next few games, Bael and Ollin nearly won. None of the Travelers had come so close to winning, but in the end, the humans always prevailed." Fury paused for the briefest of moments, giving everyone a chance to soak in the story.

"It was at this point," Fury said with an evil grin, "that Titan decided he would win, regardless of the cost. In order to win, he put far too much of himself into creating the penultimate race; magnificent creatures of immeasurable beauty, power, and grace capable of incalculable devastation. The race would destroy the humans and every other race in the world. He created the dragons, and from the dragons, he chose the most beautiful and the most dangerous, and elevated him even further. He created Ouroboros, the original Dragon Lord." When several of the listeners gasped, Fury gave a nod of appreciation.

"It was at this moment that Tyr saw his chance. The Travelers had finally made a mistake big enough to undo themselves. Ouroboros was too powerful, too perfect. If he had sided with the Fates, together they probably could have destroyed the Travelers, but only if they could isolate them, fight them one-on-one. But alas, poor Tyr couldn't coerce the Dragon Lord to his side. However, he could convince him to create a protégé, to create a being who would work with the great dragon, to overthrow the world, and claim it as their own. He created a creature of immeasurable grace and beauty. He created... perfection."

"Let me guess," Kit said, rolling her eyes. "He created you."

"Ah, you see the truth in things." Fury said, preening himself as he did. "You knew it was me because I am perfection personified."

"What does any of this have to do with King Faol and Gorgaraeth?" Kit asked, growing weary of the tale.

"It has everything to do with him, but I just thought you'd like to hear how I came into being." Kit's eyes narrowed at the comment.

"Fine, I'll speed things up. Try to pay attention. The dragons, with Ouroboros and myself at their lead, would have destroyed everything on the planet. Titan would have won, and the Travelers would have lost interest in the game. It was only fun for them because they were forever losing. To prevent us from winning their game, Tyr sought Ollin and Bael. He told them of their parents' trickery and how they had cheated; that if they didn't cheat as well, Titan and Orth would win, and the game would be over."

Kit yawned and stretched dramatically, letting out a loud moan as she did. Where most of the people gathered laughed, Fury did not.

"This didn't go over very well with them. They both set out to create their own races that would rival us magnificent dragons. Bael created demons. He used the molten rock and metal from the world's core to fashion them. He created them to be impervious to fire and poison, two of the dragons' most potent weapons. From the demons, he chose the one who showed the most promise, the one who was the cruelest, most sadistic of all demons. He chose Gorgaraeth, and into him he fused even more of his essence. He created a demon lord of such immense power that Ouroboros quaked in fear." The draken shuddered at the thought of his master being afraid of anything.

"And while Bael was busy creating demons, Ollin took a different direction. Rather than creating horrors unlike anything the world had ever seen, he created beauty; he created the Elves. The god wanted to create a society that could live in harmony with nature, a people who could leverage the world's resources, without destroying them. He wanted a race that could survive anything. But something unexpected happened when he created them. Gaia stepped in and manipulated his actions."

"The Earth Mother changed Ollin's magic; she made it so that two races were created instead of one," Coldforge said with more than a hint of pride in his voice.

"Yes," Fury said, "she twisted the magic to create twins. The elves were tall and beautiful and the dwarves... were not. It was like everything that was wonderful and wholesome was infused into the elves and everything that was left over got stuffed into the dwarves, the dark elves."

"This is all fascinating," Kit said, stifling a yawn. This was a boatload of information, and her brain was turning to mush. "But what does this have to do with Gorgaraeth?"

"I'm almost finished," Fury said, shaking his head. "So, I'm reasonably confident that all of this is accurate, and now I can only provide conjecture as to what happened next. It is my assertion that Ollin believed the elves and the dwarves could not stand against the dragons and the demons. He conspired with Orth to prevent Ragnarök, the end of days. He made a deal with Ouroboros that, in exchange for an amulet that would make the Dragon Lord more powerful than Gorgaraeth, he would have to leave the elves and dwarves alone, that he could not destroy them. My lord foolishly accepted the gift. As soon as he placed the amulet around his magnificent neck, he doomed all dragons to be forever locked within their mountain ranges. When Titan learned his dragons were thwarted, he went mad and threatened to destroy the world and every living thing on it, except he couldn't. He was so weakened by creating the dragons that he could not carry out his threat. Together, Ollin and Orth conspired against Titan and, in his weakened state, entrapped him in his icy prison."

"I thought it was Ollin and Bael who trapped Titan," Kit said, her eyes wide in disbelief.

"No, Kitten, I don't believe so," Fury said. "But this was when things got interesting. It was at this point that Tyr's plans were foiled. The Fate, for all his trickery, never expected the Travelers to be thoughtful." The draken took a deep breath and continued.

"As soon as Bael discovered the dragons were trapped, he sent his demons into battle. He made his play to win the game. Tens of thousands of demons spilled upon the earth, pouring up from the Underworld, laying waste to everything in their path. The world united and fought back." Fury paused for a moment as he considered the carnage. "I wish I could have seen it."

"We dwarves took the brunt of the attack," Coldforge said. He looked like he was about to be ill. "Them sulfurous creatures bubbled up in our mines. We teamed up with the Hobgoblins and the Grimmorcs and we fought them off. Tens of thousands of us died in the wars. We killed just as many of them demons, but many got past us, including Gorgaraeth himself."

"And with Titan imprisoned, Ollin and Orth worked together to defeat the demon lord. A great battle took place near to where Silverhawk now stands.

Gorgaraeth smashed Ollin to the ground with such force that a great rent opened across the land. It was so deep that when the two Travelers pushed Gorgaraeth into it, they pushed him straight to Helja. As they escaped, Ollin put up a barrier, the Veil, to hold the demon lord in Helja. In doing so, he also trapped Bael who had remained there while the battles raged on. But the Veil wasn't strong enough to hold them both. They battered the barrier, intent on destroying it. But, before that could happen, Orth fused her essence with the world. She drew power from the earth, and with the help of Gaia, they strengthened the Veil making it impossible for either Bael or Gorgaraeth to break through. The world became Orth. Orth is the world."

Kit's eyes widened at the revelation. She had always wondered why their world was called the same name as the god. "And somehow, Gorgaraeth's shade could get through the veil?" she asked, her face etched with worry.

"The veil is failing," Fury said. "It's the only plausible explanation. And if it falls, Ragnarök, the end of days, will be upon us once again. Except this time, I doubt Bael is going to stop until he's destroyed all life on the planet."

"Are ye tellin' me that because this Bael fella was pissed at his brother, he's gonna kill everyone?" Coldforge asked.

"I can't say for sure," Fury responded, "but it seems likely to me. The Travelers didn't concern themselves with the lives of lesser beings."

"So, if the Veil falls, life on Orth will end?" Lin asked. "And we're worried about slavers? Shouldn't we be doing what we can to stop the Veil from falling?"

"We're already doing that," Indie said, scrunching up his face as he did. "If the demon god was working with Faol, it's because he's the key to bringing down the Veil. Think about it. He desperately wants out of Helja. If he sent his shade to Faol, it's because he thinks the vampire king can help make it happen. If Faol is building an army, it's a part of their plan to bring Gorgaraeth back to Orth. We're cutting into his food supply, which means we're already helping to stop that from happening."

For several seconds, the room was utterly silent, everyone staring transfixed on Indie as they pondered the ramifications of what he had just said.

"Okay then," Kit said. "Now we know that we're not just saving the people from the slavers. We're trying to save the entire world."

"And if you hadn't helped to rescue Treedale," Lin said. "We never would have gotten here."

"And you and I need to talk," Kit replied to Lin. "You know a lot more than you've ever let on and you're going to tell me everything."

"Tell *us* everything," Indie said. "Who the Helja are you?"

CHAPTER NINE

ARTHURE LOGNER

The group had just finished their meal in the captain's stateroom. Runt and Lump were sleeping soundly by the door while everyone else was engaged in conversation. The sunshine came through the cabin's windows, lighting up the bits of dust that swirled about the room each time someone moved. The winds had died down and the Gaelinora Sea was, once again, an infinite stretch of calm. It stood in stark contrast to the churning acids inside Lin's stomach.

"I have never lied to you, Kit," the woman said, wrapping her arms around herself. "But there is much that I've never shared with you."

"You had better speak true," Kit said. "If you are the friend you portend to be, you will tell us *everything*."

Lin blew out a deep breath, trying to calm her shaking hands. She wanted to curl up into a tiny ball and simply vanish. The weight of the eyes on her was crushing her soul. Her life story wasn't something she wanted to share. She was embarrassed by much of it. Through her actions, she flirted with becoming like her father, a man she despised with all of her being. Each time she did, it was as though she was distancing herself from her mother, a woman she loved and respected, although she had wed *that man*, as her Grams used to call him.

"What do you want to know?" she asked, her shoulders sagging, her face going slack.

"Everything," Indie said, cocking an eyebrow. He folded his arms across his chest and scowled.

"What is your father's connection in all of this?" Kit asked, giving Indie a look that told him, in no uncertain terms, to lighten up. Lin closed her eyes for a moment, gathering her thoughts. She was counting on Kit's ability to distinguish lie from truth. She desperately wanted her approval, a sign that she wasn't the horrible person her father was.

"My father, Lord Arthure Logner, is a cruel, horrible man," she replied, staring down at her knees. "His soldiers are as cruel as their lord, carrying out whatever deeds he demands of them. Most of them enjoy it, even revel in it." Lin shuddered just thinking about it. She looked back up, seeking Kit from the many onlookers. Her voice cracked as the next words came out of her mouth. "My father is a weapons dealer. He can find and buy the best weapons on Orth. The man is indiscriminate about who he buys from and to whom he sells. It doesn't matter who he hurts, so long as there is profit."

"And King Jordain benefits from the weapons and armor he can purvey for him?" Kit asked. "Surely the king has the resources to craft his own arms." Lin shrugged and shook her head. Coldforge spoke up.

"Nah, he can't. The best arms come from three places on Orth. The dwarves make the finest heavy arms this world has ever seen. We will not sell what we create, not to humans at any rate." His bushy orange eyebrows gathered above his nose until it looked like he had a single, giant, fuzzy worm sitting on his forehead. "The elves, as useless as they are, craft the finest light arms and bows. I suppose it's not too surprising that we share this trait, seeing as how we're all kin."

"And who else do you believe makes the finest arms in all of Orth?" Fury asked, his scaled chest puffing out when he asked the question.

"The Arachne, the children of the spider queen, of course," Coldforge said, his whiskers dancing merrily on his face. "Their *spidersilk armor* is, without a doubt, the most resilient light armor ever created." Fury's scales shifted from their normal iridescent blue to a deep green. His lips peeled back, exposing his terrible, needle-sharp teeth.

"Ye got to admit it, my big lizard friend. By Gimlie's beard, none can compare." The dwarf's eyes were spinning in his head. Fury's scales were now shifting from dark green to nearly black. At the sight of the draken's lower jaw quivering, Coldforge burst out, his laughter filling the stateroom like a tidal wave breaking upon the shore. Fury's growl was drowned out by the rolling waves of laughter as everyone caught on to the joke.

"Ah, lighten up ye big bag o' scales," Coldforge burst out, clapping the draken on the thigh. "Everyone knows yer kin make the finest arms and armor in all the lands. But it's not exactly fair, now is it? Yer the only ones who have access to those amazing scales of yours. And yer the only ones who can heat a forge hot enough to work them."

Fury's facial expression shifted from unbridled anger to a sneer, to a smile, and then to a full-on laugh in the time it took for him to clap Coldforge on the back, sending him head over arse into the cabin's wall, nearly shattering the windows. Even from his precarious, upside-down position against the bulkhead, the dwarf continued to laugh. He gripped his belly tightly while he squeezed tears out of his eyes.

"Are you two quite finished?" Kit asked. The draken, and the dwarf locked eyes for a few moments before bursting out laughing again. It took them nearly a minute before they got control of themselves.

"Sorry, Lady Aithlin." Fury tilted his head and bowed lightly. "I meant no disrespect." The draken's lips pulled up at the corners again, for just a moment, before settling down.

"As I was saying, my father is an arms dealer, and he's exceptionally good at it. He would often put some of his finest pieces on display at the manor whenever he and my mother were hosting a party. He was showing off, I guess. My friend Martelle would show me his newest arrivals. They were so beautiful. The details carved into the pieces, the way the metals were folded and forged, created intricate patterns, making each piece a unique work of art."

"Were you not at the Temple?" Tym asked, scratching at the base of his neck. "How could he show you things in Two Peaks if you lived in Aarall?"

Kit replied to Lin's questioning look. "Because Lin and Martelle had seer's crystals; small magical devices that allowed them to communicate over great distances." Fury cleared his throat and glared at the little priest. "Sorry, Fury;

dragon's tears are the crystals' correct name. And these particular crystals were created by Fury himself." The draken smiled and inclined his head.

"And why did your father allow your friend to roam about his manor?" Tym pressed. "The way you describe the man, it seems doubtful that he'd allow a child free run of his house."

"Martelle's mother and my father were close friends. They visited my father often. Martelle's mother was exceptionally beautiful, and she had a knack for gathering information. I never knew for sure, but I believe Martelle is the bastard son of my father. It's the only reason I can think of that could explain why he had the run of the house. I remember my mother being furious anytime he was around. She hated me playing with him. After I moved away, he continued to stick around and shared whatever information he uncovered. When opportunities presented themselves, I took advantage of them."

"And what does that mean?" Kit asked, her jaw clenched, her tone accusatory.

"It means I used it to help me start a life of my own, away from my parents and away from the Temple. I've told you, Kit, that I was never suited to being an acolyte. No matter how Grams tried to help me have faith in Titan, I just couldn't connect with him. So, if I wasn't ever going to be a priest, I was going to be an enchanter or an alchemist. Martelle helped me, and I helped him. While he learned how to get access to the things my father was trading in, I was learning how to deal with the merchants in Aarall. We were going to be partners." Kit scoffed at the last comment.

"I think you were learning how to work in the shadows, just like your friend. You were learning how to be a criminal."

"I was never dishonest," Lin said, her back straightening. "No one ever got hurt, and I cheated nobody. I learned how to make deals with people where everyone came out ahead. The information I provided helped the merchants do a better job serving the Temple. Brother Powder couldn't get access to the better reagents for the apothecary. Not everybody is a follower of Titan. Many nonbelievers don't trust those who are, and those people wouldn't sell Brother Powder the better ingredients. I helped him get those. I was not a model acolyte, but I treated people fairly, unless they tried to hurt or cheat me. When they did…" her eyes glazed over as she recalled a vivid memory. "When they did, I delivered justice upon them, just like the Temple taught us."

"You killed them?" Indie asked. Up to this point, he had been silent, drinking in all the information. When he asked, Kit's eyes widened. She didn't believe that was what Lin was saying at all.

"Yes. Those who were evil, and those who sought to harm me or others deserved exactly what they got. I have never regretted my actions and I have never lost a minute of sleep over them." Lin's pulse raced when Kit scowled at her, the young priest's eyebrow cocking. "You have no idea how cruel these people can be. You have no idea what lengths they'll go to for a bit of gold. Don't you dare judge me." Kit's mouth flopped open and then slammed shut.

"I guess we've both found evil in the world, even if we weren't exactly looking for it." Kit's expression softened, and she looked down at her feet. "Passing judgment is exactly what we were taught to do. Whether your heart was filled with Titan's righteous fury or not, I know you believed you were doing the right thing. There is no sin in that. The city was likely a safer place because of your actions."

"I like you, girl," Coldforge said. "You have the heart of a dwarf."

"I would say she has the heart of a dragon," Fury said, nodding his approval. "Perhaps I should have chosen Lin as my apprentice." Where Lin's eyes lit up at the comment, Indie scowled. Kit watched her friends' reactions and then glared at Fury.

"That's the second time you've said that. What do you mean, apprentice?"

"Apprentice, somebody you teach. A dragon chooses an apprentice if he, or she, deems a person worthy."

"Worthy of what?" Kit asked. The intensity of her stare was increasing exponentially.

"Worthy of my time," Fury responded, crossing his arms over his scaly chest. "Are you jealous that I didn't pick you?"

A scowl appeared on Kit's face, followed by her hands flaming. "Breayn needs her rest and we have work to do," she said, storming out of the cabin.

"Can you have two apprentices?" Lin asked as soon as Kit left. "Indie wouldn't mind." She grinned at Indie, raising her eyebrows, daring him to say he would.

"It would be unprecedented," Fury replied, "but you are both worthy candidates. I will give it some thought."

Chapter Ten

Ryn and the Crows

"Hurry, leave it all behind and run!"

The Berrat herded the children out of the cavern; the food being left over the fires was sure to burn. Many hadn't eaten, and all were still hungry. While some of the younger ones protested, adults took them by the arms and dragged them outside. The older children, the ones who understood what was happening, did their best to encourage the littles, to let them know everything would be okay, as long as they moved quietly and didn't waste any time.

Ryn watched the treeline as the families headed south through the thickest part of the forest. Its Berrathian pines offered a good deal of cover, masking their movements and their sounds. Thick branches laden with long needles made a natural sound-break. A leaf-covered ground muffled every step. As the last of the children were shepherded away, he and the rest of the warriors made ready for the Crow soldiers, who were only five minutes from overrunning their camp. With his people all in position, the Berrat leader changed into his great white bear form and bellowed out a challenge to their attackers.

The first of the Crows, a band of six black-feathered scouts, broke into the clearing. The bear snarled and charged, mauling the first of the Crows before backing away. He slashed out with his paw at the next Crow who neared, removing her head with a single swipe. Ryn continued to move backwards, away from where the Crows had entered the clearing. He bellowed out another challenge as two more Crow parties came forward in groups of six. Like the first half dozen, these slavers were dressed in black feathered capes wielding scimitars or small axes.

Ryn reared up on his hind legs, easily standing three times higher than the largest of the attackers. He peeled back his lips, exposing his massive set of teeth. With his eight-inch clawed paws held over his head, he appeared all the larger. With his full weight, he brought his bulk back down to the ground. The surrounding earth shuddered when his paws landed. The bear huffed and retreated a few more steps, drawing the Crows in towards himself. They were trying to flank him, spreading out in a circle around the great bear. As they closed, the bear leapt up and transformed into a falcon. With a quick beat of its wings, it lifted skyward. As soon as the bird was high enough, dozens of arrows sped across the clearing, striking most every one of the Berrat slavers. A moment later, another volley of arrows followed, dropping those who were still standing.

The falcon swooped low, shifting back into Ryn's natural form a few feet from the ground. As he did, his warriors poured out from the trees, daggers drawn. Any Crows who were still breathing were immediately sent to the Beyond.

"Ulip would have enjoyed this," a young warrior said, her excitement fueled by adrenaline. "He couldn't have set this up any better." The girl looked at Ryn; her eyes filled with much more than simple adoration. She had long white braids, deep olive skin, and hardly any leather clothing to hide her shapely curves. The man swallowed hard as she slunk across the blood-stained ground, her intentions obvious.

"Breayn would have as well," he said, rebuking the girl before she got too close. Since his ascension to the leadership of their clan, she had been relentless in her pursuit. No matter what he said or did, she would not be denied her prize.

"But she's not here," the girl purred, running the backs of her fingers down the nape of her neck, letting them linger just above her ample cleavage. She wiped a bit of sweat with her fingertips and licked them clean. The girl was barely of age, but she dripped of sensuality, and she knew exactly how to put it to her advantage. The leader swallowed hard and took a slow, unsteady step away from the girl.

"Lyta, enough!" a young man called from across the clearing. "If you can't control yourself, I'll bind you until you're nothing more than a shriveled old woman."

"Shut it, brother," she growled back. She gave Ryn a quick smile that said *this wasn't over* and moved to the nearest fallen Crow. She stripped him of his cloak and searched him for anything of value.

"Can we get the children? Is it safe for everyone to return home?" another warrior asked as he wiped the last of the blood from his dagger. "Supper is going to burn."

"Bring them back," Ryn said. "We'll eat and spend the night. At first light, we're leaving. This place is no longer a secret. We're not safe here."

Chapter Eleven

Amilta and the Dog Soldiers

Danny had his feet up on a table strewn with documents. King Karter's ledger was laying across his lap and each time he turned a page the scowl on his face deepened. He ran his fingers through his long, flame-red hair. His normally hazel-green eyes were bloodshot, thick bags hanging below them, looking like overripe plumbs.

"Why don't the manifests line up with what's in the ledger?" he asked, frustration oozing from every pore in his body. "I can't tell which ones are right and which are not." He rolled his heavy shoulders and tilted his head side to side, hoping to work out the stiffness that had been creeping into his muscles.

"We have to assume the ledger is accurate," Rusty said, scrubbing her face with her hands. "My father wouldn't have made the entries in the ledger if they were wrong. He just wasn't like that." The woman rolled her eyes and turned away from Danny. *"Yes, I know he wasn't you,"* she growled, *"but I don't know how else to refer to the person who has been in your body all these years."*

"You and your father are having words again?" Danny asked, slamming the ledger shut. Rusty nodded curtly and stood from her chair. She straightened out her deep red surcoat and slid a thin gold ring onto her finger. The tension in her face bled away as soon as she slipped it on.

"Yes," she said, looking at the tiny gold ring with a hint of disgust. "Not that I blame him, but he's always angry, and he disapproves of everything I say or do. Bloody Helja, he disapproves of everything I think."

"Have you talked with him about what's going on here? Does he have any advice?"

"Yes, I have, and yes, he's full of suggestions on how I should do things." Danny waited for the woman to finish her thought, but wherever her mind was, it wasn't in the here and now.

"Care to share?" Danny asked. He waited patiently for several seconds. "Rusty? What does your father suggest we do?"

"He wants me to merge our forces with Aurora's Guard, the Free Traders Union, and Mortem Lupus. He thinks we have enough strength to sail into Ravenlord and crush it." The tone in Rusty's voice suggested she didn't agree with her father's advice.

"With King Faol's army there, it would be suicide. I thought he was a good leader." Danny moved from the document covered table and threw himself into one of the war room's over-stuffed chairs. His eyes never left Rusty as he waited for a response. "Rusty?"

"I know it's suicide. The man's angry and he wants revenge. He said that his body is there in Ravenlord, and he wants it back." Rusty moved to the chair next to Danny and threw herself into it.

"How does he know that his body is there? Can he sense it?" Rusty glared at the young Berrat.

"Who knows? All I can say is, he won't shut up about it."

"I'm thinking it's no picnic for him, being inside your head." The woman glowered at Danny for his comment. "Oh, I didn't mean it like that. I just meant that he's a man being forced to listen to the thoughts of a woman." Rusty's look intensified, her hands balling up into tight fists. "Sweet Gaia, woman, stop it. He's your father, and he's been having to listen to all of your deepest, most personal fantasies. No father should have to know whom his daughter is dreaming about, lusting for, missing so desperately that she can't think straight." The woman's look of derision melted away, and she blew out a long breath.

"Does it really show that much?" she asked, scrubbing her face yet again. She let her hands stay over her mouth as she tried to stifle a yawn. The question made

Danny laugh out loud. "Even if your father was right about attacking, we don't have nearly enough ships to send our army south."

"And most of them are not ready to fight," she said. She sounded worn out, defeated.

"Are the Berrat still giving you fits?" Danny pursed his lips, his eyes alight with mischief. "We Berrat are set in our ways, but if you can tap their potential..."

"I've got Treedale and Mukale working with them." Rusty tried to straighten out her jerkin. It had gotten twisted up while she'd sat in the overstuffed chair. "That young Nomad and his Berrat friend seem to communicate well with them. Even still. Even if they can be trained and readied for war, I don't know how to use them."

"I know some people," Danny said, leaning forward in his chair. "They're natural leaders and they've been running a team of guerilla warriors, Berrat warriors."

"Where are these people?" Rusty asked, throwing her head back, covering her eyes with the crook of her elbow.

"One is in Taseko, and the other is, Gaia knows where." Rusty sat up and stared blankly at Danny, shaking her head.

"That's not very helpful, now, is it?"

Danny shrugged at the comment. He could fly to Ryn and get him to Cormorant in less than a day, if he would willingly leave his people. Breayn, too, would make a good leader for the Berrat, but now that she had her mother's spirit within her, she would want to return to her mate as soon as possible. What Danny really wanted, more than anything else, was Ulip. The giant was a force of nature, commanding the respect of everyone around him, at least he used to. A shadow at the doorway caught Danny's eye.

"My pack caught this lot," Amilta said, leading five people bound and gagged into the room. "They were snuffling around the Berrat camp outside the city walls." It was Danny's turn to blow out a long breath. He didn't really care if she had captured somebody snooping around. If they weren't causing any harm, why bother? Maybe they were just...

"Sweet Gaia!" Danny laughed as he hopped out of his chair. He was near hysterics at seeing the looks on the faces of the prisoners. "You were caught by a child. A girl of only eight cycles."

"Nine," Amilta corrected. "I celebrated the anniversary of my birth two days ago." Danny felt bad that he didn't know the young Berrat was starting a new cycle, but the look of shame on the prisoners' faces washed the feeling away.

"Hello, Calian," he said with a broad grin. "Aput, nice to see you and your... pack." Calian was trying to speak, but the cloth gag in her mouth muffled the words, making them incomprehensible. Danny turned back to Amilta. "You caught yourself a pack of dog soldiers. That's not an easy feat."

"Dog soldiers?" Rusty asked. "Do you mean to say they're Lycosians? They're werewolves?" Danny waggled his eyebrows and moved towards Calian. Aput thrust himself forward, blocking Danny's progress.

"Now, now, Aput," Danny said, holding his hands up defensively. "I was just going to remove her gag, but if you insist on speaking first, I can start with you." Harsh sounding noises poured out from the man's mouth. Based on the look of fury in his eyes, none of the words were... pleasant. With his lips pursed, Danny reached up and pulled the gag from Aput's mouth.

"We were not bested by a child," the bald, tattooed man said, sneering at the small girl. "To further our agenda, we allowed ourselves to be taken captive. It was the quickest way inside."

"Sure, you did," Danny replied, a laugh in his voice. He pulled down the gag from Calian. "Nice to see you again. What's your excuse for being captured?"

"This child is a remarkable girl," Calian said, nodding her head to Amilta. "You have some interesting friends. I can honestly say I didn't expect to find you settled into a slaver's manor."

"Its owner is no longer here," Danny said, turning to Rusty. "This is General Karter, the former owner's daughter and leader of Kit Standing Bear's army."

"Yes, we know all about the little priest," Aput said. His expression was too flat to get a read on what he was thinking. "This small girl talks too much."

"You asked me questions. I gave you answers. I didn't see the harm," Amilta said with a thick pout, her face reddening. "It wasn't like you were going to get a chance to tell anyone."

"Who are these people?" Rusty asked, clearly not liking the way Aput was talking about Amilta.

"Friends," Danny said as he moved to the other dog soldiers, pulling their gags from their mouths. "They're members of Mortem Lupus, if I recall correctly." Calian nodded her agreement, drawing a growl from her older brother.

"Mortem Lupus? So, they are werewolves." Rusty gave a weak smile as she took a step back. "They don't look like werewolves; at least not like from the stories I was told when I was young."

"We are among the few who can control our wolf selves," Calian said. "Or, in the case of me and my brother, our dire wolf selves." Rusty's skin went pasty at the mention of dire wolves. She was comfortable being around Runt because she knew him and trusted him, but dire werewolves were an uncommon thing altogether.

After Danny had finished removing everyone's gag, he untied their bonds. When he got to Aput, he found his bonds had already been broken. The big man scowled when Danny cleared his throat at him.

"What happened to the silvered weapons?" Aput asked, rubbing his wrists. "We saw that the black ships are still in the harbor."

"They're all safe and accounted for," Bango said as she came strolling in with the Ashtown twins at her side. At the sight of guests, Cilya flicked her golden locks over her shoulder and raised her chin, so she could look down on the new arrivals. Ashlay, seeing her sister's behavior, mimicked it perfectly.

Rusty tugged at her earlobe. "Cilya," Rusty asked, "these people say they're members of the Mortem Lupus. Can you think of anyway to prove it?" The woman's face screwed up as she concentrated on the question. Her tongue poked out the side of her mouth as she tried to figure out a solution.

"No, not really." Cilya looked over at Pana, her eyebrows now raised. "Maybe if you asked him, he could tell you."

"You know this man?" Danny asked, pointing to one of the dog soldiers. Cilya frowned, crossed her arms over her chest, and nodded.

"How?" Bango asked, putting some space between herself and the woman.

"We met at the headquarters at Sea Haven." The dog soldiers snarled at the woman's revelation. "What? They all know where your base of operations is."

"Helja, Cilya," her sister said, "do you not understand what the word secret means? It means we don't share information with just anyone."

"I didn't share it with just anyone. I shared it with our friends. If they trust us enough to tell us you're in Aurora's Guard, surely I can trust them enough to tell them about the Mortem Lupus."

"You? You are friends of Aurora Windsong, the celestial?" Aput's eyes roamed around the room, like he was taking it all in for the first time. "By Medeina, it's true then. She's actually fighting for our side."

"It's more like we're fighting on her side," Bango said. She had a look of resignation on her face. The secret was already out and if they were members of the Mortem Lupus, they would be powerful allies. "The woman who controls this city is Aurora's daughter, Sister Kit Standing Bear."

"I'd like to meet her," Calian said. "She sounds like an amazing person."

"You don't know the half of it," Danny said with a guffaw. "She's off on a mission right now, on her way home to Aarall."

"What's happened to the masters?" Aput asked. "Why have they let this Kit person take control of their city? House Hanse pretends they're in charge here, but we all know it's the vampire king who's pulling the strings, making his puppets dance."

"Those puppet masters had their strings cut," Bango said. "Between Kit and her canine companions, they really stood little chance." The comment of canines got the dog soldiers' attention. Amilta smiled at their interest.

"Her pack is most impressive," the young Berrat said. "Runt, the son of Amaruq, the Alpha Prime, is among her followers. She also has a wonderful wolfdog named Lump. With Sister Kit at their side, they are a formidable pair." Calian snorted at the comment.

"I'd say your pack is impressive as well." Calian walked over to the girl, sniffing the surrounding air.

"Enough of this," Rusty said, taking on an air of authority. "Why are you here?"

Aput leaned his head over to his left shoulder, the bones in his neck popping. With each crack, Rusty flinched. "We're here about the silvered weapons. We had meant to prevent the ship from leaving port, but we were too late." The slightest hint of a smile appeared at the corners of his mouth. "But it looks like it doesn't matter. Had those weapons made it to Ravenlord, all hope would have been lost."

"You say the weapons are secure," Calian added. "They should be destroyed. Even if you think they're protected, they're too dangerous to be kept."

"They're also too fine to destroy," Rusty said. "We're having their nature *changed*, so that they can't be used against your kind. The properties that make them deadly to you are being made..."

"Inert," Bango finished. "The dwarves and the Hobgoblins are working on them as we speak." The mention of the Hobgoblins drew the dog soldiers' attention. Pana, in particular, seemed stunned at the comment.

"You have elementals here?" he asked, his face slack. "How many?"

"Elementals?" Rusty asked.

"Those you call Hobgoblins," Aput answered. "They are elemental wizards, creatures naturally imbued with the power to control fire, water, air, and earth. These people do not unwillingly go anywhere."

"The Hobgoblins have been working with the dwarves, enchanting weapons and armor," Rusty said. "According to my... friend, they are the best enchanters she has ever seen."

"How many?" Calian asked again. "How many are here?" Danny shrugged.

"Thirty, maybe," he said. "Why does it matter?"

"They're trying to break through," Aput answered. "It's the only thing that makes sense. King Faol is trying to bring down the Veil and free Bael and Gorgaraeth from Helja." Danny swore, using phrases nobody understood.

"More gods?" He spat the words out. "We're already up to our necks in them, and King Faol is trying to bring more?"

"What do you mean, more?" Calian asked.

"We're already fighting Ymir and, who knows what side Tyr and the other Fates are on?" He threw his hands up in frustration and stomped about the room.

"We have Fenrir to aid us," Amilta added. "As well as Fury, and Aurora, and let's not forget about Kit herself. I pity the foolish person who tries to cross her."

"What do you mean, Fury?" Calian asked. "Do you mean the dragon lord? He's free from his mountain prison?"

"It's complicated," Rusty said, spinning the tiny ring on her finger. "But we have a piece of him. He's with Kit and the others." None of the dog soldiers seemed to accept the general's assertion. Either that, or they didn't understand.

CHAPTER TWELVE

LORD ASTER AND MARTELLE

While Breayn rested in the *Mysty's* captain's quarters, and everyone else went into the city, Kit brought Lord Aster to the ship's upper deck. With his hands shackled behind his back, he struggled to climb the steep ladder out of the ship's hull. When his head poked out from the hold, he turned away, shielding his eyes from the brilliant light of the sun. It was hanging low, setting the sky ablaze in oranges and bright reds.

"What will you do with me?" Aster asked.

"It depends on what you can do for me," Kit said, holding the man by the scruff of the neck, pushing him up against the ship's rails. Aster struggled briefly to back up when the silver-blue back of a Makara broke the surface of the water.

"You wouldn't," the man stammered as a second Makara joined the first.

"Without hesitation," Kit said. "If you lie to me or if I don't like what you're saying, I'll toss you over the rail and never give you a second thought."

The lord whimpered. "I never wanted this. I don't want to die like this."

"Continue," she growled.

"I was told that I had to move prisoners in and out of my port. If I didn't, they'd kill me, and my people would suffer."

"Who told you this?" Kit demanded, pressing the man harder against the rail.

"The king," Aster responded, his eyes wild as another Makara broke the surface.

"The king told you to do this personally?"

"No, of course not." Aster swallowed hard. "His emissary came here a little more than a cycle ago. He brought an army with him, I guess to prove that he was who he said he was. In payment, he brought me a chest of gold dragons. I had no choice but to accept this gesture in return for the use of our harbor. If I didn't, he would sack the town, and they'd do what they wanted, anyway. What else could I do?"

"How did Xin become a vampire?" Kit asked.

Aster's eyes became glassy. "The day after Pental came, a woman showed up. A terrifying woman. She said we were too weak and that we needed help. There was a vampire with her. The creature turned Xin and then she tried to turn everyone in the town's guard. All but six died. She said we were still too weak, so she summoned something. It took Xin over, strengthened her, but it wasn't Xin anymore. She became cruel, twisted, keeping blood slaves for herself and her vampires. What they did to them, to us, was sick, perverted beyond measure."

"Did this woman give her name?"

The lord nodded frantically. "Annabella," he ground out. "Annabella Illum. She's the daughter of King Faol."

"And now the king wants to make you lord of Aarall? Why?" Kit asked.

"Because he can bend me to his will, unlike the previous ruling body there."

"What do you mean, the previous ruling body?"

"Father Hoarfrost and Captain Harding," Aster said, shaking his head. "They refused him, so he removed them."

Kit's hands shook badly. The lord, too, whimpered, fearing she was about to toss him into the monster-infested waters.

"When? How?" she finally asked. "Aarall's walls are nearly impregnable. The king would have had to send his entire army to take the city."

"From within," Aster said, trying to put some distance between himself and the ship's railing. "The king has people in the Temple, and in the City Watch."

Kit trembled as the blood rushed from her face. "What? How?"

"I don't know the details of what happened. I just know it did. The emissary from the king was here the day after the city fell. His name was Lord Martelle, the bastard son of Lord Arthure. He told me to make ready to relocate to Aarall."

"Martelle? He was here, in Templeton?" Kit asked, her fury rising uncontrollably. "How long ago did he leave?"

"He didn't," Aster said, his eyes glued to the flames on Kit's hands, especially the hand still holding onto him. "He's at my manor. Please don't burn me."

⸎

Angel skidded to a stop in front of the lord's manor, amidst the bodies of nearly a dozen guards. Several had arrows sticking out of them, while others had been hacked, slashed, or torn to pieces. Kit instructed Angel to let her know if anybody was outside as she dashed up the flight of hand-carved stone stairs to the manor's front door.

As soon as she entered the building, she could hear screams coming from the floor above. With her hammer drawn, Kit bounded up the stairs three at a time, following the source, until she came upon a large sitting room.

"What are you doing?" Kit shouted as she entered. Her friends were all there, standing menacingly over Martelle, who was tied to an exquisitely crafted wooden chair. The boys were standing guard by the door. Lin's sword was embedded in the man's shoulder, his blood staining his tunic, his trousers, and the room's tiled floor.

"I'm finding out why he betrayed me," Lin yelled back, twisting her blade. The man bellowed out in agony once more, begging for her to stop.

For the next several minutes, Indie, Lin, and Coldforge talked over each other, trying to convey what had happened since they'd arrived at the manor. It wasn't until Indie said that Father Hoarfrost had been murdered did any of it seep in.

"Father's dead?" Kit asked, her voice thin and hollow in her ears. Again, her friends were speaking to her, talking over each other, trying to explain what Martelle had told them. Nothing they were saying was registering with her.

Their voices sounded like they were underwater, their words almost indiscernible.

"Back away from him," Kit demanded.

Lin glared at her before turning her gaze back to Martelle. She yanked her sword from his shoulder, twisting the blade as she did. "Bitch," the man cried out, earning him a kick to the face, toppling him and his chair over backwards. Before Lin could thrust her sword into him again, Kit grabbed Martelle by the front of his tunic, pulling him and his chair back into an upright position. The prisoner's face was in ruins. Without warning, Kit punched the bloody mass, which used to be his nose.

"Tell me how Father Hoarfrost died," she growled. "How did you best the most powerful priest of Titan in all of Arnnor?"

"We killed him, simple as that. There's nothing else to be said about it."

"You're lying," Kit ground out, as a flood of relief blossomed in her chest. Martelle laughed at her assertion, declaring that she was wrong and that she just didn't want to believe it. Even though she sensed he was lying about Hoarfrost's death, what he was saying now was true. As Kit pondered his words, she struck him in the belly with all her might. The man doubled over in his chair, gasping for breath. It dawned on her that Martelle believed he was dead, but he didn't know for sure. It was the only explanation that made sense to her.

"Tell me how Father Hoarfrost was killed," Kit said, her eyes flashing golden.

"We poisoned him, and then we hung him." The words made Kit grimace. They were part truth and part lie, but she couldn't tell which was which. The fact that there was truth to either of the statements made her panic.

"And you witnessed it? Personally?"

"Of course. I watched it happen." Martelle gave her a smug look.

Another part truth.

"Why? Why did you need to kill him?"

"Because people would rally behind him. They'd follow him blindly to their deaths, all in the name of your false god."

Sweet Titan. The words were all true.

"Why would the king want to unseat Father Hoarfrost and Captain Harding?" Kit asked, her eyes once again flashing golden.

"Power," Martelle replied, as though the answer was obvious. "Power and everlasting life."

"Immortality? Who could promise that?"

"Bael and Gorgaraeth," Martelle answered, licking the blood from his upper lip. "When Ragnarök, the end of days, is upon us, they will reward those loyal to them."

Kit's face darkened considerably. More gods. More people willing to sacrifice others to benefit themselves.

"Last question," Kit said, putting her thumb over the open wound left by Lin's sword. "Tell me of Captain Harding. Is he also dead?"

"Your father is dead," Martelle replied with an evil smile. "He was of no use to us, so we hung him next to Father Hoarfrost." His smile disappeared as Kit dug her thumb into his shoulder, squeezing it until the man blacked out from the pain. His body sagged forward in his chair, pulling against his restraints.

"Almost every word out of his mouth was a lie," Kit said to Lin. "What do you want to do with him?"

"You know for sure that he was lying?" Lin's lower lip twitched. When Kit nodded yes, Lin's jaw hardened and her lips went so thin, they disappeared.

"You'd like me to ask him something... specific?" Kit asked, sensing Lin's desire.

"I want to know why he betrayed me. Why my parents used me. Why they would have me do terrible things... for them." Lin's sword-hand was convulsing as though she was holding herself back from bringing her weapon to bear on her half-brother.

Kit bent down over Martelle, her look one of pure disdain for the man. When she jammed her thumb into his shoulder wound again, his eyes snapped open, and he screeched out.

"Why did you betray your sister?" Kit asked, bits of spit flying from her mouth.

"She is no relation of mine," Martelle replied, blinking rapidly. "She's just another bastard, the result of her treacherous mother's dalliance. My father should have killed them both."

"Is that true?" Lin choked out through her tears. When Kit nodded, Lin stepped over Martelle and spat in his face.

"Who's my father?" she screeched in his face. "I thought we were friends."

"We were never friends," Martelle said, curling his split lip, baring his bloody teeth. "You're the bastard child of the king. Your mother was nothing more than a trollop, a plaything Jordain kept around. When she became pregnant, he kicked her out of the palace. My father wed your mother, took you in, raised you as his own." Lin looked at Kit, who lowered her eyes, unable to answer the question.

Without notice, she jabbed the tip of her blade into the man's eye. When he squirmed, she placed her boot across his throat, pulled the blade out with a twist, and rammed it into his other eye. After a short, garbled yelp and some leg spasms, his thrashing stopped.

"I'm sorry," Indie said, pulling Lin towards himself. He didn't really know what else to say to her, but she gladly accepted his comfort, burying her face in his shoulder. She mumbled incoherently until she said that she would make her father pay. She would make them all pay.

Chapter Thirteen

The Warrior and the Wise One

While the group boarded the *Mysty*, Kit hung back on the beach, taking a few minutes to herself. A tightness had crept into her chest. It found a home there, twisting her heart until it was on the verge of collapse. She patted Angel's neck, drawing strength from her small roan. Somehow, the horse helped ground her.

"Don't lose hope," Angel said through their bond. Kit always found it amazing how comforting her voice could be. *"Your people may yet be safe. You won't know the truth of it until we get back to the Temple."* Kit knew she was right. Much of what Martelle had said was the truth, or he, at least, hoped it was so. She had difficulty discerning between an actual truth and wishful thinking. But the man's outright lies told her he was filling his story with things he hoped were fact. Why did the problems of the world always seem to rest on her shoulders, crushing her under their weight? As the group climbed the gangplank onto the *Mysty*, Kit looked up at the pale-yellow moon, a thick crescent in the night sky. Beyond the small wisps of clouds, she spotted the Warrior and the Wise One.

"What are you telling me, Gaia?" Kit wasn't exactly expecting a response, but shook her head just the same. With effort, she tore her eyes away from the stars and blew out a breath. There was so much happening. She straightened her shoulders and made her way back to the ship. She slipped off Angel when they reached the docks and led her to the gangplank. Swirls appeared at the ship's edge, their ripples spreading outward, refracting the moon's weak light.

When Kit stepped onto the ship, the boys came bounding across the deck to greet her. Captain Windspeak gave her a tired smile while he waited for Runt and Lump to finish saying hello.

"Xin's soldiers are now your soldiers," Tym said in a flat, matter-of-fact tone. "Apparently, they had tried to rise against Xin at some point, and many of them paid the ultimate price for their actions. Everybody else fell in line and did what they were told after that."

"Should we take them to Cormorant?" Kit asked, rubbing the back of her neck. She was neither a commander nor a planner, and she didn't know if having soldiers in multiple locations was a good thing or not.

"Some may want to," Tym said, rubbing the stubble of his chin. "But most of these soldiers are regular people who Xin conscripted into her army, likely against their will. If the king decides to attack when he finds out what's happened here, they won't be able to effectively defend the town. They'll all die."

"What if you and your soldiers stayed here and trained them?" Indie asked. "We could use the Mysty to transport anybody who wouldn't feel safe back to Cormorant."

"It's not a bad idea," Tym said, looking at Kit for her approval.

"I don't want to force anybody to be away from their families," Kit said, directing her comment at Tym, knowing that if he stayed, he'd be away from his wife and daughter for an extended period.

Tym shrugged. "It's a soldier's life. Getting sent away on campaigns is what we do. But if our families could join us here…"

"Everybody who'd like to bring their family here is welcome to," Kit said with a warm smile. "You all know the risks of bringing them. If they want to come and be a part of this community, I see no problem with that." Tym looked across the sea, his face unreadable.

"Can I leave it with you, then?" Kit asked. He didn't look at Kit, but he nodded slowly, perhaps still considering what his own choices might be.

"What are you going to do with Lord Aster?" Lin asked, clenching her hands into tight fists. "Will you deliver justice unto him?"

"I do not think he's a wicked man," Coldforge said. He had been standing by the railing during the entire conversation, watching small waves come rolling in, listening to them lap against the side of the ship. "Sometimes good people are forced to do bad things. I wouldn't think twice about killing someone to protect me kin."

"I will question him." Kit patted the head of her hammer. "I will know his heart. If he is still the man I thought he was when we first met, he can stay and care for his people."

Even in the night's relative darkness, Indie's reddening face was obvious. He lowered his eyes to avoid her gaze, avoiding eye contact.

Knowing there was no more they could do that night, Kit suggested they eat, sleep, and head out at first light. As the group moved towards the captain's quarters, Kit took Lin by the elbow and asked her to stay back with her. Indie stopped and stared. Kit inclined her head slightly, her eyes boring into his.

"I just need a moment with Lin. Can you bring up some food from the hold?" Without a word, Indie changed directions and made his way to the hatch leading down into the ship's belly.

"Are you okay?" Kit asked her friend. "Martelle's story must have been upsetting."

"You mean finding out that my father isn't my father?" Lin's voice dripped with venom. "I couldn't be happier. The man is a blight and knowing I'm not his child, well, it's the best news I've heard in an exceedingly long time."

"And what about Martelle?" Kit asked, knowing this was the real sore spot.

"We were close, and he betrayed me." Lin's lower lip quivered. "I felt like he stabbed me in the heart. He opened my eyes to my father's treachery. Permanently closing his eyes gave me more pleasure than it should have."

"I'll do what I can to make it right," Kit said, embracing her friend tightly. Kit still didn't fully understand Lin, what she'd been up to, and how she fit into the attack on Aarall, but right now, all she wanted to do was comfort her. When she felt Lin's body finally relax, she broke their embrace and brushed Lin's hair behind her ear. "Go inside. I'm going to go have a chat with the fallen lord."

Without a word, Lin nodded and moved off toward the stateroom. As Kit made her way to the ship's hold, she crossed paths with Indie and a ship's hand. Their arms were laden with trays of food. "I just need a minute with Lord Aster," she said, giving her man a peck on the cheek as she walked past him. "Make sure the boys save me some food."

Kit stepped into the hold, igniting Fury's light, chasing away the darkness. The sailors had chained Lord Aster to a crossbeam, where he was dangling precariously. He was, by design, made to be as uncomfortable as possible without actually hurting him.

After a long, and heated discussion with the man, Kit believed Lord Aster had his people's best interest at heart and that he should continue running the town. The lord objected strenuously to having Captain Windspeak and his soldiers staying behind, believing they were there as his babysitter. His objections died off when Kit suggested a life-shortening alternative. She had his jailer remove the heavy padlock that held his chains in place.

"Go home," she said. "Care for your people. If I find out that you betrayed me, there is nothing that can protect you from my wrath." Kit's eyes slipped into their inky blackness. Fury's flames burst outward, forcing the lord to either back away or burn.

CHAPTER FOURTEEN

LUPIEN AND THE SPIDERWOOD FOREST

The early morning had long since passed by the time the Mysty had set sail for Cormorant, returning with Breayn and a few soldiers and townspeople who'd felt it was too dangerous to remain in Templeton. Once the ship had reached open water, Kit and company prepared to make their way to Aarall.

Passing through the Templeton's front gates, Kit grimaced as the group rode by the giant rift she had created when she'd faced Pental, the murderous fiend who had forced her hand. This was where she had killed so many innocents. Even if they were under the vampire's control, their minds warped by his compulsion, they didn't deserve death. Father Hoarfrost had forgiven her for her actions, telling her that there was no other solution, save for letting the people kill her. She desperately hoped Martelle's words were wrong, that Father Hoarfrost lived. How would she continue without his guidance? More than anything, she wished to have more time with the man. There was still so much to learn.

Char's hoofbeats drew Kit's attention. She gave Indie a small smile as he rode up beside her, his long legs dangling comfortably down his great black stallion's flanks.

"A lot has happened since we first visited this town," he said. How he could manage such a quiet grace was beyond her, but his presence comforted her. "I still have trouble believing you did this, created this giant hole." The comfort he had provided vanished before he finished the sentence.

"Men," Angel said. *"Why can't they just stand around and be pretty? They'd be so much easier to deal with if they'd keep their mouth shut."*

"I can't really hold him at fault," Kit replied. *"More often than not, I don't think about my words before I let them spill from my lips."* Angel nickered. Char responded in kind. Indie gaped and cocked his head to the side.

"I just wish Char would stop worrying about me," Angel said. *"When I'm with you, riding into adventure, I'm at my happiest. When you're with me, I fear nothing. It's just so wonderful to run."*

"I think I'd like to run," Kit said to Indie just before Angel broke into an easy gallop. Char followed suit, with Lump and Runt instantly giving chase. Coldforge whooped as the dire wolf surged forward. He grabbed a thick handful of the wolf's fur to stop himself from rolling off. The two had formed a strong bond over the past few days. Kit could only guess it was either Coldforge's playful demeanor, or the dwarf's willingness to give the boys snacks anytime there was food around.

"Not too fast," Lin called out as she spurred Whistler into action. With her horse's speed enchantments, she could keep up with her friends, so long as they didn't push too hard. Lump circled back, nipping at Whistler's hooves, driving her to speed up. The golden retriever's brown eyes were bright and filled with joy, while his tongue lolled out the side of his mouth like a great, pink flag.

They had been running at a steady pace for a while before Kit veered from the road, turning toward the woods to their right. At a distance, the ferrous-wood forest looked black and foreboding. Her heart pounded at the thought of entering it again, but it was the fastest way to Aarall, even if it was the most dangerous.

"Kit, no," Indie called out. "We're not going through the Spiderwood Forest again. Remember what happened last time?" Even the boys seemed reluctant to re-enter the spider-infested woods.

"What's the problem, lad?" Coldforge rode alongside the Nomad. "It's just a bleak, black forest. Surely you've been in such a wood before."

"I've been through many woods," the young tracker replied. "But none as deadly as this one. It's infested with spiders big enough to eat a horse, even mine."

"Really? That big? Ye know, I have little use for me cousins," the dwarf said as he scanned the treeline for any sign of spiders, "but those tree-lovin' arses could probably clean this forest out in a fortnight."

"Your cousins?" Lin asked absentmindedly as she, too, scoured the trees for signs of spiders.

"Them pointy-eared elves," Coldforge replied, his wild orange beard twitching as he spoke.

"I don't expect we'll see a single spider," Kit said as she nodded towards a large gray wolf that appeared off to their left. "I expect they'll make sure we travel through safely." Even though wolves inhabited the forest that would protect them, nobody, except for Kit, seemed any more at ease. Ignoring her cohorts' concerns, Kit pushed Angel forward.

"I sure hope you know what you're doing," Angel said, her voice filled with trepidation. Kit could feel her worry, perhaps because she remembered what had happened to Kit's mount the last time they had traveled through here. She certainly didn't want to be a meal for a group of forest crawlers and wolf spiders.

They were only a hundred feet into the woods when it became so dark, they couldn't see fifteen feet ahead of themselves. Kit ignited the light of her hammer. Its brilliant white light burst outwards, penetrating the darkness, illuminating the game trail for thirty paces in front of them. The forest's canopy was a dense tangle of huge leaves, preventing even a single ray of sunlight to penetrate down to its leaf-littered floor. Without the sun's warmth, the temperature dropped drastically, forcing everyone to pull their traveling cloaks about their shoulders just a wee bit tighter. Lump, Runt, and Coldforge seemed unaffected. Coldforge didn't even seem to mind the oppressive darkness that drew in around them.

"It's like being back in the mines," he said, sniffing at the air. "But it doesn't smell as nice. Everything here stinks of must and decay. And where are these giant spiders ye all were worried about?" He had his war ax hefted over his shoulder, using his other hand to maintain his grip on Runt's fur.

"Keep your voices down," Indie suggested, his eyes straining to see into the blackness. "They're just as attracted to sound as they are to movement. If you keep talking, you might as well ring a dinner bell."

The deeper the group traveled into the forest, the more Kit's nerves were on edge. Her senses were on high alert, which drove Angel's own anxiety up. Coldforge and Runt took the lead, able to move at the very edge of Fury's illumination. The way the dwarf was rocking side to side on Runt's back, Kit thought he was singing quietly to himself, almost dancing to some dwarven tune he was playing in his head.

The rest of the trip through the wood continued without incident, except for when they came too close to a grizzly bear and her cub. When she decided that Kit and her cohorts posed no real threat to her, the bear bounded off into the underbrush, her cub bawling as it followed.

When the group finally exited, they stopped at a stream that ran near to the forest's edge. The animals needed to be watered and everyone was ready to eat. Despite knowing that there were wolves providing them protection on the way through, everyone was relieved to leave the accursed forest behind. Judging by the fact they could easily see the river's rocky bottom and that leaves were only slowly floating along the surface, it would be safe for the horses to cross. Lump, in human form, told the group it would be unlikely that any Kappa, the river monsters Kit had encountered in the rift just south of Silverhawk, would be there. The water was too clear and too shallow for them.

"What happens when we arrive at Aarall?" Indie asked as he cleaned up the camp. "If the Watch is under the king's control, they're not going to just let us come through the front gate."

"There is a way into the temple through the cemetery," Lin said, drawing yet another look of surprise from Kit.

"How could you possibly know that?" she asked, raising her eyebrows. Lin's face reddened at the question.

"What will we do inside the Temple?" Lin asked, tugging on a stray lock of hair that was hanging across her face.

"Stop avoiding my question," Kit said, pursing her lips.

"I found the path while I was... exploring. It was the first time I'd ever found a way off the Temple grounds without being seen."

"So that you could smuggle things in and out of the Temple?" Kit didn't know how to react. It seemed there was always another facet to Lin's indiscretions.

"Not just *things.*" Lin waggled her eyebrows, her lips in a thin, tight smile. While neither Indie nor Kit found this amusing, Coldforge's laughter boomed out with enough force that it may well have carried for miles in every direction.

"You will bring the king's army down on us if you can't stay quiet," growled a voice from behind the group. They turned to see several wolf-man creatures walking towards them. They were dressed in studded leather armor and had short, curved blades hanging from their belts. At their back, a large pack of gray wolves followed close behind.

"Hill Gizmos." Indie drew his swords. The boys moved forward to block the gizmos' progress. Neither was growling, but their bodies were crouched low, ready to strike if necessary.

"That is an insulting word," the largest wolf creature said, watching the boys. "If you're unable to call us by our proper name, then don't bother speaking at all."

"And what is your proper name?" Kit asked, resting her hand on Indie's forearm. She gave him a look that said to be calm.

"We are Lupien." The gizmo stood proud; his lips pulled back enough to expose his teeth. "And if it wasn't for the wolves, you'd not have made it through the forest alive." The alpha wolf padded up beside him. "I am Akh'lut, and this is my pack." The Lupien was large, almost as tall as Indie, but he looked to be substantially heavier. He had silver-gray fur and many battle scars across his face and arms where no fur had ever grown back. At his waist was a pair of curved blades, too long to be daggers, but too short to be called swords. Kit didn't really understand why he had such weapons when he had teeth and claws that rivaled Runt's.

"My name is Kit Standing Bear, and these are my allies." Both Runt and Lump relaxed at Kit's words, sensing no hostility coming from her. "Are you suggesting the wolves protected us from the giant spiders?" The question made Akh'lut laugh, although it sounded more like a strange bark.

"The spiders were the least of your problems. Had the wolves not told us who you were, we'd have killed you for bringing a dark elf into our forest." Coldforge sputtered with outrage. In a heartbeat, he had his ax drawn, and he was striding toward the wolf-man, ready to remove his furry head from his furry body. With just a look, Kit told him to stand down.

"And what exactly is your problem with dwarves?" Kit said. "Calling my friend a dark elf is... insulting." Akh'lut smiled. His expression looked so much like Runt it made her laugh to herself.

"They destroy our lands, the hills, while they dig up whatever shiny metals they can lay their grubby little hands on."

"Me hands are big enough ta throttle ye, wolf," Coldforge said, sheathing his ax. "I don't need no ax to handle the likes of you." When Kit glared at him, the dwarf's orange beard twitched, likely hiding a scowl. "He started it," he muttered, "and I'd be happy to finish it."

"And yet, you carry steel weapons," Indie said, moving in beside Coldforge. "You sound like a hypocrite." The Lupiens' ears all pinned back at the insult.

"They are not metal." Akh'lut's hackles rose high enough that they stood taller than his ears. "Like your head, they are made of wood. We craft them from fallen branches and polish them with spidersilk. They are both beautiful and useful, unlike your head."

"Then how did the wolves save us?" Kit asked, trying to diffuse the situation.

"You are known to them. You are, *Wolf-friend*." Runt barked out, raising his head proudly. "And this one, he is not as he seems." Runt barked again, as though agreeing with the assertion.

"This is Runt, son of Amaruq, the late Alpha Prime," Kit said, bowing her head respectfully at the great wolf's passing. As she said the words, Runt's illusion fell away, showing everyone his true form. While the wolves and the Lupiens all dropped low to the ground, Akh'lut stood still, his eyes wide. A moment later, he, too, bowed deeply.

"Lord Runt," he said, his eyes lowered, and his ears pinned back. "We wept at the news of your father's passing to the Beyond. May he forever run in its fields of green, beneath its skies of blue." Runt lowered his head at their words before letting out several high-pitched barks. The group of Lupiens and wolves all barked back in reply.

"How can we help you?" Kit wondered why they had come out to speak to them. The wolf-man shook his head.

"We do not need your help, but the offer means much to me." He stepped forward, his eyes turning toward Aarall. "We came to warn you away from the city. It's no longer a safe haven. The man who declares himself king of these lands has corrupted it. His warriors forced us from the hills beneath his stone den, turning us into homeless wanderers, seeking shelter where we can."

"How can you know the city isn't safe?" Kit asked. "What else can you tell me about it? Is Father Hoarfrost truly dead? What of the captain of the City Watch?"

"I know nothing about those people," Akh'lut replied. "A young Tahr came to us two days ago. She had several children with her. Apparently, it was no longer safe for them in the city. The other children, the orphans, had been moved underground." Kit's jaw tightened as he told the story.

"Was the Tahr's name Iba?" The girl's name left a sour taste in her mouth. That obnoxious goat-girl had been nothing but a pain in her backside since the day Kit had arrived at the Temple.

Akh'lut shrugged in response. "Perhaps." He turned to one of his cohorts, who nodded slowly. "Apparently, yes. Is she a friend?"

"Hardly." Kit scoffed. The question was absurd. "But it seems she is more than I realized."

"It might surprise you then, to hear that she spoke highly of you. She said that if you showed up, the city might have a chance." Kit snorted. The idea that Iba would say anything kind about her, well, was absurd.

"Kit, we need to get moving," Indie whispered. "We have much to do and little time to get it done." When Kit finally got control of her emotions, she nodded her agreement.

"Thank you for the warning," Kit said, inclining her head. "May Gaia keep you safe. May you forever walk in Fenrir's protection."

"A strange blessing from a priest of Titan," Akh'lut said, inclining his head, "but I appreciate the sentiment." As soundlessly as they had arrived, the group left, heading back towards the trees. In an instant, the forest swallowed them up, hardly leaving any trace that they had been there at all.

Chapter Fifteen

The Crystalline Palace

The late day sun streamed through the curtains, casting a golden glow across the room, forcing Danny to squint as he peered into the dragon tear. He rolled his shoulders, trying to loosen the tightness that had been creeping up to the base of his skull. He took a long drink from his earthenware mug, hoping to ease the incurable dryness in his mouth.

Where are you, Kitten? Why aren't you looking at your crystal?

"Oh, sweet Gaia," Breayn said, averting her eyes as she stepped into Danny's bedroom. "Put some clothes on, cousin. We're gathering in the war room." As fast as she entered, the woman disappeared. Danny glanced down at his bare chest and shrugged. It's not like he was naked, not entirely anyway. He gave the dragon tear one last check before tucking it into his pocket. Not wasting a moment, he snatched up the green tunic he had laying beside him and headed out the door. His heart thumped erratically in his chest, wondering why his cousin was back without Kit and the others. He was still buttoning up his shirt when he entered. The war room was abuzz when he stepped inside, the chatter dying off moments later.

"What?" he asked, looking down to ensure he had properly buttoned his shirt.

"It's not good," Breayn said. "Come in and I'll explain."

"Explain what?" Danny asked, looking to Rusty, trying to gauge her demeanor.

"Aarall has fallen." Breayn's voice was level but absolute. "Father Hoarfrost is dead." Danny's knees buckled beneath him. Other words followed, but they were muffled, like they were coming from another room. He wanted to keep moving, but his legs refused to listen.

Kit, is that why you're not answering? His pulse was thrumming in his ears. Each beat of his heart was like the hollow thump of a war drum.

"How?" was the only word Danny could seem to manage. The room spun again, his stomach along with it. He was about to collapse. Unbidden, the phoenix within him burst forth, pushing away his anxiety, replacing it with steely determination. His back straightened.

"How can you know this?" Flames licked at the corners of Danny's eyes, turning the room into shades of oranges and reds, and all the people within, a bright yellow. "Were you there? Did you see with your own eyes?"

Breayn shook her head. "No, I did not see, but your friend, Kit, she interrogated a man who told her everything. He wasn't lying. His words rang of truth. Jordain Cloudweaver, the king of Arnnor, would seem to be in league with Faol. Without Father Hoarfrost and the Temple of the Fist to stand against the king, there is no hope for the kingdom."

"What of Kit?" Danny asked.

"What of Lin?" Rusty asked, stepping in front of the young Berrat. "Where is she? Is she safe?"

"When I left Templeton, they were on their way to Aarall," Breayn said. She showed no sign of concern or worry for the others. Danny couldn't tell if she was putting on a brave front or if she honestly believed they would be okay. "Most of the soldiers we took south stayed to garrison the town. Some returned. We brought back several hundred Berrat who were too afraid to remain." The woman moved closer to Rusty. "Captain Windspeak, Tym, stayed behind. He asked that we bring his family to Templeton. Many other soldiers asked the same. They want to be with their families if the end is upon us."

"The end?" Danny stepped out from behind Rusty. "This is just the beginning and we have not yet begun to fight."

"They have demons." Breayn gave her cousin a challenging look. "And vampires, and... demon possessed vampires. The vampires were weak, but the demon made them nearly unbeatable." Danny's ears pricked up at one word, separating it from the rest of what his cousin had said.

"Nearly," he said, his voice full of hope. "That means Kit and the others beat them. I refuse to yield. I refuse to believe that we can not beat them back, defeat them."

Aput took a seat; his head hung low. "How can you possibly think your friends can retake a fallen city? I agree we cannot stop fighting because the alternative is unthinkable. But we will perish. We cannot stand against gods, and Fates, and demons, and whatever else King Faol has in his arsenal."

"Whatever Faol has at his disposal, its far away from us." Breayn sniggered. "A good part of his army is in Ravenlord, cut off from the king and his vampires. If they cannot cross the Gaelinora Sea, they cannot help him. We can scuttle their ships if we can't defeat them outright. Without ships, they would be forced to march there. It would be winter by the time they made it to Arnnor."

"How many ships does the Fair Traders Union have?" Rusty asked Cilya. The woman's face paled, her eyes were unfocused. "Cilya? How many?"

"I don't know exactly, thirty or forty?" She had to swallow hard before she could get the words out. "I think they're spread out, though. There might be ten warships at Sea Haven."

"We have over one hundred," Aput said, "they're not large, but they're fast. We have over one thousand dog soldiers, but we need to wait until the moon is nearly full. Right now, my people aren't much stronger than the average human. When the moon hangs fully in the night sky, we will be a force to be reckoned with."

"How many of King Faol's soldiers are in Ravenlord?" Danny had been trying to figure out what their combined strength was, and it was making his head hurt.

"Thirty thousand," Aput replied, "with a fleet of over one hundred ships."

"That makes no sense," Rusty said. There was something different about her. Her mannerisms and her bearing were different. Danny didn't need to see her hand to know that she was no longer wearing the ring that kept her father's soul at bay. "With that many soldiers and that many ships, Faol didn't need to go to Ravenlord. You said he was having silvered weapons delivered there to arm his soldiers. You thought it was to destroy the Mortem Lupus. With thirty thousand soldiers, they could have wiped your group off the face of Orth without even slowing down." Rusty tapped her finger to her chin. She stopped for a moment as though to feel her skin. "I need a map of Lycos and Berrathia. If it has Arnnor as well, all the better."

Bango sprinted across the room before rustling through an enormous pile of papers on one of the dining tables. She pulled out a large, rolled up parchment, unfurled it and tossed it to the side. She pulled out another larger roll. Again, she unfurled it enough to inspect the map, her eyes lighting up as she did.

"Here." Bango waived Rusty over. "This map is of the northern half of the eastern continent. It includes everything you asked for, plus the kingdom of Faol, as well as some of the Great Eastern Forest, the Elven kingdom."

Rusty continued to stroke her chin and cheeks, nodding as she did. "I believe he plans on invading Lycos. Look here." She was pointing to where Ravenlord was on the sea's western shore. "If his army is equipped with silvered weapons, it would significantly improve their chances of defeating the lycans, even if the moon was full. From Ravenlord, he would travel down the coast to Ashenburg, then on to Port Jevline, and then up the Praetorian Straits to the Lycos capital, East Den." Rusty's face turned ashen. She smoothed down the map, letting her finger move past East Den to a dark green blotch a small way below it. She rapped her knuckles on it several times. "He's not after Lycos. He seeks to take control of the Crystalline Palace here in Brightwood Forest. Titan, save us all."

"What's the Crystalline Palace?" Danny asked. "Why would Faol want it?"

Aput didn't look well. The conversation seemed to give him a sour stomach. "Because it's the home of Aldur, the eldest son of Arcanus Illum, the one and only emperor of Orth, before he abdicated. Aldur is the source of Lycosian magic. It was he who created the first... werewolf. He is King Faol's eldest brother."

"Who is Aldur and the emperor person?" Danny surveyed the others, looking for an answer. "I've never heard of them." Calian shook her head at the question.

"Emperor Arcanus Illum is at the heart of our world's problems. Ever since the Great Games began, he was involved. The stories say that the Fates chose him to lead the humans. They aided him, making him the most feared general who had ever walked the lands. He led his armies against whoever Titan and Orth threw against them, and he prevailed every time. When the emperor ascended to Autoria, the realm of the gods, he split his empire among his seven sons. Aldur is the eldest and Faol is the fourth, the middle child."

"Another god?" Danny ran his fingers through his hair and groaned. "This is ludicrous."

"He's not a god," Calian said. "But before he ascended to Autoria, he was a wizard of unparalleled power. His children are formidable wizards in their own right, but they are not their father."

"How can you know this?" Bango had stayed back from the rest of the group. She was seated on a couch with Amilta sitting in her lap. "I have never heard of such tales, and Aurora makes a point of keeping us informed."

"We thought they were just folktales," Calian replied. "Until we met your friend here, The Phoenix." Rusty lost her balance, knocking many of the parchments from the dining table. Her hands were shaking badly.

"My father," she said, her voice shaking as terribly as her hands. "My father's soul, or whatever was trapped in that container, heard things. He, he didn't understand what was being said, but I think he does now. Ragnarök is at hand. He thinks that they're trying to build an army strong enough to defeat the humans, once and for all. Aldur is the eldest. If they can kill him, it may cause enough of a ripple that the other brothers will not fight, that they will lose hope."

"I think it's more than that," Aput said. "We... Lycosians are deadly to the vampires. With us fighting against them, we would dramatically reduce their chances. I think General Karter was right the first time. The soldiers in Ravenlord. They're going to wipe us out and then they'll move on the Crystalline

Palace. The lycans will be gone and the vampires will have little in the way of a unified opposition."

"We steal their ships," Danny continued running his fingers through his long red hair. "If we can't steal them, I'll set them all ablaze and we can watch them burn."

"Better yet." Breayn had a nasty, thin-lipped grin on her face. "We steal some ships, get the others to chase us, and then we set them ablaze."

"And just how do you propose we do that?" Rusty asked.

"I know how." Cilya flipped her long blonde hair over her shoulder. Most everyone, including her sister Ashlay, gave her a dubious look.

Chapter Sixteen

The Griffin Riders of Silverhawk

The door burst open, making half the patrons of the Crimson Ale yelp and the other half draw weapons. It was difficult to tell who was standing at the door. The taproom was darker than usual. Ever-burning streetlights back-lit the man whose body filled the doorway, casting his face in deep shadows. Light from the few braziers and torches within, reflected off the man's blade. It was at least five feet long and a full hand wide.

"Hold," the man called out, his voice strong and confident like he was accustomed to giving commands and having everyone listen. He strode inside, the bright silver of his armor and the blue of his surcoat marked him as a griffin rider. The large circular epaulets that secured his gold cape identified him as the high commander, the leader of the city's entire air force. Behind the man, six more people followed, all dressed in regular City Watch uniforms.

Carver, the round bellied bartender, flinched when the commander turned his gaze upon him. The balding man kept an ax behind his bar, ready for any sort of trouble. His hand twitched several times as he considered his actions. After a moment, he wiped his hands on his filthy white apron and splayed his fingers on the bar. Reaching for his weapon would likely have been a fatal move.

"Everybody," the commander said, his voice firm, "put away your weapons and press your arses against the wall."

While most of the patrons did as the commander said, Jayne kept her butt firmly planted on her stool, her elbows resting on the beer-stained bar. She shared leadership of the tavern with Sellina and neither of them was the sort to back down, especially from a pompous man. Even though Carver was supposedly in charge of the Auctioneers, Silverhawk's slaver organization, he looked to her for instruction. She tucked an errant lock of her mousy brown hair over her ear and sighed.

"Have we not paid the Watch enough coin to keep your ugly mutt faces out of here?" Jayne didn't bother to look directly at the commander. She polished the bar with a filthy rag.

"You will move against the wall with the others, or I will pass judgment upon you, right here, right now." The commander pointed his great sword at the insulant woman. She was dressed in brown leather pants, a white linen shirt, and a brown leather vest. On her face she wore a look of indifference.

"I think it's best that you and your people leave." Sellina stepped in through the swinging doors that led to the kitchens. "I'll make sure the next tithe includes an extra bit of coin for you." The man's already dark complexion turned scarlet. With a swing of his sword, he sliced cleanly through one of the thick wooden tables.

"Listen, commander." Jayne's voice was authoritative, her posture sure and fearless. "If you haven't received your due, that's not our fault. Speak with your captain if you must. But know this, if you continue with this idiotic bravado bluff, you and your people are going to die, and I'd rather not have to be bleaching the floorboards again."

The captain snatched the woman up by the front of her vest, hoisting her in the air like she was nothing more than a small satchel. With a simple push, he launched her into the darkened area of the tavern, her body slamming into tables and chairs, scattering them across the room. Before he could take a step, Sellina leapt onto his back, wrapping her arm under his chin, pressing with all her might against his windpipe.

The commander tried to reach behind, to grab his attacker by her long, straw-colored hair, but she evaded each attempt. The pressure on his neck was relentless. He stumbled forward, trying to steady himself. He waved his great blade about, his actions appearing desperate.

"Carry me into the darkness," Sellina whispered into his ear. *"What are you doing here?"*

The commander stumbled further towards the rear of the tavern, landing on top of a table, sending himself and Sellina sprawling across the floor. The back of the tavern was nearly pitch-black, masking their actions from any who may have been watching. Jayne drew herself up off the ground, grabbed a chair and threw it at the commander. He ducked easily, the chair crashing against the bar.

"Commander?" one of the City Watch called out.

"I've got this," the big man bellowed back. "I can handle two bar wenches, you fool."

"Ow." Sellina continued with the charade, screeching out her words like she was being injured. "Okay, I'll come quietly." Jayne tossed another chair, slamming it against the wall. She pushed a table over, scattering more chairs across the floor.

"You need to come with me," the commander whispered. "I'll take you to the barracks where we can talk."

"Punch me." Jayne pointed to the corner of her mouth. "Right here, in the face. Make it hard enough to draw blood."

"No. I can't. I won't."

"You can't take us to the barracks. The hawk riders, we've bought them all. They'd attack you on sight, even if you're their high commander." Jayne knocked over another table. "Now punch me and make it good. Interrogate us here, away from the others."

"I will not strike you," the commander said, looking back to where his people were. Most were looking their way, squinting to see into the darkness.

"Oh, sweet Titan," Sellina ground out. She didn't hold back, smashing her fist into Jayne's nose. Blood sprayed in every direction, covering the three of them with crimson spatter. "Now call for your people to detain me." The words had only just left Sellina's mouth when she bolted for the front of the tavern, making her way to the exit.

"Stop her," the commander bellowed out, snatching Jayne by the collar of her leather vest. A pair of City Watch guards tackled Sellina to the ground and pinned her there. One had his knee jammed into the back of her neck while he ground her face into the rough wooden floor.

"Okay. I yield." Sellina struggled to speak under the pressure of her captor's knee and hand.

The commander dragged Jayne out from the darkness. He nodded to the man holding Sellina to the floor. "Let her up." He turned to Carver with a deep sneer. "You. Do you have the key to the cell?" The bartender's eyes narrowed, wondering what the griffin rider had in mind. Jayne, with blood flowing down her nose and over her lips, winked, the action not lost on the balding man.

"Yes, I do." Carver folded his arms across his chest, jutting out his chin defiantly.

"Unlock the cell and put three chairs inside." A wicked smile crept across the commander's face. "I'll start with these two and if I don't like what I hear I'll work my way through the rest of you."

"You should start with him." Jayne gingerly touched her nose, wiping the blood on her trousers. The taste of copper flooded her mouth. "He knows way more than we do. We're just barmaids. He's in charge here. He knows everything." The bartender blinked rapidly at the words. His gaze moved from her, to Sellina, to the rest of the Auctioneers who looked just as dumbfounded. Carver's mouth opened, closed, and opened again. He made a move towards his ax but stopped when Jayne furrowed her brow and pursed her lips.

"Make it four chairs then." The commander motioned with his head for the bartender to get moving. "I said, let her up." The big man bared down on the corporal who was still choking the life out of Sellina. When he finally released the pressure on her neck, the woman rolled onto her back, her nose bleeding badly, and she had a deep cut on her lower lip. She stayed on the floor for a few moments before hoisting herself to her feet. She spat a thick wad of bloody mucus at the man who had trapped her, earning her a backhanded cuff to her cheek that sent her back to the floor.

"Enough!" The commander looked ready to rip the guard's head from his shoulders. "You," he said, pointing his calloused finger at a woman in his group. "Grab that torch and lead us to the cell." The soldier, a lanky woman with a nose that had likely been broken several dozen times, snatched a torch from a sconce and moved towards the back of the tavern. As she walked into the darkness, the battle between the commander and the two bar wenches became apparent. A good deal of furniture had suffered heavily, a few tables and chairs ruined.

"Unlock the door." The commander waited impatiently while Carver pulled the key from around his neck and popped open the thick iron padlock. The bartender had pushed open the door when the commander, using Jayne like a battering ram, pushed the two of them forward. He glared at Sellina as she slunk into the cell.

"Chairs. Four," the commander said to his soldier, taking the torch from her hand. "No, make it five. You can stay." The soldier nodded and dragged chairs into the small cell. The commander bared his teeth at the other Auctioneers who were pressed up against the far wall. "Any of you do something stupid, I will kill them without a second thought." He turned to his own people. "If any of them do something stupid, you will exact judgment upon them, immediately and without remorse." The guard who had pinned Sellina to the floor nodded. He clearly wanted one or more of the prisoners to do something stupid.

The griffin rider stepped into the cell after his corporal had finished bringing in the chairs. He slammed the door hard enough to shake dust from the walls. Sellina and Jayne were glaring at the man. Their eyes darted between him and the corporal who was standing by the door, her hands on her hips.

"She's okay." The commander kept his voice low. "Corporal Longshoe, Dawn, is my eyes and ears in the Watch." He gave the raven-haired woman a smile, motioning to the door. "Keep an eye out. Make sure nobody comes near." She nodded and looked out the small, barred window. Sellina cocked an eyebrow. To be able to see out the door's tiny, barred window, the woman had to be well over six feet tall.

"Commander, what are you doing?" Carver curled his right hand into a tight fist.

"Commander Bishop?" Sellina touched her swollen lip and grimaced. The man stared back, considering the question. He scratched at the side of his neck and groaned. The woman's eyes bulged when he didn't respond. "Billy, why are you here? You could ruin everything we've accomplished."

"It's necessary." He slid his great sword back into its scabbard behind his back and scrubbed his hand over his short-cropped hair. "The king's army has been mobilized. They're heading down from Two Peaks. It seems they're on their way to Aarall."

"That's excellent." Jayne's voice was nasal. She was holding her head back, pinching the bridge of her nose, trying to stem the excessive bleeding. "Maybe they're finally going to move on King Faol. If the bulk of his army is in Ravenlord, they may finally put that bloodsucker down."

"No, we don't think that's what's happening." Billy sighed and hung his head. "Faol's army is bivouacked just south of the Arnnor border. It's hard to say for sure from two leagues above them, but I'd say they're waiting for King Jordain's soldiers. I fear they're going to merge, not fight."

"What of the northern raiders?" Carver asked. "Have they all been taken care of? Are we looking at a reprisal from the masters?"

"That's a part of the mystery," Dawn replied from her place by the door. "Ever since we started rounding them all up, we haven't seen a single vampire, nor have we seen a single member of the Scarlet Tide."

"Are they headed south?" Sellina directed the question to the commander.

"Hard to say," Billy replied with a shrug. "If we can't see them, we can't say where they're going."

"They're likely headed to Cormorant." Jayne knitted her brows together. "They're likely going to mount a counterattack, to take the city back."

"I still can't believe that little girl took down an entire city." Carver shook his head in disbelief. "I know she's tough, but she's barely old enough to..."

"Yes?" Sellina's head snapped back. "Barely old enough to... what?" Carver's face reddened as he squirmed in his chair.

"She's young is all I'm saying." He dropped his voice down to a whisper. "Even if her mother is... you know who." The commander took a menacing step forward, his hand pulled back to unleash a punch.

"Shut it, fool." Billy stole a look over his shoulder at his corporal. She turned away, looking out the window, turning her head left and right, ensuring nobody had snuck closer.

"There is no one within earshot, Commander. Whatever secrets I might learn, I will take to my grave. On that, you can be sure. I don't know who Sister Kit's mother is, but if that young woman will risk everything to save people she's never met..."

"I trust you." Billy nodded to his corporal. "But some information is too dangerous to know. Under compulsion or even a strong complacency potion, words can leak out. Even if you'd rather die than share them." The soldier nodded briskly.

"Yes, Commander. I understand. Would you prefer I leave, so that you can speak more freely?" Billy rubbed his square chin for a moment before shaking his head.

"No, I want you here. Just... keep your eyes on the others." The woman nodded and turned fully to the door, looking out at the City Watch members and their prisoners. Nobody was getting out of line and the guards were standing at the ready should that change.

"What of Lord Stout?" Jayne sat upright after her nose had finally stopped bleeding. "Have you been able to discover his involvement with the slavers? None of my people can find anything on him."

"That pompous ass," Billy said with a harrumph. "He takes being Lord of Silverhawk quite seriously, throwing parties and siphoning off as much coin as he can, taxing the citizens. Besides the toll he exacts, he augments with his association with the Thieves' Guild. He bankrupts the poor and steals from the rich. The man and his entire family are a menace, but as far as I can tell, they're not slavers."

Sellina tilted her head to the side and cleared her throat. "Okay, Billy. You never answered my question. Everything you shared could have gone through normal channels without risk of exposure."

The commander dropped his voice low and set his jaw. "I want to stage a coup. I will invoke martial law and take full control of the Silverhawk military."

Jayne stood from her chair. "To what end?"

"To take them to Cormorant. The Split Crows are making a play, a big play. There is an armada from Wantage headed their way, big enough to carry ten thousand troops, or more." The commander motioned for Jayne to sit, but she refused, crossing her arms over her chest to make the point clear. "Sister Kit has assembled a formidable army there, but most of them are too green to fight effectively."

"You have little more than a hundred soldiers here." Carver cleared his throat and pressed his lips together into a thin line and stood, joining Jayne. "What difference would you make? You'd leave this city unguarded. We Auctioneers outnumber you nearly thirty to one. Since we've started our raids, our numbers have swelled well beyond expectation."

"Ten to one." The commander shrugged. "We are nearly three hundred. With your people, we are well over three thousand."

"You plan to enlist the Auctioneers? Why would they fight for you? They're mostly thugs and brigands. Almost all are facing death sentences for their crimes. It's why they've joined the Auctioneers, to avoid being hung."

"I will grant full amnesty to everyone who fights with us." The commander nodded at his statement, perhaps hearing the plan aloud for the first time. "They can either die at the end of a rope or live with a spear in their hands. If you back my words, they'll join." Carver looked to Jayne and Sellina, both of whom agreed it sounded like a viable plan.

"What of the city? Without the Watch..." Carver left his words hanging.

"What do you care?" Billy raised his eyebrows, challenging the fat man. "Have you suddenly grown a conscience?"

"As a matter of fact." The bartender rubbed his thick arms like he was cold. "I've learned a lot about... caring... in the last few weeks. It turns out, I prefer to not let people suffer needlessly."

"If I declare martial law," Billy said with a smile, "then I will control the Assassin's Guild. They will have no difficulty keeping order in the city."

Jayne swallowed hard. "There's an Assassin's Guild? I've never heard of them."

Billy grunted at the woman. "It's not too surprising. They work for Lord Stout. He uses them to keep the rich in line. Their presence alone is enough to dissuade any of the lords or ladies from having delusions of grandeur. The guild will take control of each of the nobles' personal guard. All tolled, they likely number over five hundred soldiers."

"You've thought this through then." Jayne retook her seat. "Our benefactor trusts you, so I trust you. When do we move out?"

The commander nodded at the comment. "At first light, the hawk riders will fly ahead to make sure there are no ambushes set along the way. We'll meet you in Cormorant at nightfall."

A Change In Directions

After everyone had eaten and had drunk their fill, they mounted up in preparation to move out. It was now midday, and the sun was high in the sky. An occasional line of clouds blocked the sun, giving the group a temporary respite from the heat. Nobody was going to miss the Spiderwood Forest that loomed dark at their backs.

"Kit?" Indie gave her a pensive look as he rode beside her. "Do you think we can make a slight detour? I'd like to stop at my village, to make sure everyone is okay."

"We don't have time." The look of concern and disappointment on his face crushed Kit's heart.

"We can go and then meet up with the group before they reach the city," Angel said through their bond. *"It would mean a lot to him to know if his people are safe."* Kit nodded lightly.

"Continue towards the city." Kit gave Indie a crooked smile. "I'll go to your village. If you get to the city before me, wait outside the cemetery. I'll meet you there."

Indie shook his head. "You're not going without me. I need to see firsthand."

"Then you'll go on your own and we'll enter the city without you. We won't wait for you."

"But..." Indie's expression was a mixture of anger and dismay. He stared off toward his village and then back at Kit.

"But nothing," Kit said. "I will tell you everything that is happening at your village." Indie just shook his head.

"I need to do this for myself." He stiffened his back. He was not taking no for an answer. "They need to take refuge, to hide. They need to leave their homes and they might not listen to you."

Kit stared blankly at the man, unsure what to do. Finally, she relented. "Fine. Go. We will wait for you at the cemetery for as long as we can. If you're not back in time, you'll have to find your way to us." Indie nodded in response. Without instruction, Char wheeled around and sped off at a full gallop.

"Hurry back to me," she whispered, watching her man disappear in the distance. "Be safe."

***

Kit grumbled to herself the rest of the way to Aarall. Coldforge had come whooping up as he and Runt were zigzagging across the countryside, Lump barking merrily along with them. As soon as he was within earshot, the young priest suggested that, if the dwarf couldn't be quiet, she would have to stuff her boot in his mouth.

"Lighten up, would you?" Lin road Whistler alongside her friend. "There's nothing but grass and rolling hills for as far as the eye can see. It's not like there's anybody who can hear him." Kit shot her friend a pointed look that suggested she might stick a boot in her mouth as well. Whistler shied away, putting some extra distance between herself and Angel. "He's going to be fine, and he'll be back on time."

"And what do you know of men?" Kit's lip curled up enough to show her teeth. The comment drew a sneer from Lin.

"More than you, it would seem." Her voice carried a tartness to it. "The man would literally walk through fire to be with you, and you're worried he might be late?"

"I'm worried he might walk into trouble, and I won't be there to help him. All because..."

"Because you want to make sure the city is safe; the Temple is safe; that Father Hoarfrost and your father are both safe." Lin's tone softened as she listed off

Kit's loved ones. "Indie is resourceful. If there is any hint of trouble, he'll either take care of it or he'll stay clear of it. He doesn't need you to protect him."

"I know." Kit dropped her chin to her chest and sighed. "I'm just worried." The girl's words fell away as the muffled voices of Coldforge and Runt drew her attention. The two of them each had one of the dwarf's boots in their mouths. Their insane antics pushed aside Kit's melancholy, and she laughed despite the situation.

Without another word, the group picked up speed, galloping along the countryside. The verdant green of the meadows and the swaying grasses with their tan colored seed-stalks resembled rolling waves. A flock of butterflies that was trying to forage nectar from a patch of yellow flowers filled the air as Lump raced through them. The boys and the whooping dwarf chased them about, their movements as haphazard as the insects they were pursuing. Was this what it would be like to watch her own children playing? She liked the idea of having children, sharing the experience with Indie, guiding them through their younger years. Memories of her own mother, Riva, came flooding into her consciousness. Kit wondered if her mother still worried about her, especially with her ability to glimpse into the future.

⌒⌒⌒◇⌒⌒⌒

The group slowed as they approached the cemetery, which was located outside the northernmost end of the city's western wall. Beyond the forty-foot-high wall lay the Temple grounds. Even under the warmth of the late afternoon sun, the graveyard looked cold and desolate. There were no mourners and there were no guards at its north gates.

"It's not a good sign." Lin moved in beside Kit. "There should be people here. There are always people here." Kit nodded silently. "Do you want to wait for Indie, to give him a chance to meet up with us?"

"Yes, but we can't. We need to keep going. We have no time to waste."

"It's not wasted," Lin said. "We don't know what we're getting ourselves into and we need him. You need him." Kit cocked an eyebrow.

"You think I need a man to protect me?" The question made Lin scoff.

"Hardly. But if he's not with you, you'll worry about him and if you're worrying about him, you won't be at your best." Kit blinked, her expression flat. Lin poked her above her left breast. "Your heart will be with him and not with us."

"It was his choice to leave." Kit slipped down from her horse. "We need to continue."

"He won't know how to get to the Temple from the mausoleum," Lin said. "At least let me leave him a map."

"Fine." Kit gave Lin a hint of a smile. "Angel, Lin will give you the map when she's done. You make sure Indie gets it when he shows up." The horse nickered in response, seeming to surprise Lin.

While Lin worked on the map, Kit and Coldforge stepped in through the cemetery's main gate. They walked amid the graves, keeping a wary eye out for any signs of trouble.

"It's good that ye give yours a proper burying." Coldforge slowed to inspect one of the larger headstones. "How some folk carry on about ye northerners, you'd think you are savages or something."

"What do you mean by that?" Kit hushed her words, signaling the dwarf to keep his voice down.

"No offense." Coldforge bellowed the words out, throwing his palms up as though to ward off an incoming blow. "Just sayin' that people think up terrible things about people and places they know nothin' about. I knew ye were good people as soon as I met you."

"You really have no idea how to sneak, do you?" Kit scolded the dwarf while keeping her voice low. "Sneaking involves being quiet. Why is that so hard for you to understand?"

"No more sneaking." Coldforge whiskers twitched as he waved his arms about. "Dwarves meet our foe head on. We don't do... this."

"Perhaps you'd rather stay with the horses then?" Indie asked, scaring the life out of both Kit and Coldforge. "If we fight these people head on, we'll all die."

Kit screeched out, punched Indie in the shoulder, and then promptly wrapped her arms around his neck.

"It would be a glorious battle though," Coldforge mumbled back. "Just sayin'."

"How long have you been here?" Kit asked, her voice coming out breathless.

"Thirty minutes," Indie replied. "I was scouting around, trying to see if there was anyone hiding here."

"You could have told us." Lin's eyes bulged as she glowered at her drawing. "I drew you a nice map and everything. What a waste." Kit ignored her friend's frustration and groaned when Lin ripped it up into tiny pieces.

"What happened at your village? Is everyone okay? Are they safe?" Indie nodded his head; a hint of shame in his eyes.

"They had no idea anything was amiss. Everyone was going about their lives like nothing had happened."

"Did you tell them to stay away from the city?" Lin placed her hand on Indie's shoulder. "I hope you told them to at least wait a while." Indie rolled his eyes.

"Of course, I did. I would not let them just walk into trouble."

"How did you get here ahead of us?" Kit was baffled by how he got there first. They hadn't rushed, but they hadn't doddled either, and their path was direct.

"I nearly killed Char." Indie's eyebrows gathered together, his hands dropping limp by his side. "I pushed him beyond his limits to make sure you didn't go in without me."

Kit reached out through their bond with her horse. *"Angel, find Char and make sure he's okay,"*

"Whistler and I are with him now. He's fine. He's bragging that he's faster than me." Kit chuckled at the comment.

"Let him have that. I'd say he's earned it." Kit could hear Angel groan, making her laugh aloud.

"Something funny?" Lin asked. "Care to share?" Kit pursed her lips to stop smiling. She craned her neck up to Indie.

"Char will be fine. He will do anything for you."

"And I will do anything for you." His expression melted Kit's heart.

"And I'm going to puke." Lin shook her head and walked towards a large white-stone mausoleum. "This way."

Coldforge gave a low whistle as they approached the crypt. He marveled at the thick, ornately carved pillars holding up the massive portico and the two statues of Titan at each corner. They were the replica of the gargantuan ice statue of the god who used to glare down at Aarall before it melted and turned into Lake Titan. He ran his fingers over the pillar's gray granite stone, impressed that there wasn't a single seam visible over its entire length. He smiled up at the stern face of Titan that stared out over the cemetery.

"Fine dwarven craftsmanship. Ye truly know how to honor those who came before you."

As he continued to move between the statues flanking the main entrance, he ran his fingers along the highly polished iron-bound doors. His hand fell onto the brushed silver door leaver. With another nod of approval, he gave it a push. When the handle refused to yield to his touch, he put more strength into it.

"It's locked, but I don't think it's magical."

Kit put her hand on his shoulder when he pulled out his massive battle ax. She shook her head. "Put that away. We've got someone who can get past that."

"Please, step aside." Lin waved her hand, dismissing Coldforge. "I need some space."

As the woman stood before the door, she moved her fingers, forming intricate patterns as she did. Tiny wisps of smoke came spreading out from her hand and entered the keyhole. In a moment, there was an audible *click* as the door unlocked.

Kit chuckled lightly. "It bothers me you can do that so easily, but it sure has been coming in handy lately."

Lin pushed on the lever, and the door easily swung open. Giving Kit a wink, she stepped into the mausoleum.

"Grab her!" someone yelled from within.

CHAPTER EIGHTEEN

THE TRUTH OF THE GIZMOS

The glow of firelight erupted from within the mausoleum, followed by a shriek and a cry of pain. In moments, Kit was through the door, her hammer in hand, wreathed in blue flames.

"Lin!" Before she could finish her sentence, the sight of her friend engaged with two soldiers came into view. Her twin long swords were aflame, cutting through the air, leaving red and yellow trails behind them. The soldiers were equipped with chain mail and short swords. They got more than they'd bargained for when they attacked the short-haired woman.

Rather than try to close the distance, Kit threw her hammer at the two men. "Fury, hold them." Just before the hammer struck one soldier, the visage of the draken appeared and snatched the other man by the throat. His blade bounced ineffectively off Fury's dragon hide scales.

A clash of steel to Kit's right drew her away from Lin's fight. Indie and Coldforge were fighting off four more soldiers while the boys were darting in and out, biting at the enemy, harassing them until ax and sword cut the soldiers down.

The soldier tried to break Fury's grip. "Let me go. I am a member the king's royal guard, and you will be executed for your actions." The other man with whom Lin had been in combat was lying in a pool of blood on the ground.

"Shall I bite his head off?" The man squealed at Fury's question, making Kit smile.

"Why are you here?" Kit picked her hammer up off the stone tiled floor. She gave it a shake and its blue flames ignited, casting her face in an eerie glow. The man's eyes were wide and wild. Whichever direction he turned, certain death stared back at him.

"Tell me true and you will live. Lie to me and my big friend here removes your head." A dripping noise drew Kit's attention towards the floor. She sneered as a puddle spread out from beneath the man.

"This is where I was assigned. My lieutenant posted us here, to make sure nobody came in. He ordered us to capture anybody who tried to enter."

"Where's Captain Harding?" Kit pulled back the hammer; the flames dying off immediately.

The guard stammered, struggling to get the words out. "I don't know. Please, don't kill me. All I know is that he was taken prisoner. Maybe he's in the Watch dungeons."

"If the captain's been taken prisoner, who's running the Watch?" Indie's voice smooth and low, making it sound even more threatening.

"Lieutenant Karr. I mean, Captain Karr." The guard continued trying to wiggle out of Fury's grasp.

Kit swore under her breath. "Titan's snowballs. I knew it. I knew he was a traitor. Why didn't I trust my instincts? When he killed the Moreden twins..."

Lin's eyes widened, and she shook her head. "I didn't know. You know I'm telling the truth, right? You know I didn't know that Karr was working with Martelle?" Kit ignored Lin's questions, her eyes remaining focused on the soldier.

"How many of the king's men are here?" Indie ignored Lin's protestations of innocence.

"I don't know. I swear. Father Hoarfrost killed many of them when he collapsed the Temple."

Kit staggered backwards at the man's words. She had hoped beyond reason that Martelle's stories were not true and that he only believed that Father Hoarfrost was dead. Before she realized, Kit's hands were ablaze, and she was reaching out for the soldier, her red flames licking out towards his face. The soldier's screams redoubled at the sight. He thrashed against Fury's dragon grip. The draken smiled at the futile attempt to break his hold.

"You promised." He flailed madly, renewing his attempts to escape. "You promised to let me live if I told you the truth. By all the gods, I swear, I never lied to you."

Kit's body was shaking uncontrollably as she pulled her hand back. A low growl emanated from her chest. "Bind him." Before anyone else reacted, Lin ran her long sword through his heart. The man twitched a few times before she extracted her blade.

"What have you done?" Kit growled at her, rounding on Lin as though she was about to attack.

"If she hadn't, I'd have killed him meself." Coldforge stepped between the two women. "The man was a coward. He'd have told anybody willing to listen that we were here, if he thought it would save his miserable skin."

"He's right, Kit," Indie said from behind her. "Nobody can know we're here."

"Had any of you even considered that I might have had more questions for him?" She turned her glare on all three of her cohorts. "Did you? Any of you?" The boys pushed past the group, rubbing their shoulders against Kit, each of them whining softly. She sheathed her hammer and let her hands run through their thick, silky fur. In less than a minute, the stress drained from her face and her breathing returned to normal.

"Where are the stairs into the crypts?" Kit turned to Lin, waiting for an answer. The woman recoiled a little but regained her composure.

"They should be right here." Lin pointed to the solid stone floor. "I've only ever opened them from the other side of the trap door though. I'll have to figure out how to open it from this side."

"Can you use that magic trick to find the lever?" Kit asked, her mouth drawn tight.

"Ye say this is where the door is?" Coldforge examined the floor, running his toe along any visible seams. When Lin nodded, he walked over to the wall opposite the entrance door. Running his fingers along the narrowest of cracks between each stone, he laughed to himself. After giving the knuckles on both of his hands a good cracking, he pushed on two stones that were eye-level with him. They slid in easily, and a moment later, a stone slab in the floor dipped down and retracted under the floor. He peered over the edge, down the flight of polished stone stairs. Turning back to the group, he gave everyone a broad, toothy smile, and extolled the many wonders of dwarven architecture.

"Let me scout ahead." Indie took first position at the top the staircase. "We don't know if there will be more guards waiting down below."

"We're stronger together." Lin looked to Kit for agreement. When everyone nodded, Indie shook his head and insisted that he take the lead. Before everyone headed down, Kit asked Coldforge to lock the entrance door. She had considered trying to conceal the dead bodies, but there was so much blood on the floors and walls that it would do no good. As soon as Coldforge closed the doors, the room went pitch black. Kit once again ignited her hammer, casting eerie, dancing shadows across the walls.

⸎⸎⸎⸎⸎

Against Indie's protestations, Kit led the way down the stairs into the catacombs. Since she was carrying the only light-source, her glowing hammer, it made the most sense to everyone, except Indie.

Kit slipped down the stairs, careful to keep her steps quiet. The boys rushed past her, nearly sweeping the young priest's feet out from under her. While everyone else descended quietly, Coldforge's feet slapped hard on each step, drawing a look of ire from Lin. When they reached the bottom, the glowing battle hammer lit the narrow corridor, illuminating the tunnel about twenty paces out in front of the group. Where the mausoleum's upper floor was tile and stone, the lower level was constructed of wood and dried mud. Along each wall, for as far as Kit could see, were shelves hosting the remains of those long since passed. Most of the corpses were wrapped in shrouds, but many had been disturbed by rats and other vermin. The cloth had been eaten away, revealing the darkly stained bones beneath.

A thin fog swirled around the party's feet as they moved along the corridor. The pungent scent of death and decay, with a heavy dose of mildew, filled the air. Lin couldn't hide the sour face she was making when she suggested that the air tasted as bad as it smelled.

There were five shelves on each wall, made of rough-cut timbers. The wood showed signs of insect damage, but they still looked like they would last a thousand cycles. Time and moisture had worn the floor's thick wooden planks. They were badly twisted, making the footing treacherous. Before she realized it, Kit was muttering prayers as she walked, while her fingers lingered over the dead.

Indie wrinkled his nose. "These aren't much better than mass graves. I'm guessing many of these are the people who died during the Gizmo uprising."

"Ye've mentioned that event before, or at least the captain did." As usual, Coldforge's voice was much too loud.

"It was a dark day for Aarall," Indie said. "For all of Arnnor, really."

"What happened?" the dwarf pressed.

"I was just a small girl," Lin's eyes turned dark as she recalled the memories. "My Grams had brought me to the Temple the season before. When the Temple's warning bells pealed, we were all shepherded into the Temple's larder. It was the only time I ever saw Sister Nevara look scared."

"What made them attack?" Coldforge asked, even more interested in the tale.

"The king," Lin replied, as though it was enough of an explanation. When the dwarf tilted his head to the side, she elaborated. "The gizmos in Arnnor almost always kept to the hills, mountains, and tundra. Those who learned the common language would come to the cities and villages to barter for anything they couldn't make themselves. In the mountains that range between Two Peaks and Aarall, a huge gold deposit was found."

The dwarf's eyes lit up when Lin mentioned the gold. He leaned in closer, hanging on the woman's every word.

Indie shook his head at the dwarf and added his own experience to the story, recounting the tales he'd heard while training with the Watch. "The gold was in the Capra Mountains, mountain gizmo territory. When the king sent a mining crew to dig, the Tahr, the mountain gizmos, killed them all. In retaliation, the king installed a new City Watch commander in Aarall. His name was General Sheteo, the head of the king's personal guard. He was a renowned hunter, and a known friend of the gizmos. Upon arrival, the general's first order of business was to bring a Tahr delegation to Aarall, to discuss an arrangement that would allow the king to mine in their territory. The Tahr came, but they refused to allow the king to send miners into their lands. Against the Tahr's wishes, the general sent another group of miners into Tahr territory, except this time, two dozen City Watch guards accompanied them. The gizmos killed them all. They planted the soldiers' heads atop spears along the roadway leading to their mountain range as a warning to others who might trespass on their lands."

"We'd have done the same." Coldforge wrinkled his brow, his hands clenched into tight fists. His thick orange whiskers hid whatever else his face was showing. "Ye don't take somebody's land from them, especially if it's filled with trea-sures."

"Not long after, the general himself led a cohort of the king's personal guard into the Tahr's territory." Lin scowled at Indie for interrupting her story. "The general and his people slaughtered hundreds of Tahr, maybe even thousands. They killed them all, adults and children alike. Not a single one was spared."

Lin paused for a second, and took a deep breath, as though recounting the story was causing her physical pain. "People believe that some of the mountain gizmos survived, and that they spread the word of Sheteo's treachery. On the night of the next new moon, the Gizmos attacked Aarall. A group of Tahr broke in through the roof of the City Watch barracks, into the general's quarters. They dismembered him and tossed his body parts out the window to the training field below. They worked their way down to the officer's sleeping quarters, cutting their throats while they slept. Kit's father, then Lieutenant Harding, woke before they could murder him. He single-handedly killed the entire lot. He was the one who raised the alarm, waking everyone before the bulk of the gizmo army had breached the city walls."

Indie's expression darkened. "The battle lasted thirteen days. Thousands of people died, most of them were gizmos."

"Are you sure? That's not the story the priests tell acolytes." Kit's face took on a green tinge, like she was ready to throw up. "I was told it was the gizmos who started the war. I was told they couldn't be trusted."

"Nobody wanted to admit it," Lin said. "Over time, the story kept changing, likely at the king's bidding."

"I believed those stories," Kit continued. "I've hated gizmos, all the gizmos, because of a lie."

"And now you can right that wrong, too." Coldforge's excitement grew. The talk of gold and battles had gotten the dwarf's blood up, and he was ready to get moving.

The discussion came to a halt when Lump and Runt came bounding down the tunnel.

"Where were you two?" Kit's scolding tone made Lump recoil a little. His ears drooped before he switched from dog to human form.

"While you were busy talking, Runt and I went scouting on ahead. Runt could hear people coming so we came back." Kit took a battle stance, her eyes straining to look down the hallway. Lump shook his head. "It will be a while before they get here if they're coming this way at all. There is a room not much further down this tunnel. It's filled with crates and tools for digging. We can hide there."

Not wanting to waste any time, Kit had Lump show them the way. They continued down the corridor until it ended, branching off to the left and to the right. Lump turned to the right and loped down the tunnel until he came to the room filled with the digging tools.

As he had said, there were crates, shovels, picks, and wheelbarrows from one end of the room to the other. Indie, noticing that one crate was open, reached into the straw packing material, and pulled out a tall, thin ampoule of amber liquid.

"This looks like dragon brandy." He tried to pull the vial's cork. In an instant, Fury appeared next to him, startling him so badly that he nearly dropped the bottle.

"Give it to me." Fury raised his muzzle and held out his clawed hand. He held the bottle up to the light of Kit's hammer. "This is not dragon brandy. I suspect it's a transformation potion."

"What sort of transformation potion?" Lin thrust her hand out to the draken, waiting to inspect its contents. The draken reluctantly passed it to the woman. He frowned at her, daring the impudent human to provide a better insight into the thick, viscous liquid.

Lin popped the cork and sniffed lightly. "You're right. These are transformation potions but they're not complete. They smell like they need another ingredient before they will be active."

The draken scoffed and held out his clawed hand. He gave the contents a sniff. His eyebrows raised, he drew back his lizard-lips, revealing a mouthful of razor-sharp, pointed teeth. "I think I might have chosen the wrong apprentice."

The draken's words made Lin blush, Indie scowl, and Kit growl.

"That's the second time you've mentioned Indie being your apprentice." Kit stared up at the now feigned-innocent face of Fury.

"I am training your boyfriend to become a Dragonheart," Fury said, as though it was a simple matter of fact.

"A Dragonheart?" Kit's eyes burrowed into Indie's.

"The dragon lords take humans, and bestow gifts upon them, in return for *favors.*" Indie gave his feet a good hard look.

Kit wheeled around back to Fury. "And what sort of favors did he promise you?"

"Only that he'd help me escape the bonds holding me in my mountain prison." The draken lifted his hands, palms turned upward. "It's unlikely it will ever come to pass, but if I can turn him into a Dragonheart, he will be well suited to help me if the time comes."

"And what exactly is a Dragonheart?" Kit continued.

"The original Dragonhearts were an ancient sect of humans who devoted their lives to the dragon lords. Most were bestowed gifts of strength, endurance, and an exceedingly long life. We gave some of them dragon attributes, like extremely strong magic. Those who were particularly devoted, well, we granted them the gift of flight; actual dragon wings."

"And what *gift* did he offer you?" Kit asked, bearing down on Indie, forcing him to back into a stack of crates.

"They're coming," Lump interrupted. "You best be quiet." He shifted back into his golden wolf-dog form.

SAY IT ISN'T SO

The group ducked down behind the crates as the footfalls neared. Everything brightened as people carrying torches entered the storage room. Shortly afterwards, Indie held up four fingers. Kit nodded to him before moving to the corner of her hiding place, trying to get a look at the strangers. She couldn't see them from her vantage point, but from the sounds of it, they were gathering tools and wheelbarrows. She glanced back at the others and motioned for them to follow her lead. Slipping between two of the crates, Kit ignited her hammer and stepped out.

"Hold or die." The four strangers practically jumped out of their skin. The people all had their backs to her. One of them was huge, her head almost brushing the ceiling.

"Amara! Silverleaf!" Kit squealed at the sight of her friends.

"Kit? Is that you?" the giant asked. "Sweet Titan, what are you all doing here?"

"Hello, Iba." Kit stared at the tiny Tahr when she turned. The girl was full of surprises. "I certainly didn't expect to find *you* here."

"And we didn't expect to see you here either." Silverleaf's eyes bulged. Slate dropped the pickaxe he was holding. The boys raced over to greet the newcomers, bouncing between them, giving each of them exuberant, wet kisses.

A crooked grin appeared on Iba's face. "Hello, Kitten. I'm glad to see you. We could use your help." Kit's jaw practically bounced off the rough wooden floor.

The last time she had talked with the Tahr, Iba had threatened to kill her. But Kit could feel the honesty in her words. She was genuinely happy to see her.

"Hullo, lad." Coldforge stepped up towards Slate, regarding his orange hair. "What clan are ye from? Orange beards like ours are not so common."

Slate thumped his fist on his chest. "I am an acolyte, a member of the Fist of Titan." Coldforge chuckled at the boy's enthusiasm.

"You two can catch up later." Kit cut off the dwarves' conversation. "What are you all doing down here?"

"We're breaking Sister Gale and Brother Snowpack out of their cell," Amara said. "Once we have them..." The giant's words faltered.

"What?" Kit's stomach dropped when Amara's eyes welled up. "Is it Father Hoarfrost? He's dead, isn't he." Amara nodded. That one simple action crushed Kit's spirit.

"Yes." Iba's voice was full of venom. "No thanks to your traitorous friend." Her big, round goat eyes fixed firmly on Lin. "She's in league with them. She sold out the Temple. For what, a pile of gold?"

"Liar!" Lin bolted towards Iba, grabbing her by the throat. The pair slammed into a wheelbarrow, sending them both careening across the floor. "I never did those things, you lying crap-stain." Before Lin could stab her with the dagger she had drawn, Amara snatched her up by the back of her armor.

"What do we do with her?" the giant asked, turning to Kit. "She needs to pay for what she did."

"Put me down," Lin yelled, kicking, and flailing about, trying to get Amara to release her hold on her.

"Sister Kit?" Amara scowled at Lin who was trying to bite her.

"Put her down, Amara. She's not working with them. She was duped, just like we all were."

"How can you be sure?" Silverleaf asked, his brow furrowed.

"Because I know her heart to be true," Kit said. "I saw how Martelle's deception crushed her."

"We have questions for him, too, when we catch him." Iba picked herself up off the floor, brushing off her dust-covered clothing.

"Well." Kit grimaced while she pondered what to say. "Dead men tell no tales."

"You killed him?" Amara shook her head in disapproval.

Kit motioned to Lin. "She did, right after we found out that he had been using her for his own gains."

"Just like the man I thought was my father." Lin was still dangling a few feet above the ground, clawing at Amara's outstretched arm.

It took several minutes for everyone's blood to settle, but once they were reasonably calm, Kit needed to ask the question she'd been dreading. It couldn't be put off any longer.

"What's happened to Father Hoarfrost? Is he... truly dead?" Her eyes welled up as the words passed her trembling lips.

After several seconds of silence, Silverleaf finally answered. "I'm sorry, Kit. I know how close you were to him. They poisoned him. I did everything I could to reverse the effects. Iba and I snuck into the apothecary. We grabbed every potion I thought might help. I didn't know what they had given him. He called for you. Even though he was delirious, you were his last thought."

Kit's heart pounded in her ears. She wanted to cry, to grieve for the man who had cared for her and had mentored her for so many cycles. The man who had willingly endured all of her acts of defiance, who had loved her even when she was, unlovable. Her jaw quivered as the weight of her past actions smothered her.

I should have stayed here. I might have prevented it.

"He asked for the strongest rejuvenation potion I had," Silverleaf choked out, rousing Kit from her ruminations. "We both knew it would kill him as soon as the effects wore off. We also knew the poison was going to do the same thing. When I brought him the potion, he told me to clear the priests and acolytes from the entire Temple. He told me to tell everyone he had passed to the Great Cycle."

"That was the very moment that Karr acted," Iba continued. "The king has been sending his people here for the last moon, disguising them as merchant guards. As soon as Silverleaf said that Father was dead, they started taking everyone prisoner. Karr sent hundreds of soldiers to storm the Temple."

"When the king's people entered the nave," Slate interrupted, "they found Father Hoarfrost standing before the statue of Titan. When the soldiers attacked, he called upon our god."

Kit had difficulty standing, the story sapping the last ounce of strength from her. Indie moved to her side, offering her support and comfort. The boys followed suit, leaning against her, letting her know they were there for her, too.

"He immolated himself." Tears continued to stain Amara's cheeks. "Father communed with Titan one last time. He brought the Temple down on the soldiers and killed almost every single one of them."

"How do you know this?" The pain in Kit's chest was nearly unbearable. Her brain wanted to deny what she was being told, but her heart ached for her mentor.

"I was there when it happened," Slate answered. "I was still in the Temple when it came crashing down. As soon as Father started his final spell, I escaped through the back of the nave. Father died so that we might live."

Kit's heart was now beating so fast she feared she was going to pass out. Her chest was on fire, her daemon self begging to exact vengeance on those who had harmed her mentor. Silence fell upon the group as they processed the dwarf's words.

"What's with the transformation potions?" Lin, still dangling above the ground, broke the profound silence that had fallen over the group. She, too, was wiping tears from her cheeks. Kit motioned for Amara to put the woman down.

The half elf walked over to another crate and pulled out a vial of dull black liquid. "We found them in the apothecary. Along with this. I can't say for certain, but I don't think it's the poison that was used on Father. It smells of nightshade and something else. I think they're using it to keep the prisoners quiet."

"Let me see that," Fury said, popping out next to the half elf. Iba bleated at the draken's sudden appearance, went stiff as a board, and flopped onto her face.

"Sweet Titan, what happened to her?" Kit knelt beside the Tahr. Fury was chuckling while everyone else stood dumbfounded. "And how is this funny? What happened to her?"

"I frightened her." Fury pulled his lizard-lips tight over his teeth. His shoulders were still jouncing as he tried to contain his laughter. "It's an uncommon condition among the Tahr. I haven't seen that happen in ages." The draken's shoulders were still bobbing. "It will pass in a few minutes."

Iba bleated again and popped to her cloven feet, her eyes still wide and wild. Fury bowed to the girl, still trying to suppress his laughter.

"My apologies, little sneak. I did not intend to startle you." Iba glared at the draken in response.

Indie pulled a vial of the black liquid from the small wooden crate. Lin snatched it from him, giving Indie a look that he didn't fully understand.

"Why did you call her a sneak?"

"Because the Tahr are the best sneaks in all the world." There wasn't a hint of humor in Fury's voice. "They have served us dragon lords very well over the millennia."

Iba gaped at the draken. "You're a dragon lord? You don't look..."

"No, I don't. I am Fury, or at least a part of myself."

"Nightshade and grave dust," Lin said. "This potion isn't meant to kill. It's meant to render the victim catatonic, a sort of *undead* state, caught somewhere between life and the Great Cycle." Lin's assertion drew Fury's attention away from Iba. The draken took the vial from the still dumbfounded Silverleaf and gave its contents a sniff.

Fury grunted and gave Lin an appreciative nod. "You are a gifted alchemist, and you are quite right. If given in the correct dosage, this could render a person inert."

Kit pondered the word for a moment. "Inert? What in Helja does that mean?"

"It would neutralize any magical ability the person has and make them docile." The draken handed the potion back to the slack-jawed half elf.

"Well." Amara rubbed her chin and nodded. "That explains why none of the priests are trying to break out of their cells."

"The priests are in dungeon cells?" Kit asked. "Are they in the City Watch dungeons?"

"They're being held down here in the catacombs, in a make-shift dungeon," Silverleaf said. "The king's soldiers had cells built in one of the newer tunnels. It's why we're getting the tools. We're going to dig them out."

A strangled sound leaked out from Indie's throat. "Won't the guards notice they're missing? As soon as they check on them, they'll see they're gone."

"They'll still be there." A smile tugged at Silverleaf's lips. "We replace them with their own people. Transformation potions make them look like the priests we took out." His eyes brightened. "We should bring these nightshade potions with us, too, to keep them quiet. We knocked out the first lot, but when they wake up, they'll likely start a ruckus."

"You've already rescued some of them?" Hope sprung in Kit's chest, chasing away the daemon's hold on her. Amara nodded.

"We were aiming to free Sister Gale, but somebody took us in the wrong direction." Amara glowered at Slate. He blushed under her scrutiny.

"I was under a lot of pressure," he said, primarily to the elder dwarf. "I miscalculated by two paces, and we broke through into the wrong cell." He paused for a moment before turning to Kit. "We saved two priests and two acolytes though. So that's something, right?"

"Where are they now?" Indie asked. "Why aren't they helping you?"

"I don't know how to wake them." The shame in Silverleaf's voice was not unlike his dwarven friend's. "We've got them stowed by some shelves, right near the cells. There are bodies of the more recent dead in that section. They're still decomposing, and nobody goes there because of the horrible stench."

"Sweet Titan." Kit's head snapped back. "You've hidden them among the dead?" The entire lot of them nodded.

"They don't move at all, and we had no place else to take them." Iba was still eying Fury, her pink nose twitching frantically.

"How's about we get to it then," Kit suggested. "It looks like you were on your way when we interrupted you."

Silverleaf and Amara exchanged a look.

"What?" Kit asked. While Silverleaf's face blanched, Amara's hardened.

"It's nothing," she said. "We'll get Sister Gale out and then we can talk about it. First things first."

"Tell me." Kit's face paled and licks of flame burst from her hands. Slate stumbled backwards, throwing up his hands in defense.

"Titan's snowballs. When did you learn to do that?"

"Tell me." Kit took a menacing step towards Silverleaf, a low growl rumbling from her chest.

"Your father, Captain Harding. He's being held in the ceremonial altar room. They're torturing him, trying to get him to switch sides. As long as he fights against them, his men won't follow Captain Karr."

"They're not just torturing him, Kit." Slate took an apprehensive step forward. "Other people are being brought in, City Watch members, priests, acolytes. They're torturing them, too, in front of Harding, hoping he'll change sides to protect them."

"I've heard they're looking for his family, his wife and daughter." Iba's comment about Kit's stepmother and half-brother raised her ire even further.

"We rescue Captain Harding, my father, first." Kit turned her attention to Amara. "Why did you keep this from me?"

"We can't get to him, not yet." Amara took a knee before Kit, meeting her at eye level. "There are too many battle mages guarding him. They are incredibly powerful, and they wield dark magic. We need more priests to help fight them."

"I don't need more priests." Torrents of flames danced around Kit. The intense heat pouring off the girl's body forced Amara to retreat.

"If we can't get them all at once, they might just kill your father outright." Amara turned her face away from the heat of Kit's flames. "We need to plan this attack carefully and Sister Gale is the best person for the job."

"Kit." Indie placed his hand on Kit's shoulder and grimaced. Golden scales instantly covered his skin as her flames tried to consume him. "Amara's plan makes sense. You need to listen to her."

Chapter Twenty

The Best Laid Plans

With Silverleaf and Amara at the lead, the group moved through the catacombs. They paid little heed to the dead bodies that flanked them on both sides. The rhythmic beating of their feet on the tunnel's wood planks concerned Kit, but nobody else seemed bothered by it. She kept her hammer at the ready, just in case.

"Aren't you concerned about the enemy seeing your torches?" Lin asked. "Between our feet bouncing on these wooden planks and the light from the torches, we're signaling everyone that we're coming. Maybe we can just use Kit's hammer? At least she can control how bright it is."

Amara stole a glance over her shoulder. "Nobody comes through these tunnels. We're not on any of the main pathways." Silverleaf's head bobbed frantically in agreement. The pair stopped at a doorway to another set of stairs.

"We'll need to extinguish the torches before we head down this last flight. We're going to have to pass through one of the extensively used tunnels. I'm going to cast a silencing spell so that nobody can hear us." Silverleaf pulled out a small scroll from a pocket within his priestly robes, holding it up for Kit to see. When she finally noticed what Silverleaf was wearing, the girl's eyebrows shot up.

"How do you know these warrens so well and why are you wearing priests' robes?" Kit's voice was a hoarse whisper. Her eyes shot over to Amara. "You, too? You're both in priests' robes."

Silverleaf's chin pushed forward and his back straightened. "Father promoted us both to priests. We stopped a necromancer who was raising an army of the dead." Kit's eyes widened at the comment.

"It wasn't an army," Amara said with a deep, scolding tone. "We don't really know why he was raising the dead. We didn't really have time to ask him." Silverleaf shrugged, a bit disappointed Amara was downplaying their adventure.

"It's why we know the catacombs so well. We followed them in through the mausoleum and down to the altar room, the same room your father is being... held."

Kit's face darkened. Silverleaf cleared his throat and unfurled his scroll.

"We can tell you more when we have time." The look of rage on Kit's face didn't abate. Silverleaf swallowed hard and motioned to his scroll. "Now, the silencing spell has a small area of effect. It only spreads out a few paces around me, so we need to stay close together. We won't be able to talk to each other once the spell is active, so if you've got anything more to say, do it now."

"When we get to where we're going." Coldforge held up his pickaxe and gave it a shake. "Let me and the lad do the diggin'. Ye others are just going to get in me way." Amara shrugged and rested her pickaxe over her shoulder.

Kit ignited her hammer, keeping its light to a dim glow. The others all extinguished their torches, leaving the group in a soft, yellow aura.

"Okay then." Silverleaf grinned and rubbed his hands together. He read the words on the scroll, unleashing the spell contained within. A soft, gray-green light pulsed out from where he was standing and disappeared just as quickly. With a wave of his hand, he beckoned them all to follow. Coldforge, who was within an arms-length of the half elf, opened his mouth in a soundless scream. A joyous look spread across his face while his head and shoulders bobbed, his mouth opening and closing all the while.

The last flight of stairs they took were badly rotted, and they sagged under their weight with each step they took. When they reached the bottom, the stench was enough to elicit gag reflexes from everyone. The bodies here were newer, more recently buried. Silverleaf's spell silenced any noise caused by their movements, but it did nothing to abate the disgusting odor of mold and decay as they traveled deeper into the crypt. As the Temple needed more burial space, they simply dug deeper, creating additional levels to store the dead. The floors here were hard packed dirt, rather than wood-plank like the upper floors. Iba scampered to the front of the group and motioned for everyone to stay put. A moment later, she bolted ahead, disappearing into the darkness. The boys gave chase, racing after the Tahr. Kit gave Amara a questioning look, but she nodded back, indicating that everything was okay.

They waited for several minutes until Iba returned with the boys running ahead of her. She motioned for everyone to follow before she took the lead.

The group traveled through the catacombs until they arrived at a place where new, freshly dug tunnels began. Eight people were slumped against the wall; two priests, two acolytes, and what looked like four guards who were bound and gagged. Sister Caribou, the theology teacher, was among the lot. Kit burst ahead and dropped to her side. While Silverleaf and the dwarves got to work digging, the rest of the group followed Kit.

"Sister?" Kit whispered, now outside the spell's range. "Sister!" She gave the woman a bit of a shove, trying to rouse her.

"No need to worry," Amara whispered back. "It's the influence of nightshade. She won't wake anytime soon, not until we learn how to dispel the effects of the potion." Fury unexpectedly appeared next to Kit. Not far behind, Iba bleated out.

"How would you counteract this potion?" Fury asked Lin. The woman rubbed her chin, pondering the question. A moment later, her shoulders slumped.

The draken sucked in a disappointed breath. "Medeina's Grace. It would be best, but its exceedingly rare. Sorrowsage will work, too, but the recovery process will be much slower."

"I have sorrowsage in my cell." Lin hoped she could get herself back in the dragon lord's good graces. "But I don't have any Medeina's Grace. It doesn't grow in Arnnor. Brother Powder's apothecary might have some though." Fury nodded.

"Sneaks, do you know the way to the apothecary?" He frowned at Iba, lying face down on the ground, her arms and legs rigid. "It seems I frightened her again."

Kit motioned to the guards. "Who are these people?" She waited for someone to tell her, but Amara had joined Silverleaf and the dwarves, who were actively digging a hole in the wall. Indie appraised the unconscious people.

"I'm guessing they're going to be used to replace the priests we're about to rescue. I hope someone remembered to bring the transformation potions with them."

Iba bleated and hopped to her feet, looking equal parts annoyed and disoriented.

"Sneaks, can you find the apothecary?" Fury asked her again. When she nodded, the draken continued. "Can you look for Medeina's Grace and bring back as much as you can find?" The girl nodded and disappeared down the corridor.

"I should have gone with her," Lin said. "I might have found other useful things while I was there."

⚬⚬⚬⚬⚬◇⚬⚬⚬⚬⚬

After an hour of digging, aided by Fury's flame-breath to soften the dirt, the dwarves broke through the wall into one of the dungeon cells. Slate peered into the hole and pulled his head back inside. With frantic motions, he pointed towards the opening, making signs with his hands; perhaps like he was trying to yell. Kit didn't fully understand, so she poked her head inside the hole.

In the cell next to where the rescuers had come in, were four prisoners banging on the iron bars. They were flailing their arms wildly above their heads. Their mouths opened and closed repeatedly as their gaze moved between Kit and the doorway leading into the room. It was Sister Caribou, Sister Snaer and two acolytes. The sight of the two priests confounded Kit for a moment before she realized what was happening.

Sweet Titan, those must be the replacement prisoners, and they're awake. They're calling for help.

Now, rushing against time, Kit used her battle hammer to knock the cell's brick wall inwards, affording her enough space to squeeze into the room. Lump followed, squeezing his body through the hole. Runt trailed closely behind, taking down a large piece of the wall as he pushed his oversized dire wolf body through the too-small opening.

Sister Gale and Brother Snowpack were lying against the bars of their cell. Two other priests were with them. Kit recognized their faces but didn't know them by name. As she stepped forward, the voices of the other prisoners rung out.

I must be outside the range of the silencing spell.

"Don't make me come over there." Kit rested her hand on her sheathed battle hammer.

Sweet Titan, I sound like Sister Miyuki when she scolded me as a child.

"The guards are going to be here any second." Indie could not keep the panic out of his voice. "The other prisoners are making too much noise."

Amara moved in beside Kit. "We're going to get caught. Let's get our people out of here and get going." Looking like she was picking up two sacks of flour, the giant grabbed Sister Gale and Brother Snowpack by their robes and hoisted them off the ground. Slate and Silverleaf were pushing replacement prisoners through the hole, unaware of the cries of terror coming from the adjacent cell.

"Indie, help Amara get everyone out." Indie nodded and dragged the other priests towards the hole. As soon as the last priest was out, he, too, went through the hole to grab the last pair of replacement prisoners, leaving Kit and the boys alone in the cell.

"Fury, can you shut them up?" Kit asked. A moment later, the draken appeared in their cell, fueling the prisoner's cries all the more. As he closed in on them, the prisoners scrabbled to get away, continuing until they pressed themselves against the far wall. Fury followed until he was too far from the hammer and unexpectedly disappeared. The prisoners' look changed from terror to confusion, and they once again renewed their screams.

A guard stepped through the stone archway of the make-shift dungeon. "Shut up! You should all be asleep." His face went slack as his eyes fixated on the huge black wolf in the cell that had previously held four other prisoners. "Dire wolf!" The guard fumbled, trying to pull his crossbow from his back and cocked it.

In seconds, there were six guards standing outside Kit's cell. The king's men in the cell next to her were still screaming at the top of their lungs, yelling for them to shoot. While the first guard was taking aim with his weapon, the others loaded their crossbows. Before Kit had a chance to react, the man unleashed his bolt at Runt.

At the sight of the guard pulling his crossbow trigger, the world around Kit slowed. She could see with painful detail, the weapon's string pulling the bolt along its slide. The guard's aim was not at Kit, it was at Runt. The dire wolf flexed his muscles, as though bracing for the impending impact. From the corner of her eye, Kit caught sight of Lump. His haunches coiled; his muscles were ready to carry him across the cell in a single leap.

Even though everything was appearing in slow motion, Kit was frozen in place while she watched helplessly as the bolt, Runt and Lump converged. When the bolt struck the leaping Lump just behind his front shoulder, Kit's heart shattered. The wound would be instantly fatal.

Before a tear could fall, Kit's vision went dark as tiny tendrils of inky blackness crept across her eyes.

Acting now purely on instinct, she found herself outside her cell bars, next to the guard who had shot Lump. The man's mouth dropped open, perhaps in shock or perhaps to yell for help. Either way, his moment of abject terror ended abruptly when Kit slashed at his throat with her bare hand. The force of the blow removed his head from his shoulders, sending it sailing into the other guards who were still busy trying to load their weapons.

As one guard recoiled from the severed head, Kit swept towards two others, her hands a frantic blur, becoming drenched in the blood of her enemies. As two more of the guards tried to flee, she closed in on them, slamming their heads together, caving in their iron helms.

When Kit turned, there was only one guard remaining. His weapon clattered on the stone floor.

"I beg you." The man dropped to his knees. His last word was one of pleading. Whatever it was he had said, it went unheard.

Kit stared down at the six mutilated guards, her lips pulled back in a feral grin. She wheeled around, striding across the make-shift dungeon's blood-soaked floor towards the noisy prisoners. When she approached the bars to their cell, they screamed out yet again, but this time they were pleading for their lives.

Kit didn't remember how she'd escaped her own cell, but this time, she was going to take a different approach. Grasping the door's large iron padlock, the girl's hand erupted into deep red flames. As the inferno engulfed the lock, she kept her eyes focused on the prisoners, reveling in their terror.

As molten iron splashed on the floor at her feet, Kit inspected her hand. Her skin was bone white, covered with intricate black etchings. Her fingers, which typically had rough broken nails, were tipped with obsidian-black claws. The tiny priest chortled, as she pulled open the barred door.

"Please, no!" The prisoner's cries for mercy were cut short. Kit plunged her hand into his chest, crushing his heart in her fist. With her hand still wrist-deep in the man's chest, she turned her pitch-black eyes on the remaining prisoners. Their cries abated. They crab-walked away from the blood-soaked crazed woman, whimpering, speaking unintelligible gibberish.

With imperceptible speed, she fell on a woman prisoner. Grabbing the woman by the throat, Kit slammed her head into the cell's iron bars with enough force to cave in the back of her skull. The woman spasmed, her arms flailing by her side, her hands twitching uncontrollably.

One of the other people in the cell, the largest male prisoner, jumped Kit from behind, wrapping his legs around her waist, locking his thick muscled arm around her neck in a blood choke. His joy at capturing the woman turned to ash, literally, when Kit erupted in a swirling mass of red and blue flames.

The second last of the prisoners, another woman, screeched out in terror as Kit turned her gaze on her. Her cries ended abruptly when Kit grabbed her by the tunic and slammed her head into the wall with enough force to crack the brickwork.

The last prisoner, another westerner, backed up against the bars separating his cell from where Kit's allies had been. When Indie grabbed him through the bars, the prisoner wailed, crying uncontrollably as Kit walked towards him.

"Kit! Don't kill this one." Indie waved frantically, trying to get Kit's attention. "We can question him."

The man nodded feverishly, crying, screaming, pleading that he would tell them anything they wanted to know so long as they kept the abomination away from him. The man's choice of words would be his last regret. When Kit was close enough, she clawed wildly at him, raking her talons across his face, neck, and chest. Each attack dug deeply into the man's flesh, exposing the muscle and bone beneath.

Kit's eyes, now obscured by the sprays of blood from her victims, couldn't make out the man on the other side of the bars, calling for her to stop. But her rage had taken hold of her heart and mind. She snarled at the enemy standing before her, pleading with her to spare his life. With a single swipe, she reached through the bars and opened the man up from cheek to chest.

Passing through the bars, as easily as one may pass through an open doorway, Kit entered the cell, moving in on the man. She found her way blocked by a massive black wolf. It was snarling at her, with foam and saliva dripping from his enormous canines.

A voice from somewhere deep within Kit's mind broke through to her consciousness. *"My strength is your strength. My heart is your heart."* She hadn't heard the voice in a long time, but she recognized it. She knew who it was. *"Return from the darkness. You have lost your way."*

Kit's blind rage passed as fast as it had begun. As it did, Runt's snarls changed to submissive whines as he crawled on his belly up to her.

"Thank you." She stroked the wolf about his head and ears. "You are the bravest friend a person could ever have."

Indie squirmed on the floor, his blood-soaked hands covering his face. Her heart sank as she remembered her attack on a man, a man she believed was an enemy. She dropped by his side, revolted by the excessive damage she had done to him. It took all her willpower to not wretch. She had split the man's face in two; one of his eyes was gone. Blood spurt from his neck with each weak beat of his heart.

"Sweet Titan, no." The sight of the man crushed Kit's spirit. "What have I done? Indie! What have I done?"

She called on her healing power, but it wouldn't come. She frowned at her bone-white, rune covered hands. After several more attempts to call on her healing power, she whimpered. "Titan, hear me."

Tears of joy sprung forth when her hands took on the once-familiar soft yellow glow of Titan's healing powers.

"Unto you, I give thanks." She put her hands across the wound and let her faith flow through her.

"Unto you, I give thanks," she repeated as the spurting blood slowed a bit. Kit's heart continued to break as her love's face lost its color. It was only then that Kit realized her hands had changed from bone-white to pale gold. She called upon her own healing powers again. The pale-yellow glow was instantly replaced with a vibrant gold, that spread across Indie's face, neck, and chest.

As her healing powers took hold, Kit's body stiffened. She bellowed out in agony as she took the pain from Indie. With each beat of the girl's heart, her suffering renewed and redoubled. Even knowing that she was on the brink of passing out, she poured more and more of herself into her efforts.

"*My strength is your strength. My heart is your heart.*" The voice in her head again called to her again, bringing her back from the brink.

When the haze obscuring Kit's vision cleared, Indie lay unconscious on the floor, but fully healed. A large, wet tongue scraped across her face. She was about to push Runt aside. Her heart stopped. Her breath hitched. It wasn't Runt licking her. Tears poured down her cheeks when she looked into Lump's deep brown eyes, her heart exploding with joy.

"I thought you were dead." Kit desperately clutched the wolfdog. She stroked his neck, pausing as her fingers ran over sleek scales instead of his silky, thick fur.

Fury appeared behind Lump. "Amazing, don't you think? I expect it's the result of him drinking the magicked ice and the dragon brandy. He looks... splendiferous."

"Are you a dragon?" Kit cupped Lump's face with her hands.

Lump's long pink tongue lolled out, his dark brown eyes sparkling as he stared back at Kit. The dragon-dog took a step back as large golden wings sprung forth from his back.

A leathery wing whacked Coldforge in the head. "Frookin' Helja!" The dwarf had been trying to climb through the hole, into the cell.

Lump tucked his wings back in and shook like a dog trying to dry out his wet coat. As he did, the scales melted away, replaced with his luxurious, long golden fur.

"Why would you lower yourself back to your dog form?" Fury's voice was a mixture of confusion and disappointment. "You were a beauty to behold. Not so glorious as I was in my true form, but marvelous nonetheless."

Kit wrapped her arms around Lump's neck, placing herself between Lump and Fury, as though to shield him from the draken's words. The shaggy gold dog nuzzled Kit's neck, giving her a tiny lick.

"What now?" Indie propped himself onto his elbows. His voice carried a significant edge to it. "The plan was to free some allies and replace them with enemies."

Kit slid from Lump to Indie. "I'm sorry." She couldn't help but cringe when Indie traced the small remaining scars on his cheek. He popped up to his feet and stepped away from the girl. If he'd clenched his jaw any tighter, he would likely have shattered his teeth.

"We continue with the plan." Amara's baritone voice broke the awkwardness between the couple. "Get hair from Sister Gale and the others to complete the transformation potions. Once we have them, we can create their replacements."

"We still have nothing to cure the effects of the nightshade potion," Lin said.

"I got some Medeina's Grace," Iba said, poking her head through the hole. "There wasn't very much of it, and it's dried, not fresh."

"I can work with that," Fury said. "Lin, borrow Kit's hammer and come with me. I'll show you how to make the antidote."

"We don't have any alchemy equipment here." Lin held out her hand for Kit's hammer.

"You are an excellent alchemist, but you have much to learn." The draken gave Lin something resembling a smile. "We can use what's in the storage room upstairs. If the half elf can finish up with the prisoners, we can start reviving the priests." Fury snatched up two of the priests like they were bags of grain. "Amara, you and the others gather up the rest of the sleeping priests."

Kit handed Lin her hammer, but she was still carefully watching Indie.

"How did you do that, Kit?" Silverleaf's voice was a mixture of awe and disbelief. "How did you turn into smoke?"

"I turned into smoke?" Kit held Indie's gaze. "When?" The half elf clutched his chest.

"While you were fighting. You turned into wispy, black smoke. Then you just slipped through the bars and turned back into, well, whatever you were."

"She turned into a daemon." Indie crossed his arms in front of himself. Everyone gasped at the revelation. "Kit's half celestial and half daemon."

"That's not quite right," Lump said after shifting to human form. "She *is* part daemon, but she's mostly angel. Daemons and angels are both celestial beings."

"I couldn't control it." The comment garnered a dark look from Indie. "Whatever happened, it seems to show up when I get emotional."

"You're always emotional." Indie marched across the cell and picked up one of the unconscious priests. He threw the man over his shoulder and stormed off to the opening in the wall.

"You all head upstairs," Coldforge said. "Me and the lad here will repair the wall. Nobody will ever know we were here."

"They're going to notice the padlock missing on the other cell," Slate added. "What are we going to do to fix that?"

"Sure." Iba looked at the two dwarves like they'd lost their collective minds. "They'll notice a hole in the wall, and a missing lock, but they won't notice the eviscerated bodies and the blood-soaked walls and ground."

"If we fix the wall, the guards won't know how we got inside," Coldforge said. "It will look like someone came in and murdered all the Temple priests." Iba shook her head. Even though Coldforge might have had a point, she didn't see the sense of it.

"Do what you want, I'm going with the others. Be quiet about it though. There's no silencing spell to hide the noise."

Chapter Twenty-One

Treedale and Mukale

"No, no, no." Mukale waved his arms about, trying to get the trainees' attention. "You'll never consistently hit your target like that." Before he could stop him, the Berrat trainee released his arrow. The two of them watched the projectile fly a good eight feet over the target that was a mere fifteen paces away.

"Everyone, stop." Treedale combed his fingers through his ponytail. "I'm going to show you again. For those of you who are struggling, don't worry, you'll get this." He held out his hand to the young Nomad girl who was standing next to him. She handed him her short bow and a blunted arrow from her quiver. She blushed as his hand touched hers during the transfer. He gave the girl a quick wink and stepped in front of the group of trainees.

"There are a few steps in the process but the first thing you need to do is relax. You're all too stiff when you draw back the bowstring. Your shoulders are creeping up to your ears and that's no way to shoot a bow. Now, I know some of you have spoken with the other soldiers and they have told you a different way to shoot, but while Mukale and I are your instructors, you'll do it the way we say. Understood?" The young man waited patiently until all of his students were nodding their understanding.

"First, relax yourself and nock your arrow. Be sure a fletching is pointed towards you." He shook his head when two of the trainees nocked arrows. "No, don't do what I'm doing. Listen to what I'm saying. If you're busy trying this out, you will not hear my instructions. There aren't many, so you should be able to remember what I've said when I'm finished." The pair of eager trainees stuffed their arrows back in their quivers and gave their instructor their full attention.

"Okay." Treedale wrapped his hands behind his head and sighed. "Grip your string with three fingers. One on top and two below the arrow. When you've got your grip, breathe, and relax your shoulders. Now, raise your bow arm until it is level with the ground. As you do, draw back the arrow until your fingertips are just brushing your chin. Remember where you're making contact. You want to come back to the same point every time you shoot. The hardest part about learning to aim is learning how to repeat what you're doing. Make sure your shoulders are kept low and not creeping up to your ears. Watch your target with both eyes. Exhale and release the bowstring." As soon as he'd finished speaking, he performed the actions, exactly as he had described them. The arrow thumped into the bale of straw, striking the middle of the red circle painted on it. "Mukale will now demonstrate, repeating exactly what I just did."

The Berrat drew an arrow from his quiver, nocked it, raised the bow, and drew his arrow back. As soon as his fingers touched his chin, he exhaled and released. The bow thrummed, and the arrow struck the target less than a finger's width away from Treedale's arrow. The Berrat trainees oohed and aahed at the display. With an air of authority, the pair of instructors strode behind the trainees.

"Begin." Mukale called out each step and the trainees following along as he did. When he told them to draw back on their bow, two of the would-be soldiers' forms deteriorated, their shoulders pulling up to their ears. Of the eighteen students, fourteen of them hit their targets, with two of them striking near-perfect bullseyes.

"Without an arrow." Mukale stood in front of the two Berrat trainees who had struggled with their form. "Draw back your string to your chin and hold it for me." As they did, their form faltered. "Okay, slowly release the tension." He moved in behind the first of the struggling archers. He placed his finger behind the shoulder blade of the Berrat male.

"Do you feel where I'm touching?" The man nodded. "Okay, when you draw your bow back, try to trap my finger, pull your muscles back through here." The man nodded again, his back muscles flexing as he did. Mukale observed carefully as he went through the motions. "Okay, let's try this again. Nock an arrow and pull back on your bowstring. When your fingers touch your chin, release." Again, the man nodded. He followed the instructions perfectly, released the arrow and struck the target. It was not perfect by any means, but it struck the bail and that was a vast improvement over his previous attempts. The instructors showed each of those who were struggling with form how to improve. Within an hour, the entire group was consistently hitting the bails.

As the lesson was ending, Treedale addressed the group with a cheery grin on his face. "The muscles you're using to shoot a bow, they're not muscles you use every day. You're going to be sore tomorrow. I want you to repeat this exercise every day, twice a day. Without an arrow nocked, draw your bow back like you would when you shoot. When you touch your chin, hold the arrow for three slow breaths. After three breaths, release the tension on the string. Wait a minute and repeat the process ten times." The group enthusiastically nodded to what the young Nomad was saying, all of them excited for having achieved so much progress in so little time.

Mukale gave the trainees a small round of applause. "That's it for today. I want you to practice shooting at least thirty arrows a day, besides the exercises that Lieutenant Treedale gave you. In five days, we will test you. Tomorrow, if you're struggling to hit your target, come find me and I'll help you with your form. Dismissed."

"They're coming along well." Treedale tried to sound hopeful, but he doubted the students would be ready for a while.

"Hopefully, they won't need to fight anytime soon. Under pressure, none of them will hit their target. They're more likely to shoot an ally than an enemy." Mukale laughed weakly at his friend's joke.

"Maybe the next group will be better." Treedale groaned as eighteen more eager trainees came striding into the room, each with a new bow and a quiver full of arrows. At least half had incorrectly equipped their quiver. Several had their quiver hanging off the wrong shoulder. The lone human amid the Berrat was wearing full plate armor. The pair of instructors groaned in unison.

Chapter Twenty-Two

ASHKEY AND THE SPRITES

The boy stopped at the hanging potted plants before opening the door. Clutching a tiny parcel to his chest, he stretched out to sniff the delicate yellow blossoms. Their scent was subtle, but the flowers still warmed his heart and calmed his mind. With the tiniest hint of a smile, he pulled the latch on the door and stepped into the colorfully painted house. The walls, the ceiling, the door, and the window frames were all the same bright yellow as the tiny flowers that grew outside the home's front door.

Grams stepped in from the kitchen, carrying a steaming mug of coffee. "What have you got there?"

"Summer berries." Ashkey opened his cloth-wrapped parcel, holding out his treasures for the old woman to see. "I found a large patch in the fields beyond the road." Grams' eyes lit up. Her skin was weathered and wrinkled, but she had the eyes of a child, full of life and love. The boy grinned with delight as the woman inspected his prize. "I picked them for Triss, but there is plenty enough to share."

Grams clutched at her breast; her heart filled with joy. It had hardly been a few hours since the boy's broken mind had returned from the abyss. He had seemed to be living in a trance, barely aware of those around him. The only person with whom he had appeared to make any connection was Triss. The old priest believed the trauma of witnessing the little mouse-sprite being brutally beaten had permanently warped his perception of the world. Feigh's mate had tirelessly worked her special magic. Day and night she sang to the boy, infusing him with hope and a promise of better days to come. After a week of no visible response, he awoke at the sound of Feigh preparing to leave. By the light of a single candle, he caught sight of the little sprite. He appeared worried as he took a long look at his wife. With the softest touch, he had kissed his mate goodbye. Ashkey's concern for his friends drove the darkness from his mind, freeing him of the burden that had been weighing on him.

"No, child. Save them for Triss. They will make a lovely breakfast for her when she wakes." Ashkey beamed at the old woman, carefully wrapping the berries once again. "I have made some hotcakes if you're hungry. They're stacked up in the kitchen next to the stove." The boy nodded and dashed into the kitchen. A minute later, he returned with a plate full of hotcakes, his cheeks bulging from the one he had already stuffed into his mouth. Ashkey had hardly eaten at all since he'd arrived from Silverhawk and desperately needed many good meals.

"Not too fast now," Grams whispered, her lips puckered into a tight bow. The boy nodded and swallowed the rest of the hotcake in his mouth.

The boy paused between bites. "When will Feigh be back? The sun wasn't even up when he left."

"Soon, I hope." Grams sat in a chair at the large wooden table and invited the boy to take the seat next to her. She took a sip from her steaming mug, careful not to burn her lips. The aroma of the fresh coffee carried her worries away on a cloud of caffeine induced bliss. "He's gone to spread the word to his kin."

The boy took a large bite of another hotcake. "What word, Grams?" Grams regretted letting that slip. The boy didn't need to hear that and no good would come of scaring him in his fragile state. Ashkey dropped the rest of his hotcake onto his plate. He got a far-off look in his eyes. "Darkness is coming. It will spread across the lands like a spring flood, destroying everything it touches." The boy had almost no emotion in his face or in his voice. He spoke of doom and he acted like it didn't affect him at all. Tears welled up in Grams' eyes. She didn't know how to react. She didn't know what to say.

"Don't worry, Grams." Ashkey reached out and took the old priest's hands in his. "In the darkness, the light shines its brightest. As long as there is hope, there is life. And where there's life, there are limitless possibilities." The tears in Gram's eyes overflowed. She reached out and took Ashkey, pulling him close to her. He was so warm, so filled with hope, so filled with life.

"Where did this come from?" Grams held him away from herself so she could look into his eyes. It was the first time she noticed they were so dark they were almost black. The boy shrugged.

"I don't know." Thick wrinkles appeared on his forehead as he considered the question. "While I was sleeping, I heard a voice tell me. It told me to not be afraid, that we can only see the stars when the night is at its darkest. The voice told me to have hope."

A squeak came from the sofa, drawing Grams' attention away from the boy. Triss was perched upon a bright yellow pillow, stretching and yawning. When she spotted Ashkey at the table next to Grams, she hopped down from the couch, scampered across the floor, and leapt up onto the table.

"You're awake." The mouse-sprite's beady black eyes were wet with tears. "You came back." The boy nodded and raced from the table into the kitchen. A moment later, he returned with his gift for the tiny mouse-sprite. The boy unwrapped the package, its bright red berries spilling out onto the table.

"I picked these for you. I heard they're your favorite." The boy bit his lower lip, clasping his hands behind his back. "To say thank you. You gave me hope when I needed it most. It's a small gesture, I know. But one day, I'll return the favor." The tiny sprite startled him when she jumped from the table, landing on his chest. As best as she could, she draped her arms around him, nuzzling her face against his soft, white tunic.

Triss' voice hitched. "Seeing you back as you were before." She clambered up his chest to his shoulder, perching comfortably next to his neck. "This is all I could have ever hoped for."

"Try the berry." Ashkey presented the largest of the fruits to her. The sprite grasped it in her little hands and sniffed. The floral fragrance flooded her senses. Triss smacked her lips, anticipating the berry's natural sweetness. The tiniest bit of drool appeared at the corner of her mouth. She opened wide and took a huge bite, spraying its bright red juice everywhere, staining the boy's once-white shirt.

She sniffed back tears as she savored the tangy-sweet flavor, finishing the berry in just a couple more bites.

⚜

"Come on Midnight, you need to put it behind you. I'm not holding any grudge against you for swiping my locket."

The dark blue rabbit just stared, his tiny black nose involuntarily twitching. He narrowed his pink eyes and placed his hand on the handle of his sword. He tucked his white-feathered wings tight to his body, making sure they wouldn't interfere with his weapon.

"You cheated me, Feigh. You and that stupid deck of cards. I want my staff back." Feigh seemed to reach into the ether and pulled out a gnarled stick with a thick bulbous head on it. As Midnight's eyes fell upon it, his nose twitched faster, and his grip on his sword tightened.

"If you recall, I didn't want to bet you, but you insisted. I just wanted to spend time with my friend but... you had something to prove. You wanted to show off in front of Triss. You wanted to show off how powerful your magic was." Feigh twirled the tiny staff in his mouse hands, pinning his round mouse ears to his head. A wicked smile crossed his lips as he unfurled his own fluffy white set of wings. He was challenging the rabbit to take the staff by force.

Midnight drew a few inches of his blade from its scabbard, the weapon's bright-white metal catching the moon's rays. A slight glow on the steel made the sword look even more threatening. The rabbit-sprite returned the mouse's grin, his buckteeth giving the animal a maniacal look.

"Oh, here." Feigh rolled his eyes and tossed the staff to the rabbit. "I had never meant to keep it, but you were such a sore loser. You made it too easy for me."

Midnight slipped his sword back into his sheath and caught the staff. He stared down at it, adjusting his grip like he was hugging an old friend. When he raised his eyes, the maniacal look on his face became... truly unsettling. His pink eyes darkened. His long, near-black ears laid flat across the back of his skull. A ghastly green glow ran up the length of the weapon's gray wood. His smile changed to a sneer as he pushed the staff out in front of himself, sending a cloud of blue-green smoke at the mouse.

"Gaia, save me." The mouse-sprite recoiled from the stench, waving his hands in front of his face. Feigh's normal gray-brown fur changed to a putrid yellow. He covered his nose with his paws and turned away. He took a few steps, distancing himself from the rabbit, and then a few more, and then broke into a run. As he increased the distance between himself and Midnight, the cloud of noxious fumes followed him. The rabbit couldn't stop laughing as the mouse tried to chase away the thick green fog that remained attached to him. "Come on Midnight, stop it. I yield. I yield."

"Apologize," the rabbit-sprite said. "Say you're sorry and I'll call it off."

"I'm sorry. Now stop it."

"Swear to it." Midnight hopped around in a small circle. "Swear to me, you're sorry."

"I'm sorry. If I'm lying, may my ears fall off and my tail shrivel." The cloud dissipated. Feigh dropped to his knees, his chest heaving as he tried to fill his lungs with the fresh, night air.

"Why are you here?" Midnight rapped the mouse-sprite on the back of his head. "I'm sure you didn't just come to give me back my staff. You want something." Feigh rubbed the back of his head, wincing at what he perceived to be a lump.

"That hurt. And that disgusting cloud trick of yours is..." The mouse scrubbed his nose, running his paws over his muzzle, hoping to ease the stink.

"Disgusting? Yes, it kind of is. That's the point of the spell. I like the way it heightens your senses, too. It really lets you enjoy the fragrance. I guess that's why your head hurts, too. I hardly touched you."

"You're an ass."

"And you're a jerk."

They both crossed their arms and glared at one another. They held their stare for several minutes before Feigh finally relented.

"I missed you. With all my heart, I'm sorry that I took your walking stick."

"Well, to be fair, I might have deserved it." The rabbit preened his ears and cleared his throat. "So? Why are you here, old friend?"

"Grams says that Ragnarök is coming. It's time we Sprites pick a side."

"Our kind doesn't play the game of the gods. We hide and we wait. It's how we've survived through all the cycles." The rabbit plopped onto his butt, resting his staff across his legs. "Grams knows that. Why would she ask us to pick a side?"

"She said this one is different. She said if we don't stand together, all will perish. The gods won't let any race live this time." Feigh sat beside his friend, wrapping his long tail around the both of them. "We've got a champion, though, someone who will fight for us. She'll fight for everyone."

"Misty isn't a champion. She's become a recluse. Nobody has seen or heard from her in many cycles now." Feigh's ears dropped at the sound of the girl's name. The three of them had been inseparable for many summers, until, as Feigh had said, *that damned, thick-necked squirrel came along.*

"That's not who I was talking about." The mouse-sprite gave a shallow sigh. "But it would be good to see that lynx again. That girl's smile could brighten up a thunderstorm. If I ever see Hob again, I'll cut off his damned tail and choke him to death with it. It was his fault we split up."

"And after we split up, you met Triss." Midnight's eyebrows shot up, like he was daring the mouse to deny it. "Maybe you should thank Hob. Maybe he's the reason you got the best girl in the entire world." The two sat in silence for many long minutes until Midnight broke the spell.

"So, if your champion isn't Misty, who is it?"

"Her name is Kitten, but don't call her that." The mouse chuckled to himself. "She gets really mad." His chuckles turned to a full-on laugh. "Call her Kit, or Sister Kit if you want her to like you."

"Tell me you're not talking about that zealot, priest of Titan." The rabbit popped up to his feet, looming over his mouse friend. "You think that foolish little girl is going to be our champion?" The mouse nodded furiously.

"I gave her our mark." His beady black eyes held the rabbit's dark pink gaze. "She is so much more than she seems." Midnight was about to cast another spell, something far less playful.

"She's a stupid, idealistic, human girl. I bested her with ease. Had I wanted, I could have run her through a dozen times before she even pulled out that ridiculous hammer she carries."

"In your dreams, Midnight. I saw her in action. That girl saved Triss and took over the Crimson Ale in an afternoon. She has immeasurable compassion and steadfast friends who would lay down their lives for her. In every sense of the word, she is a champion."

"You gave our mark to a human. Now she can see us wherever we hide. None of our magic can fool her. If you're wrong, you've doomed our kind."

"I'm not wrong. Kit saved Triss' life and Treedale's life. She saved a broken boy, his mind lost beyond hope. I owe her my life and I trust her to keep it safe."

"You're a sentimental fool, Feigh."

"And you're my best friend. What does that make you?"

"A moron." The pair laughed. It was an uncomfortable truce, one that Midnight feared would bite him in his fuzzy tail one day.

"We're going to need Misty," Feigh said. "Even if nobody has seen her in many cycles, you can find her, can't you?" Midnight scrunched his nose, sucked in a deep breath, and blew it out. He stared at his oversized feet for several moments until his shoulders slumped.

"I know where she is, but you can't come."

"I'm coming."

"No, you're not. Go home to the Great Scar, where the grass tastes best. Get the rest of the sprites living there and I'll meet you at your home."

"I'm coming."

Midnight's staff glowed that familiar, frightening ghastly green color. "No, you're not." As the spell was being cast, Feigh threw himself at the rabbit. He grabbed onto Midnight's ear just before they both vanished.

Chapter Twenty-Three

A Path Less Traveled

Fury snapped the handle off the shovel and blew a fine gout of fire at the metal spade until it was glowing. He worked the near molten metal in his clawed hands with remarkable dexterity, folding and shaping it until it was a perfectly balanced crucible. He blew on the still-glowing iron until it turned a dull black.

"I have alchemy equipment and sorrowsage in my cell," Lin said. "I can be there and back in less than an hour. Wouldn't it be better if I go get it? There isn't enough Medeina's Grace to make more than a couple of antidotes."

"I can make three." Fury gave Lin a scathing look for a moment, then his eyebrows shot up. "We can use them to rouse some priests here, but if you insist on going to your place of sleep, then maybe you can bring me a set of scales and a copper alembic, and some blightroot, if you have any."

"I have a little," Lin said. "I have some belladonna, too. It will help stretch it out to make more potions." Fury's neck elongated just before his lips pulled back, exposing his toothy grin.

"Your knowledge of plants is quite impressive, especially for a human. Take Sneaks to scout the way for you."

"I'm coming, too," Kit said, "in case there's trouble."

"Just be sure to leave your wondrous hammer behind." Fury motioned to the weapon on the table beside him. "I need to finish preparing to make the antidotes." Kit gave the draken a sheepish grin and a small shrug.

"Indie." Kit was having difficulty making eye contact with the man. "Can you go check on Slate and Coldforge? They should have been back by now."

Without a response, Indie grabbed a torch and left. Kit stared at the empty doorframe as his footsteps receded down the hall.

"Boys, go with him," she said. "Make sure he comes back safely." Lump and Runt bolted out of the room, each jostling with the other to see who would take the lead. Kit continued to stare at the space before blowing out a heavy sigh.

Lin took Kit's hand and gave it a light squeeze. "Give him time. You two have been through a lot in the last few weeks. He loves you as much as you love him. He'll come around. Men aren't as resilient as we are."

"Sure." Kit's eyes never left the door. "Let's get what you need from your cell."

"What do you want me and Silverleaf to do?" Amara asked. "Maybe we should go with Indie as well?"

"No," Fury replied with something of a hiss. "Stay here. There may be a need for muscular hands and the half-breed can help me prepare the herbs."

"I wouldn't mind watching Fury." The half elf ignored the draken's half-breed comment. "There is much I could learn, even if I prefer making scrolls over potions."

"You would need a dozen of your lifetimes to learn all I could teach you." Fury straightened his long lizard back. "I am versed in the creation of both potions and scrolls, but for now, you'll be in potions class." Amara shook her head and rolled her eyes.

"Go. We'll keep the *master* company while you're away." Amara's voice dripped with sarcasm, but Fury either didn't notice or he didn't care what the giant thought.

Lin grabbed a torch and headed out the door, turning in the opposite direction that Indie had taken.

⚜

Lin led Kit and Iba through the halls of the dead, passing by the tunnel that led up to the mausoleum. They took a flight of wooden stairs down one level before heading down another death-filled hallway. The guttering light of her torch lit the corridor to about ten paces ahead of them. The dripping water did an excellent job of masking their footfalls.

"I'll go scout up ahead, to make sure the coast is clear," Iba offered. "This torch is going to announce our arrival long before we see anyone coming."

"How can you do that?" Kit asked. "Without the torch, it will be pitch black."

"I have excellent dark-vision," Iba replied. "I don't need light to see."

"No need to scout ahead," Lin said. "We're going down, not forward."

"Down?" Kit asked. "There are no stairs here." Lin held her torch near the floor, illuminating a small stream that ran beneath the floorboards. There was no packed earth beneath the wood, just an open space.

"We're going to follow that stream. It leads under the city walls, and it will take us to the Temple grounds."

"How do we get down?" Iba asked. "There's no way to get there."

Lin smiled at the Tahr and moved to the side of the corridor. She pressed her foot against the board closest to the wall and jounced on it. The board popped up from its place and Lin easily pulled it up. She reached under the shelf holding the remains of people long since passed and pulled out a second, wider board.

"Follow me." Lin slipped down through the hole in the floor. "There's a platform here to stand on. Drop to the ground below. Try to land next to the stream. You're going to want to avoid stepping in it." Iba was about to ask why as she slipped down the hole.

"Titan's snowballs," she bleated out. "Is this runoff from the sewers? It smells worse down here than it did with the dead bodies up there." Kit followed the Tahr down the hole, covering her mouth and nose with her sleeve. It was even worse than the aroma of Blue Yeti cheese, and she thought she would experience nothing so pungent for the rest of her life.

"Breathe through your mouth," Lin offered as she moved the floorboards back into position. "It tastes as bad as it smells, but at least you won't pass out. I'd say you'll get used to it, but I'd be lying."

"How do you know this tunnel exists?" Kit had an accusatory tone in her voice. Lin's eyebrows shot up at the question. The girl blew out a breath. "Never mind."

"Tell me," Iba bleated. "I could have used it to get more children away from the city."

"That was a good thing you did, getting those children to the Lupiens," Kit said. "They'll be safe now."

"Thank you," she replied, "but it wasn't enough. I have a lot of destructive behavior to make up for."

"What you did in the past isn't nearly as important as what you do in the present." Kit lowered her head respectfully.

"That's remarkably deep." Lin's voice was wrapped in a hint of mockery. "Your philosophy is usually grab and bash, not whatever that was."

"Those were Father Hoarfrost's words to me," Kit replied, profound sorrow seeping into her voice. "Father always told me to look forward and not dwell on the past. He always seemed able to overlook my faults if I would work on them." The girls shared a moment of silence for the fallen high priest before continuing through the sewer.

After thirty excruciatingly long minutes, Lin stopped at a set of iron rungs that were affixed to a stone wall. A thick rust clung to the metal, but hopefully they were still solid.

"These will lead us up into Sister Nevara's classroom. From there, we can take the back stairs up to the dorms. After the gizmo uprising, she had this escape route built."

"That term is offensive," Iba said. "You know that, right?"

"I meant no disrespect." Lin tucked her hair behind her ear. "It's what everyone calls your kind."

"Just because so many will call us by that vulgar name, doesn't make it any better. We are *Inua Gharzhimoh*." Lin tried to speak the words and failed miserably. Kit also tried and butchered the words even worse.

"That's unpronounceable with a human mouth," Lin said. "And the last part sort of sounds like *gizmo*. I can understand how the name stuck."

"Just because you can't say it properly, doesn't give you license to use such a foul term."

"I'm sorry that the name is offensive," Kit said. "I truly am, but can we get moving? We're wasting precious time right now." Iba nodded briskly and scampered up the iron rungs. When she got to the top, she used her head to butt the trap door open.

⁂

Sister Nevara's classroom was empty and unnaturally quiet. Exceptionally boisterous children of most every race imaginable typically filled the room, often making it the noisiest place in the entire Temple, perhaps in all of Aarall. Vividly colored murals and festive decorations covered the walls. Statues of Titan, Fenrir, and Ymir filled the back corner of the room. Their menacing appearance was out of place in the otherwise vibrant, cheery setting.

Kit growled at the statue of Ymir. "Too bad I don't have my hammer. I'd like to smash the head off Ymir." Iba's eyes bulged out of her brown and white, fur-covered face.

"He's a traitor to Titan," Lin said.

"And to Fenrir as well," Kit added. "Titan chose poorly when he picked him to be his servant. Forget him. We need to keep going."

"I'll scout ahead. We'll take the western stairwell, behind the nave, up to wash-out alley." Iba glared at the statue of Ymir. Kit took a quick glance at Lin to see if she was offended by her dorm being referred to as washout alley, a place for failed, overage acolytes. "I'll come back to you if I see any trouble."

"Don't get too far ahead of us," Kit said. "If you run into danger, we need to be close enough to help." Iba nodded and bolted for the door.

"We'll need to run if we're going to keep up with her," Lin said. "At least I will, anyway."

Despite Iba having cloven hooves for feet, she made no noise, running over the tiled floors as she ran for the stairway up. The girl seemed to blend in with her surroundings as she moved, making it nearly impossible to spot her, even though she was only twenty paces ahead.

As they climbed the stairs up to the main level, Kit's heart raced. They were about to pass by the nave, the place where Father Hoarfrost had made his last stand against the king's soldiers. She exited the stairwell to look, immediately regretting the decision. Stone and debris filled the place of worship. At the periphery of the giant pile of rubble, broken bodies were laying half-buried by large blocks of granite and precious stone.

"Kit, we need to go," Lin whispered from behind her. "Iba will wonder where we've got to." Kit nodded, struggling to pull herself away from the sight. In a moment, the pair were climbing the stairs to the acolytes' level. Iba gave them a scolding look when they stepped out into the hallway.

They moved to Lin's room and slipped inside. Kit was still amazed by the shelves upon shelves of potions and reagents that covered every wall. Knowing that volumes of books were hidden behind them only made the room that much more impressive.

"Behind that shelf." Lin pointed across the room. "There's a case with my alchemy equipment. Fury only wanted the scales and copper alembic, but we might as well bring it all. It might be useful."

Kit nodded and pulled open the bookcase, revealing the shelves behind. They were jam-packed with books. A leather case sat on the bottom shelf. It was the sole thing here that wasn't a book, so she pulled it off. It tinkled as she tipped it. She grimaced and turned to Lin, fearful that she may have broken something.

"Don't worry," Lin said. "The vessels inside are extremely durable, almost unbreakable." Kit blushed, despite her friend's words.

"You're a strange woman, Aithlin." There was a touch of awe in Iba's voice. "And all this time, I believed you were just a suck-up, the way you were always following Father around."

"She was using him for information." There was more than a bit of hurt in Kit's voice.

It was Lin's turn to blush. She pulled a case of vials from one of her many shelves and handed it to Kit. "You can't keep healing us all the time. I don't care how powerful you are. Healing us hurts you, and at some point, you will not have it in you to do what you do." Kit put down the alchemy case and pulled out a vial.

"What are these?" She inspected the swirling gold-orange and red fluid liquid within.

Lin winced at the question. "It's something I worked on with Powder." Rejuvenation potions were all but forbidden, except under exceptional circumstances. More often than not, they caused more harm than good. "These are a mixture of healing and rejuvenation potions. The rejuvenation aspect replenishes your strength and vitality, while the healing aspect cures your wounds. The healing part of the potion also helps prevent the energy crash when the rejuvenation part wears off." Lin smiled brightly. "They're far safer than the regular ones."

"What about the sorrowsage?" Iba had moved into the hallway, her eyes darting up and down the corridor. "It's what we came for."

"Right! Of course." Lin threw a couple of potion bandoleers over her shoulder. She rushed over to another shelf, running her fingers along the boxes and sacks stored within.

"Sorrowsage." She pulled down a small sack and stuffed it into a satchel, "and belladonna, and the blightroot that Fury asked for." The girl's eyes lit up when they fell upon a nondescript jar filled with ivory-colored crystals. "Ooh, this might come in handy, too." She pulled the reagent off the shelf and rolled it in her hand. "Corpseflower pollen."

"What's that for?" Kit looked up from the alchemy case she held.

"It's an ingredient in shield spells. It's better when used to create scrolls, but Fury can probably use it to make protection potions. Maybe he'll even show me how." Lin's eyes sparkled as she stuffed the pollen into the satchel with the other herbs. Iba poked her head into the room.

"We've got to go." An obvious panic permeated her voice. "There are people coming up the stairwell. It sounds like there are four of them." She pulled her head out of the room and surveyed the hallway. "No, wait. There are five."

"That stairway is the only way down from here." Kit wished Fury was with her.

"I'll lead them away," Iba said. "As soon as the path is clear, head back to the others. I'll meet you there." She was gone before Kit could object.

"Close the door," Lin said, "but leave it open a crack so we can hear."

CHAPTER TWENTY-FOUR

THE TRAITOR AND THE DAEMON

Mail-clad boots came clattering down the stone hallway. Lin unloaded the supplies from her arms and drew her twin long swords. She offered one to Kit, who considered it for a moment before shaking her head.

"Where did she go?" a husky voiced woman called out. "She was just here."

"She must have gone this way," called out another.

In a moment, the clomping of feet continued, nearing Lin's cell. They seemed to pick up speed. She held her breath, leaned into the door, and closed it without a sound. The footfalls were only paces away.

"I saw her!" A voice called out from the end of the hallway, away from the stairwell. Whoever had neared the door broke into a run. The footfalls receded, echoing off the walls.

"Now or never." Lin slipped her long swords back into their scabbards and picked up the crate of potions. "Can you get the rest?" Kit nodded. With the alchemy set in one hand, she scooped up the satchel of the supplies in the other.

Neither of them moved.

"I'll get the door," Kit whispered, putting down the alchemy set. "We'll head down the stairs to the basement and then straight to Nevara's classroom." Lin nodded and Kit opened the door, letting her friend take the lead. The young priest picked up the alchemy set and backed out the door, using her toe to pull it closed behind her.

"Kit," Lin whispered. "Behind you." Kit turned to see a figure dressed in flat-black armor and cape standing at the end of the hallway. His open-faced helm showed him to be an older man, perhaps in his thirties. His skin was dark and unshaven, giving him a sinister appearance. He held a spiked mace in his right hand, which was swinging lazily by his hip. His left hand was stretched out before him, covered in a pulsating black aura.

"Run," Kit said. "Follow the plan and don't look back."

"Kit, you have no weapon!"

"Run!" Kit bellowed over her shoulder. "I'll hold him off."

"Kit, look out!" There was no time to react to Lin's warning as a sphere of darkness washed over her. The sensation was hard to describe, but it left Kit feeling like the situation was hopeless.

"Run!" she bellowed again, this time not waiting to see if Lin would obey. Kit dropped the alchemy kit and the knapsack of herbs. She wanted to run as well, but her feet had other ideas. Despair swept over her as she suddenly believed that she had wasted her life. A profound feeling of hopelessness wrapped around her heart, while utter desperation gripped her very soul. She watched helplessly as another dark sphere slammed into her, increasing her feelings of dread and anxiety.

Unbidden, she burst into deep red flames.

The feelings of hopelessness diminished somewhat, but it wasn't enough to let her move. She wanted to let her anger take hold, to let the rage engulf her, to fill her with resolve, but she couldn't. The man released yet another swirling orb of gloom.

Her flames burst out brighter, hotter. The spell struck the inferno. Her firestorm consumed some of it, but much of its debilitating effects got through. She wanted to give up. She wanted to die.

It was difficult to see beyond the tempest of flame that surrounded her. Whether she was seeing it, or only imagining it, a tiny figure leapt up from behind the man in black. In rapid succession, it brought its hand down upon the man's neck. The shadow continued to attack until the man sank to his knees and fell over onto his face.

Kit's flames abated and she, too, dropped to her knees. The tiny figure was now racing up the hallway towards her. It was going to end her life in the same way that it had ended the man's.

Kit didn't care. She welcomed death, if only as a reprieve from the constant violence and sadness that had filled her life. There was no future for Orth. All would perish. The currents of oppression and death would sweep it all away. She dropped on all fours, awaiting the inevitable.

"Kit, get up!"

She didn't want to get up. She wanted to stay there and join the Great Cycle.

"Kit, we need to leave. The others are coming."

Who cares? Let them come. They're going to win, anyway. There is no reason left to fight.

"Kitten, you sniveling coward. Get off the ground and get moving."

I'm not a coward.

"If you don't move, your friends will all die. The priests will all die. Indie and the boys will die."

No.

"Kit, now!"

No.

A tiny light of hope sprung up in her heart.

No. They won't die. I won't let them.

Kit dug her fingers into the stone floor. She drew a deep breath, letting the air fill her lungs. The hope in her chest grew, pushing out the despair, pushing away the hopelessness that had taken hold of her. As she lifted her head, big brown eyes stared at her.

"Welcome back," Iba said. "Can we leave now? There are two more battle mages looking for you."

"You said there were five people." Kit rocked back, sitting on her heels. She blinked a few times as she tried to clear her head.

"There were. Now there are two."

Kit and Iba caught up with Lin, who had been waiting for them in Sister Nevara's classroom. She blew out a sigh of relief when the pair came through the door.

"I've got my supplies stowed in the tunnel," she called out just before she ducked down the trapdoor. The light from a torch lit the tunnel below. Kit dropped the alchemy set to Lin before heading down the ladder.

"Close the door," Lin called to Iba as she came through the hole. The young Tahr rolled her eyes before pulling the trap door closed.

Kit grimaced with every step. The stench in the tunnel was no better than it had been before. The lingering effects of the spells still chewed at her confidence, but they weren't so debilitating anymore. She reeled as the putrid aroma permeated her nostrils. It brought back the desire to curl up and die.

Sweet Titan, it smells horrid down here.

The group continued along the stream until they reached the entrance to the catacombs. Lin put down her crate of potions and wormed her way up into the hallway above. Kit passed her the crate, along with the alchemy set and the satchel of herbs.

"Ensure the way is clear," Kit said to Iba. "We'll be right behind you." Iba gave a bit of a grin before she scampered up to the tunnel. By the time Kit got herself through the hole, the Tahr was gone. While Kit collected her bundles, Lin replaced the boards, leaving no trace they had come that way.

They traveled through the warrens without incident, finding Iba already in the storage room with the others. Sister Gale was sitting on a crate, looking worn out but otherwise unscathed.

"Hello, Sister Kit." There was a deep sadness in the sister's voice. "Welcome home."

"Our home is infested with vermin," Kit replied. "Perhaps you'd like to help exterminate them?" The combat instructor nodded and hopped down from the crate. She was too subdued.

"Here, Sister, drink this up." Lin offered her a small vial. "It should return your energy to you." The priest gave Lin a questioning look before unstopping the tiny bottle and downing the contents in a single gulp.

"Tasty." She ran her tongue over her lip and gave a weak smile. A moment later, her eyes widened, and she gave her head a shake. "Titan's grace! That's... invigorating."

Seeing Sister Gale bounce back so quickly, the spark in Kit's heart brightened further. "Fury, do you have everything you need to wake the other priests?" He was busy unpacking the various implements from Lin's apothecary kit. He nodded without looking up. When he pulled out the Corpseflower pollen, he clucked his tongue.

"To make shield potions," Lin said. "I thought they might come in handy." The draken grunted in response.

"Okay then," Kit said. "I'm going to look at the altar room, to see what we're up against."

"Let me," Iba said. "I'll give you a full report on their strength." Kit shook her head.

"I want to see for myself."

"As do I." Coldforge hefted his double-bladed ax over his shoulder. "I'm tired of waiting for the fight."

"Absolutely not," Kit and Indie said in near perfect unison. They stared at each other for a moment before Kit continued. "You might be the worst sneak in all of Arnnor." Kit stared at the shaggy dwarf, daring him to disagree.

"I'm coming, too," Indie said. "If you get into trouble, you're going to need some help."

"As am I," Sister Gale said. "Your big friend here woke me up so I could devise strategies. I need to see what we're facing if I'm going to plan anything."

"And I'm the only one who knows the route," Silverleaf added. Amara cleared her throat, making the half elf cringe. "Amara and I are the only ones who know the way." He gave Amara a smile after correcting himself.

"Titan's snowballs," Kit said, scrubbing her face. "I just want to get a look at the room and the numbers."

"Sister Kit," Sister Gale said in her teacher's voice. "You have a team who are willing and able to assist you here. You can't take everything on yourself. Let us help you." She paused for several seconds, her expression turning dark. "If your father is being held there, you're going to need support. You're going to need people with you to stop you from rushing in on your own."

Kit glared at Indie.

"Yes, he told me about your special powers." A crooked smile pulled at one side of Sister Gale's mouth. "It explains so much about you. From the first time you stepped into my classroom, I could tell there was more to you. Now, let us help you."

Kit blinked back tears that wanted to spring forth. "Fine. Silverleaf, you and Iba scout ahead. Sister Gale, Indie, and I will follow behind you. Don't you dare go inside without us."

"Here." Coldforge's bushy orange eyebrows knitted together, looking like a fuzzy worm across his eyes. "Take me ax. But I want it back in one piece. If you break it or lose it, I'm taking that fancy hammer of yours."

"Thank you." Kit accepted the weapon and dipped her chin. "I'll do my best to return it safely to you."

"And I'll get your hammer, right?"

"I cannot agree to that." She held the ax out for the dwarf to take it back. "It's not a *thing* I can just give away. Fury goes where he wants to go." The dwarf blew out a breath, making his facial hair look like a party favor.

"Fine. Keep me ax. May it serve you well." Fury gave Kit a nod, acknowledging what she'd said about him and his autonomy.

"If everyone's ready." Iba grabbed Silverleaf by his cloak-sleeve and headed for the door. Sister Gale followed shortly behind them, with Indie at arm's length behind her.

"Thank you." Kit grasped the sleeve of Indie's tunic. "Thank you for staying with me." The man gave her an unreadable expression and headed out the door. A knot grew in Kit's stomach. It wasn't clear if it resulted from Indie's reaction or if it was because she was headed to the altar room where her father was being held and tortured.

Kit, Indie, and Sister Gale moved through the tunnels and down several flights of stairs, never more than a hundred paces behind Iba and Silverleaf. Each time they needed to turn a corner, Iba waited until they could see her, to see which direction she had gone. They were about to follow her around a corner when Iba came jogging back to the group. "Leave your torches behind. The tunnels ahead are all lit. You're going to want your hands free for weapons. There are four soldiers guarding the altar room's entrance." Kit's face blanched.

"Are they like the man in the black armor?" She pulled out Coldforge's ax.

"No, they're not battle mages. They look pretty green." Iba shrugged. "I can lead them back to you. It would pull the fight away from the entrance."

"If the guards are missing from their post," Indie said, "someone's going to notice."

"We have no choice," Sister Gale said, speaking Kit's thoughts aloud. "We're going to need to risk it."

"I don't like it," Indie replied. "Why don't we..." Silverleaf burst around the corner, waving frantically for everyone to get back.

"They're coming," he yell-whispered. "Four guards..."

"Head back to the last bend," Sister Gale hissed. "We'll attack as soon as they round the corner. It's not safe here. We're too exposed."

Indie nodded and readied his bow. "I'll take one down and then let them follow me."

"No," Sister Gale said. "Right now, they've only seen one of us. We can't let them know our numbers. They may alert the entire army if they know there are more." Indie growled, acknowledging his understanding. Silverleaf never slowed. He kept running past them, only pausing when he got to the next turn in the hallway.

The group had just gotten themselves around the corner when the guards came pounding down the tunnel. They did not mask their footfalls, making it easy to tell how close they were. Sister Gale held up a hand, telling everyone to wait. Indie's bow was nocked and drawn, just waiting for her signal.

The priest dropped her hand just before the first guard rounded the corner. When he came into view, Indie sunk an arrow into his chest. His forward momentum sent the man crashing into the wooden shelves, dislodging one of the dead bodies. Tumbling out of its wrapping, its desiccated body draped over the fallen guard.

The next guard, who was distracted by the macabre scene before him, was met by a kali stick Sister Gale had fashioned from the handle of a shovel. As the man stumbled face forward, Kit brought her ax to bear, sinking it deep into the man's back, just below his neck. Iba greeted the third guard, scurrying up his body before sinking a tiny dagger into the side of his neck. She pulled the dagger out and stuck him with it again, and again, and again.

The fourth guard didn't appear. Indie stepped past the mayhem and into the hallway. He raised his bow and loosed his arrow. There was a solid whump when the arrow struck its target. Indie pulled his dagger and dashed down the hallway, assumably to finish the job.

Sister Gale gave Iba a look of disapproval. "Is that another vorpal weapon? Like the one that got you expelled." Iba shrugged and pushed it into a holster that sat low on her hips. Kit had never noticed before, but the Tahr had six such daggers adorning her belt.

"It wasn't the weapon that got me expelled." Iba raised her chin ever so slightly. "It was because I tried to stick it into Kitten." She blinked at Kit. It was hard to tell, but she might have been grinning, just a little.

"Such weapons are exceedingly dangerous," Sister Gale continued. "Wounds from them don't heal. Unless treated, they will continue bleeding until you die. Just a nick can be fatal, eventually."

Iba reached around behind her back and pulled out a tiny brown leather bag. "This stops the bleeding. I might have nicked myself once or twice in the past." She gave the sister a rueful look and slipped the tiny bag behind her back again. "Let's get a look at what we're facing, shall we?"

Iba scampered around the corner.

"Let's go," Kit said. "Indie's probably already scouting ahead."

"Indie's right here," he said, stepping back around the corner. "Iba's gone though. If she hadn't spoken to me, I don't think I'd have even seen her go past."

In minutes, they were approaching the entrance to the altar room. Kit's heart was racing out of control. The effects of the battle mage's spells had worn off, but the memory of them was still fresh. The idea of finding her father, savagely beaten or dead, reunited her with the deep feeling of despair brought on by the spells.

"Go get the others. Hurry!" Iba raced out from the altar room. "The numbers are in our favor. We need to act now."

"To plan a strategy, I need to see what the room looks like." Sister Gale scratched at her scalp. "We may only get one chance."

"Now's the time," Iba said. There was a profound sadness mixed with her insistence that everyone hurry. "Unless there are more hidden, there are only eleven soldiers inside. Based on what they're wearing, six of them are battle mages. Four of them look to be personal guards. One is..."

"What is it? One is what?" Kit asked.

"One of them is a priest of Titan. It's Brother Powder." Kit's mouth dropped open and her skin paled.

"Are they torturing him?" she asked. "We need to rescue him." Iba shook her head, her body trembling.

"He's interrogating your father." Big tears were in the Tahr's eyes, about to flow down her cheeks. "Sister Miyuki is there, too. I think she's dead." Kit's skin turned bone white, covered in dark ruins; her golden eyes instantly replaced with inky blackness.

"Get the others," Sister Gale said to Silverleaf as Kit ran into the altar room, yelling out something akin to a war cry. "Hurry!"

CHAPTER TWENTY-FIVE

THE ALTAR ROOM

Sister Gale stood transfixed before the entry to the altar room, stupefied by what she had just witnessed. She watched from the doorway as Kit, now a human fireball, was racing headlong towards the enemy. The girl's skin had transformed to a bone white, covered in black runes. The ax she had borrowed turned to ash and molten metal. Indie followed the inferno, his bow at the ready. He rushed to keep up with her, his body reflecting the flames. His skinned appeared as though it was covered in shiny, golden scales.

"Sister, they need you." Iba bolted into the fray. She was only ten paces away before she seemed to just meld with the darkness of the room. In the distance, Kit was engaged with someone dressed in black armor. She lit up the area around her like a bonfire. The man before her shrieked in agony and terror as she wrapped her arms around him, lighting him up like a piece of kindling.

Indie had nocked and released two arrows in the meantime. One struck Brother Powder high on his shoulder, the impact slamming him to the ground. A soldier standing next to the brother was clutching the shaft of the arrow protruding from his own chest.

Iba seemed to appear and disappear just as quickly. Twice she appeared beside a soldier in black, stabbing him and then disappearing once again.

"Titan, frost bolt," Sister Gale intoned. A thick layer of ice crystals formed about her hands. She knitted her fingers together and pushed the power outwards, aiming it at one of the three guards about to swarm Indie. The bolt sizzled through the air, changing direction to follow the intended target. A moment later, it struck a female guard high in the ribs, sending her skidding across the room's tiled floor. In moments, the soldier's skin turned blue and then white.

"Aura of healing," Sister Gale called out. A deep green ring appeared around her, spreading out three paces in all directions. She pulled her kali sticks from her belt and raced towards one of the black armored men.

"Don't let their dark magic touch you." Iba blurred past the priest. Sister Gale nodded and moved to a flanking position. Her target, one of the three remaining battle mages, was locked on Kit, throwing swirling purple-black spheres at the girl. It was impossible to tell if they were hurting the little priest or not. They seemed to disintegrate on contact with her swirling inferno. But with each strike, Kit seemed to slow, her steps appearing to be labored.

Closing in on the battle mage's rear flank, Sister Gale delivered a series of rapid blows about the man's head and neck, but it seemed to have little effect against his armor. She changed tactics as the man turned towards her, attacking his knees with a flurry of kicks. Despite the grimace of obvious pain, the battle mage called upon his powers. A surge of lightning crackled around his gauntleted fists, and with a sneer, he struck out at the female priest standing before him. Sister Gale leaned back, allowing the strike to arc harmlessly past her face. As soon as the man's fist was clear, she struck his elbow multiple times with her kali sticks before giving him a sidekick at the back of his leg. There was a loud crack, followed by a bellow. As the man dropped to a knee, she brought her right leg around, raising it until it was straight over her head, and brought her heel down on the man's shoulder, knocking him face first onto the floor. She placed her hand across the nape of his neck, gripping it tightly.

"Freeze," she yelled. The man's body instantly went rigid. When she pulled her hand back, his neck was a solid block of ice.

"Sister," Indie warned, drawing her mind back to the battle. A heartbeat later, an arrow whizzed over her head, striking the guard that was standing over her. The arrow embedded itself into the man's wrist, forcing him to drop his raised blade. Sister Gale picked up the sword before it bounced a second time and rammed its point into the man's throat.

Sister Gale pulled her blade from the soldier's neck, seeking her next opponent. None could be seen. Kit wailed, standing near the altar atop a raised dais. She peered up at her father, her body shaking uncontrollably. The man was dangling by his feet from the ceiling, his hands bound behind his back, slowly spinning like meat on a spit. His near-naked body was a mass of deep gashes, ghastly bruises, and dried blood.

"Oh, sweet Titan," the combat teacher said when her eyes fell upon the body of Sister Miyuki. She, too, was dangling from the ceiling by her neck. Her face was a battered mess. They bound her hands behind her back. Her feet and the bottom of her robes were black, covered with burns and scorch marks.

"Indie, help me," Kit wailed. She was reaching out for her father but unable to place her hands upon him. She was still wreathed in flames. "Indie, please," she called again. Indie threw his bow aside and sped up the stairs to the dais. All he could do was support Captain Harding, to take some pressure off the chains that were wrapped around his ankles.

"Take his weight," the deep, baritone voice of Amara called out, as she and Lin came through the doors into the altar room. "I'll release the lock holding him in place."

Indie adjusted his grip, wrapping his arms around the enormous man's chest. With a grunt, he lifted him high enough that the chains holding Kit's father slackened. "Now," he groaned out, signaling to Amara. The giant pulled a lever on the opposite wall. The spool spun freely, allowing the man to be lowered.

"Amara," Sister Gale called out. "I'll get Miyuki." The teacher bolted up the dais and folded her arms around the rotund sister's legs. When she was ready, Amara pulled a second lever, releasing the chains. Despite the excessive weight of the Temple's head baker, Sister Gale caught her and lowered her gently to the ground.

"Here." Lin handed the combat instructor a vial. "It's a healing potion."

Sister Gale questioned whether the potion was what Lin had said it was, but it didn't matter. Sister Miyuki had already passed on. There was no potion, or spell, or miracle that could bring her back.

"Oh, Miyuki." Sister Gale tried to tidy the woman's hair that was stuck to her battered face. "Why would they do this to you? Why would anybody hurt such a tender soul?" She pulled the woman to her breast, wrapped her arms around her, and wept uncontrollably.

⚬⚬⚬⚬⚬◊⚬⚬⚬⚬⚬

"Father," Kit howled, the last of her flames finally subsiding. When her fires had fully abated, she rushed to the man's side. His injuries were severe. He had bruises so deep they could be seen through the caked blood that covered his skin. Without thinking, Kit called upon her healing powers, but they would not come. She stared down at her still rune-covered hands. She wanted to call on Titan's healing graces, but it wouldn't be enough. Slipping her hand under his body, she pulled the big man up, placing his head on her lap.

Kit scowled at her bone-white fingers as they ran over her father's forehead. Her daemon self gave her tremendous power, but it came at a heavy cost. While under its influence, she could not heal, and she could not tell lie from truth. Oh, but sweet Titan, it gave her power. The daemon's raw, undiluted wrath cared not about right and wrong. It suffered no regret. It was just blind rage. But this man lying before her didn't need that girl. He needed the angel, the person who could deliver justice but still see the goodness in people. He needed the girl who could heal him.

Once again, she called upon her healing power. She could feel its spark building in her chest, but she could not release it. The faintest of auras appeared around her hands, her still bone-white hands.

"Kit, wait." Lin took a knee beside her and held out a pair of deep red vials. "You don't know how grievous his wounds are. Give him these first." The woman's dark brown eyes reflected the flickering torchlight that surrounded them. "If nothing else, it will save you some pain when you... do your thing."

Kit nodded and accepted the two potions. She carefully poured the liquid of the first over the most severe wounds. With each drip, the skin knitted together, and the bruising lessened. Kit's chest was heaving as she watched her father's health return. After finishing the contents of the first vial, she lifted her father from her lap. She carefully tilted his head back and opened his mouth. In a similar fashion, she poured the contents of the vial over his lips. Holding her breath, she waited for him to swallow.

Seconds ticked by. When the captain finally swallowed the thick red liquid, Kit squealed with joy. As her father's eyes fluttered open, she begged him to finish drinking the potion, pouring it faster now. Within seconds, the color in his face returned to normal.

Still cradling her father in her lap, Kit's own healing powers burst forth, unbidden. Like a cascade of molten gold, her aura spread over the man. She squeezed her eyes closed just before she buckled over him. As the moments passed, Kit straightened up, her chest heaving from the exertion.

"Your hair." Her father looked up into the golden eyes of his daughter. His brow furrowed, thick wrinkles gathering across his forehead. "How did you get here?"

"It's not important right now." Kit placed her hand on his forehead. "All that matters is that you're alive." The big man's face crumpled. With effort, he pulled himself from his daughter's lap. Indie tried to offer him a hand up, receiving a glare from the captain for his efforts.

"There's something I need to tell you." He helped his daughter up from the stone floor. "Father Hoarfrost..." The man's voice fell off, unable to finish what he'd started.

"I know." Kit stared down at her feet. "I don't know what I'll do without him."

"We will carry him with us." Her father raised her chin, tipping his head to the side. "And we will use what he taught us. We can mourn him later, but right now, we will avenge him and Sister Miyuki." Kit nodded and wiped the tears from her cheek. She paused for a moment and stared up at her father. Her stomach knotted, and her mouth went dry.

"What of her?" she croaked out. "What's happened to Miyuki?"

"He murdered her," Sister Gale ground out. The priest was on the far side of her father. Kit pushed past the man to find Sister Gale clutching the head baker, rocking the woman in her arms like a mother would hold her infant. She spit on the body of Brother Powder, who was only a few paces away.

Kit stood motionless, trying to take in the scene before her. She couldn't understand what she was looking at. Why would anybody hurt Miyuki? It made no sense. She was the kindest, most caring person in the Temple. How?

"I'm sorry, Kit." Her father wrapped his arm around her shoulder. "They tried to use her to make me change sides. They wanted me to... Brother Powder kept healing me. He continuously tortured me. When that didn't work, he tortured the others in front of me."

"I understand," the girl replied, her voice calm. She shrugged her shoulders to free herself from her father's embrace. Her light golden skin paled as it, once again, turned bone white. The black runes followed shortly thereafter, covering every inch of her body. She strode across the dais, stopping when she was standing over the fallen brother. He had an arrow embedded into his shoulder, just above his collarbone.

"Why?" Kit asked. "What could anyone offer you to betray your family?"

The man laid still. Kit nudged him with the toe of her boot, but he didn't stir. He was still breathing, but his breaths were shallow, almost invisible. Feigning death was not a good look on a priest. Kit's own breathing was less shallow.

"Maybe you'll answer me now." She bent over, grasped the arrow embedded in his shoulder, and twisted it. The man's eyes flew open, and he screeched out. He tried to grab Kit's wrists, to stop what she was doing to him, but his efforts were futile. With a shove, she pushed the arrow deeper until its tip protruded from his back.

"Stop," he begged, turning his face away from the searing pain.

"Did you stop when your prisoners cried out?" She pulled the arrow out of him, cutting muscle and tissue along the way. "Did you give mercy when they begged you?" The man was now whimpering. Words came from his lips. They were incomprehensible gibberish. Kit pushed the bloody tip of the arrow against his throat.

"This is the last time I'll ask you nicely," she said. "I've got a full case of your special healing potions. I'm guessing I could keep this up for several days before it runs out."

"They want to overrun the city," he said. His eyes were swollen and red and they were totally crazed. "What did it matter? I might as well be on the winning side. I chose to live. They said I would want for nothing."

"You sold out everything you stood for, for gold? You betrayed the Temple in return for a rich-man's life?" Kit's eyes widened. "You poisoned Father? How could you do that?"

"Hurting Father Hoarfrost is my only regret." Powder's mouth screwed up as though he had just taken a bitter pill. "But as long as he breathed, the city would stand."

"You poisoned him, and then you gave him a rejuvenation potion." Kit remembered the tale Silverleaf had told her. "You could have given him an antidote instead." The man's lower lips quivered.

"I couldn't. If I had... I just couldn't. Everything was already in motion. If I had cured the poison, everyone would have known it was me. They'd have known I did it."

Silverleaf burst into the group. With all his might, he kicked Brother Powder in the ribs. "You made me help you kill him. He didn't need to take that rejuvenation potion. You could have stopped it." Silverleaf kicked him in the ribs again. "He killed Father! This useless sack of crap poisoned all the priests and acolytes! He murdered Sister Miyuki!" The boy was wailing at the top of his lungs. He was moving in for another kick before Amara restrained him.

"No," she whispered. "No. Beating him is not the answer. Killing him will serve no purpose." Silverleaf tried to reach out and grasp Brother Powder, but Amara's grip on him was too tight.

"Here." Lin held the dragon hammer out to Kit. "Cast judgment upon him. Letting him live will serve no purpose."

"Perhaps now is not the right time to decide," Kit's father suggested.

Fury appeared beside Kit. Captain Harding yelped at the sight of the draken. Brother Powder relieved himself, soiling his priestly robes. Kit took her hammer from Lin, her expression vacant.

"Why should he live?" Fury stared down at the man, considering Captain Harding's words.

"Because the transformation potions won't work if he's dead." Silverleaf's voice was muffled from within Amara's embrace. "We can use his form…"

"To find out the king's plans," Indie said. "We could get someone on the inside. Right now, we can only guess what's happening."

"Give him a complacency potion," Silverleaf added, now free of Amara. "He'll tell us everything he knows, and then we can use that information."

"I'd rather just kill him." Kit placed her foot across Brother Powder's throat. "I don't care what the king's plans are. We'll cast judgment on them all." She scanned each of her cohorts, looking for their reaction. Nobody would say anything, but it appeared they agreed with Silverleaf's plan. Kit shook her head and took her foot from the man's throat.

The cords in the little priest's neck pressed against her skin. Her head swiveled around. "Where are the boys?" Her voice was shaky, her eyes wide. "Where are Lump and Runt?"

"They never returned." Fury looked back at the entrance. "You sent them to check on Coldforge and Slate."

"Holy Helja," Kit growled. "Somebody take Powder to the storage room. I'll go see what's going on with the boys." Indie didn't wait to see who was going to take Brother Powder. He took off after Kit, followed by Lin and Sister Gale.

Captain Harding looked to the others, who were still standing around. "Who's Coldforge?"

Chapter Twenty-Six

All for One

If there were any more soldiers in the catacombs, Kit didn't see any as she raced up to the storage room. She had the light of her hammer on full, illuminating her path with blinding brightness. In the distance, she could see people coming towards her. They were too far away to make out who they were. If they were more of the king's soldiers, she would release her daemon and tear through them without compunction or remorse.

Kit lifted her hammer to shoulder height and increased her speed. It didn't matter that she was running down a hallway filled with the bodies of those long since passed. She was going to add a few more, and that suited her just fine. A pair of jade-green eyes stared at her from the darkness. Her footsteps slowed. A heartbeat later, her hammer's light fell upon Runt and Lump rushing toward her. She dropped her hammer to the ground, freeing her hands to embrace the furry pair as they knocked her to the rough wooden floor.

"Holy Helja," Coldforge yelled out. "And ye complains that I'm loud."

"Where were you?" Indie said, shaking his head at Kit as she rolled around on the tunnel floor with the boys.

"We came back with stacks of priests, but there was nobody there. Went back to get more," Slate said. He had a wheelbarrow with four people stacked up like sacks of wheat. "This is the last of them."

"How many did you bring back?" Sister Gale asked. Lin was at her side, puffing heavily.

"All that were there," Coldforge replied. "By my count, fourteen."

"That's all?" Lin asked. "There were only fourteen, and you got them all?" Kit lifted her head from Lump's fur, still scratching both of the boys.

"Where are the rest of them? There should be over two hundred." She turned to Indie, a profound sadness in her eyes. "You don't suppose they killed the rest of them, do you?"

"No," Sister Gale said. "I don't think so."

"Me neither," Slate added. "I think they've got the acolytes in the dining hall. It's the only place big enough to hold the lot of them." Sister Gale nodded in agreement.

"Once Fury awakens the priests, we can go rescue them," Sister Gale continued. "They're going to need an army to stand against a coordinated attack from us. We know the dining hall well. We can make a proper plan of attack this time."

"I say we go in through the main door and kill them all." Kit continued to let her fingers run through the boys' fur. "There can't be that many soldiers left. There were only a handful guarding Powder and my father. I think Father Hoarfrost took down a good many of them when he brought the nave down on their heads. No one could have survived that." Her throat clenched tight as she remembered the dead bodies crushed beneath the fallen stones, knowing that her friend and mentor was still buried beneath the same pile of rubble.

"They have hostages," Sister Gale said. "If we rush in, they might start killing them."

Lin smirked. "I doubt it. If they see Kit and Fury come bursting through the door, I expect they'll soil themselves the same way Powder did."

"I am a sight to behold." Fury appeared within the circle of cohorts, running his clawed fingers over the iridescent scales on his head. "If Lump here arrives in his dragon form, there won't be a tight butt-hole in the house. I've seen it happen before." He pulled back his lizard lips, exposing his long, pointed teeth. Kit could only surmise that this was his version of a smile. It did, however, also look like his snarl.

The rest of the group arrived a few minutes later. Captain Harding had a bound and gagged Brother Powder over his shoulder, while Amara was cradling the body of Sister Miyuki. Kit struggled to hold back her tears at the sight.

"We need to bring her to the Temple cemetery," Amara said. "So she can be properly buried."

Sister Gale nodded, her jaw firm. "We need to get Father's remains as well, so he can join his family."

A snarl crept across Kit's mouth. "We'll do all of that as soon as we rid the city of the king's people and everyone else who's helping them." She picked up her hammer and slid it into its sheath. "Fury, how long until you can awaken the rest?"

"With Lin's help," the draken said, "an hour or two, at the most. Her alchemy equipment is top-notch."

"Me and the lad can tear down the cages, like me kin did in Cormorant," Coldforge added. "We can make a good number of weapons from the steel."

A look of hopeful expectation appeared on Kit's face. "Indie and I can search the area to ensure there are no other soldiers patrolling the catacombs." Before the man could answer, Iba pushed through the crowd.

"No need," she said. "I've searched every bit of these crypts. There isn't a living soul anywhere to be found. Do you want me to search the Temple as well?"

"You searched the whole crypt?" Silverleaf said. "There are more tunnels down here than I could count."

"I didn't need to search everywhere." The Tahr placed her hands firmly on her hips. "Most of the tunnels have a thick layer of undisturbed dust on them. Nobody has been down those halls in many moons. I followed all the trafficked corridors that led to the Moreden mausoleum entrance, as well as the tunnels that lead to the Temple's crypt."

"The Temple crypt?" Kit asked. "Is that where Father's family is buried?"

"Along with every high priest who's served the Temple," Lin said.

"And every priest who died in the service of Titan," Sister Gale added.

It took longer than expected to revive the rescued priests and acolytes. There were also more questions than anybody had time to answer. Each time a priest was awakened from their magicked slumber, they wanted to know what had happened to them. After telling the same story for the third time, Sister Gale insisted the explanations wait until everyone could hear them, all at the same time.

There wasn't a single priest or acolyte who wasn't in agreement. They would pass judgment on every person involved in the coup.

"We can use the tunnels to take us to the Temple Mausoleum," Lin said, "or we can follow the river to Sister Nevara's classroom."

"It's not a river." Iba shook her head like she was still trying to chase the memory of the stench from her mind. "It's sewage runoff, and it's disgusting. I have an extremely sensitive nose."

"I think it's best we stick together," Sister Gale said, "smelly river or otherwise."

"There is strength in numbers," Captain Harding said, considering his options, "but if the rest of the Temple's faithful are being held in the dining room, we can split into two groups and attack from both sides of the hall, simultaneously. It's difficult to defend on two fronts."

Indie scrubbed the back of his neck. "What if, instead of attacking simultaneously, one team attacks first, coming through the main entrance? The king's people will react to the assault. If there is anyone guarding the back way into the dining hall, they'll likely leave their post to respond to the immediate threat. The second team can then attack from the rear. We'll likely catch them off guard."

"The lad's a natural tactician." Coldforge nodded. "I like his idea, but whoever goes through the main doors first is going to face a firestorm. I want to be on that team."

Every person in the group demanded they be a part of the vanguard. Kit tried several times to get them to settle down, but there were too many forceful personalities, and nobody seemed willing to compromise. A gout of blue flame from Fury brought the conversation to an immediate halt.

Kit blew out a breath. "Sister Gale, the priests have the best defensive spells of us all. I suggest you lead that team to breach the main entrance. The rest of us will come from behind and take them from the back." Kit turned to the priests. "Be wary of the soldiers in black armor. They're battle mages and they cast dark magic. It gets into your head and breaks your will. The magic makes you just want to give up and die."

"The shield potions I made might help against that," Lin said. "I could only make six vials, so we should save it for whoever plans to enter first." This brought about another burst of arguments between the priests, each of them vying for the role of being first through the door.

Fury blew another gout of flame over everyone's head, once again bringing the conversation to a halt.

Sister Gale tried to keep her voice as calm as possible. "Sister Kit, I will usher the priests through the main doors. I will decide who will have the honor of breaching the entrance. You take the acolytes and your menagerie up the back stairs. Wait until we are fully engaged and then make your attack."

"Sister Gale," Amara interrupted. "If it's all the same to you, Silverleaf and I want to stay with Kit." Silverleaf acknowledged his agreement, nodding his head frantically. Sister Gale grinned in response.

"You inspire loyalty among your friends, Sister Kit. It might be best if they stay with your group. They can provide your team with magic support."

"We're going to be going up against fully armed and armored soldiers," Captain Harding said. "And outside of Kit, Lin, and Indie, nobody else is wearing any armor or carrying any weapons of note. We have two crossbows and some steel bars. Do you not think we should stop by the Temple armory and get some actual equipment?"

"The armory is in the basement." Sister Gale wrinkled her nose. "It looks like we're going to take the smelly river to Sister Nevara's classroom."

"Where is Sister Nevara?" Kit asked. "She wasn't a captive." Brother Snowpack stepped forward, his wild set of braids bobbing atop his head.

"Nevara escaped with the children at the first sign of trouble. I expect they are all safely ensconced in her secret chambers. She will either wait there until they run out of food and water, or until someone goes down to tell them the threat is over. But nobody, save Father Hoarfrost, knows where the room is located."

"That's not entirely true," Lin said. "I know where they are."

"As do I," Iba added. Kit didn't know that Iba was even in the room with them. She had been so quiet. She had disappeared shortly after the arguments had broken out. "And, if anyone's interested, I estimate that you'll be facing eight battle mages, and about a dozen soldiers."

"How can you know that?" Sister Gale asked, taken aback by the information the Tahr was providing.

"I just came back from the dining hall," she replied with a grin and a shrug. "I had nothing to do for the last while, so I went to scout on ahead to see what we were facing."

"You are a credit to your race, Sneaks," Fury said. "That's just one of many reasons we dragon lords like your kind."

"They've got the numbers and they're in an entrenched position," Captain Harding said, scrubbing his face with his thick, meaty hands. "We'll have surprise and confusion on our side, but if we don't do this properly..."

"There's more to tell," Iba said, interrupting the captain. "There are two priests with them. The way they were interacting with the battle mages, I think they're working with them."

"Who?" Kit continued scanning the priests present, trying to see who was missing.

"Brother Rimes, and an old priest that I didn't recognize. He was wearing robes of white and green."

"Sweet frookin' Helja." Kit burst into flames at the news. Those priests who were unaware of Kit's special abilities backed away and took a battle stance. One went so far as to start casting her battle magic. She only stopped when Sister Gale told them to be at peace.

"Tyr is working with Brother Rimes." Kit spat out the words. "I'll crush the pair of them. I'll bet Rimes was behind Miyuki's death. She had suspected that he was up to something. And I'll bet Tyr's been pulling the strings all along."

"You can't fight a god or a Fate, or whatever he is," Indie said. "We stand no chance against them."

"I don't care!" Kit's eyes were black as the abyss itself. "I will either destroy him, or I'll die trying. You people can stay here and cower, but I'm going."

"Your mate is correct," Fury said. "We cannot face Tyr. Even if he was alone, without the support of battle mages and soldiers, he could decimate you with a thought." Kit scowled at the draken, drew her hammer, and threw it across the room. Fury disappeared, only to reappear beside the hammer.

"You can stay here, too." Kit pulled her lips back in a snarl. "I'm going, with or without you." Runt and Lump ran to her side, whining at the flames that were swirling around her. Lump changed into his dragon form and stepped inside the ring of fire. He stared up at her with his big brown eyes. He unfurled his wings and wrapped them around her. Kit's flames died out.

"Didn't you say that Tyr isn't allowed to interfere?" Indie stepped in close. "You said he can only influence things. He can't act directly. We might not need to fight him." Kit glanced over at him, and a profound sadness swept across her face. The blackness in her eyes melted away, leaving behind the pools of gold.

"If you're going to fight Tyr, then I'm going to fight with you. If I die by your side, then so be it. I wouldn't want to live without you anyway." Kit's breath hitched at the man's words. With everything she had done to him, he still loved her. He still wanted to be with her.

"Ye saved me life, so I'm already on borrowed time." Coldforge bowed his head. "I will follow wherever you lead." Runt barked his agreement. After switching back into dog form, Lump did the same.

"You won't face Tyr alone." Her father wrapped his arms around Kit. He surveyed the group, nodding to each person who stepped forward. "I'm fairly certain that everyone here will fight by your side, regardless of the odds."

CHAPTER TWENTY-SEVEN

AT ANY COST

Although nobody balked at it, there wasn't a cheerful face among the lot as they wended their way along the underground stream that reeked of sewage. It was a necessary evil they needed to endure if they were going to retrieve weapons and armor from the Temple's armory. From the tunnel, they emerged into Sister Nevara's classroom. From there, they continued on through the basement corridors until they arrived at their destination. The room was immense, holding an impressive arsenal. With practiced precision, the priests spread out across the room, equipping themselves with either hammer or ax, a large heavy shield, and splint mail.

Coldforge was forced to get himself yet another new ax, after Kit had once again incinerated the one she had borrowed. He found a double-sided ax that was very much to his liking. There was also a variety of bows and arrows present, but not a single priest nor acolyte showed any interest in them. Indie and Lin replenished their stock, choosing the broad-tipped hunting arrows. Silverleaf, unlike the other priests, selected a hunting bow for himself. Like Indie and Lin, he also chose broad-tipped hunting arrows.

Silverleaf motioned to a huge glaive on a rack of pole arms. The weapon was at least twelve feet long, with an enormous blade at one end. The other end of the weapon featured a steel spike. "I think they made this one for you," he said with a hint of a smile. Amara blew out a long breath and took the weapon.

Leaving the armory, they traveled farther towards the dining hall's front door. Kit suggested that her team wait in the stairwell until they heard Sister Gale's team start their attack. Once they were engaged, they'd come up the stairs and enter through the rear of the hall.

With everyone in agreement, Kit and her cohorts split off from the priests and made their way to the stairway that would take them from the kitchens up to the back of the dining hall. Kit's stomach twisted as they moved through the galley, knowing that she'd never again have a meal with her friend, Miyuki. The woman's death spurred on Kit's desire to annihilate every enemy present, especially Brother Rimes and Tyr. She would grieve for her friend later.

The group came to a sudden halt when they encountered a wall of thick iron bars barring their way up the stairs.

"Now what?" Indie asked. "We don't have time to go back to the main hall and we can't get up this way."

"We'll be okay." Kit gripped one of the metal poles, her hands instantly bursting into flame. She pumped as much heat as she could into it, but all she managed was to bring about a bright red glow to the metal.

"Allow me." Fury said, appearing beside Kit. Behind the group, Iba bleated. Fury blew a concentrated gout of his blue flame at the bar Kit had been working on. The bright red glow on the iron pole became white hot. Regardless, it refused to yield.

"Runt, my friend." Coldforge's eyes were alight. "Do ye think ye can blow some ice onto this, right here?" The dwarf pointed to the still white-hot metal. Runt stepped up and blew a tight cone of frost where the dwarf had pointed. Once the thick fog had dissipated, the white-hot bar had changed to a dull black. Coldforge's whiskers were dancing on his face as he wrapped his hands around the iron pole and snapped out a sizeable chunk.

"They're made of cold-iron. They're almost impervious to fire, but the metal can't withstand rapid temperature changes. It becomes as brittle as glass." With Fury and Runt working in concert, in minutes they had snapped off enough pieces that they could easily get past.

"Nobody makes a sound." Kit followed her father as he led the group up the stairs. "Nobody acts until Sister Gale and the others are fully engaged." Coldforge nodded and put his hand over his mouth. When they'd made it to the rear entrance of the dining hall, everyone prepared themselves, waiting for the priests to come in through the main doors.

They continued to wait. And then they waited some more, and then some more. Minutes passed like hours.

"What's taking them so long?" Indie whispered to nobody in particular.

"Maybe the way is barred, like ours was," Lin offered, her voice no louder than a soft breath.

"I had followed soldiers into the hall," Iba said. "There were no bars, but maybe they've magically locked the door?"

"How long do we wait?" Coldforge tightened his grip on his war ax. He thumbed the weapon's edge, testing it for sharpness.

"Someone's trying to breach the door," a voice shouted out from within the dining hall. "Make ready," another person called out. "Start with flame spells and then switch to necrotic. Guardsmen, hold until we've launched our attack."

"They're going to be eviscerated," Captain Harding growled. "We need to distract the battle mages before Sister Gale comes through those doors." The words had only just formed on the man's lips when Coldforge blew past the group, riding atop a snarling Runt. Lump, who had already changed into his gold dragon form, was close behind them.

"By Gimlie's beard, you will pay," Coldforge yelled, followed by a series of whoops, barks, and roars.

The others may or may not have heard Kit swear as she ignited her hammer and followed Coldforge and the boys into battle. Lin and Indie, with their bows nocked, followed her with Captain Harding close behind, a massive bastard sword in his hand.

"You may need to use your glaive," Silverleaf said to Amara. "You may need to kill." Amara's face was dark. She blew out a breath and nodded.

"I'll stay with Harding. You keep with Lin and Indie," Amara said as she bolted into the fray. "Aura of defense," she called out, a deep yellow glow emanating from her body.

Silverleaf shivered. The only actual combat he had ever been in was when he had battled a necromancer and his undead minions in the bowels of the catacombs. He had never witnessed warfare on this scale. He feared for Amara, that she would not be willing to use her weapon to kill. That moment of indecision could cost his best friend her life. He was just about to move into action when a thunderous boom rocked the building. The multitude of voices doubled, some bellowing out orders while others were crying out in pain.

"Titan, ranger's mark," Silverleaf called out as he, too, joined into the fray, a pale blue-green aura clinging to him as he moved forward.

He had barely crossed the threshold into the rear of the hall as utter chaos filled the room. Allies and enemies were clashing, the deadly music of steel ringing out, reverberating off the walls. The pitched battle was in full bloom. To the side, huddled like a group of robed statues, were the acolytes. They stood motionless, clutching onto one another, frozen in time.

It took all the young half elf's fortitude to move in beside Indie and Lin, who were standing in front of the statue of Fenrir. As soon as he came into range, his aura expanded to engulf the pair of archers who were firing arrows as fast as they could draw them from their quivers.

He had never seen the Temple priests in combat before, at least not outside of the training field. They moved and worked as a unit. Those who were in melee acted as a shield for those who were casting blessing spells, auras designed to enhance the skills of the warriors they were supporting. Spells from the battle mages seemed to disintegrate as they hit the priests, apparently doing only minor damage when they made contact.

Sister Gale had split off from the primary group. She was working her way through the soldiers. She parried their attacks and unleashed her own devastating blows with her ferrouswood kali sticks. Her poise and grace in combat made her look more like a dancer than a warrior. Everything she did was one continuous, fluid motion.

In stark contrast to the woman's grace, Runt, Lump, and Coldforge more closely resembled a battering ram, crashing into the enemy with enough force to send them careening across the room. Runt and Coldforge seemed to work in tandem. Runt was blasting enemies with his frost attack while the dwarf chopped down the incapacitated target. Lump, in his gold dragon form, was flaming any enemy within ten paces. Those who were not set ablaze dove behind overturned tables, trying to escape the dragon's searing breath.

Amara and Captain Harding had worked their way towards Sister Gale. They were engaged with two battle mages who were fighting beside great hulking beasts. The captain's blade sliced deep into the creature. It bellowed out in pain just before disappearing into a puff of purple smoke. A moment later, the creature reappeared at the captain's back, swiping at him with horrible gray-green claws. Amara could deflect the creature's blow, allowing the captain to strike it once again with his bastard sword. Again, the creature bellowed out and disappeared in a wisp of purple smoke. Amara gave a look of horrified exasperation as the beast reappeared at the man's back, raking him with its wicked claws.

The giant stepped towards the beast, ready to strike it with her glaive. She changed directions, mid swing, bringing the weapon's enormous blade down onto the battle mage who was controlling the creature. The blade caught the man just beside his shoulder, splitting him in half. The summoned creature disappeared, leaving the familiar purple mist behind. This time, it did not return.

"Kill the summoner," Captain Harding ordered. "I'll hold off the beast."

Before the priest could react, Amara had already brought her glaive to bear. With a sideways arcing swing, she cleaved the second battle mage, cutting him in half just below his chest. His summoned creature disappeared in another puff of purple smoke.

Silverleaf hadn't noticed that both Indie and Lin had moved away, throwing themselves into the melee. Their bows were on the tiled floor in front of him. He had been too busy watching his friend, the pacifistic giant, who was now barrelling across the room, destroying anything and anyone who was within reach of her twelve-foot pole arm. The woman's straw-colored ponytail swung about as she moved. She did not match her combat instructor's grace, but she more than made up for it with sheer ferocity.

The half elf's eyes fell on Kit. She was beyond the dais, standing before an aged priest and Brother Rimes. Beside Kit was the floating body of Iba, a look of pure fury on her face. She seemed to be paralyzed, her arms splayed out behind her. Kit's dragon hammer was poised to strike, but she was not attacking. She was shouting at the pair of priests before her, her words lost in the battle's din. Most unexpectedly, the cacophony of sounds abated, the last of the soldiers and battle mages having fallen against the onslaught that had descended upon them. Kit's words suddenly became audible, even if they were mostly unintelligible.

Brother Rimes threw back his head and laughed as everyone moved in behind Kit. This seemed to enrage Kit all the more. She pointed her hammer at the priest and released a tight gout of brilliant blue flames. The fire parted and swirled about the priest, never coming close enough to do him harm. The old priest, the one Kit had called Tyr, had a bewildered look on his face. He seemed to find the encounter amusing or, at the very least, entertaining.

Kit lowered her hammer, and the flames died off. A moment later, Fury appeared before Kit. He took a step towards Brother Rimes and halted. A grimace twisted his face, as though he was struggling against an indomitable force. He opened his mouth, as though to release his own flame attack, but nothing happened. Motionless, he just stood there. Silverleaf looked to his cohorts, who had gathered behind Kit. Each of them was similarly frozen, as though petrified by a gorgon or a basilisk.

***

"Tyr." Kit's eyes were swirling pools of gold. "Release them. End this now. Why are you protecting this man?"

"I am doing no such thing." Tyr morphed from his elderly priest persona into that of a young, virile Nomad. "I am only observing." The Fate's comment made Brother Rimes laugh all the harder.

"Liar!" It was the only thing Kit could think to say, even though she knew he was telling the truth. There was no way Brother Rimes had the power he was wielding. She doubted that even Father Hoarfrost had possessed these types of powers. Brother Rimes turned to Tyr, his mouth tied up into a tight knot. He stared at him for several seconds while Tyr's expression remained stoic. A moment later, Brother Rimes burst out laughing yet again. His eyes were filled with tears as he threw his head back, laughing maniacally. While the man laughed, Kit walked up and punched him in the throat.

Brother Rimes clutched his neck, his mirth falling away, replaced with undiluted rage.

"You would dare to strike me?" A swirl of black smoke appeared around his feet. "You impudent child. Bow before your betters." The priest stretched out his hand over Kit. When she didn't move, his brows knit together, and a sneer contorted his mouth. Tiny beads of sweat appeared along his hairline as he pushed his magic at the girl, the veins in his temple pulsating.

"Your magic isn't as strong as you think, Brother." Kit's voice was filled with contempt.

"It's not possible," he replied, tilting his head to the side.

"I hear that a lot." Kit kicked the man just above his knee, knocking him to the ground. With a spin, she brought her flaming war hammer down onto his head. The hammer slammed into something impenetrable just before contact. The impact was jarring. It sent reverberations up the dragon-bone handle, stinging her hands. The girl's grip faltered, sending the hammer spinning across the floor. From his prone position, Brother Rimes raised his head and laughed yet again.

"And you are not as strong as you think you are." He began lifting himself up off the ground, getting as far as his knees, before Kit kicked him fully in the face, sending him, once again, back to the floor.

"Whatever you're doing to protect yourself, it's not exactly working for you." There was a hint of laughter in Kit's voice. Before the priest could right himself, she kicked him yet again, sending the man skittering across the floor. The black mist that had gathered at his feet now fully engulfed his body.

He must be possessed by a demon, the same way that Xin was in Templeton.

Kit growled and took a menacing step forward. "Foul creature, remove yourself from this man. Face me directly, if you dare." Kit's challenge made Tyr laugh.

"Be careful what you ask for," he said to Kit, his eyes fixed on Brother Rimes. "Then again, you've done more damage than either of us could have ever expected. My friend here has already broken the rules and will face the power of the four."

Brother Rimes snarled. "And if I do, I will take you with me to oblivion." The black smoke that had been swirling about him turned into a writhing mass of fireflies. They rose from the priest's body until they coalesced into a robust woman, a mass of patchwork flesh and writhing black clouds.

"Eris!" Kit roared.

A familiar voice whispered in Kit's ear. "Kill Tyr." She turned to find no one there. "Kill him and I will free you of your debt to me," the voice whispered again.

"Tiamat?" Kit spun to see where the woman was.

"The power is within you. Kill him now and I will give your life back to you. In doing so, it will upset the balance and we will prevail." Kit glanced over at Tyr, who had a bemused look on his face.

"You're lying to me." Kit was still searching the room, trying to discover the source of the voice. "I don't know who you are, but you are not Tiamat."

"Your ruse failed, Tyche," Tyr said. "As I told you, she is wondrous."

And with that, Tyr disappeared, along with the swirling mass of fireflies. In the distance, a coyote howled.

For the briefest of moments, the room was quiet and still, everything frozen in time.

When the power holding Kit's allies suddenly released, Iba crashed down to the floor. While three of the priests rushed to the Tahr's side, everyone else flocked to Kit.

"What just happened?" Sister Gale's words unleashed a fury of more questions. Everyone shouted over each other as their minds desperately trying to understand what had just unfolded before them. Lump, back in his dog form, along with Runt, pushed their way through the group, offering Kit their strength and comfort.

"Tyr is up to something, but I don't know what." Kit strode towards Brother Rimes, who was lying unconscious on the floor. "Maybe Rimes will have some answers."

"Who were those people?" Sister Gale moved to the far side of Brother Rimes. "This Tyr person seems to wield tremendous power."

"He's a Fate," Indie said. "One of the gods who has been tormenting this world."

"It's a long story," Captain Harding said, seeing the vacant expression on Sister Gale's face. "Once we get Brother Rimes safely into custody, I can tell you all about it." The man gathered the priest from the ground and tossed him over his shoulder like a sack of potatoes.

Silverleaf called out from within the gathered throng. "Kit, help me. Kit, please, Amara needs help." The young man's hands were shaking badly as he scrubbed at his chest. Kit's heart jumped up into her throat.

"What is it? Is she hurt?" Silverleaf didn't respond. He turned and worked his way back through the crowd. Following behind him, Kit's pulse thrummed in her ears. As soon as they broke through, she found Amara sitting on the ground, her arms wrapped around her knees, her face buried under her mass of golden hair.

"Amara," Kit called out to her, taking a knee beside the giant. She gave Silverleaf a questioning look, hoping for an explanation.

The half elf deflated as he looked down on his friends. "She killed two people to protect your father."

Kit's eyes went wide, her stomach knotting. With care, she took the woman in her arms. "Thank you." She pressed her lips to the giant's ear. "What you did for my father. I understand..."

Amara lifted her head, her face wet with tears, her eyes already swollen. "He was... they were going to kill him." Amara's voice was thick and gravelly. "There was no other option."

"I know." Kit's golden aura appeared, unbidden. "It was unfair that you had to do that." The golden glow poured out, wrapping itself around the pair.

"Titan should have struck me down." Amara sniffed loudly. "Killing is forbidden within my clan. I broke my vows to my people." Before Kit could speak, she continued. "But I didn't care that I broke my laws. After I murdered those men, I sought more. I wanted to kill more of them."

"Battle fever." Kit's aura glowed with increasing intensity. "The will to survive at all costs, it changes us."

"And now that the battle is over, all I feel is shame. Shame because I don't feel bad for killing them. I took two lives, Kit. I don't care that I did. Without hesitation, I would do it again."

"We do what we have to, to protect the people we care about." Kit pursed her lips. Why did she, herself, never feel remorse for delivering justice? She cherished the lives of everyone around her and mourned the loss of those who left to join the Great Cycle, but she never concerned herself about those whom she'd killed, those whom she'd passed summary judgment upon. The golden aura that had surrounded the pair of women faded away.

"Are you okay, Sister Kit?" Amara's expression was now a picture of concern.

Kit gave her friend a weak smile and nodded. She rose to her feet and offered to help Amara from the floor. "Thank you for saving my father."

"Better?" Silverleaf took his friend's hand. "Why don't we go check on the acolytes? They're going to need your strength." Amara nodded and gave Silverleaf a crooked smile.

Chapter Twenty-Eight

For the Children

The first rays of the morning's sun were just breaking over the horizon, filling the dining hall with a cold, pale-gold light. Kit and Lin were both inconsolable, lamenting over the death of Father Hoarfrost and their dear friend, Sister Miyuki. It was the first time they thought about the loss of their friends. Their grief consumed them.

Amara and Silverleaf had gone back down into the catacombs to retrieve the remains of Sister Miyuki. A contingent of priests had joined them, in case they met any more of the king's men, but mostly to *escort* Brother Powder back to the Temple. Several acolytes had been sent downstairs to the kitchens to bring food and drink. Indie and the boys watched over them, even though nobody expected any trouble. When they returned with the food, Kit couldn't bring herself to eat. She simply had no appetite.

While everyone waited for instructions on how to proceed, some of the priests busied themselves, gathering the bodies of those who had died during the battle in the dining hall. Table linens were used as burial shrouds, as they treated the bodies of ally and enemy alike, with reverence and respect.

A tightness had found its way into Kit's chest, and it refused to loosen. Her eyes were dry and swollen from tears that had refused to abate. Approaching footsteps, clomping on the stone-tiled floor, drew her attention.

"Kit." Her father's voice was full of concern. "We've interrogated Brother Rimes. He is either the best liar in all of Arnnor or he knows nothing of what has transpired. Do you want to question him and… do what you do to ferret out the truth?" Kit considered her father's words. What she really wanted to do was execute the traitor.

"No." She wiped her tear-stained face with her sleeve. Kit stared up at her father from her place on the floor. "I'd rather deliver justice upon him."

"That is probably the right course of action, but it's going to have to wait. We're going to go hunt down Karr and anybody else who's still working with him. We need to flush out the last of the king's people and release the City Watch prisoners."

"Do you know where to find Karr?" she asked.

Her father gave Kit a small nod. "I expect so. But I want you to stay here and rest. We've got this."

A thankful, loving smile crossed Kit's lips for a moment before it transformed into a deep scowl. "I can rest once we've retaken the city and destroyed the evil growing within."

"I told you so." Indie held out two vials of swirling gold-orange and red liquid.

Kit accepted the two vials and handed one to Lin before downing the other. Her body shuddered as the potion's power coursed through her. The tightness in her chest was still there, but she would use it as fuel to press forward.

"Wow." Lin sidled up to Kit. Like Kit's, the woman's eyes were swollen and red, but they were filled with resolve. "I feel like I could run from here to Cormorant. Those potions are incredible. If they don't cause you to become debilitated when they wear off..."

"Where are we going?" Kit asked her father, cutting Lin short.

"My guess is, he's taken up residence in my quarters." Captain Harding's eyes were hard as flint. "In my house... near the Temple."

"The only house near the Temple..." Kit's words trailed off as her mouth flopped open.

"Is the Royal Manor!" Lin finished. "You live in the mansion beside the Temple grounds?"

"Yes." The captain appeared rather sheepish. "It came with the post. The city built it for my predecessor General Kren Eagle Claw."

"But the Manor has always looked abandoned." Lin knitted her brow. "We used to sneak into it when I was... younger."

"That's because neither Kren nor I ever wanted to live there." The man cocked an eyebrow at Lin. "We both preferred to sleep in the barracks with our soldiers."

"Captain, the sun's going to be fully up soon." Coldforge spun his double-bladed ax in his hand, his eyes twinkling with desire, ready to put his weapon to use. "I expect we'll just parade through the front door and finish them?" The dwarf clearly liked the idea of a frontal assault.

"There's another way." Lin looked to Kit. "The exit from Sister Nevara's classroom leads to the manor's back gardens. It's just one of the many hidden paths for the sister to take to make sure the children are safe."

"And how is it you know about it?" Indie crossed his arms and ground his teeth.

"Sister Nevara told me." Lin stuck her tongue out. "Well, she didn't tell me personally. She spoke about it with Father Hoarfrost, and I was in the room."

"Why would she speak of secret exits with you there?" Indie probed further, making Lin squirm under his gaze.

"Because they didn't know I was in Father's office." Lin was turning bright red. "I was... invisible."

"What?" Kit and Indie exclaimed in unison.

"You're the reason Father Hoarfrost had the mage-eyes installed in the Temple," Captain Harding said. "He had said there were *spies* in the Temple, but he never told me who they were."

"Mage-eyes?" Kit and Indie asked, again in unison.

"They're magical devices capable of seeing through invisibility spells." Lin turned an even brighter shade of red. "They also let Father know if there were people lurking outside his office."

"That's how he knew! I thought he could read my mind." Kit blinked as her memories drifted back to all the times Father Hoarfrost miraculously knew she was outside his office or what she had been up to.

"I don't think I should go with ya." Coldforge shook his head. "You're going to be sneakin' and that's not what I do."

"I agree," the captain replied. "I think we should march up to the front door with the priests and acolytes, the same as we did here in the dining hall. While we draw their attention out front, the rest of you enter through the back."

"I've still got a few more scrolls of silence," Silverleaf said as he and Amara joined the group. He was rummaging in the sack he kept at his hip.

"I don't enjoy sneakin'." Coldforge batted the half elf's hand away from his sack of scrolls. "But makin' 'em fight on two fronts is an excellent plan. It's not very dwarven, but it's a good plan all the same."

"Lin?" Kit asked. "Can you call on Titan to cast an aura of healing or an aura of protection?"

"I've never been able to call on Titan for anything," Lin confessed, shaking her head. "I'm pretty sure my grandmother was the only reason Father Hoarfrost even let me stay at the Temple."

"Fury?" Kit summoned the draken to stand before her. "Would it be okay if I lent you to Coldforge? They could use some extra *fire power* if things go badly for them."

The sky-blue draken considered the request for a moment, giving the dwarf an appraising stare. "I would be honored to fight beside the dwarven prince. He has the heart of a dragon and the soul of a warrior."

With a bow to the draken, Kit handed her mithril hammer to Coldforge, who handed her his double-bladed ax. The dwarf was salivating as he examined the weapon, testing it for weight and balance.

"It's a bit light," he said with a hairy-faced grin.

"And yours is forward-heavy," Kit said in return, as she gave it a few tries. "Recovery from a swing will be a challenge. It's likely going to pull me off balance."

"Ye just need a bit more... muscle." Coldforge's broad smile was hidden behind his unruly orange beard.

"Titan provides," Kit said in response.

While Captain Harding, Coldforge, the priests, and the acolytes made their way through the Temple to the manor's front garden, Kit and the rest of her cohorts traveled from the dining hall to Sister Nevara's classroom. They opened the trapdoor and slipped down below. Rather than follow the path that would have taken them back to the catacombs, they went in the opposite direction. The putrid air in the tunnel was just as revolting as the last time they had used it.

"I'm going to make sure the way is clear." Iba took off ahead of the group.

"Go with her," Kit said to the boys. In seconds, the trio disappeared into the darkness.

"Will she be okay on her own?" Slate asked. Like the Tahr, he, too, had excellent night vision, a trait all of his people shared. Silverleaf snorted at the comment, drawing a chuckle from Amara.

Lin lit the fires on her twin long swords, illuminating the tunnel with their flickering orange and red flames. After following the tunnel for what smelled like an eternity, the walls changed from packed earth to meticulously crafted stone. A small bridge marked the transition, taking the group away from the fetid stream. Iba and the boys stood on the far side of the bridge.

"Not a soul," Iba said. "Outside of Sister Nevara and the children, I don't think anybody has been this way."

Kit cocked her head to the side. "Sister Nevara was here? How do you know?" Iba tapped the side of her nose in response. "Okay then," Kit continued. "If there are no enemies ahead, let's pick up the pace. We don't want my father to get to the manor before us."

The group broke into a slow run, following the stone tunnel for ten more minutes. Finally, Lin called for everyone to stop.

"The doorway we want is here." Lin handed her flaming blades to Iba.

"Where does this door take us?" Kit tugged on her shield's straps, tightening it around her forearm. She objected to Indie's insistence that she take one, but since she was wielding a weapon that she was unfamiliar with, she reluctantly accepted.

"Right out into the manor's back garden." Lin took a position in front of a solid stone wall. Without the burden of her swords, she ran her fingers along the thin mortar seams, around waist height. After several seconds of searching, she paused. With a tiny smile, she placed her hand against one of the lower blocks. She calmed herself with a deep, cleansing breath.

"For the children." Lin's voice was low and solemn. Immediately, there was a rumbling, and the wall transformed somewhat. The slightest seam appeared, revealing a doorway. Using only the lightest of touches, something akin to the strength of a small child, Lin pushed open the door, revealing a set of stairs that led upwards. She took her blades back from Iba and stepped forward. Before getting very far, Indie pushed past her, his own twin long swords at the ready.

The stairway led up to a storage shed. It was filled with tools and gardening implements. It smelled of oiled steel and aromatic cedar. The shed had two doors, one on the left side of the room and another across from where they had entered.

"Which door?" Indie asked, looking back at Lin.

"Just wait," she said with a mocking tone. Within seconds, the door on the left and the door they had come through vanished from sight.

"That's incredible." Slate was inspecting the thick wooden walls, finding no sign of a door. "Where did that door lead to?"

"That door leads down to an enchanted maze that runs beneath the manor. If you find the door and you don't know the password to the maze, once you go in, you never come out. I'm expecting Sister Nevara took the children down there." Lin's eyes got a far-off look to them. "If Sister Nevara hadn't come looking for me, I would have likely died down there."

Iba gave the door an appraising stare. "I could smell they had come this way, but I'd have never been able to find them. Praise be to Titan."

Kit took Lin by her elbow. "As soon as we secure the city, let Nevara know she can return to the Temple."

"Are you all ready?" Indie interrupted. When everyone nodded, he opened the far door and stepped into the morning light, the boys bounding past the others to take up positions on the young man's flank.

"Hey," Kit called out with a hushed voice. "I'm the one with the shield. Maybe I should lead?"

"And I'm the one who knows the way." Lin moved in beside her friend.

"I'm good in the back." Silverleaf tested the pull on his hunting bow. "I'm not sure how much damage this bow will do against a battle mage, but I can keep them distracted, if nothing else. Maybe Slate can stay with me and provide some magic support?" The dwarf nodded, his eyes downcast, his bright orange beard sagging. The half elf prodded Slate in the ribs. "I need your help. I'm near useless with this bow. If you can cast ranger's mark on me, it'll help my aim."

"I want to be up front." Amara worked her way into the lead. She turned her face up towards the morning sun. "After we've retaken the city, I'll atone for my sins."

Kit craned her neck up at her giant friend. "You have nothing to atone for. What you did was a service to this city. People will live free because of your actions. Never forget it." Amara nodded curtly and renewed her grip on her glaive, its broad blade reflecting the sun's rays.

As the group exited the shed, they found themselves behind a screen of heavy foliage, blocking their view of the rear entrance to the manor. The air was thick with the aroma of early summer blossoms, creating an almost intoxicating effect.

"As soon as we clear this trellis," Lin whispered out, "we'll be about thirty paces from the back door. There are many windows at the rear of the manor. The chance of somebody spotting us is, well, extremely high."

"Nobody's going to notice us," Kit said with a grin. "My father is going to challenge Karr. Everyone will be at the front of the house."

"Challenge him?" Indie said. "What's he going to do, call him out to fight?" As though on cue, a voice called out with such volume that the leaves on the trellis trembled.

"Karr! Meet me in fair combat and let's end this."

"I gave him my pearl necklace," Kit said with a small grin, looking to Lin. "The one you made for me, to help project my voice. He's going to draw everyone's attention. Let's go."

Chapter Twenty-Nine

The Taking of Aarall

Darting out from behind the trellis, the group sprinted across the garden, and up to the manor's back entrance. Tall stately trees, manicured shrubs, and an abundance of flowering plants filled the yard. The group stayed to the grassy area, avoiding the pea-stone walkway for fear of making too much noise if they tread upon it. For a home that was supposedly unused, its yard was meticulously maintained.

Kit exhaled when they found the back entrance unlocked. As the group slipped in through the door, they could hear armored feet running across the home's highly polished tile floors.

"This way to the servants' quarters," Lin said. "We can cut through to get to the front of the house and slip in behind Karr." She gave Indie a wink and a playful elbow to the ribs when he nodded in agreement. Kit chuckled at the guttural sound he made in response.

Following Lin's lead, the group slipped through an enormous sitting room with tall, beveled glass windows overlooking the garden. Thick wool carpets helped to mask their footfalls as they snuck to a plain wooden door. Lin carefully opened it a crack to peer within before passing through the entranceway.

The room they entered more closely resembled a hallway than living quarters. There was an exposed stone wall along one side. Lin patted it as she walked, telling Kit that it used to be the exterior wall of the Temple. At the far side of the room was a single, narrow window illuminating the quarters with a tiny sliver of the morning light.

They had almost made it to the front of the room when Captain Harding boomed out. "Lieutenant Karr. You've lost. Step outside and let's put an end to this." The captain's words were met with silence. "Karr, come out and fight me. If you win, the Watch will follow you. They'll respect you for your strength."

Even without her special abilities, Kit would have known that was a lie. The Watch wouldn't respect him, ever. Moments later, the unmistakable sound of fireballs exploding and people screaming filled the air, followed by more footfalls and the clanking of armor. The clamor was so loud it was tough to tell how many people were being sent out.

"Kill them all," someone yelled. "By the king's command, you will kill them all."

The clank of footfalls changed to the clashing of steel and screams of pain. A pitched battle was going on outside, and Kit was not a part of it. Holding her shield out in front of herself, she opened the door that led to the front room. She ground her teeth at the sight of Karr and four guards dressed in black enameled armor. One guard was wearing a plumed helm that reminded Kit of the one King Karter was wearing in Cormorant. It annoyed her greatly that Karr wasn't taking part in the fight. He was sitting back, letting others do his dirty work for him.

"There are only four battle mages," Kit said. "At least that's all I can see."

"They're going to be the best of the lot," Indie replied. "Karr's going to keep the most powerful soldiers closest to him. Don't underestimate the mages just because we beat them at the Temple." Kit blew out her cheeks and nodded. She hadn't considered that these might be more powerful than the other mages they'd faced.

"*Titan, hear me,*" she whispered as she called upon her god for his strength. A light rush pulsed through her body, but not the full power of Titan. When she remembered she could only call on Titan's strength once per moon, Kit scrunched her eyes tight and dug deeper. "*Your strength is my strength, Amaruq. I call upon you in our hour of need.*"

"*I am with you, always,*" the wolf spirit responded in her mind. Unlike the freezing cold she felt calling upon Titan, the dire wolf's spirit filled her with warmth and a calm power. The weight of Kit's ax and shield were suddenly much lighter.

Kit stepped through the doorway. Karr and his guards were so busy watching Captain Harding and his people outside that no one noticed her movement.

"You fear my father?" Kit asked, striding towards Karr. "Perhaps you'd prefer to fight a *street rat*?"

Before his men reacted to Kit's sudden appearance, the usurper put himself between Kit and his men.

"Thank you," Karr said with a smug smile. "I didn't know how I was going to make your father and the rest of those blasted priests stand down. Now I do. They'll bow to me when they see I have the *Savior of Aarall*."

An arrow whizzed past Kit's ear, aimed at Karr. With no effort, the man caught the arrow inches from his face and snapped it in his hand. Kit remembered back to the training the Watch had gone through, learning to defend themselves from missile attacks. Apparently, the lieutenant had been an outstanding student.

"Can you catch an ax?" Kit asked, drawing back her weapon.

"Seize the little priest," Karr ordered, motioning to the battle mages. "Kill the others."

Two of Karr's four guards launched fireballs at the group. Kit wasn't sure what had happened to the flaming spheres that had flown past. She was busy dealing with the mage who had just cast a web spell at her. A thick glob of goop sprayed out from the woman's hands. It expanded outwards as it neared, turning into a wall of fibrous threads. Kit ducked behind her shield, blocking most of the sticky strands. Those that passed her guard clung to her arm and neck, with a good amount getting tangled in her hair.

The fourth guard, the one wearing the plumed helm, cast an aura spell of some sort, surrounding both himself and Karr in a luminescent midnight blue bubble. The look on Karr's face suggested he was not pleased with the mage's choice of spells. He was yelling at the man, but nothing could be heard outside the blue dome.

Ignoring the fire-casting mages, Kit headed for the woman who had attacked her.

"Get 'em, boys," she chuckled as her dire wolf and gold dragon-dog went racing past her. An arrow flew over their heads and bounced harmlessly off the shimmering blue orb surrounding Karr. Filled with the strength of Amaruq, she slammed her shield into the body of her enemy, fusing the sticky web-covered surface to the woman's chest. With a yank, Kit pulled her arm free from her shield's straps. While the mage struggled to free herself from the mass of webs, Kit gave her a front kick, sending the woman skidding across the black and white, polished tile floor.

Kit took a quick check over her shoulder. The other two mages had their hands full with Indie, Lin, and the boys. Amara and Silverleaf had taken up positions behind them, using their battle spells to provide additional protection for the group. Slate stayed close to Silverleaf, providing him with magic to improve his archery skill. Iba, who had been beside Kit at the point they'd entered the building, was nowhere to be seen.

"Are you two going to hide inside that bubble forever?" Kit screamed as she swung her ax, striking the bubble with her enhanced strength. On impact, the head of the ax exploded into dozens of tiny fragments. She stared at the broken weapon for a moment before tossing the handle to the side. From within the bubble, Karr's lips were moving frantically, but she couldn't make out anything he was saying. However, judging by the egotistic look on his face, he seemed content to remain inside his cocoon.

Indie's scream of agony diverted Kit's attention from Karr. Her heart leapt from her chest. Runt was sprawled out on the ground. An enormous scorpion-like creature held Indie, suspending him in the air. It had him clutched by the waist in its pincer. The man was trying desperately to push the claw open.

"They're summoners," Lin screamed out as she fought a creature that could have just stepped out of a nightmare. It was huge, with glowing gray eyes protruding from its glistening head. Its maw was a mass of needle-like teeth. Its arms were extraordinarily long, ending with hooked, bladed fingers. The woman ducked under the creature's clawed attack. As its arm moved past, Lin swung one of her flaming long swords at the beast, its blade ringing off the creature's bony exterior.

"Kill the summoner and their creatures will disappear," Amara screamed out. "You can't kill the monsters."

Kit's daemon self burst forth, her skin turning white, covered in its black runes. With her obsidian claws extended, she dove at the mage controlling the giant scorpion. He tried to fight her off, but once her claws had dug into the man, there was no way he was going to break free. The mage cast a spell that covered his body in writhing snakes. They burst outward, biting at Kit's armor. If their teeth were penetrating her skin, she didn't notice. She just kept gathering the mage towards her until she had her arms wrapped around him, dragging him to the ground. As soon as she had a tight grip, she turned herself into a giant fireball, simultaneously consuming the mage in flame and breaking his summoning spell. Pulling herself up from the floor, she rushed to Indie's side. His skin was pale and clammy, his eyes unable to focus.

"Help Runt," Indie croaked out. "He needs you."

The creature had ripped Runt's stomach open. Blood was pouring out of him at an alarming rate, spreading out across the floor in a thick crimson slick. He had multiple injuries, including a large puncture at the base of his neck. A thick gray ooze seeped from the wound. As Kit slid over to kneel next to him, she could see that his wounds were fatal, and they'd likely kill her if she used her powers on him. She didn't care. Taking the wolf's head in her bone-white, rune-covered hands, the young priest grimaced. When she called upon her daemon self, she couldn't use her healing powers.

"Titan, hear me," she whispered. The sounds of the battle raging around her fell away as she called upon her deity. People were standing beside her screaming, but their words went unheard. "If you are the god that I pray you are, you will not let your servant perish."

As soon as a pale-yellow aura encased her hands, Kit placed them across Runt's deepest wound. Slowly, the gash knitted itself together. In moments, the aura changed to a swirling mixture of pale yellow and deep gold. Tiny tendrils reached out across the dire wolf's body, seeking damage and repairing it on contact. She grimaced as the yellow aura died away, leaving only her angelic golden glow. As Runt's life returned to him, she poured even more magic into the wolf, infusing all of herself into him. Despite her efforts, Runt didn't seem well. There were no visible wounds, and yet, he still appeared to be slipping away. Without warning, Kit's daemon self burst forth, her flames engulfing the pair in searing red flame. In seconds, the flames died away, leaving the dire wolf uninjured. With glassy eyes, the gigantic wolf raised his head as though to give thanks to his friend.

"Rest," Kit said, stroking his thick black neck fur. She turned her attention back to Indie. Silverleaf was hunched over him, reading from a scroll. As he finished, the scroll turned to ash in his hand, and he pulled out a second. Again, he read, and a pale orange aura engulfed the Nomad and the half elf.

"What do the scrolls do?" Kit knelt beside Indie, her heart racing.

"I've stabilized him," Silverleaf replied, exhaling heavily. "Help Lin!"

Slate seemed unsure what to do. He continued staying close to Silverleaf, his hammer at the ready should anyone come near.

Kit spun around, looking for Lin. She couldn't get a good look at her. She was beyond the pitched combat between the nightmarish creature and Amara. The giant poked at the creature with her glaive and retreated, drawing it towards herself. When it stepped forward, Amara stepped to the side and swung her glaive at its legs. The creature jumped easily out of the way before lunging at the giant. As though she expected the attack, Amara parried with her pole arm and moved further to the side. At that point, the path to the battle mage opened up. Lin was engaging him with her blades while Lump, who was still in his gold-dragon form, snapped at him. They were harassing the man from two sides, neither able to penetrate a barrier of thick-bladed knives that spun about him. Each time either Lin or Lump got close enough to strike, the weapons would lash out.

"Lump, flame him," Kit yelled as she bolted across the room. On command, a bright red firestorm issued forth, bathing the man in dragon-fire. Even though the barrier of blades disappeared as soon as the flames struck him, Lin was forced to retreat to a safe distance as the inferno grew. Kit, unaffected by the fire, threw herself at the mage. She had considered using her own fire against him, but seeing that Lump's dragon-fire wasn't hurting him, she tried a different tactic.

"Lump, stop," she cried out. As soon as the flames abated, she slammed the man with a frost attack, a swirling vortex of intense cold whirling up from the ground at his feet. The mage's eyes went wide as his skin turned blue. Kit continued to push a deep, relentless cold into her attack. The mage's face contorted as he tried to defend against the frost that was spreading across his skin. With effort, he raised his hands before himself, ready to unleash a spell at Kit. The action came to an abrupt halt when Amara's glaive removed the man's head from his shoulders in a single swipe. With vacant eyes, Amara turned away from the carnage she had wrought, and made her way towards the dark blue sphere holding Karr and the last battle mage.

"Don't bother trying to break through," Kit called to her friend. "You'll only end up destroying your weapon." Amara paused before striking. Her ears were bright red, and a deep flush was spreading up her chest to her neck. Her knuckles were white as she adjusted the grip on her glaive.

"Do you know what that sphere is?" Kit asked, as Lin and Lump took up protective positions next to her.

"It's beyond my knowledge," Lin said. "Maybe Lump here can flame it, to see what happens?"

"Kit, behind you," Silverleaf screamed from his place next to Indie. The young priest spun around to see the female battle mage a few feet away from her, a half dozen wolf spiders standing around her. The spiders were advancing, the horrible clicking noises of their mandibles filling the air. Slate rushed to Kit, ready to offer his hammer in the fight. Without notice, Iba appeared from out of nowhere at the battle mage's back. With a leap, she jumped at the woman, burying one of her daggers into the summoner's temple. The woman's body went stiff, and the spiders disappeared. Iba nodded briskly before vanishing. The mage's body flopped to the ground, her head bouncing off the floor tiles.

"Thank you," Kit called out, not really sure where Iba had gone to. When there was no response, she called Lump over and motioned to the sphere.

Lump moved closer to the blue bubble and rocked his neck backward. He looked to be taking a giant gulp of air. Throwing his head forward, he unleashed a thick gout of flame at the sphere. The mage's expression changed from concern to smug arrogance; the dragon fire had little effect. Where the mage appeared indifferent, Karr's expression was less controlled. Beads of sweat were forming on both of their foreheads.

"Getting hot in there?" Kit asked, as the gold leached from her eyes, replaced with their daemon-blackness. Kit stepped up to the sphere and placed her claws against the shimmering blue bubble. She raised her eyebrows and released her own inferno, her flames mixing with Lump's until the outer shell of the protective barrier lost its shape. The mage's smug look melted away, replaced first with panic and then with terror as Fury strode up with Captain Harding and Coldforge at his side. With a grim smile, Fury added his own bright-blue flames to the mix.

"I yield," the mage screamed out, his face now dripping with sweat. "Please! Stop!" Kit couldn't hear the words, but she could still make out what the man was saying.

The heat from the attack was now so intense that everyone stepped away. The sphere was no longer round but a gelatinous blob, struggling to hold its form.

"Enough," Kit yelled out, her voice almost inaudible over the blaze. One by one, they all ceased their attack. As the last of the flames died out, the mage collapsed to the ground. What remained of the sphere melted away.

"It's over, Karr," Captain Harding boomed, his voice echoing off the walls as he stepped nearer.

"The rest of the king's guard have been dispatched," Sister Gale added as she came in through the entrance. "They're much faster runners than I'd have expected, but I believe we got them all before they got too far away."

"The king will hear of this," the helmed mage screamed out from his place on the floor. A moment later, he vanished in a puff of purple smoke.

"Where'd he go?" Coldforge asked, his head spinning about as he searched for the man.

"He's teleported." Sister Gale surveyed the room to be sure the mage was gone. "We can't let him get away."

The twang of a bowstring and a scream of pain interrupted the conversation. The disappearing mage materialized a few paces away from Karr, with one of Silverleaf's arrows embedded in his back. A moment later, Iba was there, jabbing him repeatedly up under his armpit with her dagger. The man staggered for a moment before dropping to his knees and then onto his face.

"Mage eye," Silverleaf said, holding up a small green pendent around his neck. "It allowed me to see through the invisibility spell."

Captain Harding pulled Kit's necklace over his head and tossed it to her.

"You're going to tell us everything," the mountain of a man said to his lieutenant, his voice deep and threatening.

"Why should I?" Karr replied, trying to look menacing as he drew two deep-bellied swords at his waist. "You're going to execute me, anyway."

"True," the captain replied, holding his bastard sword out in front of him, the tip only a few inches from Karr. "But you can choose a quick death, or you can suffer."

"You think I'm afraid of torture?" Karr spat. "You trained me well, Captain. You can't break me."

Kit gave the prisoner a wicked grin, her eyes still pools of inky blackness. "Everyone always says that until the pain begins."

"Is the *special prisoner* still being held below the dungeons?" Indie asked, his eyebrows raised. He didn't look healthy, but he was strong enough to stand. The question made the captain chuckle as he nodded his head. When Karr realized what Indie was suggesting, he threw down his weapons and dropped to his knees.

"No," he cried out, his lower lip trembling, his eyes glassy. "I'll tell you everything."

"Too late," Kit said as she struck the man across the face with her fist, sending him sprawling across the floor.

Chapter Thirty

The Red Door

The priests were exhausted, but not a single one would admit it. Kit, too, desperately needed sleep, but their fight wasn't over yet. They still needed to free the City Watch who were being held at the barracks. Brother Snowpack and Sister Alyce had patched up the group's minor wounds, while healing potions had been administered to those who'd been injured more severely. Three priests had perished in the combat with the king's soldiers. Kit knew them by name only, but the loss still weighed heavily on her.

The city was unaware of what was happening. Except for the Temple's destruction, much of the king's incursion took place hidden from the eyes of the general populous. Whether this was by design, Kit wasn't sure.

The people of the city came out in droves to watch the parade of priests and acolytes as they marched through the streets with Captain Harding and The Savior of Aarall at their lead. The bound and gagged Lieutenant Karr was being dragged along, hidden within the ranks of the priests. Runt and Lump, in their normal doggie-style, greeted anyone who came near with wagging tails and slobbery, wet tongues. Their antics served two purposes. The boys lightened the mood and pleased the population, but they also kept them from interacting with the procession and potentially causing a panic.

"We're going to have a problem when we get to the barracks," Captain Harding said to Sister Gale as they neared their destination. "We're going to be seen by the guards at the city's front gate and by the guards outside the barracks as soon as we pass the central fountain."

"How many more battle mages do you think there are?" Kit asked.

"I can't believe there are many left," her father replied. "There can't be more than a couple at the walls or in the barracks themselves. Karr would have been more worried about keeping the priests under control. My people are much less of a threat against powerful magic." Kit nodded her understanding. What her father said made sense. She wished she had concluded this on her own, but military tactics were not her strength.

"Still, just in case, why don't you and the priests retake the barracks and I'll take Indie, Lin, and the boys to take down the guards on the walls." Captain Harding's gaze flitted about for a moment before he ran his thick fingers through his hair.

"It would mean fighting enemies on two fronts," he said, "and that is rarely a sound strategy. If only I knew what you would be facing. I really never got a sense of just how many of the king's soldiers were here. There may be hundreds on the walls."

"No," Iba said, seeming to appear out of nowhere. Even in broad daylight, she could be imperceptible. "There are only twenty soldiers at the front gate. I saw nobody on the parapets at all. There are two more guards at the gatehouse to the barracks. I didn't go inside, but I'm going to guess there are not too many within the building itself. Everything looks like any normal day. Citizens are coming and going as they please, and the marketplace is doing lively business."

"Let's just rush them." Coldforge's eyes were alight. If he was at all tired, he wasn't showing it. "We have overwhelming strength. We should use it to our advantage."

"There are too many civilians." Captain Harding furrowed his brow. "If they see us coming as a group, the soldiers may take hostages."

"Me kin would consider that to be acceptable losses," Coldforge said. "Any of us would sacrifice our life for the benefit of the clan."

"No." Kit's eyes were fierce. "We don't let people die just because it's the easy path."

"I can lead Kit up to the main gates without being seen." Lin drew her mouth into a thin line. "There's a path that will take us up to the city walls. From there, we can slip up to the gatehouse." Kit shook her head at her friend. She really knew far too many ways to breech security measures.

"I don't think we need to be so careful," Indie offered. "The king's people don't know who we are. If we split up into small groups of two or three, we should be able to just walk up to the gates without drawing attention to ourselves."

"Ye might be able to do that." Coldforge thumbed at the priests. "But this lot in their fancy white robes doesn't blend so well." Sister Gale slipped out of her priestly robes, her lithe body covered by only a thin shirt and a pair of short, baggy pants. Several others, men and women alike, followed the sister's example. They slipped out of their robes as well, showing even more skin than the combat instructor.

Captain Harding turned away and groaned. "Yes, that should draw the guards' attention. Sweet Titan, do you people have no shame?"

"Ye can't parade around like that." Coldforge's whiskers danced on his face. "Ye can't hide no weapons if yer nekkid."

"The priests are weapons," Kit said, "but I'm not doing that." Lin considered her options. She was spending far too much time inspecting the faithful and their varying degrees of nudity. Kit gave her a solid elbow in the ribs. "Are you forgetting about Rusty already?"

"I was only looking," she replied with a sly grin. "I mean, they're standing right in front of me."

"If you two are finished." Sister Gale strode forward. "Let's get moving. Captain, you need to stay back with the priests. Everyone else, split up into pairs and don't bunch up. Amara, I think you should stay behind. You will definitely not blend in." The blonde giant pulled the laces at the front of her robes, letting them fall into a pool at her feet. Beneath her robes she wore a leather vest and thin linen pants. Silverleaf gasped and turned bright red.

"I'm coming." Amara stepped forward, thumping the butt of her glaive on the ground.

"Amara." Panic rose in Silverleaf's voice. "I'm not... I don't... I can't."

"I get it." Amara smiled at her friend. If he knew what she was planning, he'd have likely run away. She let her hips sway as she strode back, grasped the half elf by the scruff of his robes and hoisted him off the ground. "You can be my prisoner, my gift to the guards." Kit couldn't get a read on the man's expression as he dangled two feet above the ground. Both Indie and Lin were laughing openly. Perhaps they saw something that she did not.

While the captain stayed back with the bulk of the priests and all the acolytes, Kit and the rest of the group moved forward. There were nine priests in various levels of undress, walking in groups of three. Kit and the boys kept a safe distance from the others, while Lin and Coldforge walked hand in hand like a couple out for a morning stroll. Iba was, of course, off doing her thing.

"I caught this one lurking up the street." Amara held Silverleaf out before her. She motioned to a guard standing at the barracks' gatehouse. "Captain Karr said we'd be rewarded if we brought in any people who were not faithful to the king." The guard was unsure of how to respond. He signaled for his partner to come over.

One of the other priests with Amara spoke up. "Karr said he'd pay us in gold." The priest was a tall, thin man with long, lean muscles. His only adornment was a simple loin cloth, and it barely covered his manly parts.

"And who are you to be bringing us prisoners?" the second guard said. His face was weathered but clean shaven. He moved like a soldier who knew how to handle himself in a fight.

"We work at the Red Door," the third priest said, her breasts swinging freely under a shirt that was no thicker than gauze. "Captain Karr favors us with his company, and we are simply returning his kindness."

"Maybe we can come to an arrangement." The first guard waggled his eyebrows at the buxom priest.

"We were promised gold." Amara pulled Silverleaf back like she was withholding a prize. The first guard put his hand on the hilt of his sword and cocked an eyebrow at her. Amara laughed with her deep baritone voice. She glanced down at herself before turning her eyes back on the guard.

"Do I look like the sort of woman who might be intimidated by a man with a sword?" A sly grin spread across her face. "I deal with men's swords daily, so they don't need to grab it themselves." The threatening look of the guard melted away, replaced with a guffaw. The second guard joined in. "Maybe we can tie up the prisoner in your guardhouse, get to know each other, and then we can see about you getting us our gold?"

The group headed into the guardhouse. Just before entering, Amara nodded to let the others know that these two guards would be taken care of. Kit couldn't hear what Amara had said to get the guards to take them inside, but she almost pitied the soldiers for what was in store for them. She turned in time to see another trio of priests, which included Sister Gale, being approached by four of the guards who were stationed near the front gate.

"Hold there," a lanky guard dressed in chain mail called out. He had a good deal of mirth in his voice as his eyes ran up and down the priests. "We can't have you walking about in public like that."

"Why not?" a second guard asked. He was thumping his fist on his black enameled breast plate to draw the nearly naked people's attention. "Beauty such as this need not be covered. It should be displayed unabashedly for all the world to enjoy."

"I'm glad you like the view." Sister Gale sidled up to the battle mage. She ran her fingers down her throat and tied her lips up into a tight bow. "But we taste even sweeter than we look," she offered, her eyes bulging as she did. "I love men in authority. Especially those dressed in black."

The battle mage's attention was drawn away, his eyes searching out the entrance to the barracks. His look darkened, and he shook his head. He pushed Sister Gale out of his way and motioned for the other guards to follow him.

"Where are you going?" Sister Gale ran up beside the man who was striding across the open courtyard, heading straight for the City Watch gatehouse. The other priests were busy sidling up to the guards, trying to draw their attention away from the barracks.

"Leave us," the mage barked back, "or I'll arrest the lot of you."

"Come now." Sister Gale sprinted to keep up with the battle mage's pace. "If you're doing something exciting, let me watch. It gets me... going." She waggled her eyebrows at the man, licking her lips to get his attention.

"Fine," he growled. "Follow. Watch. See what's in store for you and your friends if you cross me?"

Kit was watching how the main gate guards would react. A group of four were heading towards the battle mage. She knew that, even unarmed, Sister Gale could handle herself, but if this lot joined in, the numbers would be against her.

"Excuse me," Lin called out to the guards. "Excuse me, fine soldiers; over here, if you will." One guard looked to see who was calling to them. She was a heavyset woman and looked every part a soldier. Her attention lasted for only a moment before the soldier continued to head towards the City Watch gatehouse.

"Stop what you're doing and render aid unto me this instant," Lin called out, this time her voice filled with fervor. "I am Lady Aithlin of House Logner. You will stop what you're doing, and you will come to my aid this instant." The four guards stopped in their tracks and changed direction to intercept Lin and Coldforge.

"Kind of you to announce yourself." Another of the four guards drew his sword. "We have orders to arrest you and your cohorts, *Sister Aithlin*." The three remaining priests caught sight of Lin's interaction and made their way over.

"I wonder." Lin stormed towards the oncoming guards with Coldforge doing his best to keep up. "Who do you think will punish you more, my father, Lord Arthure, or my friend, Lord Martelle? Which of you will scream the loudest when they turn the wheels of the rack?"

"Take the dwarf," the guard demanded, his eyes fixed on Lin. "Kill him if you have to, but this one's mine."

"Oh my." Brother Snowpack flounced over to the group, his multitude of black braids jouncing around atop his head. "So much tension. You people need to learn how to relax."

"Back off, the lot of you." The female guard brandished her sword at the group of underdressed priests. "Unless you whores want to be arrested as well."

"Whores?" Brother Snowpack pressed his hands to his cheeks, his eyes wide. "We are worshippers of Pele, the sun god. Unto him we offer our flesh that he may nourish it with his warmth. Unto him, we offer our souls that we may feel his burning love for us."

The female guard swung her blade at Brother Snowpack, forcing him to back away a few steps.

"Ye'll not be doing none of that." Coldforge stepped up to the guard. She turned her blade on him, pointing it at his face. The dwarf reached up with one hand and grabbed the blade. With his free hand, he grabbed the woman by the forearm, snapping the bone like a twig. The woman's howl drew every guard's attention.

"Holy Helja," Kit swore, as a dozen guards came running from the city's main gate. "This wasn't the way this was supposed to go." She broke into a sprint, trying to intercept the guards before they reached Lin and the others. After only a few steps, Runt and Lump passed her by. Lump was mid-change, his body covered in a mix of golden fur and scales. Runt, now in the lead, dove headlong into the group. The guards screamed out as the dire wolf ravaged them. At the sight of the dragon, their will to fight ended, and they routed. Citizens who were crowded around the area joined in with their own screams. People were running about in every direction, trying to get away from the rampaging creatures.

"Stay with the boys," Kit said to Indie. "I'll help Lin."

"They've got it under control," Indie said. "I'm staying with you."

Kit watched, in stupefied wonder, how the group of underdressed priests, the boys, and the rest of her cohorts dispatched the group of guards with no help from either her or Indie. She hadn't seen how it happened, but the battle mage was lying on the ground with his head twisted into a horribly unnatural position. Those soldiers who had not been killed were lying facedown on the cobblestone street with their hands locked behind their heads, their fingers interlaced together.

"Well." Indie slid his swords back into their sheaths. "Not what we had planned, but it was extremely effective." Kit was still struggling to find words.

"This is all of them," Iba said as she and the boys escorted seven guards. "The others chose to fight. It didn't go well for them." She motioned to the boys, busy licking the blood from their muzzles.

"I guess all that's left is to free the City Watch." Kit's shoulders slumped.

"Oh, Kitten, don't be disappointed that they left nobody for you to bash." Fury popped up beside the young priest. Iba bleated out yet again, went completely rigid, and fell on her face. The dragon lord smiled his toothy, draken smile as he stepped over the rigid Tahr lying splayed out on the ground. "Maybe I should find a way to announce my arrival before I actually show up."

Chapter Thirty-One

Ulip and the Fire Drake

"We need to go to Aarall. This is not the right way!" Ulip's jaw was so tightly clenched he was on the brink of shattering his teeth. *"Yuka, you're supposed to carry me to Aarall."*

"That is not so, now is it?" The fire drake's voice was grating in Ulip's mind. *"Spur would let one of us bear you, but he also said that I would decide where we go and by what route."* The fire drake dipped, dropping hundreds of feet in a heartbeat before swooping back up into the evening sky. Had Ulip not been clutching her scales for fear of falling, or had his stomach not wanted to paint the world below with its contents, he might have enjoyed the brisk wind that bit at his skin and whipped his hair about his head.

"Please, stop doing that." Ulip desperately tried not to vomit.

"Relax, would you," Yuka replied. *"You will not fall, and if you don't loosen your grip, you're going to rip my scales out from my skin. If you do that, I will roll onto my back and I will shake you like an errant bit of schmutz. And if I can't shake you off, I will simply burn you to a crisp."* The fire drake inhaled a great gulp of air, stoking the fires in her chest, raising her internal temperature to unbearable heights.

Ulip released his grip on the drake's scales, and she let her temperature return to normal. *"Do you feel that surge in your belly?"* she asked, her voice turning playful.

"What surge?" The words were not yet even a thought when the drake banked swiftly to the left and then to the right. The quick change in directions

made the giant's heart race, and there was a *surge* in his stomach. Despite the maneuvers, he found his hands were resting easily on the drake's neck.

"That surge," she said with a laugh. Her laugh was joyous, sounding like hundreds of tiny bells chiming all at once. *"What you're feeling is a mix of freedom and joy. You can only get this feeling when you are leagues above the ground, with the wind racing over your body, and you allow your worries to fall away like old scales."*

"I have no room for joy in my heart. My clan is all but gone and those who destroyed it are doing the same to others, ripping them from their homes, from the ones they love..."

"Your clan is not just your kin, the people you grew up with. Your clan is everyone who cares for you and whom you care for. The people you spoke of; Ryn, and Breayn, and... Danny, they are as much your family as your kin ever were. And when you find your sister, we will bring her home and you will rebuild your village. Your kin and your friends are your family. They're the people who matter."

The giant considered the drake's words. There was truth in them, but his clan was his clan. They were decent people, and they did not deserve to be killed, or worse, taken as slaves. Another surge coursed through his blood, but this was not joy. It was the desire to bring ruin on those who'd harmed him.

"Be mindful of your emotions." Yuka banked to the west. *"The road to revenge is dark and you may lose your way. Choosing to right a wrong is a noble path, so long as your heart remains true."*

"How is it you can speak to me, in my mind?" Ulip tried changing the subject. *"How is it you know the common language?"*

"I can speak to you because Spur allows it. The old dragon has much magic and, if the cause is worthy, he willingly shares it with others." The drake flapped her wings and, with several powerful beats, the pair rose high into the air. So high that the world was obscured by thick, white clouds. Water collected on Ulip's bare skin, turned to rivulets, and flew from his body. The cooling effect was extremely pleasant.

"Why are you taking me so high?" Ulip's mind was becoming as foggy as the surrounding air. *"I'm feeling... dizzy."*

"Rest your head upon my neck," she said, her voice calm and gentle. *"We will descend shortly, but for now, we are where we need to be."* Yuka's words floated in his mind, sounding like they were a thousand leagues away. Like the words, he, too, floated lazily as the air continued to cool his skin and ease his mind.

⌘

A great squawking roused Ulip from his slumber. His heart was beating much faster than it should, and he struggled to draw enough breath to fill his lungs. The coolness of the clouds was gone, and his body was drenched in sweat. Still, the thunderous voices continued to grate at him, making his head throb. Great red shadows passed before him, screeching, pounding the ground, making it shudder beneath him. Slowly, his vision returned. He blinked repeatedly, trying to make sense of what he was seeing. Yuka was surrounded by four, or was it five other fire drakes, their long serpentine necks intertwined, the hooked claws on their wings clasping each other.

"Can you not be so loud?" he called out, clutching his head as he did for fear it would rip apart as the words left his mouth. "Please."

"You're awake." Yuka's voice remained soft and calm, in complete contrast to the high-pitched squeals and shrieks that continued on about him, driving great spikes into his brain. A moment later, the noise abated. The sudden absence of the caterwauling was jarring. *"These are my nest mates. They are the reason for not taking you to your sister."*

"These are your brothers and sisters?"

"Some are the children of my mother, but... we don't raise our children as you do. We gather all the season's eggs into a single clutch. The males take turns warming the nest, rotating the eggs every hour, to ensure healthy dragonets, children."

"You call young drakes, dragonets?"

"All species of dragons, even the lesser ones like drakes and wyverns, call our children dragonets. It is to honor the dragon lords, Ouroboros and Fury, our creators." At the mention of Fury, the other drakes screeched and screamed, each

one louder than the previous, forcing Ulip to wrap his great black arms around his ears, trying to protect his head from exploding.

"Can't you just talk inside your heads, like you're doing with me?" A moment later, the drakes' voices died away, leaving Ulip with a throbbing head and a pain that ran from the base of his skull up and around to his eyes.

"My family was telling me something, something impossible. They said that Fury had been here, on this mountain and that they'd spoken with him."

"Why is that impossible?" Even communicating inside Ulip's mind was making his skull want to explode, but since the noise had died down, so had his pain lessened.

"Because, like all dragons, he is trapped in his mountain domain. None can leave until the key is found, the key that opens the Collar of Command." Yuka sensed the Gigas' question. *"Ouroboros was tricked by the Fates, made to believe that the collar would allow him to communicate with the other dragons across great distances. They told him it would ensure his victory over the others in the ultimate battle. The dragon lord insisted it wasn't necessary, but one Fate, Tiamat, convinced him there was no other way. She told him that Tyr was cheating, rigging the Great Game so that the humans would win, like they always did."*

Ulip scratched his massive chest as he considered the drake's words. *"Those are the stories my clan tells in song, or at least, we used to. And you're telling me they were true?"*

"Where do you think you got the tales? They were passed on to you by Spur, so that you, too, would know of the burden he carries."

"Then how is it that Fury could be here if he's trapped in his mountain range?"

"That's what I'm trying to find out, but you keep interrupting my conversation with my nest mates." Ulip drew his knees up to his chest and rested his chin upon them. The throbbing in his head was abating, and with it, his heartbeat and breathing were returning to normal. He watched the drakes as they communicated with one another. Their facial expressions and gestures were so Gigas-like. On multiple occasions, Yuka's scaled eyebrows rose, and her eyes widened, like they were telling her a tale that was beyond belief. Suddenly, they all made a

horrific, yet joyful, sound. One drake sat back on his haunches, grabbed his scaled belly, and fell over on his side, rocking back and forth like a small child.

"They spoke of a young human girl on a horse. She carried a hammer that declared itself to be the mighty Fury." Yuka sat back on her haunches and shook her head. *"The hammer became angry when my nest mates didn't believe him."* The drake's shoulders bobbed up and down, and she covered her mouth with her great clawed paw. Unable to contain it any longer, she snorted and blew out a thick gout of bright red flame, igniting the ground at Ulip's feet. *"The drakes told the hammer they'd never heard of Fury. The hammer lost its mind."*

While Yuka continued to chuckle at her story, Ulip was busily trying to put out the fire that threatened to spread into a large patch of winterberry bushes. As he put out the last of the flames, he crossed his arms. "What if it was him? How do you know the hammer wasn't actually Fury? Can you imagine what would happen if your kin actually met him and rebuked him?"

The drake's shoulders ceased bobbing and her eyes widened. She swept the last of her tears away, fearful that she might start laughing yet again. Finally, she sucked in a deep breath and slowly exhaled, careful to not set anymore of the vegetation ablaze.

"If it was actually Fury, then... well... that would be bad, very bad, indeed." The drake paused; her thick, scaly brow furrowed. *"My nest mates said that the hammer and the little girl helped them defeat a hill giant. They said they had a sumptuous feast that night."* It was Ulip's turn to be skeptical. He ground his foot into a small bit of branches that had flamed up again.

"Little human girls are not warriors," he guffawed. "Even I would struggle to defeat such a creature." Ulip held his hand over his head, as though showing how tall a hill giant was. "They are no smarter than a boulder, but they are powerful and mean-spirited."

"The girl wielded the hammer and rode a horse that was so fast it could set the ground on fire. She broke the hulk's leg with the hammer, and when it fell, the others finished him." Yuka ran her claws over her eye-ridges, paused, examined one of her claws and chewed on it. When she caught sight of Ulip staring at her, she preened the creamy white scales on her chest. *"The hammer talked. I don't*

think I've ever heard of a sentient weapon before. Scale rot. What if it was him? What if, somehow, Fury was the hammer?"

"And what of the girl? If the hammer contained Fury, why would he let a little priest wield him?"

"She was a zealot, a priest of Titan, the imprisoned god."

"My sister is a follower of Titan. She serves at the temple in Aarall, where you were supposed to take me. Do you suppose the little girl is also from there?" Yuka shrugged at the question; her bright yellow eyes filled with concern.

"Can we go there now?" Ulip pressed, trying his best to wait patiently.

Yuka didn't answer. She was carefully examining the claws on her front left paw, lost in deep thought. She switched to her right paw, studying each of its twelve-inch nails.

"Yuka?" Ulip asked, his voice low and calm. "Can we go see my sister now?"

"No," she rocked her head. *"I must speak once more with my nest mates and then we have another stop to make. I need to speak with Siku. She must be told of Fury, or whoever the hammer is."* Ulip growled at the news, his stomach twisting.

"Spur told you to take me to Aarall, to my sister. Enough games. Take me there now." The big man's fists were clenched tight as he stared up into the fire drake's great yellow eyes. Yuka stood upon her hind legs and unfurled her thick, leathery wings. With a single beat, she sent Ulip careening backwards, almost sending him over a precariously steep ridge. She screeched and screamed, blowing fireballs over the Gigas' head, nearly close enough to set his hair on fire. Ulip didn't flinch. He stood up, straightened his back, and strode towards the lesser dragon and her eight-inch teeth.

"You will be a powerful chief," Yuka said, a sharp edge to the voice in Ulip's mind. *"If you live long enough to rebuild your clan. We will leave for Mount Toka shortly. I will speak with Siku. If she permits, we will travel to Aarall, and you can see your sister."*

"What do you mean, if she permits? You answer to Spur, and he bows to no one." The Gigas' assertion made Yuka laugh.

"How can your people have served Spur for so many hundreds of cycles and yet you know nothing of dragons?" Ulip's brow furrowed, his beady black eyes lost

behind his heavy forehead. *"Dragons, all dragons of all types, bow to Ouroboros, then Fury, and then the females. We bow to the males if they are stronger than us. I bow to Spur because he is a dragon, and I am a drake. Every dragon, save the dragon lords, bows to Siku."*

"Why do you need to go to Siku?"

"She will want to know of the hammer named Fury, even if he is not the true lord. I feel it in my scales. I need to seek her out, even if it will be my doom."

"You fear she will kill you? Kill us?"

"You are not coming. That is what I need to discuss it with my nest mates; if they will permit you to stay with them until I return." Ulip raised his eye-ridges, his beady black eyes reflecting the sun's dying light.

"I will be there with you," the Gigas said. "If she destroys you, she can destroy me as well."

"If I bring you, she will destroy me without question, without hesitation. She tolerates ice drakes because she needs them to bring her food. The Tahr are welcome because they are her eyes and ears beyond the mountain. I expect she has never seen one of your kind. She will probably eat you, just to see how you taste."

"Then she will find out that I taste bitter, and I will give her indigestion. I am coming and I will not accept no for an answer." The statement made Yuka laugh. With a quick beat of her wings, she lifted herself off the ground, a great gust of wind sending Ulip to his backside. In seconds, the drake was airborne, hovering several hundred feet above the Gigas.

"You will learn to deal with disappointment."

"And you will learn to live with being deemed a coward," Ulip screamed, shaking his great fist at the drake. Yuka continued to hover above the hulking man for several more seconds before she collapsed her wings to her side. She instantly plummeted to the ground, unfurling her wings at the very last second. She hit the ground next to Ulip with enough force to shake the earth. The Gigas stood tall, unflinching.

"You are either very brave or incredibly stupid." The voice in Ulip's head was filled with resignation. She lowered herself to the ground, allowing the black-skinned giant to climb onto her back.

"You will probably find that I am both." Ulip patted her scales. "You may also find out if I am tasty or not."

CHAPTER THIRTY-TWO

FATE'S GAMBIT

With the king's guards at the City Watch gatehouse and the city's main gate under control, Captain Harding and the rest of the priests and acolytes joined the vanguard.

"Not a single injury among us?" The captain surveyed the group.

"Not a one." Sister Gale slipped her priestly robes over her head. She gave her body a shake, helping to settle her clothing into a comfortable position. "I'm going to guess your people are being held in your dining hall, like the acolytes were in the Temple. I suggest we head directly there."

"Either there or on the training grounds," Captain Harding replied. "We'll have to pass through them on the way to the dining hall, so I suppose we'll find out soon enough."

"Most of your people are in the dining hall." Iba slid in beside the captain. "There are also a fair number of them being held in the dungeons. As best as I could see, there are only ten guards inside. None of them are battle mages. They're all with the prisoners in the dining hall."

"Sweet Titan," Captain Harding exclaimed, "would you be willing to work with the Watch? We could really use a person of your talents." The comment made the young Tahr smile.

"Now you can see why we dragon lords value the Tahr so highly," Fury said, bowing to the girl. "They are truly wondrous beings. I, too, would be honored to count you among my followers." Iba gave the draken a bit of a smirk and slipped out of the room.

"How's about we go free the rest of the prisoners?" Indie said. "The sooner we get that done, the sooner we can eat and sleep."

The group was well over one hundred strong when they burst through the front door of the barracks and into the indoor training grounds. As Iba had said, the place was empty and eerily quiet.

"Sister Gale." Captain Harding motioned to the dining hall entrance. "Take the priests through the front door. I'll take the rest in through the kitchen entrance. Give us a few minutes to get there and wait for our signal."

"How will we know you're ready?" the combat instructor asked, a hint of a grin on her lips.

"When everyone screams," Kit replied. "I'm guessing they're not expecting a draken, a dire wolf, and a dragon to come bursting into the room."

"Sounds like a plan," Sister Gale responded. She motioned to the priests to follow her. While they maneuvered to the front, Captain Harding led the rest of the group towards the kitchens.

"You acolytes stay out of harm's way," Kit said. She ignored the groans and protests, including the loudest complaints coming from Slate. "We are going to burst into the room and overwhelm them. I expect they will give up without a fight."

"No, they won't," a melodic voice said from within Kit's head. *"They are not as they seem. Trust not your eyes, for they will lie to you."*

"Tiamat?" Kit spun around, looking for the voice. Nobody was there. She turned towards her father with wide eyes. "It might be a trap."

"Why do you say that?" The captain looked towards the door they were about to breach.

"Someone spoke to me, in my head. She said things are not as they seem."

"Who spoke to you?" Indie asked. "Maybe it's just Tyr messing with you."

"I don't think so." Kit shook her head, her brow furrowing as she recalled the words. "What she said felt truthful to me."

"If the soldiers here are battle mages," her father said, "then we need to make sure the acolytes stay well back. We need to get word to Sister Gale. She's expecting regular soldiers, not battle mages."

"Lump, go tell Sister Gale. Tell her we're facing something more than regular soldiers. They might be battle mages. They might be something... more." The wolfdog nodded his understanding and bolted off to the dining hall's main entrance. With as much time as Lump had spent in the barracks, he knew the route well.

"How is he going to convey those details?" Kit's father asked. "You didn't give him a note to carry."

"Because that is the most amazing dog that I have ever laid eyes on." Coldforge's voice was filled with awe and admiration. "He can change into a dragon or a human at will."

"Okay then." Captain Harding gave his daughter a questioning look. "We're going to need to separate the king's people from my own. If they're battle mages, this is going to be a lot more complicated."

⸎⸎⸎⸎⬦⸎⸎⸎⸎

The group waited for Lump to return. He told them he had conveyed the message to Sister Gale before changing into his gold dragon form.

"When we step through the door, we're going to be in the open," Captain Harding whispered. "We're going to fan out so that the mages won't be able to hit us as a group with their spells."

"Fury and I will go in first." Kit's eyes were black, her voice guttural. "We'll move off to the side as fast as we can and draw their attention. The rest of you can come in as soon as we're in position."

"We talked about this," her father ground out. "I won't allow it." Ignoring the man's words, she turned to Indie.

"Stay with the boys. Make sure they're safe."

"We'll go in second," Indie said, "and move to the opposite side of the room. I'm thinking we'll be able to split their firepower."

"The priests are going to be coming in, too, as soon as they hear the noise," Coldforge said. "The mages will fight on three sides. We can take 'em up the middle." His eyes were much too bright and cheerful for the captain.

"Fine." Captain Harding was still glaring at his daughter. "Be safe."

"You, too." Kit pulled out her hammer and gave it a quick spin. "Let's have some fun, Fury."

As planned, Kit stepped through the door and broke into a run. Fury sprinted along beside her, his long claws clicking as he did. From the opposite corner, Lump issued a tremendous roar that shook the walls. He was definitely learning how to be a dragon. His roar signaled the priests to enter.

Why is nobody screaming?

Kit stole a glance at the people in the room. She was so busy getting into position, she really hadn't bothered to look around. She skidded to a halt, her feet sliding somewhat on the rough, wood-plank floor. The room was filled with City Watch soldiers, who were all seated at the rows of trestle tables. They watched the spectacle in stunned silence. The guards, who were interspersed between the tables, were positioned where they could monitor everyone in the room. They stood transfixed; their eyes locked on the many threats who had just entered the dining hall.

"Drop your weapons," Captain Harding bellowed out. "Drop your weapons or perish."

There was a loud clattering as spears and swords were tossed to the ground. The soldiers then held their hands away from their sides, offering no resistance. The priests swept through the room, gathering the weapons and securing the new prisoners.

"This isn't right," Kit said. "I know that whoever spoke to me wasn't lying. This is not what it seems." Fury scanned the room and growled.

"It's not an illusion," he said. He seemed to scrutinize every single prisoner, his sapphire-blue eyes glowing. "Everything appears to be exactly as it appears to be."

"Bring me the prisoners," Kit called out, striding towards the middle of the room. "I will speak to them."

Kit's cohorts gathered as the prisoners were brought to her. The priests took up positions around the perimeter of the room, ready to react should things move in an unexpected direction.

"What is your position in the king's army?" Kit asked the first of the soldiers, a young female with honey colored skin and dark green eyes. Her expression was serene as she looked back into her questioner's swirling pools of molten gold.

"I am Corporal Yin Chin, of my king's Royal Army." The truth in her words washed over Kit. Tension grew in the back of her neck. She had expected the woman to lie to her.

"Are you trained in the art of magic, in any way?" The woman shook her head at the question, but her movements were jerky, almost like she was cringing. "I need you to speak your answers to me."

"No," she said, standing straighter. "No, I am not."

"Are any of your cohorts trained in magic?" The woman turned to the other soldiers, who were all shaking their heads. Some reactions were almost imperceptible, while others were fervent in their actions.

"No," she replied. "Not that I am aware of." Even though her response was true, Kit picked up a tremor in her voice. A small tick in her cheek made her eye twitch.

"What are you not telling her?" Lin moved in closer. "She's being kind to you. You don't want to see her being... unkind." The guard's eyes snapped to Lin and then back to Kit. She swallowed hard. Her eyes were becoming glassy, her breathing erratic.

"Yin, stay quiet," one of the soldier's cohorts said, his voice pleading. Every one of the other soldiers had their eyes squeezed tight, as though awaiting a terrible fate.

"They aren't the threat," Kit yelled out. "It's something else. Something in this room." One of the City Watch guards screamed out, his words unintelligible. The man seated beside him reached over, grabbed him by the face, and wrenched his neck single-handedly. There was a loud snap, and the guard slumped over and fell limp onto the table in front of him. The guard who'd killed him turned to the woman on the other side of him and snapped her neck in a similar fashion. He cackled as she flopped onto the food-stained floor. Like a shock wave spreading out from its epicenter, members of the Watch turned on the people sitting next to them, killing them with little effort and no remorse.

"We can't tell friend from foe," Sister Gale called out. "Who do we attack?"

Many of the City Watch tried to yell back a response, their words dying off before they could finish. Kit threw her hammer at the man nearest to her, the one who had killed the first two Watch members. Fury winked out from where he stood beside Kit, reappearing next to the intended target. He grabbed the man in his scaled claw, his fingers wrapping easily around his neck. Terror filled the man's face as the draken lifted him from the ground. Fury bared his teeth, and, with a flick of his wrist, snapped the man's neck.

"That was too easy," Fury called out, furrowing the scaled ridges over his eyes.

The room had turned to bedlam. People were rushing about, knocking one another to the ground as they tried to escape their assailants. Some guards fought back, trying to fend off their attackers. Some of those who'd successfully defeated their attacker turned their assaults on other Watch members who were nearby.

"Kit, it's a demon spirit, or several of them," Lin yelled out, "like the one we faced in Templeton."

Kit's knees weakened at the thought. Roving spirits, or whatever they were, couldn't be caught or destroyed. At best, they could be forced to leave, but there were so many of them. They would move from host to host until every member of the Watch was dead. What if they inhabited the priests, using them as puppets?

That's not right. The demon we faced in Templeton was visible when it changed bodies.

"Tyr, Eris, whoever you are." Kit spun on the spot, looking for who was speaking. She thundered towards Fury, moving to retrieve her weapon. "Face me, you coward. You've already broken the rules. You're already facing dissolution. Why not finish me and be done with it?"

"I told you she was clever," Tyr said, appearing seated on one of the ceiling's rafters. His feet dangled below him, his expression a look of sheer delight. He was in his Nomad male persona, dressed in black leather from head to toe. His hair was pulled back into a ponytail that hung over his shoulder. "What will

Tyche think if you are too afraid to face her? He is the only Fate siding with you right now, and he is the reason you're still alive."

"Tyr," Kit screamed, as inky blackness filled her eyes. "What are you up to?" The Fate put his hand to his heart and leaned back.

"I am only an observer." He disappeared from his seat in the rafters and reappeared next to Fury. He picked up the dragon hammer and held it out for her to take. "A spectator, if you will, here to bear witness to these events."

"Eris!" Kit screamed, snatching her weapon from the Fate's hand. "You festering sack of refuse. Show yourself."

"Now, now." Eris appeared next to Tyr, pressing her voluptuous body against him. Black smoke swirled around her feet, climbing up Tyr's leg, almost caressing him as it did. Her pulsating mass of patchwork skin made Kit want to retch. "There's no need to use foul language, little daemon."

"You are breaking your own rules of non-interference." Kit tried to keep herself from losing control. She surveyed the room. Every person was still. It was only then that she realized the room was perfectly silent.

"I broke no rules, unlike our arbiter who shared information she shouldn't have. She should have been punished for her crime, but your admirers wouldn't hold her accountable. Apparently, our rules only apply to me and nobody else."

"I never acted on what Mephitis told me." Kit jutted her chin out at the woman. Truth was, she had forgotten about the conversation she had shared with Mephitis until just this very moment. At some point, though, she would need to have a chat with Lump so he could tell her about her heritage. Come to think of it, there were a few things that she wanted to question Lump about. It seemed he had much to say, but she'd always been too preoccupied to take the time to listen.

"You see?" Tyr's smirk dripped with arrogance. "I could take away Lump's ability to switch to a human, and then she'd never know. Mephitis would have broken no rules."

"Please don't." The words spilled out of Kit before she could stop them.

"It wouldn't matter, anyway." Eris strolled up to Kit, running the back of her nails across her cheek. "She broke the rules. Regardless of the effect, she should be punished. Rules are rules, after all. But neither Tyr nor Tiamat would agree."

"Because, by breaking the rules, she furthered our agenda." Tyr had a dangerous edge to his voice. He pressed his face close to the woman's, his eyes narrowing. "Every rule has caveats, exceptions to make them less rigid."

"Too bad you never apply those caveats to Tyche or me." Eris put her hands on Tyr's chest and shoved him back.

"You're both still here, aren't you? Nobody stopped you from this... charade." And with that, Tyr disappeared with a pop. A moment later, a coyote howled in the distance.

"I hate it when he does that." Eris rolled her eyes. "It's so boring."

"Why are you here, Eris?" Kit asked. "Why are you doing... this?"

Eris feigned a yawn and stretched her arms over her head. "Not everything that happens is the work of me or the other Fates. Ragnarok is upon us. I'm trying to decide whose side I will be on when The Veil falls."

"You're only on your own side." Kit gave her a disgusted sneer. "You are a self-centered narcissist, only concerned with your own wellbeing."

"I told you, Kit. Not everything is as it seems." Like her cohort, she disappeared with a pop, leaving a cloud of fetid smoke behind her. In the distance, a woman laughed. As soon as the sound of her laughter died off, the room once again became a din, people screaming, scampering about, trying to find safe refuge.

"It's over," Kit yelled. Even at the top of her lungs it wasn't enough to break through the din. The surrounding people were in a full panic. Kit reached into her pocket and retrieved her pearl necklace. She slipped it over her head, filled her lungs with air, and bellowed.

"Be at peace!"

The power behind her voice toppled several tables and chairs, bringing everything to an immediate halt.

CHAPTER THIRTY-THREE

THE HUMBLED SQUIRREL

"Feigh, you can't be here. Misty's going to lose her mind and you're going to leave with a fresh batch of scratches." The mouse-sprite paused at the natural hole in the base of the thick aspen, his huge ears twitching, trying to pick up any noises coming from within. A powerful push from behind sent his head smashing into the smooth-barked tree. He spun around just in time to duck under an incoming punch. As knuckles shattered the trunk behind him, Feigh slipped to the side, drawing two needle-point daggers as he did.

"I'm going to crush you." Hob shook the pain from his hand. "I'm going to crush you and then I'm going to hurt you, bad."

Sweet Gaia, he's gotten even bigger. What exactly does this squirrel eat to give him such huge muscles?

"Leave him be, Hob," Misty said from her perch, many feet above the melee. "You shouldn't have come, Feigh. You're not welcome here."

"I tried to tell him." Midnight rubbed his shoulder muscle where Hob had laid a well-placed strike. The rabbit-sprite's nose twitched; his pink eyes darkened. "Feigh's still just as mule-headed as when you last saw him."

Feigh slipped his daggers into their sheaths. "We need to talk, without your muscle." Feigh turned to regard the squirrel. He was never much taller than Feigh was, but the man's arms were at least four times thicker than his own, and he had no neck. Where his ears ended, his shoulders started. Hob cracked his knuckles again, just before he beat the palm of his left hand with his right fist.

"Whatever you need to say to me, you can say in front of Hob. Unlike you, he keeps no secrets from me, and I keep none from him." The cat-sprite purred the words out, but they were filled with the pain of hurts that would never heal.

"Grams needs us, Misty. We need to gather the sprites, all of them. Hiding won't be an option this time."

The cat dropped from the limb, landing softly on the thick grasses growing at the base of the tree. She stood over the mouse, lording her height over him. She leaned in close enough that Feigh noticed catnip on her breath. The girl loved that spice much more than she would ever admit.

"Why?" she asked, carefully examining his eyes, perhaps searching for deception in them.

"Because she told me to, that's why. We owe her everything and when she calls, we answer."

"That's not what I meant. I meant, why won't we be able to hide this time?"

"The prophecies are coming to pass. The three are in play and they will free Titan. When they do, the Veil will fall, the gates of Helja will open, and Ragnarök will begin. All life, in the air, on the land, and beneath the waves will perish." The cat-sprite scoffed at the words.

"How many times have we heard this? How many times were they wrong? Every. Single. Time. Whoever the three are, they will fail, like they always do. Things will go back to where they were, and the cycle will repeat." Misty licked her paw and ran it over her ear. She was about to repeat the process when Feigh stopped her.

"You're as beautiful as you ever were. There is no need to preen yourself." She couldn't help herself and smiled at the mouse's words.

"You're as smooth as ever, but it will not make any difference today."

"The Phoenix has risen," Midnight said. "It's going to be different this time." This time it was Hob's turn to sneer. "Scoff all you want. I've seen him. Just before the statue of Titan fell, she was there. You all know it. She is the harbinger of doom."

"The rumors might have been true?" Hob asked. "I thought they were just crazy people saying the sky was falling. I hate crazy people."

"Just because you don't understand them doesn't make them crazy." Feigh had a deep look of contempt on his face. "Do what you do best and bash things. Let the rest of us do the thinking. Okay, big guy?" Hob took a menacing step toward the mouse, pausing when Midnight held his staff at the ready.

"I'll talk with Grams." Misty shook her head. "If she can convince me, I'll rally the others. You know, though, we're going to need the Nymphs and we won't get their support unless the elves are with us."

"If you speak with Lady Galahdes, she'll listen." Feigh hopped from foot to foot. "The Elven queen always had a soft spot for you."

"I would like to return to the Eastern Forest. It's been too long since we walked among the Amberwood trees." Misty turned to Hob and cocked an eyebrow. "Will you come with me to see Grams?" The squirrel chittered and scratched the fur on his chest.

"I will never leave your side. Not while I'm still welcome and not while I draw breath."

"You could learn from him," Midnight whispered, digging his elbow into Feigh's ribs. "He might be a dolt, but he knows how to speak to a lady." Feigh simply grunted and headed off towards Ashcroft, the village where Grams lived.

⁂

"Grams?" Feigh called out, sticking his head in the old woman's front door. He had been pounding as hard as he could for several minutes, but to no effect. He had to, repeatedly, stop Hob from trying to bash the door down. It seemed he either didn't understand the concept of privacy, or, more likely, he simply didn't care.

"Wait here." Feigh's tone was severe enough that he was leaving no room for confusion. He stepped in the front door, finding the bright yellow room empty. A hand pressed against the middle of his back, just a moment before he was shoved into the house.

"Grams!" Hob yelled out. "Grams, we're here, just like you asked."

"You need to put him on a leash," Midnight said to Misty. "He's going to cause a fight, and someone is going to get killed."

"Hob wouldn't hurt Feigh, not really," she said with a coy smile.

"He's not the one who's going to die. I swear to Gaia, I will send him through a portal to the top of Toka, and he will never find his way home. Not before he's eaten, anyway." The cat-sprite gave Midnight a withering look.

"Why can't you just get along?"

"And why are you so blinded by him?" Feigh pulled at his ears. It bothered him that Hob had searched the house, helping himself to Grams' food stores. "He is beneath you, but still..." he threw his hands in the air. The argument was hopeless. He had had this discussion with Misty more times than he could count, but she was infatuated with the squirrel and his overly developed physique.

"I'd heard the old girl is the mayor of this village or some such nonsense," Hob called out from the kitchen, his words muffled through a mouthful of food. "You'd think she'd have a better home than this hovel."

"I like my hovel just fine, Hob. I don't recall offering my food to you, but manners were never your strong suit, now were they." Grams had come in through the back entrance with Ashkey. Triss was riding on his shoulder, still singing away to him like she had been since they'd left Silverhawk.

Hob stepped into the home's main living space with a handful of nuts and berries that he had pilfered from the kitchen. Whatever Grams had said to him went over his head, or more likely, he heard and simply didn't care. Triss squealed with delight when her mate stepped through the doorway. She hopped down from Ashkey's shoulder and raced across the room to dole out a hefty supply of hugs.

Feigh turned toward a deep, throaty grunt, like that of a bull. Ashkey stormed across the room, his face red, his hand curled up into tight fists. The last time he'd seen the boy, he was barely cognizant of people around him. He was definitely aware of what was going on around him now.

"Those were not yours to eat," Ashkey growled out until he was a step away from Hob. In a rather spectacular fashion, the boy pulled back his leg and booted the squirrel across the room, sending berries and nuts in every direction. Hob struck the wall with a solid thud before dropping to the floor, making a terribly similar sound. He popped to his feet; his thick fluffy tail raised up close to his back. It quivered frantically while his rear foot thumped the floor.

Ashkey was busy rooting around the room, picking up the fallen summer berries, examining each one to make sure it was unspoiled. Hob dashed across the floor. The overly muscled squirrel's fists were drawn back, ready to strike. He flew toward the boy, ready to unleash his fury upon him. Hob squeaked, his tiny pink tongue sticking out of his face, when the boy snatched him from the air and hurled him back against the wall. He struck it with enough force to break bones. Hob clutched onto the home's log wall with his wicked little claws. He hung there for several seconds before dropping unconscious to the ground.

"He shouldn't have touched Lady Triss' berries, Grams. They weren't his, and Lady Triss never gave him her leave." The old woman had her hand over her mouth. She stared at the boy with wide eyes. Her shoulders shook. It started small, but the shaking kept getting worse. Tears were forming in the woman's eyes and just when it seemed like she could not withstand it a moment longer, she pulled her hands from her face and unleashed the loudest, most hysterical laugh ever witnessed in the village, possibly the entire kingdom. Feigh and Midnight joined in, holding their bellies to stop themselves from falling over. Even Triss, who would normally not engage in such childish behavior, lost control of herself and laughed along with everyone else. The only people besides Hob, who weren't laughing, were Misty and Ashkey. Misty seemed torn, unsure if she should scold the boy or if she should aid the battered squirrel. The look of indecision made the other sprites laugh all the harder.

"Grams?" Ashkey's lower lip was trembling, the berries in his hands being turned to pulp in his fists. "I don't understand." The old woman's heart broke for the boy. He had no actual history with the sprites. All he had done, from his perspective, was protect the one sprite who had cared for him. He loved her dearly, and he believed they were mocking him.

"Oh, sweet child." Grams rushed to the boy, wrapped her arms around him, and poured as much love into him as she could manage. "The reason we're laughing would take a lifetime to explain, but know this." She pulled herself out of the hug and stared directly into the boy's eyes. "What you just did, well..." The old woman had to fight to hold back the laughter that was welling up within her, laughter that would only confuse the boy further. "What you did, there isn't a single one among us who isn't jealous. We would have loved to have slammed that little jerk into the wall ourselves. He's had it coming for a good long time."

"Thank you," Triss said, standing at the feet of the boy. "Thank you for standing up for me. You are the best protector a girl could have."

It was hard to say whether it was Grams' or Triss' words that had gotten through to Ashkey, but a bright smile split his face. He offered his hand to Triss, lifting her to his shoulder. "I love you. Nobody will ever hurt you while I'm around."

"I believe that." Feigh stole a peek at Mysty before addressing the boy. "You can't imagine how happy I am to see you up and doing well, my friend. If you don't mind, I'd like to introduce you to my kin. This here is Midnight. This lovely lady is Misty. And this rude ball of muscle that you so handily dispatched is Hob." Feigh stared at the stricken squirrel a bit longer, nodding his head appreciatively. "You're the first person I've ever seen get the better of my cousin. You're some kind of special."

"Yes, he is." Triss patted the boy's shoulder.

"I guess I should go help Hob." Grams was clearly not really that interested in helping the squirrel.

"No need, Grams; I've got this." Midnight pulled his staff out of the ether. Holding it in one hand, he gestured with his other. A swirling blue sphere appeared, hovering a few feet above the squirrel. When the sphere was fully formed, the rabbit clenched his fist. The sphere lost its shape and crashed down upon the unconscious sprite, dousing him with a bucketful of water.

⚬⚬⚭⚭◈⚮⚮⚬⚬

"Never, have I ever." Hob wrung the water from his luxurious tail. More than anything, he wanted to smack the lad who had bested him in physical combat, but after his last encounter, the squirrel directed his ire at Midnight. "Where did you pull that water from? It smells of... I can't even describe it, except that it's horrid."

"You poor thing." Misty rubbed him down with another towel. She turned away and wrinkled her nose, shuddering. She narrowed her eyes and stared at the rabbit who was entirely too pleased with himself.

"There is a small pool at the bottom of the hill, just outside of town." Midnight held his hands up innocently. "I can't speak to its quality, only to its presence. He needed to be revived, and it was the only water I sensed." Misty's face contorted with rage, her hands shaking violently.

"There's a pitcher of water on the table. Right there, not two paces from you, and you pulled water from the sewage pond?" The cat's comments elicited another bout of laughter from both Feigh and Midnight.

"There's not enough water in it for me to feel it." Midnight dismissed his staff back to the ether. "I panicked. I thought our muscly friend's life was in peril."

"You're an ass." Hob shook off the last of the water. He sniffed himself and winced. "I will get you back. You know that, right?" A sweet melody filled the room. Trill notes drifted about, dancing and weaving themselves around each person. Rich tones colored the air like a tapestry of rhythms and harmonies. The tension in the room died away, leaving everyone at peace. When the music stopped, everyone was in a state of restful bliss.

"Thank you, Triss," Grams said as she entered the room. She carried a tray laden with cut up fruits and vegetables. She winced when she, too, caught the acrid scent emanating from Hob. "And as for you, Midnight, you remove that... smell from Hob, right this instant." The rabbit regarded the old woman's demands, his eyes half closed, a dreamy look on his face. With a shrug, he reached out, pulling his staff once more from the ether. With a warm smile, he reached his free hand out towards Hob. He closed his eyes and wiggled his fingers in front of himself. The calm, blissful look on his face changed to deep concentration, his eyes closing tightly, his body weaving from side to side. He groaned as he lowered his head. A dull aura appeared around the head of his staff. Finally, his posture relaxed, and a cloud of yellow-green dust, pulled from

Hob's fur, hovered for a moment above him, and then disappeared with a slight pop.

The squirrel slumped.

"Give him some water," Midnight said as he, too, slumped, leaning on his staff. "He's a bit dehydrated. Better give him the whole pitcher."

"What did you do to him?" Misty asked as she lazily moved across the room, snatching up the pitcher.

"I needed to borrow a bit of water from him, to remove the… residue. He's unharmed, I swear." Unlike all the other sprites who seemed to be in a dream-state, Midnight was himself. The exertion of his magic had washed away the spell that Triss had woven around him. He hopped over to the table, helping himself to the food that Grams had just delivered.

"So, why did you want us to come?" Midnight chewed on a thick leaf of lettuce. "It's got to be important if you're willing to put up with this lot." He motioned towards Misty, who was helping Hob drink the pitcher of water.

Grams motioned for everyone to join her at the table. She passed out small plates to everyone as they arrived, encouraging them to eat their fill.

Grams picked up the empty water pitcher. "These are troubling times. You, more than most, understand the game of the gods and what it means to the world. Most of you were around for the end of the last game. You know what to expect."

"As long as the Veil is intact." Misty sniffed an overripe Thornberry. "The end cannot come. Lady Galahdes ensures the Veil will not falter. She has too much to lose should it fail."

"Who is Lady Galahdes?" Ashkey had been sitting calmly in the corner since he'd smashed the squirrel into the wall. Triss looked at Grams, who nodded her approval.

"Lady Galahdes is the queen of the elves, a lesser god." Triss hopped down from the table and hopped up onto Ashkey's lap. She traced a pattern with her fingers onto the palm of his hand. "Ollin chose her from all the elves he had created. She would rule the children of the wood, help them grow and flourish. The god gave her unparalleled power because he felt the goodness within her. He loved her deeply, and he feared Bael and his horde of demons would defeat the Elves. Ollin feared the dragons would not side with them. He feared he would lose everything. It was no longer a game to him.”

"People will do almost anything for love.” Feigh joined his wife on Ashkey's lap, his eyes reflecting his words. "Ollin and Galahdes struck a deal with the Fates. The Fates lured Bael to visit Helja. While he was there, Ollin and Galahdes cast the greatest spell ever devised. They created an impenetrable curtain designed to keep Bael and his minions in Helja forever. But something went wrong with the spell. Some of us believe the Fates had their thumb on the scales. They warped the magic. Instead of it trapping Bael in Helja, it trapped every god who was not on Orth in whichever realm they were in. In doing so, they trapped Gimlie, the dwarven god, along with every subsurface being living in the Underworld.”

"But they saved the elves, right?” Ashkey was confused. He didn't understand the ramifications of Ollin's actions.

"Yes, they did.” Triss' eyes welled up. Her mate nodded lightly. "Do you remember what it felt like to be a prisoner?” The boy's bottom lip trembled at the question. "That's how these trapped people feel right now. They are imprisoned and they are angry. I expect they've been working to free themselves ever since, and when they get out...”

The boy motioned with his chin at Hob with a sneer. "They're going to smoosh us against the wall, like I did to him.” Ashkey's choice of words made Feigh chuckle.

"Exactly. And Grams thinks this is about to happen.” The mouse-sprite raised his eyebrows and turned to the old woman, who nodded her agreement. "Triss, my love, why don't you take our young friend here to go pick some flowers for Grams. I'm sure she'd love to have some fresh yellow daisies for her table.”

Triss looked up at Ashkey. "Would you like to do that?” The boy smiled enthusiastically at the question and patted his shoulder, inviting Triss to sit upon it.

While the pair headed for the front door, Feigh returned to the table where the others were enjoying the bounty laid before them.

"What would you have us do?" the mouse-sprite asked the old woman, a look of dread on his face.

CHAPTER THIRTY-FOUR

A FITTING FATE

They were slow to transition from panic to peace. More than a dozen guards were killed in the melee, along with several of the king's soldiers. While Captain Harding restored order, Kit and her cohorts moved from the barrack's dining hall to her father's office.

"Does anybody else feel like a pawn in the gods' games?" Kit asked, sitting on the corner of her father's desk, a heavy, beat-up piece of furniture. She stifled a yawn and scrubbed her eyes with her fists.

"What does it matter?" Lin said. "Look at what you've accomplished in just one day. The king took control of the city, sending his best people here to take it away from us, and you took it back."

"Me?" Kit laughed, a tired, pathetic laugh. "I hardly did anything. It was all of you. The priests, the acolytes, my father; it was all of you who made this happen." Runt and Lump moved up beside her, staring at her with their bright, hopeful doggy-eyes. "And you, too. You guys were amazing." She slid off the desk and wrapped her arms around their necks, taking a moment to enjoy their warm, thick coats. As she buried her face into Lump's neck, her nose wrinkled. "But you guys need a bath."

"We could all use a bath," Indie offered. He was sitting in one of the captain's guest chairs, with his feet stretched out in front of himself. "But we've got more business in front of us." He did his best to stifle a yawn and failed miserably. The need to yawn spread through the rest of the group, providing a bit of levity.

"We've got three people to interrogate," Sister Gale said. "I, for one, want to have some pointed words with Brother Powder and Brother Rimes." Somehow, the woman was still fresh and ready to fight, although her once white robes were mottled with so much brown and red it was difficult to tell the garment's original color. Kit sank down to the floor at the comment, resting her back against her father's desk. The boys settled in beside her with Lump resting his head across her lap.

"Wouldn't it be better to just pronounce judgment upon them," Kit said, yawning yet again. "It would certainly take less time."

"Easier yes, but not better," the combat instructor replied.

"We also need to take time to honor the dead." Amara hadn't changed out of the revealing leather attire, refusing to put her priestly robes back on. "Many of us passed on to the Great Cycle today." A giant knot twisted in Kit's gut at the comment. Many priests died, but it was Sister Miyuki and Father Hoarfrost who she would miss the most. They were two of the most important people in her life, and now they were gone. She should have been sad or angry at their loss, but thinking about them left her feeling hollow, like an enormous piece of her was missing.

"We need to find Sister Nevara." Lin leaned back against the far wall. "We need to tell her it's safe for her and the children to come out of hiding. I can't imagine what they're going through right now."

"They're cold and they're scared," Iba said. "But they're safe and they're whole. The experience will strengthen them. The children will know that the Temple will protect them when danger is near." Kit got the feeling there was something more to what Iba was saying, something very personal, but at the moment, she was too tired to think about it.

Kit hoisted herself up off the ground. "Iba, thank you for everything you did. Things would have been much harder for us had you not been here." The small Tahr blinked and nodded her head.

"Lin." Iba's voice was shaky. "Why don't we go find Nevara and the children? We shouldn't let them continue to worry that their world is ending. There is much to be thankful for today." Lin pushed herself away from the wall and moved towards the door. She stopped long enough to give Kit a hug before exiting with Iba.

"Take the boys with you," Kit said. "The children will enjoy seeing them." The boys darted for the door, jostling with each other to see who would get there first.

"Sister Amara, Brother Silverleaf," Sister Gale said as she, too, moved towards the door. "Would you accompany me to gather up the dead so that we can pay proper homage to them?" Without a word, the two priests moved from their spot together and joined their teacher. "You too, Slate," she added. "You can visit with your kin another time."

"I'd like to help with the preparations as well, if I may," Coldforge said. "It's only right to honor those who paid the heavy price. The lad here can see how we do it back home." Sister Gale inclined her head and led the group away.

"Let's go find your father," Indie said. "We can start the interrogations with Karr."

⸺⸺⸺◆⸺⸺⸺

It hadn't taken long for the captain to get his people organized. They were dispatched in small groups, accompanied by acolytes, to secure the city's front gates and to take up positions along the parapets. The bodies of the dead soldiers had been gathered in the barracks' training yard. Captain Harding had promised a ceremony would be held for those who had fallen, but first, he needed to make sure the city was safe, and order was restored.

At Kit's request, only Indie and her father accompanied her as she led Karr into the barrack's lower dungeons, or the cellar, as her father referred to them. On multiple occasions, the prisoner had attempted to break free, earning him a split lip and a deep gash over his left eye. They hadn't even made it to the bottom of the stairs before the air quality changed, turning dank and moist. The earthen floors of the cellar were spongy under foot, water seeping up from the ground with every footstep. The air was so thick with mildew that it coated Kit's tongue and nose with every breath she took. She smacked her lips and frowned as the taste of mold took hold.

The scent of earth and natural decay couldn't compare to the stink of putrefaction that had rolled out when Captain Harding opened the cell door. Within the large room was the vampire Indie, and the boys had faced during their training exercises. Indie used his torch to light two braziers that were sitting just inside the doorway. The fires cast the room in a flickering, deep red glow; the light reflected by a pair of hungry eyes huddled in the corner behind thick steel bars.

"Please, have mercy on me," Karr screamed out as he struggled against the bonds holding his hands behind his back. A quick jerk on the rope tied around his neck silenced the man. The vampire moved out from the back of his cell, the smell of fresh blood driving him into a frenzy.

"Come now, Lieutenant. You've been through this before." The captain's voice dripped with sarcasm. "This should be easy for you." An evil look crossed the captain's face. "Then again, perhaps it won't be as easy as it was in the past. I've disabled the protection spell that would keep the creature at bay should you get too close."

"You know I couldn't." Karr continued pleading, his lower lip quivering. "You know I failed these tests. Without the spell…"

"He'll drain you dry." Kit punched him in the face again, splitting his lip open even further. Smelling the fresh blood, the vampire *thing* behind the cage screeched. It yanked at the bars, while continuing its high-pitched, blood-lust wails.

"I'll tell you everything, I swear," Karr screamed again, trying desperately to escape his bonds.

"One chance." Kit's eyes flashed golden. "Tell us true, or you will spend what is left of your miserable life in here with this… thing."

"I am working with Martelle and Aithlin." Karr's eyes were glued on the desiccated face of the vampire as he stretched his clawed hands out through the bars. Kit flinched when he spoke Lin's name.

"What was Lin's role in this?" Kit dragged the man closer to the cage.

"She provided information." Karr's eyes were wild as he resisted against the rope around his neck, strangling himself in the process. "Her and Martelle, they were bringing in rare weapons from Two Peaks. I helped them steal the weapons, and they gave me information on what her father and the king were up to."

"Lin betrayed us to King Jordain?" the captain asked through gritted teeth.

"No." Karr's voice came out between choked gasps. "She only wanted to hurt her father, to ruin his reputation as a supplier of rare and valuable weapons. It was Martelle. He used her to his advantage. He duped her."

Kit's heart leapt for joy at the man's words. He was speaking the truth, at least to the best of his ability. His words corroborated Lin's story. Even though she didn't detect any deception from Lin, hearing it from Karr directly removed any doubts Kit had about her friend.

"Martelle wanted to rule Aarall," Karr continued, until he was cut off by Kit.

"I thought Lord Aster was to rule Aarall," she growled.

"He was." Karr's voice was becoming shrill. "But only as a figurehead. Martelle would have been ruling from the shadows, much like he did while he was in Two Peaks."

"Are you suggesting that the king is Martelle's puppet?" Captain Harding scoffed. "I find that very difficult to believe."

"No, not like that." Karr's voice returned to normal. "He knows people, powerful people. He whispers in their ears, sowing seeds of doubt and mistrust. Each time the nobles quarreled, his station in the capital rose. But, as a bastard son, he could never receive a seat at the Council."

"Is King Jordain in league with Faol, the Vampire King?" Kit asked. All the details were coming in too fast, and she was struggling to keep it straight in her head. But she was going to milk the man for every drop of information.

"Yes." Karr lowered his head, his eyes cast down at his feet. "Faol promised to not attack Arnnor if the king never interfered with his plans. But when people fought back against the slave trade, Faol insisted the king provide him with slaves as well."

When Karr raised his eyes, he looked like he'd just bitten into a lemon. "I wanted no part of that. I only wanted..."

"Power," the captain interrupted. "You wanted to be the head of the City Watch, but you couldn't do that if I was here. All because I'd never take a post in the King's Guard."

"You hold the highest seat in the city," Karr said with a disgusted sneer. "And yet you live like a common soldier, bunking in the barracks with the rest of us. You could have been showered in luxury if you'd only accepted it."

"We're soldiers," Captain Harding growled at him. "We swore an oath to defend the people of Aarall, not to enrich ourselves."

The captain clenched his massive hand into a tight fist and smashed it into the lieutenant's face. Blood from the man's mouth and nose sprayed across the room, with a good amount of it landing on the ground near the caged vampire. The creature dropped to the earthen floor, trying desperately to lick up the blood. While the vampire was busy trying to suck up the last drips of crimson from the steel cage, the captain tied off the end of Karr's rope to the bars of the cell.

"No!" Karr screeched. "You promised me a quick death. Don't do this."

"I promised you nothing." The captain gave the lieutenant a look that suggested he reeked of refuse. "I'll come back tomorrow. If you're still alive, I'll give you a merciful death."

"The vampire will drag him into the bars," Indie said. "We should at least give him a chance to withstand the creature's compulsion. Having that *thing* in your head is far worse than being killed by it."

Kit drew her dagger and cut the lieutenant's bond, holding him to the cage.

"Like your captain said." Kit threw the sniveling man to the ground. "Survive until tomorrow, and I'll make sure you get a quick death."

As Kit pulled the door closed, the wails of Karr and the animalistic screeches of the vampire filled the air. She stared at the closed door for several seconds. "For Father Hoarfrost and Sister Miyuki."

As the trio made their way from the cellar, Kit's heart shattered. A wave of intense sorrow washed over her, consuming her. She was never again going to enjoy the love and company that Father Hoarfrost and Sister Miyuki had so willingly given her. Never again would her mentor share his wisdom. Never again would Kit get to enjoy another meal with the woman, who happily gave her time and energy to see that she was happy.

Sensing Kit's internal grief, both Indie and her father placed a comforting hand on the small priest's shoulders. She reached out, grabbing them both by the waist, drawing them next to herself. Her chest hitched as she tried to find the words she so desperately needed to share with them.

"I love you both very much." Tears threatened to pour from Kit's glassy eyes. "If I don't tell you often enough, I'm sorry."

⸎

The trio walked in silence, climbing the stairs from the dungeons. Wordlessly, they made their way outside to the barracks' gatehouse. It was well past midday. The sun was warm, peeking out from behind a single bank of dark clouds.

"Can we leave interrogating Powder and Rimes until tomorrow?" Kit asked, leaning into her father. The big man patted her shoulder and grunted.

"It's best we let them stew for a while. I need to go back to my people and make sure everyone is okay. We lost too many souls today, even for soldiers."

"I'd like to go to the Temple. I need to see..." her words died off before she could finish. Beyond reason, she hoped that Father Hoarfrost was still alive. Seeing his broken body would shatter that dream, as unlikely as it was.

"I'll take her," Indie whispered to the captain. "I'll make sure she gets some rest, too."

"Stay safe." The captain nodded. "You never know what other dangers may have been left in the wake."

"We will, Captain." Indie clasped the man's arm. "May Titan guide and watch over you." The captain gave the young man a look of surprise. Indie shrugged in response. "Since Ymir seems to be a traitor, I might as well follow the same god as Kit."

"What do you mean, Ymir's a traitor?" The captain's eyes were wide in disbelief.

"It's a long story." Kit sighed. She was utterly exhausted. "He seems in league with King Faol, but it's hard to know for sure where a god's loyalty lies."

"It's a strange world we live in," the captain said, staring aimlessly out across the courtyard. "The rumors of Ragnarök may well be true."

"End of days or not, I'm not giving up." Kit gave Indie a wistful smile. "I've got too much to live for."

"*Don't we all,*" Angel said through their bond.

Kit squealed with joy at the sight of Angel, Char, and Whistler, as they came trotting up from the main gate. Pulling away from her father, she raced towards her little roan, wrapping her arms around her neck. Indie moved to greet his stallion, albeit with a more subdued reaction.

"Perhaps you can take us to the stables? It would be nice to have fresh hay and oats. The wild grasses are okay, but it's a lot of work to get enough to satisfy me. After all, I'm eating for two."

"You're pregnant?" Kit let out another ear-piercing squeal. When Angel whinnied in response, Indie gave Char a knowing look and patted him on the neck in congratulations.

"Here." Kit reached out to unbuckle the horse's saddle. "Let's get this off you."

Angel snorted. *"I am still quite capable of carrying you. We horses are not as fragile as humans. If you don't ride me, I'll only get fatter."*

"Okay." Kit gave her horse a kiss on her soft, warm muzzle. "And for the record, you've never looked more beautiful."

"Why don't we get them to the stables?" Indie chuckled. "You wanted to visit the Temple, anyway, didn't you?"

Chapter Thirty-Five

Titan Provides

The ride back to the Temple went without incident. Mostly, the citizens appeared to be going about their lives as though nothing had happened. It dawned on Kit that the people had their own lives and their own worries. The affairs of lords and ladies and of priests and soldiers were of little concern unless they directly affected them.

At the foot of the Temple stairs, hundred of mourners had gathered, crying, and wailing, praying to Titan for his salvation. As Kit approached, they flocked to her.

"Savior of Aarall! Acknowledged of Titan!" many of them were screaming out, with tear-streaked faces and outstretched hands, hoping that she might bestow her blessing upon them.

"You need to say something," Indie urged Kit. "They're desperate for comfort, for reassurance."

The young priest moaned audibly before slipping her necklace on.

"Titan's faithful," she called out from her roan's back. "We have all endured hard times, and yet, we continue on. We continue on because we know Titan is with us, that he watches over us, and when ill befalls us, it is a part of his grand design. When we pass, any of us pass, we join Titan in the Great Cycle. Our spirit, our essence, returns to our creator."

When Kit finished speaking, the people were all kneeling before her, their foreheads pressed to the ground. Slowly, they rose and as they did, they gave Kit the greatest gift she had ever received. In their eyes, she saw hope.

"May Titan's peace and grace be upon you." Kit spurred Angel forward, slipping off her necklace. She'd lost count of how many times this small gift from Lin had helped her.

"*We can find our way to the stables. Taking us there is well out of your way.*"

"If you're okay with that." Kit slid down from her saddle and patted Angel's neck. "I'll send some acolytes to check in on you."

Kit shuddered as she stood before the Temple's massive oak doors. The thought that her mentor had died within its hallowed halls crushed her spirit. With a trembling hand, she reached out to push the door open.

"Let me." Indie took her hand in his.

Kit gave the man a weak half smile. "I need to do this." Her voice was wavering. "But thank you."

Kit drew a deep breath and pushed on the heavy iron-bound door. It groaned as it opened. Dust swirled out from the opening like spirits trying to escape from an ethereal prison. The entrance to the Temple was typically dim, with the only light coming from braziers that lined the vestibule's outer walls. But now, there were no fires to brighten the hallowed halls. There were no window slits to let the smallest amounts of light into the room. There was only darkness, and death's rank stink.

Kit wrinkled her nose and coughed as another cloud of dust swirled about them, raised by a warm breeze that had followed them inside. Pulling her hammer from its sheath, she called upon its light to illuminate the room. From beyond the entrance, doors opened to the nave.

As Kit had witnessed earlier, blocks of granite and precious stone filled much of the Temple's main hall. Several of the primary support pillars were gone, but the lofty roof appeared to be intact. Kit pulled her eyes away when Indie drew a sharp breath.

"Look." Indie pointed to a section of fallen debris off to Kit's left. From beneath the boulders and rubble, a pool of blood had poured out, now dried to a sickly red-brown color.

"The reports would seem to have been accurate." Kit moved closer to inspect the carnage. "Father took down a good number of the king's people when he…"

"He made it possible for us to retake the city." Indie tried to comfort his love. "Like you, he willingly offered his life in the service of others."

"Where was Titan?" Kit dropped to her knees. There was a hard edge to her voice. Her skin was turning pale, her daemon runes spreading across her hands and face. "Why didn't he save his most faithful servant? What sort of god lets the head of his church die like this?"

"Titan didn't decide, Father did. Just as you would have, too, if it was the only way you saw to save the people of the city." The runes died off and Kit's skin returned to its pale gold color. She sniffed and wiped her nose with her sleeve.

"Come on, Kit," Indie took her by the hand. "There looks to be a path around the outside of the rubble. We might make it to the eastern hallway, to Father Hoarfrost's office."

With the man's aid, Kit picked herself up off the ground and strode along the path between the fallen stonework and the walls. Just before reaching the hallway's entrance, Kit paused and held up her hand.

"I hear voices," she whispered.

"They sound like," Indie said, his eyes narrowing as he strained to listen. "They sound like children."

"Nevara!" Kit bolted around the corner, finding her friends accompanying Sister Nevara and a large group of children.

"Sister Kit," the severe-looking priest called out. Her hair, which was typically pulled back in a tight knot, was bedraggled. The woman looked to have been to Helja and back, but she was otherwise healthy and whole. She broke into a run, and reaching Kit, she grasped onto the young priest as though she were a life preserver in a turbulent sea. The elderly priest babbled incomprehensibly as she continued clutching onto Kit.

"I know." Kit stroked the woman's hair. "We're going to set things right."

"Ye know," Coldforge said as he entered the Temple's main hall. "Me kin could fix this up in no time."

"What?" Kit and Nevara both asked.

"It's not so bad." The dwarf surveyed the expansive hall. "Most of the main pillars seem to be intact, and there are no collapsed walls I can see."

"Then where did all this stone and rubble come from?" Indie asked, scrubbing the back of his neck. "This looks like an entire building came down on the enemy here."

A raspy voice called out from within the depths of the rubble. "Titan provides."

Kit's eyes went wide as she bolted for the pile of debris, scrambling up and over it until she disappeared beyond the ridge, with only the light of her hammer letting everyone know where she was.

"Father's alive! He's alive!"

⁂

Kit's heart was beating so hard and so fast, she could hardly breathe. Beneath the Temple's main altar laid Father Hoarfrost, his skin a deathly shade of gray, his arm and leg pinned beneath a massive piece of Titan's statue.

"Peace unto you." The old priest gave Kit a thin-lipped smile.

"Shh, Father," Kit said, calling upon her healing powers.

"Don't." Father Hoarfrost shook his head.

"I can fix you." Tears were dripping from the tip of Kit's nose onto her injured mentor.

"It's not possible. I can't be healed while I'm pinned under... Titan. It doesn't matter, anyway. The poison I was given... I can't cure it." The thought that Brother Powder had poisoned him made Kit's blood boil.

"Help!" she screamed out. "I need help!"

Within seconds, Indie, Coldforge, and Lin came scrambling down, Silverleaf a short distance behind them.

"He's trapped beneath the statue. The poison Powder gave him, it's killing him," Kit said to Lin, hopeful that she had a potion to cure the old priest.

"I have nothing for the poison." Lin handed Kit one of the special rejuvenation potions. "It won't cure him, but it will help restore his health somewhat."

Taking the stopper from the tiny flask, Kit poured the concoction into Hoarfrost's mouth. As soon as it touched his lips, the old man's eyes brightened. A moment later, he screamed out in pain.

"We need to get the statue off him," Kit said. "As long as he's trapped beneath it…"

"If you can lend me yer hammer." Coldforge ran his hand over Titan's stone arm. "It's about ready to split on its own."

"Be careful to not hurt Father." Kit trembled as she handed the dwarf her weapon.

"Wait." Silverleaf was rummaging through his sack of scrolls. "I have scrolls of protection from poison. They might help."

"We remove the statue first." Kit gave the half elf a gentle look.

"We can pour healing potions onto his leg and arm." Lin handed Indie a small crystal vial full of deep red liquid. "These are the strongest healing potions I have."

Kit nodded to Lin and closed her eyes for a moment in prayer, her hands igniting with her familiar golden aura. "Whenever you're ready," she said to Coldforge, holding her hands a few inches over her mentor.

"Gaia, guide my hands," Coldforge whispered, before bringing the hammer down on the statue. There was a deafening crack and a burst of brilliant white light as the hammer contacted the stone. Hoarfrost's screams of agony echoed off the Temple walls.

Kit poured herself into her healing powers. Pain exploded through her, her body wracking in response. Somewhere within the man was an injury that she could feel but could not heal. It evaded her. It seemed impossible to hold on to. Just before giving up on it, something from within herself reached out and grasped hold. The injury, whatever it was, burned into nothingness.

Kit's face was scarlet, dripping with sweat when she opened her eyes, unable to focus through her tears.

"Father?" she called out, clearing her vision with her sleeve.

"Hello, Sister," Father Hoarfrost said, giving Kit a warm smile. "I knew you'd find me."

"We were told that you…" Kit's vision once again blurred by her tears.

"Immolated myself? That was my plan, but Titan had other ideas." A sudden pang of regret ripped through Kit's chest. She had assumed that Titan had let his priest die. But here he was, alive and mostly whole.

"I don't understand," Kit said, sniffing noisily. "Immolation, it's a final spell."

"I was going to." The old priest propped himself up into a seated position. "Then I thought of you, and how you saved the city. I brought Titan down on those who would desecrate the Temple. I swear, it was as though he pulled me under the altar, just as his statue exploded into… all of this."

"We need to get Father to the infirmary," a red-faced Sister Nevara called out from the top of the rubble pile.

"There is no need for that. Thank you, Sister," Father Hoarfrost called back. "I've received all the healing I require, and then some."

Father Hoarfrost stroked Kit's flaming red hair. "You'll need to tell me about this," he whispered, "and your healing power. I saw the pain in your eyes. You were not channeling Titan in your spell."

"I'll tell you about all that, and more." Kit kissed the old priest on the cheek. "So much has happened. I don't know where to start."

"Ye can start by calling yer firebird friend," Coldforge said. "If we can get me kin here, we can have this Temple restored in no time."

Chapter Thirty-Six

SIKU

"You didn't take me up into the clouds like you did when we arrived." Ulip breathed in the cool evening air. In the moments between the drake's flaps, the only sound was the air rushing past the giant's ears. Everything was peaceful in the sky, his troubles simply flitting away in the wind. He allowed himself to relax, riding on Yuka's back, his hands by his sides and his feet dangling comfortably on either side of the drake's neck.

"If you're going to die anyway, there is no need to hide my nest mates' location."

Ulip didn't know if she was joking with him or if his life was nearing its end. Either way, he didn't care. For a moment in time, he was free, and he was happy.

"Thank you." He raised his chin and closed his eyes. *"If I am to die when we meet Siku, then I want to tell you now. Thank you for bearing me."* Yuka sighed. It was no fun if he didn't take her threats of death seriously.

"Do you truly not fear death, or do you simply no longer wish to live?"

"I neither seek death, nor do I fear it. I have committed terrible sins against my people's ways. Even if the cause was just, it was wrong that I felt joy in killing. At some point, I will pay for my transgressions."

"Who have you killed and why did you do it?" Yuka's voice in his head was softer than normal.

"Slavers. I killed those who stole the lives of others and ruined them for profit. They came into our lands and took our people. They killed any who fought back. Even though my clan didn't resist, they're still all gone."

"I'm sorry for your clan. They were good people and did not deserve their fate. Your laws allow you to fight to protect yourself or to protect your clan. It is not a sin to take pleasure in a task." Yuka banked to her left, carrying the pair due south. In the distance, a rugged, snow-capped mountain came into view.

"I was no longer protecting my clan." Ulip's voice was resolute. *"I was seeking revenge on the slavers for killing them all."* Yuka chuckled at the Gigas' words, drawing the big man's ire.

"Everything you just said was wrong on so many levels. No wonder your mind is so badly twisted." Ulip paused at the drake's words, unable to process their full meaning. *"Not every member of your clan was killed. Because your lives are so short, you see things from a warped perspective. Everyone who is born will die, eventually. Some of us live longer than others. People leave us and new people join us. Our clan, the people we love and care for, changes over time. Some of your clan have left, but new people have joined your life. The community of Berrat that you built. You gave them a home, and you gave them hope. By killing the slavers, you protected your clan. It protected many people who you never even met. Do you not believe that is a good thing?"*

"How? How do you know that?"

"Very little happens in Spur's realm that he does not know about. We who serve him see much of what happens. It is the reason I offered to bear you. I understood your plight, and I was willing to help."

"Then why don't you help us destroy the slavers?" It didn't matter that his voice was lost in the wind. He needed to scream.

"Because killing the slavers does not further our mission to free Spur. Your people's best hope is to free the dragons so that they might bring order to the land. The dragon lords are your salvation." Yuka beat her great wings several times, carrying them higher into the sky. It was only as the air thinned did Ulip realize they were circling the summit of Mount Toka. A shimmer, less than fifty paces away, caught his eye, but there was nothing there. Another shimmer, this time even closer, appeared to his left, creating something of a silhouette against the darkening sky.

"We are being guided in." There was a hint of worry in her voice. *"Whatever anger you feel towards Spur for not helping you kill slavers, let it go. If you carry it with you when we meet Siku, you* will *die."* A screech off to Ulip's right seemed to punctuate Yuka's comment. A second and a third screech followed, one to Ulip's left and another from above. They were clearly being shepherded by what Ulip could only guess were ice drakes.

"Yes, they are ice drakes. Now, clear your mind of any hostility. Think of your sister and how desperately you want to see her again. Hold tight." No sooner had her words entered Ulip's mind, Yuka changed the angle of her wings, slowing her speed dramatically. With a few controlled wingbeats, she dropped onto the snow-covered ground, steam bursting out where her clawed feet hit the snow. She dropped to her belly and laid her unfurled wings across the ground, creating even more steam, covering Yuka and her rider in a thick fog.

"Bow!" Yuka dropped her chin and lowered her eyes. Ulip could see no one around him, but he followed the fire drake's actions, spreading his arms out to his side and lowering his head.

"Speak your purpose," a thunderous but feminine voice called out in the common tongue. "Why have you entered my realm? Why have you brought me this creature as an offering?"

"I am no offering." Ulip lifted his chin to whomever it was before him. He still couldn't see anybody.

"Silence," Yuka screeched in her native language, knocking Ulip from her back, flaming the snow at his feet. *"How dare you speak in the presence of the great and powerful Siku, goddess of the skies, master of wind?"*

"You will speak aloud and in the language of his people." Siku rose from the snow, an avalanche pouring off her ice-blue body. The dragon seemed to just keep getting bigger and bigger until she was the size of a small mountain. Spur was an enormous dragon, but Siku utterly dwarfed him.

"Warrior of flame," the great dragon continued, "I will ask you again. Why have you brought me this offering?" She pulled back her lips, exposing her small, needle-like teeth. She moved her long neck forward until her head was only five paces away. On closer inspection, her teeth were not that small. They were likely ten feet long. Inside a head that was almost the size of Spur's whole body, they didn't seem that large. Ulip swallowed hard, crossed his arms over his chest, and defiantly raised his chin.

"Oh, wondrous queen of the north, I bring you Ulip, Clan Chief, and tidings from Spur, The Terrible." The great ice dragon burst out laughing, the power of her breath knocking Ulip off his feet.

"Children, and their silly names." Siku laughed and laid herself on the ground. The snow immediately gathered around her, wrapping the dragon in a thick blanket of white. "Spur did not spend enough time with his mother before we were trapped in our mountain homes. He did not benefit from her wisdom." The great dragon addressed the fire drake. "And, speaking of mothers, is yours well, Yuka?"

The fire drake bowed deeply to the dragon. "Very well. Thank you for asking. She is guarding her newest clutch of eggs, while the dragonets torment her constantly. I know she is happiest when her family is beside her, even though she protests bitterly." Yuka stopped speaking and lowered her head. "My deepest apologies, goddess of ice, I forgot myself."

"Arise, Yuka. I will be with my family again some day. I trust Ouroboros is caring for them, as best as he can." Ulip couldn't be sure, but he could have sworn the ice dragon rolled her eyes at him. "Please tell me, what does your dragon master wish you to share with me. I hunger for news from the north."

"My people are in peril. Slavers raid and kill. They must be stopped at any cost." Ulip thrust his great blade over his head and stepped toward the great dragon. A deep rumble came from Siku, shaking the ground, clearing her body of the snow that had continued to gather around her. Despite struggling to maintain his balance, Ulip strode forward and shoved his blade into the ground at his feet.

"Forgive him." Yuka threw her body between Ulip and the dragon. "He has the fever and cannot control his actions." The ground shook at the fire drake's words as Siku chuckled.

"He is like most men, who are all unable to control themselves." Siku blew out a stream of frosty air, knocking Ulip backward several dozen paces. "But if this child of the northern realm cannot learn to hold his tongue, I will cast him from this mountain without concern or remorse."

"Are you no different from those with power?" Ulip brushed away the ice that clung to his clothing. "Would you simply destroy anyone who stands against you, like the slavers did to my clan?" Siku narrowed her ice-blue eyes and placed her chin on the ground in front of Ulip.

"The plight of the children has not gone unnoticed, Chief of the Fire Drake Clan. But the problems they are facing are only one small, but not insignificant part of what evil has befallen the lands. With the tiny people of this world, my kind and I cannot tell friend from foe. We cannot flame any without killing the evil and the innocent alike. But if we cannot free ourselves of our bonds, the entire world will burn, and all will perish. Can you put aside the hatred that clouds your mind for one moment so that you might see the scale of what the people, all the people, are facing?"

The Gigas paused and considered the dragon's words. After several moments he stepped closer to the wall of teeth in front of him. "I am not a dragon, nor can I change the world. But I can change the world of the people I care for. I will do what I can, for I can do no more."

"Because you are a man, you cannot see beyond the tip of your tiny sword." Yuka laughed at the dragon's choice of words, making Siku smile. "But truth be told, you have started something much bigger than yourself. Like the little girl who dwells in this land, you tiny creatures have proven yourselves capable of doing remarkable things. I can respect that." Ulip lowered his eyes and took a knee.

"I am unworthy of your respect, great dragon. I have done very little except shame myself by taking joy in killing." The dragon raised her head from the ground, lifting it nearly one hundred feet into the air. With it looming over the Gigas, she inclined it to him.

"If I believed you were being insincere, our conversation and your life would have ended. You lack perspective. From your place on the ground, you can only see that which is directly in front of you. From the sky, you see the entire world at a glance. What you see are your own problems. What I see are the ripples you have caused across the lands. Berrathia, as you know it, is rising against its oppressors. Your actions were no small part of that. You inspire those around you, coaxing them on to be bigger than themselves. But, let it be known, you can win a battle and still lose the war. Even now, great armies grow south of here. They will march before the moon is full and many people will die. They seek to destroy the Veil and to bring an end to this world. If that happens, all but the gods and their foul minions will perish."

"My queen." Yuka lowered her eyes. "I wish I had more news to share with you, but it seems you already know everything of what is happening in Spur's territory." The great dragon smiled; her large scaly eyebrows upturned.

"I didn't know how you were doing, child. Nor did I know that your mother is brooding another clutch of eggs. It was news of you and your life that I wanted to hear about." The dragon considered the Gigas standing beside the fire drake before returning her attention back to the drake. "It would seem that your mother raised you well, as I knew she would."

"What would you have me do, my queen?" Yuka bowed low. "How best may I serve?"

"Seek the key that will free us from this wretched prison and protect the one you carry. He is more important than I believe anyone realizes. I don't know why, but my heart tells me so. I always trust my heart." A wistful look crossed the great dragon's face. A moment later, it was gone.

"May we spend the night in your mountain home?" The drake stepped closer to Ulip. "I have flown far this day and my wings are weary."

A hint of a smile crossed the dragon's lips. She spread her wings out and a great wind swirled about the Gigas and the fire drake. In a moment, they were cocooned with a magnificent dome of ice and snow, a small vent at the structure's peak.

"You and your Gigas friend will always be welcome in my domain," Siku said, her voice sounding like a purr. "Rest now. The new day will bring new opportunities."

Chapter Thirty-Seven

HOPEFUL SIGNS

"Breayn," Danny said, strolling into the war room, the ledger tucked up under his arm. "I need to show you something."

"We're trying to make plans here, Danny," she replied, looking up from the maps she had strewn out on the table in front of her. Rusty was using one hand to stop the parchment from rolling back up and the other hand to move two black ship models to the coast, just off Seahaven, the Mortem Lupus stronghold.

"Rusty, can you leave, please? I really need to speak with my cousin." Both women looked up from the map and glared at the Berrat. The young man pulled the ledger from beneath his arm and held it up. With his head tilted towards the book, he stared intently at his cousin.

"Fine," Rusty said, releasing her hand from the map, allowing it to roll up and spill the small ships that sat upon it, all over the table. "Considering it's my father's book and I'm in charge of the army, you'd think I might be included in a conversation about its contents."

"Thank you," Breayn said, resting her hand on the woman's arm. "As soon as we're done, I'll come get you. We need to complete our plans." Rusty shook her head and swept out of the room, pulling the door shut behind her.

"I found them," Danny said, patting the top of the book. "I know where they are."

"Who, Danny? Who have you found?" Breayn rolled her eyes and flopped onto a couch. She yawned and scrubbed her face, trying to chase away the fatigue that had set in. She gave her cousin a weary look and invited him to sit beside her.

"Our parents," he said as he sat on the couch, carefully opening the tome to where he had placed a bright blue ribbon between the parchments. "I've found them, all of them." Breayn's head snapped back. Her eyes welled up, blurring her vision. She swiped the tears away, her body swaying. She pressed her palms on the couch cushions to steady herself.

"You're sure?" she asked, her voice shaky. Danny nodded as he ran his finger down the ledger, stopping at a line near the bottom of the page.

"I had trouble understanding the earlier entries. These are not like the others. They're not a simple accounting of what has come in and out of Cormorant. It's almost like a diary. I'll try to translate for you."

The boy was taken beyond my reach to where I cannot touch him. The master's power is too strong there. His followers are too devout.

"That's me he's talking about. I'm sure of it." Danny's eyes were wide as he gauged Breayn's reaction. She was still staring at the ledger, refusing to lift her eyes. She took a deep breath and swallowed hard. "There's more. Here, look." He moved his finger down a few more lines.

The parents will make do. If I can't have the boy, maybe they'll have what I need; what he needs.

"Those are my parents he's talking about, and this is King Faol. I'm sure of it." Tears rolled off Breayn's cheeks and onto her lap. She closed her eyes.

"That could mean almost anything." Danny shook his head, but his cousin couldn't see his reaction. She was staring at her hands, examining her nails.

The sisters are the two purest. The daughter of the eldest may, too, hold the key.

"And here," Danny said, flipping to a page he had marked with a deep red ribbon. "This is the proof."

The husk was delivered, her essence held back for leverage. King Faol may be powerful, but he lacks vision. Only I thought to remove the soul from its vessel. When I discover how the key works, I will rule all while the others rot in their prisons for eternity.

"It has to be them," Danny said, pleading with Breayn to believe him. "He pulled your mother's soul, keeping it for himself. Whoever's inside Rusty's father, he sent her body to Faol, without her soul. He has to have my parents, too."

"Is there more?" she said, taking a deep, shaky breath. "Does he speak of my father?" The woman's neck was bent forward. She scrubbed her hands against her pant leg. When she raised her eyes, they were a deep gray, but there was no storm brewing behind them.

"This was all I could find," he replied, closing the book.

Chapter Thirty-Eight

The Calm After the Storm

It had only been two days since Kit and her cohorts had retaken Aarall. They had held profoundly solemn ceremonies to commemorate the deaths of the Temple's faithful. Father Hoarfrost presided over the entombment of Sister Miyuki and the other priests and acolytes, all of whom were memorialized for their service unto Titan.

With the High Priest at his side, Captain Harding held a vigil for the fallen members of the City Watch. Unlike Titan's faithful, who were entombed, the bodies of the City Watch members were burned upon huge funeral pyres. Unlike the Temple's ceremonies, which were private, the final send-off for the City Watch was a public affair held beyond the city's walls, near Lake Titan. The vast majority of the city's population attended the service, paying homage to those who had made the ultimate sacrifice in service of the people.

In honor of Sister Miyuki, Sister Nevara and the surviving kitchen staff put together a meal reminiscent of the Feast of Titan's bounty. While everyone ate, Kit told Father Hoarfrost everything that had happened since she'd left the city. The children, who had gathered around Kit while she spoke, sat in silent rapture as the young priest spoke of bravery and honor, and of those who had sacrificed their lives in service of the oppressed.

"You need to sleep." Nevara shooed the children away from Kit. "You all do."

Whether it was the copious amounts of food that Kit had eaten, or whether it was the rejuvenation potion wearing off, she could not resist the siren's call of her bed. Taking Indie's hand, she gave Nevara a warm smile.

"I agree, Sister. Thank you for everything. We'll help you clean up and then we'll get some sleep."

"You'll do no such thing," Nevara said, waving her arms at Kit and the others. "You sleep. When you wake, we'll have a suitable breakfast prepared for you."

"Father?" Lin asked. "Do you need help to return to your quarters? The poison..."

"No need to worry, Aithlin." The old priest gave a weak smile. "And I believe the poison has been neutralized. This is the best I've felt in ages, thanks to you, Brother Silverleaf, and our very own little angel."

"I can't be sure, Father," Kit said, her eyes downcast. "It's possible it was my daemon half that cured the poison. When I called upon my healing powers, I felt something different. Something told me, instinctually, to allow it to work its magic."

The elderly priest flexed his newly healed arm. "Don't think of it as angel or daemon. It's just *you*. No more, no less. Your heritage has blessed you with powers beyond what Titan offers us, but it's how you put them to use that defines you as a person. I've always known that freeing Titan would require inhuman abilities. When I look upon you, I now understand why."

Kit stared blankly at her mentor for several seconds before speaking. "Which path lays before me? Am I to free Titan, or am I to free the people?"

"Your path lays to your quarters." Father Hoarfrost inclined his head. "Let's leave the big questions for tomorrow, after we've all had some sleep."

Without another word, Kit and her friends headed for the staircase leading up to the dormitories. Lump and Runt had been comatose beneath a dining table, their stomachs distended from consuming so much food. Captain Harding grabbed Coldforge by the arm as he followed them. "We can sleep in the barracks. The dorms are for priests and acolytes only."

"But Indie..." Coldforge clamped his mouth shut before he finished.

"Priests, acolytes, and their *guests*." A hint of blush appeared on the captain's cheeks.

"My guest quarters are much closer," Father Hoarfrost said. "No need to walk across the city for a bed." The dwarf smiled and grabbed a tray of meats.

The boys lifted their heads when he ripped off an enormous chunk from a roast, its bright red juices splattering on the ground.

"I've got enough to share," the dwarf said to the boys, "if'n ye want to keep me company." In a heartbeat, the two canines were by Coldforge's side, with long bits of slobber hanging from their mouths.

As Kit and her friends made it to the acolyte level, Kit wished them all a pleasant sleep before she guided Indie up the next flight of stairs. She growled loudly when Silverleaf made kissy noises, earning him a cuff to the back of the head from Amara.

"Sorry, Sister Kit." Amara had a broad grin on her face. "We'll leave you in peace." She grabbed Silverleaf by the back of his robes, hoisted him into the air, and led Slate and Lin to the acolyte's cells. With everything that had been going on since they'd been promoted, neither of the two priests had received their new quarters yet.

"I need a bath," Kit said as they reached the top of the stairs leading to the priests' quarters.

"I'll wait in your cell," Indie said with a coy smile. "Don't be long."

"You need a bath, too." Kit pinched her nose with her fingers.

"I smell?" Indie asked, taking a step away from her. His expression made her think she had just kicked a puppy. Kit took his hand, ignored his protestations, and guided him to a rustic-looking door with a cold-iron ring on it. After rapping lightly, Kit pushed the door open, revealing a pitch-black room within. She dropped her hammer outside the entrance and coaxed Indie into the darkness.

"Wait out here," Kit said to Fury. The battle hammer laid lifeless on the ground, making the girl smile. "Thank you," she added just before closing the door.

"I have much better control," Kit cooed. A long, slender flame appeared in her free hand. As she increased the size of the red dancing flames, the light showed a utilitarian room, nearly devoid of furniture. On one wall was a large stone tub with thick copper pipes over one side. Next to the tub was a wooden stand suitable for holding clothing. On the opposite side of the tub was a table laden with rough-spun gray towels.

"Put a plug in the tub's drain." Kit pointed to a conical shaped piece of granite. "I'll light the braziers."

Indie looked around the softly lit room. "There are no pails."

"Pull that lever." Kit gave the young man a warm smile. "It's a part of the dwarven design. There is a large cistern on the top of the Temple. It catches rainwater."

When Indie pulled the lever down, torrents of water came gushing from the copper pipes, filling the large stone tub. Indie shivered as he placed his hand into the icy flow.

"Is it too cold?" Kit asked playfully as she pushed the lever, shutting off the stream of water. She plunged her hand into the tub. A burst of flames ignited beneath the surface, turning the water a brilliant red. In seconds, the water bubbled. "How about now?"

Kit's fingers trembled as she unbuckled the clasps of her crimson jacket. Indie's face blanched.

"Do you trust me?" Her jacket fell to the ground at her feet.

"With my life." Indie pulled open the front of his tunic, sending buttons scattering in all directions.

Kit's eyes were glued to the man's burly chest. He was *definitely* more mus-cled than she remembered during their last *attempt* at intimacy. With a pull of a thin leather rope, she unfastened her trousers, allowing them to fall in a puddle around her ankles. Her face reddened as she realized she had not yet removed her footwear. As she tried to pull one of her boots off with the toe of her other, she lost her balance and crashed to the floor.

"Kit!" Indie rushed to help her up.

"I got this." She playfully pushed him away. Her butt ached, but she would not let him see her discomfort.

Now chuckling uncontrollably, the young man gave Kit some space as she pulled off her boots and tossed them against the far wall of the chamber. When she'd finished, she raised her chin to find Indie, dressed in nothing but his small clothes, clearly *ready* for Kit to remove the tunic that covered her from neck to mid thigh.

"I don't want to ruin my clothing the way you did." Kit deliberately unbuttoned the topmost clasp on her shirt. With painful slowness, she continued to the next button, and the next. With each deft movement, she revealed more and more of her cleavage. Just as she was about to undo the last clasp that held her tunic in place, Indie let his small clothes drop to the floor. With a shrug of her shoulders, Kit's blouse fell from her back, revealing her nearly perfect but heavily scarred body. Wreaths of flame ignited around her, covering her in a dazzling display of orange and red fire.

Stepping over the edge of the tub, Kit slid into the water, her flames extinguishing as she did.

"Tell me if it's too hot." She beckoned Indie to join her.

The man winced as his toes penetrated the surface. Almost instantly, the skin on his leg was transformed into brilliant gold scales. As he put both feet into the water, the scales traveled up his thighs, stopping just above his waist.

"It feels good." He gave Kit a small smile, desperately hoping she would not disapprove of his metamorphosis.

"You're beautiful." She drew him closer. Flames lit on her hand, and she reached out for his skin-covered upper body.

She pressed her flame covered hand to his chest. "Does this hurt?" On contact, Indie's skin transformed into more golden scales, radiating outward to the base of his neck.

"It's pleasant," Indie said, with no hint of deception. "Actually, it's much more than... *pleasant.*"

Kit let her flaming hand move up the man's chest until she slipped it behind his neck. As she did, his golden scales moved with her, spreading up his neck to his face and head. Indie's hair transformed into soft, spikey scales, resembling the ruff of a male lion.

"So beautiful," she repeated as she pulled his body against her own. Her hands slid from Indie's neck down to the small of his back. As she drew him nearer, Kit let her legs slip around his waist. Her chest heaved with short, desperate breaths.

"I love you." She squeezed her legs, drawing Indie into her. Her back arched, and she gasped.

"Don't hold back," Indie moaned in response. "You can't burn me."

Kit burst into flames, filling the chamber with steam that smelled of sulfur and tasted like honey.

THE STORY CONTINUES...

The story continues with *Wrath of Titan,* the next and final novel in the Priest of Titan series.

AFTERWORD

Thank you for reading my novel. Reviews are critical to the success of every indie author. I would ask that you leave a review on Amazon, GoodReads, and Book-Bub. If you have any thoughts or comments that you'd like to share directly with me, I would love to hear from you. You can email me at paul@paulmouchet.ca.

Do you want more stories? You find links to all my novels on my website. You can also sign up for my newsletter, Marvelous Mondays, which I send out every other week. They're full of fun pics, snippets of what's going on in my life, and book news.

Also, if you'd like to discuss my stories with me and other fans, in a safe, friendly environment, please connect with me on my Facebook group ~ Paul Mouchet's Reader's Group.

You'll find the link to all my social media accounts on my website. I look forward to chatting with you.

Happy Reading!